OATH
KEEPER

OATH KEEPER

DEATH SMITH BOOK 3

Joost Lassche
aka Osirium Writes

Podium

Published in 2024 by Podium Publishing
www.podiumaudio.com

OATH
KEEPER

Prologue

May, 14 AR
GRRO Main Office
London, England

SAMUEL

Samuel Jones, the head of the London branch of the Global Rift Response Organization, pinched the bridge of his nose, feeling his headache intensify as he glanced at the sealed folder beside him. The meeting he was currently in had been going on for an hour already. Many of the findings presented by the investigation team had been being disputed and rejected by the officials in the room.

I can't blame them for disagreeing, Samuel thought. *The claim that the Bulgaria incident originated from a Rift, the assertion that there are similarities with recent incidents in Albania and Croatia, and the suggestion that more incidents will follow . . .* If he had heard these claims from anyone else, he might have dismissed the report altogether.

"It doesn't matter what you think. The facts don't lie, and it's clear that these are not just incidents but attacks. They are getting more refined, showing that this threat is becoming more familiar with us and more surgical in its methods. And it's moving west," Daniel Wells said, slamming his hand down on the stack of papers in front of him that he and his team had brought.

Some of the officials shook their heads, clearly unconvinced. One of them pushed the papers he had received back toward Daniel. "This is a waste of time and paper. Why are we listening to this former baker? We're talking about three isolated incidents. These incidents lack any common characteristics—"

"Except that Rifters died en masse in all three locations. You people don't know what it would take to eliminate a group of well-trained Rifters like that," Daniel said as he slid the pile back to the official, almost daring him to return the gesture. "And if you insult my former profession again, I'll give you a firsthand demonstration of what a proper incident looks like."

"Enough!" Samuel said, silencing the room. "We'll take some time to digest all of this and convene again in a few hours. Until then, you can all cool off outside. . . . Now." He closed his eyes, trying to suppress what he knew would turn into a full-blown migraine before the end of the day. Samuel stopped Daniel before he could leave the room like the others. "Not you."

The Rifter clicked his tongue as he closed the door and took a seat next to Samuel. "I'm not apologizing."

"Stop being a child," Samuel said. He knew that there was no hope of changing or tempering Daniel. There had already been a dozen HR grievances filed against him for his brutally honest comments, and the fact that he threw knives around in his office. The official complaints from Bulgaria's foreign affairs ministry were even worse. *That'll teach me to put a bloodhound in charge of an official investigation.*

Despite all the trouble Daniel had caused, his results for the GRRO couldn't be denied. Three cases had already been closed thanks to his efforts, and he had achieved remarkable results in the Bulgaria incident, despite the red tape. "I'm removing you from the case."

"Now who's acting like a child?"

"I'm serious. The GRRO is giving the case to someone else, and I'm giving you a new assignment. Closer to home this time. You'll be working with Interpol to locate and detain a Rifter." Anticipating Daniel's reaction, Samuel held up his hand to silence him and slid a thick folder toward him, keeping his finger on it to hold it in place. Samuel hesitated before releasing it, knowing that he had set something in motion that was beyond his control.

Samuel watched as Daniel opened it. "They're calling the Rifter in question the 'Demon of Dublin.'" He knew the man would scan the summary on the first page. It mentioned the possibility of multiple casualties, although they had only recovered one body so far. There were reports of two heavily injured or murdered individuals being taken from the scene. The crime scene was a mess, with blood and tissue samples that made little sense.

Worse still were the reports of a terrifying, unnatural roar heard by witnesses, and the descriptions of a "demon" clad in armor who had dragged the two missing individuals away from the scene. Despite the damage to the footage, investigators were able to identify one of the injured as a known assassin with ties to several high-profile individuals. "We've identified the other wounded man as Lance Turner."

Daniel was silent for a few moments before he closed the folder and suddenly stood up. His face remained impassive as he left the room without saying a word. Samuel realized that he had misjudged the situation.

I mistook a sleeping wolf for a bloodhound.

CHAPTER ONE

Weightless

Somewhere Above the North Sea

LANCE

Perhaps you were born under a bad sign . . .

Lance pushed the lingering memory aside as he inhaled sharply and tried to ignore the taste of his own blood in his mouth. He spat out as much as he could, adding to the mess in the sink. He steadied himself and opened his eyes to face his reflection in the mirror in the cramped airplane bathroom. He looked like a mess, standing there as the metal world around him occasionally shook.

I've definitely looked better. He touched the scars on his chest, recalling the pain he had experienced when Iyas repeatedly stabbed him. Despite having encountered the horrors of the Rifts and the monsters within them, the dagger had been the most terrifying thing he had ever experienced. *At least the stitches are out*, he thought.

Lance's lips curled in disgust as he said, "Iyas . . ." The word felt like poison. He could still remember every moment of his betrayal, the nonchalant way the man had killed Mira and cut the white-shard out of her. Weeks later, he still wasn't free from his memories of the assassin, or the poor girl. Just as with Thomas, Lance could feel the remnants of Iyas and Mira in his own mind. He frequently had dreams of their lives, glimpsing brief moments and interactions, or even experiencing their deaths as if they were his own. The connection wasn't as strong as with Thomas, but it was still there, threatening to contaminate his thoughts or control his actions.

Lance tried to reassure himself as he washed the blood from the sink, saying, "At least the coughing is getting less frequent." He wasn't sure if it was due to an injury he had sustained or if there was something else wrong with him. He feared it was the latter, since he had experienced similar symptoms when he first created Ash, although it hadn't been as bad then. *It's only pain. Push onward.*

Then he accessed his Inventory and went over his equipment, supplies, and the remnants of Iyas and Mira. He forced himself to stare at their icons for a while, demanding that he adapt and numb himself to them. He *had* to because he couldn't go back to being the person he was before. If he did, he knew he would lose more people he cared about. It was a painful realization but one that he had to accept.

Lance tried to push aside his regrets and focus on the task at hand as he rinsed his teeth one last time before getting dressed. It felt odd not to put on armor when facing danger, but he knew it would only hinder him for what was to come. *Don't look back. You have a job to do,* he thought solemnly.

Mend Wounds
[You have used Mend Wounds Level 2 at the cost of 15 Mana]
[Current Mana 330/345]

Lance's body glowed blue as a wave of healing energy knit together his minor injuries. He could feel the tingling sensation around his chest, indicating that he had not fully healed from the damage Iyas had inflicted on him. As the light faded, it took the fatigue with it, and Lance stepped out of the lavatory, feeling renewed but tense.

Glancing out the window as he headed toward the cockpit reminded Lance that he was in the sky, relying on a chunk of metal to stay aloft. He tried not to think about it. Arriving at his destination, he found Brian and the pilot. Brian, his personal fixer, had his feet propped up against a window while sipping on a beer. A half-empty bag of chips lay discarded between Brian and the pilot.

"Morning, sunshine. Did you have a pleasant nap?" Brian greeted Lance with a smile. He seemed relieved to have some company, especially since their pilot couldn't speak English. He had assured Lance that he completely trusted him, even though the man smelled strongly of alcohol, more so than Brian did himself.

"It's past midnight."

"Alright, we can skip the pleasantries," Brian said, exhaling briefly and clearly suppressing several swear words. "I guess you're a nervous flyer. Alcohol can help with that. It has something to do with the altitude," he lied, pulling out a flask and drinking nearly half of it before offering some to Lance. When the young Rifter declined, Brian offered it to the pilot, who finished the rest. Brian then returned to his beer.

"Are we nearly there yet?"

"Deset minuta. Postoje lakši načini da se ubijete," the pilot said, tilting his head toward Lance. He then held up ten fingers to indicate that they had ten minutes left until they arrived at their destination. Afterward, the pilot shook his head in disapproval.

"What was that about?" Lance asked as he shifted his attention toward Brian.

The fixer simply shrugged his shoulders as he finished his beer. "Something about the weather?" He gave Lance a reassuring smile, as if to say that he had everything under control. "Just get that hell-spawn friend of yours ready in the meantime. I'll join you in a minute."

Taking one last look around the cluttered cockpit, Lance saw that the seats were held together with duct tape and that there were Post-It notes with scribbles on them next to important-looking instruments. He hated flying under the best of circumstances, but this . . .

He shook his head as he left the cockpit and walked down the length of the plane. There were crates and boxes everywhere, all securely fastened as well as two vintage cars. Brian had told him that he was transporting these cars to sell in Norway, in order to make the flight seem as legitimate as possible. Lance caught sight of Ash sitting in one of the cars, "practicing" his driving skills.

Lance shook his head and got into the passenger seat. "Are you ready?" he asked. His silent companion just nodded. Ash had grown a lot since Lance first created him through his "Death Forge" Skill and was getting better at expressing himself. However, he didn't experience fear. While he had a self-preservation instinct and did his best to avoid injury, he would never hesitate when the situation called for it.

"Good man," Lance said as he Ash shifted gears. He couldn't help but think, *At least he isn't getting any worse,* remembering the one time in Ireland when he had allowed Ash to drive. He was just about to give him some pointers when he heard Brian's footsteps coming closer.

"Just a few more minutes, kids. Gear up. It's time to strap into those panties and put on your Dora the Explorer backpack," Brian said, trying to lighten the mood. He stopped when Ash made eye contact with him, his gaze devoid of emotion. "Or you could continue to traumatize me with that stare of yours. It's not like I wanted to sleep peacefully ever again."

Lance patted Ash's shoulder and signaled for him to get ready and stop teasing Brian. He wasn't sure why, but Ash seemed to have taken an instant dislike to the fixer. *Is it because he sees Brian as a threat, or is it something innate?*

They both wore civilian clothes suitable for colder weather. Ash had on a jacket with a hoodie that covered much of his face, but his pale skin was still noticeable.

Lance had dyed Ash's hair and eyebrows brown and applied some makeup. The goal was to make his companion look as normal as possible. In the first few days after being stabbed, Lance had kept Ash on standby in his armor. Once he had felt strong enough to walk on his own again, he had gone shopping and given Ash a makeover. However, the changes were not permanent, as they would be erased when Ash was returned to his Inventory.

No doubt Brian was already suspicious of his ability to store and retrieve monster corpses, and the fact that Ash never spoke—nor ever seemed to let down his guard—didn't help the situation. To avoid raising Brian's suspicions any further, Lance chose to keep Ash close and in civilian attire.

"Speaking of gear, are you sure you got everything that I asked for?" Lance asked as he watched the fixer produce another flask from his pocket and start drinking again. The man held up a single finger to let Lance know that he was getting to it.

Brian wiped his mouth on his sleeve and stashed the flask away. "Yeah, I did. Fergus delivered the items you wanted a few days ago and secured transportation and housing for you. Only the best, of course." The fixer then retrieved a parcel from his jacket and handed it to him.

Inside, Lance found several passports for him and Ash—American, German, Greek, Andorran, and even Brazilian ones—as well as a list of points of interest and several stacks of Norwegian currency. "Andorra?" he asked, glancing at the unfamiliar country listed on one of the passports.

Brian explained, with a smug, satisfied expression on his face, "Andorra is a micronation nestled between France and Spain. It's landlocked and not officially part of the EU, the GRRO, or any major Rifter agency. That makes it perfect for someone like you to hail from, without too much paperwork attached to your name. Clever, right?"

"Yes, I'm impressed. Did you make them yourself?"

Brian shrugged and said, "No. I don't know the guy personally, but I know someone who knows someone who's related to a friend's sister's friend. You know how it is. Here," he added, handing Lance back his cracked smartphone. "Your phone isn't as high-tech as I would have liked, but my friend made some adjustments to it so it's as anonymous as can be. You can still take it with you into a Rift. I've already programmed in the important numbers and coordinates for your pickup in a few minutes. Any questions?"

"Did you do all this sober?" Lance asked.

"Well, I'm not a two-pot screamer, that's for sure," Brian replied with a grin. He raised an eyebrow when he noticed that Lance didn't understand the reference. "Just trust me, kid. You came to me for a reason. I might not always act like it, but this is what I'm good at . . . And let's face it, you don't have any other options."

"And what about my other request?"

"That will take some more time," Brian said, his smile fading. "It's doable, but it's hard to make from scratch. I know you're set on the specifications, but the thing you're asking for will probably break your arm the first time you use it . . . If it doesn't just blow up in your face first."

"Don't worry about my arm," Lance interrupted. "Just finish it as soon as you can."

A moment later, flashing lights in the cargo hold signaled their approaching destination. Brian grabbed two bundles and oxygen masks. *Here we go,* Lance thought, his stomach churning as Brian prepared for their departure.

Lance stood at the edge of the rampart, peering over the edge into the darkness. Clouds streaked by, and he could feel the primal pull in the back of his mind, urging him to jump out and spread his wings. *Don't forget you hate flying,* he thought, even while simultaneously having to resist the strange temptation.

Lance noticed Ash out of the corner of his eye, standing at the edge of the rampart beside him. As always, his companion showed no fear nor hesitation. Both were equipped with parachutes, oxygen tanks, and masks—though the latter two were unnecessary for Ash. Still, Lance wasn't about to broadcast to the world that his friend didn't need to breathe.

"Are you sure we can trust these?" Lance asked, speaking through the small communication device beneath his mask. He shifted his gaze toward Brian, who had strapped himself into a seat and was giving him the OK signal with his hands.

"It's fine," Brian reassured him. "And the equipment is made from Rift-materials. Hell, I packed it myself. Trust me, it should be fine."

"*Should?*"

"It's okay. How hard can it be? It's basically just falling for a short time before you pull on a cord. It's not rocket science, right?" Afterward, the fixer struggled to keep his oxygen mask in place, quickly taking a few swigs from his now-half-empty flask.

Brian's involvement in folding and packing the parachutes made things even more unsettling for Lance. He had to suppress the desire to get back into his seat and demand that Brian find him another way into Norway. He understood why they had to do it this way—to leave no trace, they had to jump out of the back of a cargo plane in the dead of night.

Louis . . . Connor . . . Kira . . .

Hearing the names in his mind stirred something within him. The remnants of his friend began to surge upward, invigorating him with anger and the desire to act. It was still an unfamiliar feeling, but he had gained a better grasp of what was happening to him over the last few days. He understood that it was a side effect of using white-shards and his Class, but he was grateful to have even just a small portion of his friend's emotion and courage with him.

"Are you ready?" Lance asked Ash as he flicked the switch on his communication device to remove Brian from the call. He was grateful for what the fixer had done for him thus far, but he wasn't looking forward to more of the man's "helpful tips." He still remembered the vague description he had given him about their jump altitude and the best time to pull their chutes.

Ash nodded and held out his hand, making a fist. Moments later, Lance did the same, fist bumping while staring into the dark abyss below. When the bell rang, Ash simply stepped off the edge, followed by Lance, who had to practically throw himself out of the plane.

[You have retrieved an item 3x]

A few seconds later, Lance was grinning from ear to ear. A large part of him was still screaming in terror, but too many of Thomas's and the birds' memories and emotions were at the forefront of his mind. He saw Alpha and Bravo gliding past him as they basked in the freedom of the open air.

He chuckled as the two crows drifted toward Ash, who was falling with all the grace of a bag of dirt. No doubt Ash was unconcerned by this. The man was simply observing the ground approaching him and waiting for Lance's sign to pull the chute.

Lance reminded himself once more, *I hate this,* as he felt another surge of avian memories and instincts. In the corner of his eye, he saw something speeding by, only to slow down and drift toward him. *Icarus,* he thought. He admired the way the peregrine falcon soared through the sky and occasionally showed off its skills before shifting its gaze toward the ground beneath it.

"Almost," he said through the communication device while also making a hand signal to Ash to prepare. He wasn't sure at exactly what height he was supposed to pull his parachute, but he didn't want to take any huge risks. Not with zero skydiving experience, in the dark, and above unfamiliar terrain.

"Now!" Lance yelled as he pulled his chute and soon after felt a strong force seizing him by the shoulders.

A few minutes later, Lance and Ash were sitting on a boulder beside a dirt road. Lance stored his avian companions, the oxygen tanks, masks, and parachutes in his Inventory. They had buried the communication devices because they didn't possess any Rift-materials so couldn't be stored. It was still pitch black, but due to their attire, they would look like normal hikers to anyone who might happen to pass by. The only thing out of the ordinary was Ash's steel axe, which he was sharpening.

"Are you okay?" Lance asked when he noticed Ash repeatedly pausing to look upward. No doubt the man was still trying to process his journey from the back of a cargo plane without having ended up splattered on the ground.

"Yes." Ash's voice was as deep and unnatural as ever.

"That's good to hear," Lance said as he went over the plan with Ash again. They would be picked up within a few minutes by Fergus and two locals. The latter, Brian's right-hand man, had overseen getting everything Lance needed to a secure, mobile location. The fixer had assured Lance that he had carefully chosen the locals and that everything from transportation to facilities would be top-notch.

Still, I have a bad feeling about all of this, he thought as he remembered the worn-out state of the cargo plane that had transported them from Ireland to Norway. Brian had smuggled Lance and Ash on the plane, with no paper or electronic trail that could connect them to the aircraft itself. *The thing with that fixer is that he does what he promises. . . . . .but only just barely. That cheapskate better come through.*

He would be able to have a fresh start in Norway as long as he kept a low profile. He needed a little more time to become strong enough to take down Kira and the others. A while later, they saw lights in the distance, indicating that their ride had finally arrived. Even with Lance's heightened Perception, he couldn't make out the car due to the bright headlights and the darkness.

"Just as we discussed. I'll do all the talking," Lance said as their ride pulled up in front of them. When he saw the car, his expression turned sour, and he cursed under his breath. It was a white Citroen AX, the ugliest two-door he had ever seen. It had dents on the back and a mismatched red door on the right. It was also making a sound as if it were begging to be put out of its misery.

In the front of the car were Fergus and a Norwegian lad who looked barely a day over eighteen. Both men looked terrified to be picking up two Rifters in the dead of night. Ash's unnaturally pale skin, intimidating stare, and the fact that he was sharpening his axe only added to the tension. The only saving grace was that Fergus looked even more scared than the Norwegian lad.

"Ash, remind me to punch that fixer in the mouth the next time we see him."

CHAPTER TWO

Acoustic Communication

Two hours later
Base Camp, Norway

The ride to the base camp was uncomfortable for multiple reasons. With Ash and Lance in the back, the car was cramped, and Fergus kept looking over his shoulder with a worried expression, occasionally scratching the back of his bald head. The Norwegian driver was constantly checking the rearview mirror, as if he were seeing Rifters up close for the first time. The whole time, Ash never put away his axe, instead inspecting it and testing its grip. *I almost feel sorry for Fergus. His seat must be soaking wet at this point,* Lance couldn't help but think as he struggled to contain a small grin.

Lance spent his time studying the documents that Brian had given him, including passports, Rifter IDs, information sheets, and a small book to help him learn basic Norwegian. He struggled to make sense of it all, thanks to the additional letters the language used.

"That book isn't going to do you much good, sir," the youth said, glancing at Lance through the mirror. When Lance raised an eyebrow, the young man continued. "It's teaching you Nynorsk, which is only used by ten percent of Norwegians. Norway has two languages: Bokmål and Nynorsk. You're trying to learn the one that's mostly spoken in the west, which is a long way from where we're headed."

Lance sighed and closed the book, throwing it onto Fergus's lap. *Either that fixer is inherently incapable of doing things correctly or he just takes pleasure in causing me problems.* "What's your name?"

"Reidar, sir. Reidar Kristiansen," the young man said with some concern in his voice, likely worried that he had offended the Rifters in the back with his comment.

"Thanks for pointing it out, Reidar."

Shortly afterward, they stopped at the base camp, and Lance and Ash got out to stretch their legs. Despite having lowered his expectations due to the old cargo plane, the beat-up car, the fixer's constant alcohol consumption, and the unreliable advice from the man, Lance was still disappointed by what he saw.

In front of him was an old motorhome that seemed older than he was. Behind it was a small storage trailer, and parked behind that was a truck with a cooling unit. Having already witnessed the fixer's cheap, greedy nature over the past few days, Lance was far from shocked, but still disappointed.

The old biscuit factory in London looked better than this. At least it won't spoil me, Lance thought as he opened the back of the truck and saw the bits of meat hanging on hooks and stored in boxes. It took him a few minutes to locate and open a hidden storage compartment. *I should be able to fit three or four regular-sized monsters in there. Or one larger one.*

Brian had come up with the idea of using a meat truck to store the monster corpses. This would allow Lance to keep them hidden while Fergus or one of his lackeys drove the truck to a location where they could be collected. This would keep Lance out of sight and away from the attention of the GRRO and other agencies. If he had the Inventory space, Lance knew he could fill several trucks with monster corpses, but he didn't want the fixer to know this. He hoped that by making him believe each corpse was a rarity, he could temper the man's greed.

As he closed the door of the truck, a high-pitched scream caught his attention. A young woman ran out of the motorhome and threw herself into Reidar's arms, speaking rapidly in Norwegian. Just as Lance was about to ask who she was and what was wrong, he saw a confused Ash walking out of the motorhome, still carrying the steel axe. *Ah, that makes sense.* Lance called Ash over and attempted to calm the situation.

"Ash, put the shotgun down. You're frightening the children," Lance said a few hours later as he watched Ash fire the last shot and then pick up the empty shells. The shotgun was a present from Lance to Ash for rescuing him in Dublin—one of the first things Lance had asked Brian to get for him. While it would enhance Ash's combat potential in the next Rift, Lance had truly meant it as a gift.

Like Thomas, Ash had a fondness for movies featuring certain types of weapons, such as grenades, revolvers, and shotguns. "There's still a lot of Thomas in him," Lance thought as he watched Ash return to the camp, carefully checking to make sure the weapon's safety was on before handing it over. "Did you have fun?" Lance asked as he stored the weapon in his Inventory and activated his Skill.

Repair Item
[You have used Repair Item Level 1. Reducing Stamina and Mana regeneration by 25% until completion]

The shotgun and ammunition were an exorbitantly expensive purchase, since Rifters rarely found guns within a Rift, and resources to make more ammunition were scarce. He had purchased thirty-two buckshot shells and eight slug shells in case Ash needed to take down a larger monster. Just these forty shells would've set him back nearly twenty thousand pounds, but luckily, Lance had persuaded Brian to purchase it in exchange for some goodwill and the prospect of getting more intact monster corpses.

In addition to the forty shells that Ash could take into a Rift, Lance had also ordered approximately five hundred rounds of regular shells that weren't made from Rift material. He had figured that Ash needed some actual hands-on experience shooting the weapon without wasting thousands of pounds in expenses. The only downside was that Ash's constant shooting wasn't helping the atmosphere around camp. *Luckily, I can repair most of the damage Ash has done to the weapon. How many shells did he go through?*

In addition to the shotgun, Lance had also put in an order for a small pistol with two spare magazines. He was sure he'd be able to handle the lower-level Rifts without it, but he knew he needed more experience with guns as well, both to know how to use them and how to fight someone with one. It was expensive, but he wasn't training so hard just to earn a living or to save up. He had an oath to uphold.

"Why doesn't he speak? Is he mute?" Eirin Kristiansen asked after Ash had walked over to their bags to check their equipment one final time. Eirin was Reidar's older sister by two years and had nearly had a heart attack a few hours ago when she woke up to see Ash standing above her with an axe in hand.

"No, he's able to speak. He just chooses not to," Lance explained as he heard Fergus and Reidar come closer, no doubt curious to learn more about Ash.

"Why not?" she asked carefully.

Lance smiled as he looked over at Ash, who was going over their gear as he had taught him. "Some people just like the silence," Lance lied. It was only partly true. Ash wasn't particularly talkative, but Lance had instructed him to keep to himself because the man's communication skills still resembled a combination of a death metal band grunting and a demon from Hell. *Maybe someday he'll sound normal enough not to frighten people.*

"I think it's neat. A warrior doesn't need words to fight!" Reidar said as he watched Ash from a distance, his eyes filled with awe and admiration.

Both Reidar and Eirin were in their early twenties and had bright blue eyes and blonde hair. From what Lance had learned, the two siblings frequently took on transportation jobs or helped tourists navigate Norway, being proficient in

Norwegian, German, and English. Although this was their first time working with Rifters, Lance had found them to be reliable and competent, if a bit innocent.

In truth, they were a far cry from the "professionals" Brian had promised. It hadn't taken much questioning before Fergus revealed that the fixer had found the siblings through an online advertisement. Despite this, they were being paid generously, and the fear of incurring the wrath of Rifters would likely foster a sense of loyalty.

Lance had made sure to eat and drink as much as possible when he arrived at the camp. With the next Rift a few hours away, he was confident that his body would be able to retain what he had taken in.

"Ash, gear up," he called out as he left the others behind.

As they gathered their gear and checked their weapons, Ash and Lance prepared for the Rift. Lance had knives in sheaths on his belt, wrists, and boots, and a pistol in a holster on his upper right leg. He planned to wield Dieter's old mace with both hands, knowing from experience how devastating it could be when heated with Mana. Ash could wield it as well, yet sadly the man lacked the ability to produce Mana, making the weapon less effective.

With his shotgun on his back and the steel axe and excavation tool in hand, Ash was ready to face the Rift. Both he and Lance were protected by steel and leather armor that could absorb many hits. Their backpacks were filled with food, water, and bone javelins, ensuring they were well-equipped for the journey. As Lance looked at Ash, he was reminded of the ambition he and Thomas had once had to become "true Rifters." The memories brought forth a mixture of joy and shame.

"Reidar, start up the engine," Lance instructed, nodding to the young man. He then turned to Eirin and said, "I want you to set up the base camp at the coordinates we discussed earlier. You have plenty of time, so don't rush it." Seconds later, Lance saw Reidar running toward the white Citroen, fumbling with the keys.

It took several hours to reach the Rift site. Lance knew he should have napped in the car, but he found the country's rolling hills, dense forests, and intimidating mountains fascinating. Reidar had shared some information about the country, its people, and their approach to Rifts and Rifters. He told Lance that the country was over 30 percent larger than the UK but had only a few million citizens.

Lance was aware that Norway was not a member of the GRRO. Instead, the military was responsible for the security and monitoring of Rifts within the country. The government would offer contracts to Rifters to clear the Rifts, with the payment amount based on its difficulty level. Due to the size of the country and the scarcity of Rifters within it, there were often many foreign Rifters active in Norway. As Reidar drove slowly toward the Rift site, Lance thought to himself, *At least we won't stand out as much.*

The military had installed a tall steel fence around the Rift and flattened the surrounding area, though it was not as protective as the nets used by the GRRO. Lance knew that the chance of a civilian being hurt by debris expelled from this Rift was astronomically low, given that it was in a remote location. *No doubt they would have more security measures in place if the Rift occurred within a city,* Lance thought as he got out of the car with Ash and grabbed their gear. Two soldiers from the gatehouse approached them.

"You guys are here early," one soldier with a thick Norwegian accent said. "What time will the others be arriving?"

"We like to be early," Lance said, not knowing who the soldier was referring to. He figured it was probably a guild or party that had accepted the contract for the Rift and would be clearing it around this time. He handed the soldier two forged German Rifter IDs and waited for them to be checked. It didn't take long before Lance saw the confusion on the soldier's face. *No doubt our names aren't on the list,* he thought as he held out his hands to retrieve their IDs. Before the soldier could ask any questions, Lance was already moving toward the gate, projecting a confidence that was unlike him. "Last-minute changes. We got flown in a few hours ago. The rest of the team will be here shortly." In the background, he could hear Reidar starting up the engine and driving away.

Lance made sure not to lie to the soldier. While there was no law in Norway that prohibited Rifters from clearing a Rift without a contract, it would be highly unusual and would likely irritate the guild or party that had claimed the job. Everything Lance had said so far was true: they had just arrived by plane and the rest of his team *would* be there. He had simply left out the minor detail that he kept the rest of his team in his Inventory.

"Mind getting us some coffee while we check out the Rift?" Lance asked as he walked past the confused soldier. He was glad his helmet concealed his nervous expression. He saw a few shipping containers nearby that held a small barracks, bathroom, and sleeping quarters for the soldiers, as well as private booths for Rifters to change and shower.

Lance did his best to appear relaxed. He pointed out a few things to Ash as they made a circle around the massive Rift, as if they were studying it. In the distance, he could see the soldier approaching them with two cups of coffee before the Rift itself blocked their view.

[You have retrieved an item]

"Are you ready?" Lance asked, his posture changing as he retrieved his mace. Ash nodded, equipped his axe and excavation tool, and stepped closer to the Rift.

"Yes."

Lance gave Ash a fist bump before they calmly entered the Rift on their own. Seconds later, the soldier on Earth dropped two cups of coffee as the Level-Two Rift he had been guarding flared up and became unstable, indicating that the two Rifters had entered.

"Jeg er i så mye trøbbel!!"

Lance and Ash blinked into existence and stopped on the muddy ground, scanning their surroundings. The ground beneath them was like that outside the Rift, but a short distance away they saw a sudden change in terrain. As far as they could see, it was a dry landscape with rock formations and numerous small crevices.

"You alright?" Lance asked his companion as he held up his hand. Ash nodded, and he smiled back.

[You have retrieved an item 3x]

Three birds materialized and soared upward, gaining momentum and elevation. "Alpha, cover my six. Bravo, protect Ash. Icarus, have fun," Lance said before moving toward Ash and lifting Ash's helmet to reveal pale skin and gray hair. "Like I thought, the Rift burned away the makeup and hair dye. When you get out of the Rift, you'll need to cover up again until I make you all pretty again," Lance said teasingly before hearing Icarus call out to let them know monsters were approaching.

"Alright, we should be fine. They have the numbers, but we should be faster and stronger," Lance said. He and Ash had researched this Rift and its monsters. Lance had chosen this Rift for three reasons: there were many weaker monsters, so he would gain a lot of black-shards; he had seen these monsters before, when Daniel had slaughtered them easily in their second Rift; and the considerable time difference between this Rift and Earth meant that Lance could spend extra time here training and healing without feeling like he was wasting time.

[You have retrieved an item]

"You get to pick this time," Lance said as he handed Ash his smartphone and watched him browse through the music collection before choosing. Afterward, Ash tucked the phone under his armor to keep it safe.

"A guitar duet, really?" Lance asked. Ash merely shrugged before the first wave of monsters reached them. The fur-covered creatures hissed and snarled at them as they encircled Lance and Ash. *Gnolls*, Lance thought as he inspected the canine-like monsters.

Ash quickly killed the first one by throwing a crude bone javelin through its torso. Seconds later, another monster fell, though it did not die immediately. Determined not to be outdone by his brother in battle, Lance dropped his backpack and removed the javelins he had stored there, sticking them in the ground before throwing them one by one.

Detonate

Unlike Ash, Lance's javelins hit a Gnoll and exploded violently, and the bone shrapnel that flew out proved very effective itself at taking down more monsters. Although they looked emaciated and were relatively weak, they still had the numerical advantage over the Rifters. Lance was grateful to have the Detonation Skill at his disposal. He knew he and Ash could clear the Rift without it, but it would mean engaging with more monsters at close range and dealing with bruises and minor cuts afterward. Lance had studied the Skill extensively while recovering, but seeing it in combat was a unique experience.

[Detonate: Level 1]
[Cost per usage: −25 Mana per usage]
[Allows the user to detonate an Item within a few seconds]
[Level 1 detonates the Item, dishing out 50% damage of the Item's durability]

While Lance was using the javelin and Detonation Skill to take out groups of monsters, Ash had switched to his axe and pickaxe, hacking through them in a whirlwind of blood and gore. He occasionally switched to his shotgun when a pocket of monsters lined up and he couldn't control himself anymore. Any monster that tried to sneak up on Ash suddenly had a crow on its face, scratching and pecking until Ash could turn around and deal with the threat. Occasionally, a Gnoll would simply drop dead from a broken neck after something fast and gray dive-bombed into it from above.

Amidst the brutal battle and the screams of dying Gnolls, the cheerful sound of an acoustic guitar duet could be heard, setting the mood.

CHAPTER THREE

Firstforged

Three days later
Inside Rift 13

As she carefully sank the knife deeper into the monster's corpse, the pale woman applied more and more pressure. The knife easily cut through muscle, veins, and other vital anatomy as she extracted the black-shard. Following their established routine, she then stood up and walked over to the growing pile of black-shards. Although she still stumbled occasionally, her movements had greatly improved over the past three days.

"Well done, M—" Lance started before quickly correcting himself. "Well done. You can move on to the next one now." He observed as the gray woman nodded and walked over to the next corpse, sinking the knife into the monstrous flesh. The woman's dull overalls were now covered in blood and gore, but she didn't seem to mind.

Standing off to the side was a taller individual with pale skin. He was dressed in the same gray uniform, though his was stained brown from all the dirt he had moved. He had used Lance's excavation tool to dig empty graves for basic pitfall traps, and to start a small trench line.

Lance couldn't help but feel a sense of deep hatred and disgust when he looked at the man. Initially, he had allowed both the man and the woman to use knives to cut out black-shards. However, he had put an end to it when he saw how quickly the man was becoming more skilled with a knife.

"Alright, that's enough for now," Lance said as he saw Ash approaching in the distance. His friend had been going on hunting trips nonstop for the past three days, while Lance had gotten some time to rest and heal. Ash only returned when he ran out of javelins, needed repairs, or had filled his backpack with black-shards. The pale man wasn't as strong as Lance was, but the quality of his equipment and his increased speed more than made up for it. And Ash never went out without Bravo and Icarus, with one serving as a scout and the other as an offensive companion.

"Looks like you had a good time." Ash was covered in dirt and grime, indicating that he had gotten quite up close and personal in fighting. Lance briefly checked him and his equipment for damage but found only minor cuts and dents on the armor. "Take these two and get cleaned up. Have them carry some water back with them."

[You have stored several Items in your Inventory]
[You have retrieved an Item 2x]

Lance watched as Ash's gear disappeared from his body, replaced by two empty jerry cans. Moments later, Ash handed the empty containers to the pale man and woman before pointing toward a rock formation in the north where a small pool of water was located. Lance wasn't sure if the water was entirely safe to drink, but he mostly wanted the new additions to his team to practice and learn by getting water for themselves.

"Mira . . . Iyas . . ."

The words felt strange on Lance's tongue as he said them aloud, because both were dead, but he could still see their figures in the distance following Ash. It was like what had happened to Thomas. Both Mira and Iya's reforged bodies were now devoid of color, had a gray-shard in each one's chest, and showed no signs of being alive. They didn't breathe, sleep, drink, or eat. It was almost the same as what had happened when he had made Ash, but there was a crucial difference.

Revenants.

Lance watched as the three of them peeled off their muddy, bloody overalls and bathed in the pool of water. He made a mental note to get rid of the water, as his companions had started filling the canisters after contaminating it with blood and dirt.

Compared to how Lance remembered him, Iyas was now bulkier and no longer the lanky person he had once fought. His build was now closer to Lance's. With armor and a helmet on, Lance thought they might look identical. Mira now had two functioning legs, appeared a bit taller, and had gained more muscle. *Is it because of Thomas's template?* Lance wondered, once again considering the subject. He was grateful that his forging skill had rebuilt Mira's second leg. *At least her body is whole again.*

I suppose the extra muscle and athletic build will improve their baseline, making them more effective in the field. That will also create a sense of uniformity. It might even help with standardizing their gear? Lance looked away from their naked frames and turned toward the east, where he could feel the pull of the Rift-event.

While Lance was confident that he and Ash could handle this Level-Two Rift, he was less certain about the more challenging Rifts ahead. However, he knew that having two extra human companions would give him the confidence to take on a Level-Three or Level-Four Rift.

According to the GRRO Handbook, at his current Level of thirty-two, it would be advisable for him to stick to Rifts between Level One and Six, with more party members added as the Rift Level increased.

He knew that if he wanted to mimic having a skilled squad of Rifters, he needed to both provide his companions with equipment and make them as skilled as possible. *First things first . . . Shards,* he thought, as he went to the others and told Ash to oversee training and protecting of Mira and Iyas while he went out to hunt for more shards.

Rock, dirt, and sand were all that Lance could see. After two hours of hunting, the landscape appeared the same no matter where he went. The little vegetation there was in this place was hidden inside steep-walled, eroded cracks in the earth, which were difficult to spot from a distance but dangerous when he encountered one.

Some cracks were small, only able to fit a leg inside, while others were large enough to hold a bus, with a dangerous drop. The worst part was discovering one of those cracks filled with a dozen monsters, ready to throw crude spears or axes, or use their bows. However, with Icarus and Alpha at his side, Lance could avoid most surprises.

By the time Icarus returned to signal the presence of another crack, Lance had already cleared the second one. He quickly followed the bird and spotted the third crack he would clear out today. With a crude bone javelin in hand, he peered over the edge for a moment and saw seven Gnolls. Four of them were eating something while the other three were on guard, weapons at the ready.

Detonate
[You have used Detonate Level 1 at the cost of 25 Mana]
[Current Mana 159/345]

As he looked over the edge, the crude javelin in Lance's hand started glowing. He gave himself a second to aim before throwing the weapon into the center of the group. It exploded in a wave of bone shrapnel moments later.
Now.
Jumping into the crack, he landed in the middle of the monsters. Lance spotted that several of them were wounded while the rest just looked shocked. He didn't give them a chance to recover, instead beginning to smash his mace into the first Gnoll. The skin, bone, and muscle offered little resistance as he proceeded

to stain the surrounding rocks red. Two more fell within seconds as he charged forward.

As he rushed toward the Gnolls, Lance thought to himself, *I need to keep the momentum going. I can't let them regroup.* Overpowering them left and right, the sounds of the mace slapping against their bodies being undone was sickening, but a part of him was starting to enjoy it.

Ricochet
Ricochet

[You have used Ricochet Level 1 at the cost of 25 Stamina x2]
[Current Stamina 321/530]

As he sent his mace and throwing knife flying toward the rocky wall, they bounced off faster and slammed into the Gnoll at the far end, killing it instantly. This left only one monster alive. Lance wasn't sure if the creature could experience terror, but from the way it was frantically looking left and right after seeing its brethren killed, he figured it was at least scared of him.

Ricochet
Ricochet

Throwing two more knives from the sheaths on his gauntlets, Lance missed his target completely. It was a bit amusing to see how difficult it was to hit something that was moving, ducking, and dodging. However, that amusement turned sour when three more knives missed. Deciding that was enough, Lance retrieved his pistol and fired a round into the Gnoll's stomach, causing it to fall over in pain.

"Not so quick at dodging that, huh?" he said as he approached the wounded monster and kicked it into the wall, knocking it out instantly.

As he was about to finish the unconscious creature, Lance realized that a single Gnoll might be a good sparring partner for his new companions. *They'd have a hard time fighting it on their own, but two against one and with proper weapons? They should be fine,* he thought as he prodded the Gnoll with his feet to make sure it was unconscious. "Icarus!" he shouted, pointing at the unconscious monster. "If it gets up again, kill it."

Once he had retrieved his weapons and searched for loot, Lance explored the area. Most of the monster corpses were stored for his companions to continue practicing on, and the crude axes, spears, and bows were destroyed with his Forging Skill for a chance to obtain their templates.

On the verge of leaving, Lance spotted the half-eaten animal that the monsters had been devouring. While its limbs and much of its body were missing, some of its organs were still untouched.

Must be the digestive system, Lance thought as he leaned closer and started to dissect the carcass with a knife. He knew that some predators on Earth didn't always eat everything, because of its taste, or that it could be harmful to them. As he sliced into the carcass with a knife, Lance noticed two fangs still attached to the creature's mangled head. He extracted one of them and the small sack connected to it, wondering if the animal had been venomous. He thought about how he might be able to use the venom to improve his throwing knives. *Poison is always a useful tool,* he thought before he suppressed that thought, realizing it wasn't his own.

Lance turned at the sound of a crunch behind him, finding Icarus had dive-bombed the previously unconscious Gnoll. Both the monster and the bird were now severely damaged, the monster drowning in its own blood and Icarus struggling to escape its chest cavity. It was clear to Lance that the bird had broken its wings and legs, if not more.

"I appreciate your enthusiasm, buddy, I really do. But for your own sake, we should consider improving your durability or adopt a less kamikaze attack style." He then pulled out, stored, and started repairing his favorite bird. When he had finished with this location, he went over to the next major crack in the rocky landscape, determined to wipe out any monsters that he came across.

On his way back, Lance climbed to the top of a hill and saw his camp in the distance. The combination of fertile soil, trees, and bushes against the rocky terrain was a clear sign that this was where the Rift had intersected with Earth, a hotspot for Rifter activity. With his three avian guards keeping watch from above and Ash covering his back, Lance felt secure enough to have made that spot his camp. However, he knew that in the tougher Rifts ahead, he would need to be more careful. He slid down the jagged surface, ignoring the metallic aftertaste in his mouth. Lance was still coughing up blood every now and again, but it was thankfully getting less frequent.

"Friendly!" Lance called out as he neared the camp. He was pleased to see the numerous defensive improvements that had been made, including dirt walls, traps, and other protective measures. Beyond that, it was obvious that Ash had been teaching the others how to defend themselves. "I see you've enjoyed yourselves," he remarked at the sight of the woman nursing a broken wrist and the man trying to remove an arrow from his chest.

"Sparring . . . using the bow . . . knife-throwing . . . hand-to-hand . . . they break . . . easily," Ash stated as he struggled to find the correct words and breathe life into them.

"Well, you have more experience, are faster, and can take more punishment," Lance said as he walked over to the pile of black-shards that his companions had collected. He stored them all, counting to himself, *103. Enough to upgrade some of my companions. Or should I save it up to a thousand and give Ash his third one?* A first upgrade would cost him an Item and ten black-shards. The second upgrade would be a hundred and the third upgrade a thousand. He was already dreading just how expensive it would get if he Leveled his Smithing Skill further. He then made his way over to the pale woman, placing a hand gently on her broken wrist.

Repair Item
[You have used Repair Item Level 1. Reducing Stamina and Mana regeneration by 25% until completion]

Keeping contact with the woman, Lance straightened out her wrist to accelerate the healing process. It didn't take long for it to feel more stable. "Did Ash do this, or did you manage to injure yourself?" he asked, pointing to her wounded companion.

The pale woman nodded and pointed to herself, indicating that she had a rudimentary understanding of communication. This surprised Lance, as it had taken Ash much longer to learn this skill.

Maybe Mira has a natural ability for observing behavior and patterns, like Thomas does with boxing? Lance wondered, smiling reassuringly. He held onto her wrist for a few more moments until he was confident that he had repaired it enough for now. "Great job. And here I thought you were only skilled with a rifle. Maybe a bow would suit you. Keep up the training," he said, watching as she stood up and retrieved a basic bow and some arrows.

[You have retrieved an Item 5x]

Lance brought out five more monster corpses and let them fall to the ground before turning his attention to the wounded man with the arrow stuck in him. "Quit messing around with it. Pull it out and get back to work. I need these shards," he ordered, turning away from the man and taking a seat on a nearby log next to Ash.

[You have retrieved an Item 2x]

He brought out a meal and a canteen with fresh water, but his gaze was drawn to the east where he sensed a Rift event approaching. He quickly pulled back his feet. An arrow embedded itself in the spot where his right foot had been seconds earlier. He noticed the strange, confused expression on the woman's face, almost identical to Mira's. "You could try aiming the bow away from our party members?" he suggested, nodding reassuringly as the woman turned to the side and continued practicing.

[You have retrieved an Item]

"I got you something," Lance said, handing Ash the sack of fangs and venom he had collected. "I found it on a dead creature. I was thinking we could coat some arrow tips or knives with it." He leaned back and looked up at the three gray spots circling overhead. It was strange to have six companions by his side. Despite the physical and mental pain that the forging process had caused him, he felt that the benefits were still worth the drawbacks.

"Are you angry?"

Ash's comment caught Lance off guard. As he turned to look at his friend, he saw that Ash was staring at the other two with a thoughtful expression on his face. Ash had changed a lot during the time they had spent together, but Lance had never seen him like this. "No, I'm not angry. Maybe a little stressed, but not angry. Why do you ask?"

Ash didn't answer right away, instead continuing to stare for a while longer. "You look angry . . . with him . . . but calm with her . . . like you were calm . . . with me."

Lance nearly dropped his canteen in surprise as he shifted his position to face his friend. *Where is this coming from?* he thought, following Ash's gaze to the tall, wounded man who was cutting and removing black-shards. Although he was bulkier now, he still looked so similar to Iyas. Just looking at him was enough to make Lance feel angry. Seeing the man use a knife only exacerbated that anger. "I . . . maybe? I don't really know. Seeing him like that, with the same face as Iyas, it makes me feel rage. It reminds me of bad things."

They sat in silence for a while longer before Ash resumed speaking. "Am I . . . Thomas?"

"No, you're not Thomas. You have similarities to him, but you're not him," Lance said as he felt his throat dry up.

"Then he is not . . . Iyas," Ash said, his deep, unnatural voice countering Lance's earlier comment. "We are not humans . . . We are not them . . . Not Mira. Not Iyas," Ash said softly, as if he had just come to a realization. "Not Thomas." He stood up and placed the sack on the ground next to the arrow.

"You made me . . . You named me . . . Ash . . . I'm the . . . first forged . . . by your hands. You also . . . made them," he said before moving away to assist the other two with their work, leaving Lance bemused. He began to replay the conversation in his mind.

Ash Firstforged.

CHAPTER FOUR

The Quill and the Viper

Four days later

Pick up the speed, lads," Lance said, smiling as he tucked a piece of cured meat under his helmet to nibble on. Icarus sat on his shoulder, its bright blue eyes watching him intently. Over the past few days, the bird seemed to have developed a fondness for perching there. "Just look at them, Icarus," Lance said, gesturing to the warriors a few feet ahead on the winding, rocky slope. "They're a slow but effective meat grinder."

The two men holding the line in front of him and the woman taking out enemy archers from behind made Lance feel secure. Nevertheless, the occasional stone-tipped arrow that struck his steel chest plate or helmet reminded him he was still in combat.

His conversation with Ash had helped. Although he still felt angry and disgusted when he thought about Iyas or what had happened to Mira, he had allowed himself to move on. *These are my companions that I've made,* Lance thought to himself, listing them in his mind. *Ash, Alpha, Bravo, Icarus, Quill, Viper.*

In the past, Mira had been an exceptional shooter, and that talent had carried on after the forging process. The warrior woman before him now also had a natural aptitude for the bow, leading Lance to dub her "Quill" due to the speed and precision of her shots. Lance believed the nickname suited her and was concise enough to be useful in combat situations when quick communication was necessary.

The man had presented more of a challenge to name, but eventually Lance had decided on the name *Viper,* linking his quick movements with those of a serpent. Viper was decent enough with shields, javelins, and the bow, but he had a particularly strong aptitude for daggers. The memory of being poisoned by Iyas a few weeks ago also weighed on Lance's decision.

The two pale men were fending off a group of Gnolls, armed with makeshift bone javelins and shields made from leather-bound rows of bones. The narrow, unstable terrain they were on allowed them to block the Gnolls' path with just two people.

Ash's thick steel and leather armor proved resistant to the Gnolls' weaker stone-tipped spears, knives, and arrows, with only a few causing any damage. His enhanced speed and lack of fatigue allowed him to use his javelin with rapid stabs and feints. The tight quarters of the narrow path made aiming almost unnecessary, given the large number of enemies packed together.

Ash is doing excellently, as usual, Lance thought to himself as he watched his friend shield-bash a Gnoll in the face and then swiftly stab another monster who had gotten close to breaking through his defenses. Ash then quickly returned to formation while roaring at the enemy. *I'm surprised that Viper's lasted this long.*

"Gap!" Ash yelled, his voice barely audible over the sounds of fighting and dying monsters. He slid to the side a second later. At the same time, Quill's arrow shot past Ash and into the monstrous horde. Ash then resumed his position and attacked, stabbing and bashing as rapidly as possible.

As he moved closer to the front line, Lance couldn't help but smile. He noticed a few Gnolls lose their balance and fall off the side of the ramp into the canyon below. *It looks like an old, abandoned quarry,* Lance thought, peering over the edge and taking in the rest of the large, winding ramp that led to the bottom. From his vantage point, Lance saw a Gnoll in crude metal armor down there. He assumed it was the Rift-guardian, with several other monsters serving as bodyguards. He stepped to the side to avoid another arrow. *Stubborn little buggers,* he thought to himself.

Along the edge of the ramp, Lance saw a few Gnolls armed with bows. He had confidence in his and Ash's armor, but his other companions didn't have the same level of protection. He had tried to provide some additional defense by tying bones around Viper's shins and lower arms as makeshift leg- and armguards, but he knew it was a poor excuse for a defensive layer.

"Icarus, Bravo, take care of them," Lance said, pointing at the enemy archers. He had originally assigned Quill the task of eliminating the enemy archers, but he had discovered that she still lacked the skill and experience to take out monsters accurately from that distance. Instead, Quill was targeting the Gnolls closest to her. Because of the height advantage of the spiraling slope, Quill could shoot into the mass of monsters that were being held at bay by the others.

Lance watched as Bravo flew toward the first archer and attacked its face. The crow briefly diverted its attention before Icarus struck its neck from behind, sending the poor monster over the edge and plummeting to its death. The two birds then flew upward again before identifying another target. *This combination of a defensive frontline, ranged support, and aerial precision strikes is incredibly effective,*

Lance thought with a smile. He felt Thomas's memories and emotions wash over him, intensifying the joy he was experiencing.

"Well, time to pick up my end of the sofa," Lance said out loud as he stepped forward and knelt next to a deceased Gnoll. Its left eye was missing, the socket a mess of gore and bone. "No doubt Ash killed this one." He then placed his hands on it and another corpse.

[You have stored several Items in your Inventory]
[You have retrieved an Item 2x]

Once he had stored and retrieved the monster, Lance strategically moved the corpses while channeling his Mana into them. "Ash, I'm ready on my end. Let me know when," he shouted, getting into position. He felt his body tense up, aware of the important task ahead that required a particular Skill.

"Fall back!" Ash commanded in a deep, unnatural tone as he forced Viper to retreat to Quill and Lance before he withdrew himself. The four of them regrouped further up the slope, with the shield line re-forming. The monstrous horde followed, stumbling over dozens of dead Gnolls as they rushed toward Lance and the others.

Lance smiled as the Gnolls regained a lot of ground without noticing the trap that he had set. He ducked behind Ash as he continued to count down in his mind. A few seconds later, two explosions shook the ground and then bits of Gnoll rained down from the sky.

Lance had discovered that he could use his Detonate Skill on monster corpses as well. He had to store and retrieve them to establish ownership first. The Mana cost was significantly higher for objects as large as a Gnoll, but the Damage output made up for it. Just detonating two corpses had drained half of his Mana reserves.

He watched as Ash and Viper rushed forward to attack the Gnolls that had survived the explosion, using their javelins, kicks, and shield-bashes. There were many dead Gnolls scattered across a large section of the rocky slope. Some had died from combat wounds, others from concussive force or bone shrapnel. Viper had also sustained some damage from the shrapnel, but he seemed fit to continue the fight.

"On me!" Lance shouted as he grabbed his heavy mace and charged the remaining monsters that were still on the ridge. It would only be a matter of time before reinforcements arrived from below, but during that time, Lance knew they had the advantage.

"Send them flying!" Lance shouted to his companions as he smashed his mace into the ribs of a Gnoll and sent it plummeting over the edge down to the bottom. He hoped that, with any luck, one of the falling Gnolls might hit the Rift-guardian on its way down.

Four hours passed since Lance and his companions had begun their descent into the quarry. He had lost track of the total number of monsters they had killed. Lance could only speculate about how many black-shards he would receive when everything was done. Currently, he was busy watching Ash and the Rift-guardian fight.

The Rift-guardian was a larger Gnoll, standing a head shorter than Ash but still imposing in thick iron armor. He was hacking and slashing at Ash with his sword and shield. The monster was sturdy and quick but lacked Ash's training and instincts.

Another feint from Ash was all it took to startle the Rift-guardian before he stepped in. The man dodged under the sword strike and then slammed the side of his steel axe into the monster's head, denting the helmet.

"Ouch," Lance said with a grin as Ash retreated, dropped his axe, and picked up Dieter's old mace. The weapon was a bit too heavy for him to wield properly, but he was clearly becoming more confident in his skills. At that point, both the Rift-guardian and everyone else realized that Ash was treating this as nothing but a training exercise. It annoyed Lance that the mace was just a heavy tool for Ash, as he couldn't channel Mana into it. *I wonder if there's a way for Ash and the others to actually use Mana?*

[You have repaired an Item. 'Quill' is now at 100% durability]
[You have combined and retrieved Items]

"And up you go," Lance commented as Quill appeared, clad in dull gray overalls. "Take over Viper's duties. Push all the monster corpses that still contain black-shards off the edge." She nodded and set off at a soft jog toward the ramp. Lance could see Viper further up, tipping dead Gnolls over the edge.

Blood and gore covered much of the quarry, with two crows tearing and pecking apart mutilated bodies to pull out their black-shards. *If someone else saw this scene, they might wonder who the actual monsters are.* He got up from the rock he was sitting on and made his way over to the pile of black-shards that the birds had already recovered.

[You have stored several Items in your Inventory]

When he entered this Rift, he had only a handful of shards to spare, but now he had almost 250, with several more on the way. He had upgraded none of his companions beyond what he had given Ash and Icarus in Ireland, but now he finally had the shards to do so.

Lance believed it would be more beneficial for Quill and Viper to learn about their base limits before he upgraded them. He had previously forced Quill to engage in a one-on-two fight with Gnolls, during which she had defeated them but sustained heavy damage. He reasoned it was better for them to struggle and learn from their experiences in a controlled environment.

Lance gestured toward the Rift-guardian as Viper finally reached him. "You're going to fight that thing hand-to-hand," he said. "You don't have to win. Just try not to take too much damage, okay?" He waited for the pale man to nod before walking over to Ash, who had switched to using an excavating tool to attack the exhausted, battered Rift-guardian. "Hold him down for me," Lance said as he drew a knife and circled the monster. As instructed, Ash pounded the monster until it collapsed to its knees, then held it in a painful hold.

Lance carefully cut the straps securing the creature's iron armor and removed it. He then placed his hands on the monster and enveloped it in a healing blue light that disoriented and blinded it for a few moments. "Viper, you're up," he said, signaling for Ash to step back and allow Viper to approach.

The monster sprang up and lunged at Viper, who narrowly avoided it. Lance wasn't sure if it was the healing, the sustained attacks from Ash, or the absence of armor that had fueled the Rift-guardian's rage, but it appeared exceptionally angry. "Give Viper some guidance as needed. If it looks like he's in trouble, step in and rescue him, alright?"

. . . Lance stayed to watch the fight unfold for a while longer. He saw Viper employing a range of tactics, including kicks, punches, shoves, and elbows, to fend off the guardian. The monster was certainly more powerful and hardy, but its fatigue and wounds were taking a toll on its performance. Viper's biggest advantage was his longer reach. Viper used quick leg sweeps to knock the monster's legs out from under it, stopping it from closing in. Despite this, the man took damage throughout the engagement, including the loss of a finger and multiple scratches on his chest.

As he gathered and inspected Ash's discarded weapons for damage, Lance heard more bodies being dropped from a height and others falling afterward. *Who should I upgrade first? And what should I use for the upgrade?* Picking up the weapons reminded him of a parent cleaning up after a toddler, causing him to laugh out loud for a moment. He stopped when he heard Icarus's call, signaling a nearby threat.

It took Lance a few seconds before he finally spotted the monster at the top of the quarry near the ramp leading downward. A single Gnoll wouldn't pose much of a threat to Quill, who was nearby, but Lance had sent her up the ramp unarmed. "Icarus, return!" he said, holding out his left hand. Seconds later, the gray falcon gracefully landed on his wrist and gazed at him with its unnaturally blue eyes.

[You have retrieved an Item]

A small sack of fangs and venom manifested in his right hand. "Careful now," Lance said as he placed the Item on a nearby rock and set Icarus next to it. He then gently prodded the falcon's talon through the venom sack as he coated it with the white liquid. "Scratch the monster, but don't kill it outright," he instructed his winged predatory companion. At that, it quickly took off and sped upward, likely intent on diving to attack the monster attempting to sneak up on Quill, who was working hard.

Lance had experimented with the venom in this Rift, collecting a few more venom sacks from the deceased critters he had encountered. The venom didn't seem to harm his companions much, only reducing some of their durability if applied carelessly. Lance suspected this was because his companions weren't technically alive. Coating an arrow and knife with the venom was effective, but it was difficult to accurately gauge how much additional damage the venom was causing when a monster was simultaneously bleeding out.

Lance watched as the falcon slammed into the monster's shoulder, the impact causing the Gnoll to fall. From the way it was hissing and growling, Lance figured Icarus had successfully inflicted a wound on the monster with its talons.

[You have stored an Item in your Inventory]
[You have retrieved an Item]

Lance put away the sack and retrieved his cracked smartphone, starting a timer. *Let's see how long it takes,* he thought. He then signaled to Icarus and Quill to return to the ground level and assist with cutting out and storing black-shards. While they did so, the wounded monster attempted to pursue Quill, but as the seconds turned into minutes, it lost its momentum. It seemed to have trouble maintaining its balance. Then, much to Lance's disappointment, the monster made a misstep and fell off the edge. It ended up as another red pulp on the ground.

"And there goes my test . . ." Lance said, sighing audibly. He still had some poison left, but it was a limited resource. *If I can replenish it, I can essentially coat every arrow and javelin with poison. Every minor wound could then become much more lethal,* he thought as he looked at Ash and Viper. They were taking turns beating up the Rift-guardian. Viper was missing fingers and sporting a lot of cuts, but he showed no sign of slowing down.

Lance then decided on his next course of action once he reached the pile of Gnoll corpses, tearing off a piece of muscle and retrieving a piece of bone. "Alpha,

Bravo, come here," he called out, placing both pieces next to each other. When the crows arrived, he pointed to both pieces. "Alpha, swallow the muscle. Bravo, the bone is all yours."

Lance spared himself the sight of two birds struggling to swallow them whole. He could still hear the unpleasant sounds they made, but he instead focused on how Quill was doing. He watched her sift through the gory piles to extract black-shards. The longer he looked at her face, the more he was reminded of his inability to protect those around him. Luckily for him, the two crows snapped him out of that dark spiral as they hopped in front of him.

"Ash, subdue the Rift-guardian. Don't kill it," Lance ordered. "Viper, Quill, Icarus, come here, please," he said, placing his hands on the crows. A childlike grin formed on his face when a notification appeared. That grin soured when he only noticed one notification.

[Do you wish to re-forge this Item?]
[Yes] [No]

With his Forging Skill now at Level Two, Lance should have been able to upgrade both crows simultaneously or give a companion two upgrades at once. Then why was it telling him he could only upgrade one of them? "I'm missing something here," Lance said as he went to a different Gnoll corpse and pulled out a piece of bone. Lance then pointed it out to Bravo, who immediately swallowed it. Afterward, he saw another notification appear. "So, I can only use one body part per monster corpse to upgrade you?" Lance said aloud.

"Could the upgrade require something more than just a body part? Maybe some energy released when it's dead? I should experiment with this further." With two notification screens now open, Lance's mood improved drastically. *Would the process be like what happened to Icarus and Ash? I used a Centaur-toad muscle on Ash last time. Would the effect be similar or different this time? What about using bone—*

His train of thought abruptly ceased when he suddenly felt a surge of Thomas's emotions. It triggered memories of his best friend punching his shoulder when he got lost in his thoughts again. For a moment, Lance could almost see Thomas standing next to him with a knowing grin on his face. "No point in mulling over things that no one knows the answers to," Lance said out loud as he made his decision.

[Yes x2]

CHAPTER FIVE

Upgrades, People!

Forty minutes later

[Item upgraded]

Icarus stirred to life, standing up and spreading its wings, as if testing the changes that had occurred. The falcon still looked the same, although it seemed to Lance that it was now carrying itself differently.

"Alright, buddy. Let's have a test flight," he said. The bird launched itself into the air, climbing higher and higher until it was just a dot in the sky, visible only to those who knew what they were looking for. Lance signaled to Quill and Viper to proceed. They quickly retrieved a recently deceased Gnoll and propped it up in order to use it for practice.

"Icarus!"

Lance let out a powerful cry, calling for the falcon as if he were summoning a god. On cue, the bird came hurtling toward them, striking the corpse with deadly precision. The force of the impact was enough to wrench it out of Quill and Viper's grasp and send it crashing to the ground. Lance couldn't help but feel a twinge of remorse as he watched the Gnoll's body shatter on the ground, like a tree struck by lightning.

Rushing to the falcon's side, Lance could see the falcon's broken legs, its talons twisted and bent. This one attack had cost the bird half of its durability points. But despite its injuries, the bird was still flapping its wings, responding to Lance's presence. *He's not broken. At least, not in terms of durability.* It was a far cry from what had happened in Dublin, where such an attack had destroyed Icarus.

"I'll fix you up in a moment, buddy," Lance said, feeling a twinge of guilt as he watched the injured bird slowly struggling to its feet and flapping its wings. Despite its obvious pain, it took flight again, though at a much slower pace. "Alright, that's enough for now," Lance said, relieved that the falcon could fly despite its injuries.

[You have stored an Item in your Inventory]

Repair Item
**[You have used Repair Item Level 1. Reducing Stamina and
Mana regeneration by 25% until completion]**

As soon as the falcon returned, Lance stored it and began the repair process. Meanwhile, he, Quill, and Viper stared at the ruined Gnoll corpse in silence as Ash gave a creepy smile and a reassuring thumbs up. Though Lance knew Ash was just trying to mimic human behavior to make him feel better, the pale man was doing so while sitting on top of an injured, unconscious Rift-guardian.

"It's amazing that our feathery friend can survive such a powerful attack," Lance said, as he considered the possibilities. "With more experience, Icarus could learn to minimize the damage and make that kind of attack multiple times before breaking. I know its normal attacks have also improved thanks to the upgrade." As he spoke, Lance couldn't help but imagine the many ways in which Icarus could be of use in the future.

Icarus had undergone another upgrade, building upon the enhancements he received in Ireland. His initial upgrade, a Rift-glider's eye, had not only given his eyes a striking blue hue but also enhanced his vision and allowed him to detect heat sources. This time, Lance had provided a new upgrade, a Gnoll bone, that would further enhance Icarus, increasing its durability and defensive capabilities. *I had some concerns that the upgrades would negatively impact the birds' bone structure and prevent them from flying. However, they're still as agile as ever, if not even better.*

Both Alpha and Bravo had received a Gnoll muscle and bone upgrade, serving as test subjects for his experimentation. The bone upgrade had enhanced their defensive capabilities, while the muscle upgrade had given them a slight boost in speed. Although the increase was not as drastic as Ash's speed boost from the Centaur-toad, any added speed would prove beneficial. Lance accessed his status screen to review the current condition of his companions.

Retainers

Ash	1x	Human	Rift-glider eye +2 Sight +Heat vision	Centaur-toad muscle +4 Speed +100 Durability
Quill	1x	Human		
Viper	1x	Human		
Icarus	1x	Falcon (hybrid*)	Rift-glider eye +2 Sight +Heat vision	Gnoll bone +1 Defense +120 Durability
Alpha	1x	Crow	Gnoll muscle +2 Speed +40 Durability	Gnoll bone +1 Defense +120 Durability
Bravo	1x	Crow	Gnoll bone +1 Defense +120 Durability	Gnoll muscle +2 Speed +40 Durability

"So, Alpha and Bravo have received both muscle and bone upgrades," Lance said to himself as he opened his Inventory and noted the scarcity of black-shards. He only had nine remaining, despite having double-checked the monster corpses at the bottom of the quarry. The first upgrade had cost him ten black-shards each, and the second one a hundred. With Icarus also receiving his second upgrade, he was now running low on funds.

"It's time to call it a day," Lance said, turning to Ash. "Make sure you check all of your gear and backpack. Make sure it's filled up to the brim. Viper, guard the Rift-guardian for a minute." Lance then checked his own equipment, making sure everything was in decent condition. He had filled up his Inventory with basic Items, monster parts, corpses, and other necessities, leaving him with only seven empty slots. These he reserved for his companions' gear.

I made the right choice with this Rift. Though he had spent over a week here, only a few days had passed on Earth. The time had been well used, as he had had time to rest up, use his Healing Skill to hasten his recovery, and train his new companions in a relatively controlled environment. *Even so, the Experience gain has been atrocious,* he acknowledged. Despite having defeated every monster between his entry point and the Rift-event, he had only gained two levels.

Lance had distributed the free Attribute points evenly among all the categories, as he was still uncertain about which style to choose as a Rifter. "At least clearing the Rift will earn me another Level Up," he said aloud, as he strapped on his backpack and made sure everything was secure. He then looked to Ash, "Are we ready?"

"Yes."

Lance gave a sign to his companions. One by one, he stored them in his Inventory until only Ash remained. "I'll let you have the honors this time," he said as he stepped closer to the Rift-event, the black energy proving to be overwhelming when viewed directly. So, Lance positioned himself with his back to it. Ash took hold of the Rift-guardian's head with both hands and, without warning, snapped its neck, ending its life.

Ash then extracted the Guardian-shard before grabbing the monster's discarded iron shield and sword. Though the sword was a suitable size for the Gnoll, in Ash's hands, it was more like a short sword. Ash carefully placed the Guardian-shard in his pocket and took a spot beside Lance.

The two of them paused as the world trembled and shook all around them. They cast one last look at the blood-soaked quarry floor, the winding ramp that led to the surface, and the alien sky that was unlike anything they had seen on Earth.

"We did good . . ." Ash suddenly spoke up, turning to face Lance. "No deaths . . . no problems . . . Victory." He then raised his fist toward Lance.

"Yeah, buddy, we did good," Lance said as he matched Ash's fist with his own. He realized that their connection had deepened over the last few days. It was an unusual bond, and it got weirder the more he thought about it. But he had grown to trust Ash, as a weapon and shield within a Rift but also outside of it. And with that feeling, the black energy violently exploded outward and enveloped both men in an instant.

Returning to Earth, Lance felt his feet scraping against the ground as he regained his footing. His bolstered Strength and Agility made entering and leaving Rifts easier, as long as he was stationary during the transition. He tried to shake off the dizziness that came with the Rift as he adjusted to being back on Earth. Even the gravity on Earth felt different.

"And that was Rift Thirteen," Lance said, retrieving his smartphone and waiting for it to pick up a signal. Judging by the sun's position in the sky, he guessed it was still early afternoon. "Two days have passed," he informed Ash. They had exited the Rift from the same point they had entered it. The massive, pulsating black energy obscured their view of the entrance and the barracks nearby.

Lance's smartphone started buzzing nonstop as it showed a lot of missed calls, text messages, and emails. Most of them were from Daniel Wells, his mentor, and the reason he had even survived his first Rift. *I should have called him or left him a message,* Lance thought. Since Dublin, he had been off the grid, thinking that would be the best course of action for now. He wasn't sure if there were other assassins after him like Iyas. Maybe going off the grid would keep the others safe—or it was a futile effort on his part. He just knew that he had to do something.

He set aside Daniel's missed calls and text messages for now and focused on checking up on Thomas's family. There were two messages from his dad, Jacob.

The first was an invitation to grab a meal or even stay over, and the second one was checking on Lance and asking how he was doing, mentioning it had been a while since they had the chance to talk.

I think the second message was after Daniel had spoken with him, Lance mused. He wasn't sure how much of what had happened in Dublin had reached Daniel. *No doubt finding Mira's body had forced the local authorities to work with the GRRO. Daniel would've figured out that Mira and I had just finished the same Rift.*

Then he checked the emails that Thomas's brother, Oliver, had sent him. They included a lot of news articles about Paris, new Rift sightings, and significant events happening within Rifter society. There were also lots of new music files attached to every email. Smiling, Lance downloaded them all and added them to his collection. "Ash, we've got more music," Lance said, but just shook his head when Ash gave an awkward double thumbs up before the man walked away to survey their surroundings.

Next, Lance clicked over Kate's messages and smiled upon seeing several pictures of her performing with her orchestra and one with her sitting next to her sleeping little brother Oliver, who she had picked up from the airport. Apparently, he had recently visited her. As Lance stared at her picture, a wave of emotions washed over him. Lance felt the urge to call Kate, to hear her voice.

He couldn't help but think back to all the struggles he had recently faced. He felt like he was reliving them all over again. His chest constricted and his stomach churned as the memories came flooding back, overwhelming him. *No!* He forced himself to remember the oath he had made. *I can't. Not until I'm strong enough to protect people I love.*

A few of the messages were from his neighbors, asking why his apartment was empty, if he was going to come back, or if he planned to rent it out. Brian had taken care of that for him by hiring movers to store all his possessions in a shipping container. There were also messages from the GRRO, insurance agencies, a job offer from the White Clovers, and a text from his brother Marcus, saying that their father's condition was deteriorating further.

Setting his smartphone aside for a moment, Lance turned his attention to Ash, who was moving around the unstable Rift. He was a far cry from how his companion had appeared when they first met in London. Lance still vividly remembered Ash sitting on a couch beside him with a cigarette between his lips. Back then, Ash had embodied loss, but now, armored up, he represented something else. *Ash Firstforged.*

Lance realized he couldn't stay there much longer as the personnel on the site would have noticed the instability of the Rift. "Ash, move to the side. Let them see we made it out," Lance ordered as he turned his attention back to his smartphone and sent out three text messages:

Daniel, I'm doing alright, but I need to take care of something right now. Something important. I hope that you'll understand. —Lance

I can't get enough of this music! It's been a lifesaver during the Rifts. I'm going to be swamped for a few weeks, so you might not hear from me for a bit. Talk soon! —Lance

Glad to see you're chasing your dreams, Kate. I hope I get to see you perform live someday. I'll try to scrounge up enough money to afford a ticket. Luckily, I have a decent part-time job. Hell, I might even buy a few pieces of real Italian pizza for us. Last time we had pizza, it went well, right? I'm going to be busy in the next few weeks with work. Keep an eye out on Oliver for me! —Lance

Lance hoped that would ease their worries for a few weeks. He had been cautious in his wording, as he feared that Kira or another assassin could monitor those close to him. To throw them off, he used phrasing that Iyas may have used, drawing upon the fragmented memories he could access. It disgusted him, but lately he had been doing a lot of things that went against his nature. He knew Daniel would see through it, but at least he was giving him a sign of life.

Lance considered sending a similar message to Jacob but ultimately decided against it. The lingering memories of Thomas within him made that impossible. Jacob Walker had shouldered the burden of his entire family since losing his son, and Lance couldn't bring himself to add to that burden. *He's always treated me like his own. I can't lie to him.*

I'm doing alright, despite what you might hear about me. I swore an oath to Thomas that I need to keep. To do so, I'm going to be busy for a while. You know Thomas and his wishes. —Lance

Sending the message was difficult for Lance, but he knew it had to be done. He made sure the message was intentionally vague for everyone except Jacob, who he hoped would understand its meaning. As he reviewed it one last time, his phone started ringing. It was Daniel. He silenced the phone, walked over to Ash, and asked, "Is everything alright?"

Ash simply pointed at something with his finger before speaking. "People . . . They look . . . upset."

CHAPTER SIX

A Friendly Tackle

Hmm?" Lance muttered as he walked toward Ash. He couldn't help but over-hear a commotion in the distance. He turned his gaze to a group of five individuals engaged in a heated discussion. From his vantage point, Lance could see that two of them wore the uniforms of soldiers, while the remaining three appeared to be personal aides.

"Looks like representatives from the guild or party that were tasked with clear-ing this Rift," he said as one soldier left the group and marched toward the Rift. "I'll handle the talking. Keep your face hidden." Lance took a few steps toward the soldier. He recognized the man from their previous encounter, when he had asked him for a coffee before he and Ash had snuck into the Rift. Despite the suc-cess of the mission, he still felt remorseful for deceiving him.

The man approached them, his thick Norwegian accent laced with worry. "Are you both okay?" he inquired as he approached, a small trauma kit slung over his shoulder, his eyes scanning them for any signs of injury. Lance could feel the intense scrutiny of his gaze.

Lance nodded before he spoke. "Yeah, we're fine. Sorry about before. We lost our footing and fell in." It was a lie and a bad one at that. Lance knew it, and he could tell by the skeptical look on the soldier's face that he knew it too. Lance figured that the group of people on the other side of the fence who were still berat-ing the other soldier would also likely see through his alibi.

"Good . . . It's good that no one got injured. That's the main thing," the sol-dier said as he cast a glance over his shoulder toward his colleague who the group was currently berating. "As you can see, we have a minor issue on our hands. Your incident caused a delay in the schedule of the party that was supposed to clear this Rift. Their representatives have been calling nonstop."

"I see," Lance said, looking past the soldier toward the guild representatives. "So, why are they here at the gate, giving you and your colleague a hard time?"

"It seems the Rifter IDs you two submitted were lacking in necessary contact information, beyond an email address. I assume the guild representatives wanted to be here when you returned. They probably want to get your contact information and begin legal proceedings to claim their share of the reward for clearing the Rift," the soldier clarified, his tone expressing anything but enthusiasm at the prospect. "These guys did have a signed contract with the government to clear the Rift."

"I'm sorry to have created more trouble for you. As for the reward for clearing the Rift, we don't need it. Their guild can clear it. After all, it was our mistake," Lance said, waving toward the group of people in the distance. He wasn't eager to go over there and face more questioning. There may be no law against clearing a Rift without a contract, but it had been a crummy move on Lance's part.

I'll have to get used to this. To risk irritating people and be comfortable with the potential backlash, he thought, steeling himself. He had no time to spare on reserving Rifts or handling contracts, and it would also leave a trace for others to follow. His goal wasn't just to gain the power required to seek justice for Thomas, but to do so before anyone else could reach him or his loved ones.

"We'll figure it all out. The important part is that you guys are safe. We need all the Rifters we can get." The soldier then took a few steps away from the Rift and toward the site entrance. "First, I'll get you guys a coffee before we'll let the vultures talk to you, alright?" A grin formed on the soldier's face. "I wasn't quick enough with the coffee last time."

"A coffee would be great, thank you. We'll be there in a minute. We need to check our equipment and status first," Lance said. The soldier nodded and returned to his colleague, still in the midst of a heated discussion. Even with Lance's enhanced Perception, he couldn't hear exactly what was being said, but from the nonverbal cues, he gathered that it wasn't pleasant.

[You have cleared this Rift]
[You have been awarded with a Level Up]
[You are now Level 35]
[You have three unspent Attribute points]
[You have repaired an Item. 'Icarus' is now at 100% durability]
[Repair Item has reached Level 2]

As he opened his status screen, a wave of messages greeted him. He had expected the Level Up from clearing the Rift, but the boost in his Repair Skill was an unexpected, pleasant surprise. *This will be incredibly useful in the field.*

[Agility:] [66] (+3)

He dumped the three Attribute points into Agility, believing that added speed and evasion would be beneficial in the next Rift. He then knelt down and pretended to check the condition of his boots while discreetly glancing toward the soldiers and the furious representatives.

"No doubt they'd see it as a personal insult to their guild or party. I'd rather deal with monsters than talk with those suits," Lance said, rising and pretending to examine Ash's backpack to buy himself some more time. Mentally, he also wondered what those men might do if he and Ash simply rushed past them and made a beeline for the woods. *It might be funny to see those suits give chase.* At that, Lance felt a surge of Thomas's memories influencing his own thoughts.

"We can . . ." Ash said in his deep and unnatural tone as he turned to face the unstable Rift. The black energy was violent, lashing out in all directions. It was clear that it would take time for this Rift to stabilize again.

"Sounds great, but we can't. We just cleared it," Lance said with a smile as he imagined how the three representatives would react if he and Ash simply walked into the Rift.

Ash then grabbed the Guardian-shard that he had kept secure and held it out in front of him. "With this . . . we can . . . Right?"

Lance was about to argue against it, but he realized Ash might be onto something. *The Guardian-shard allows a single Rifter entry into an unstable Rift, or exit. People use it as an emergency measure, not to skip the waiting time on a Rift. What kind of Rifter would waste it on a Level-One Rift?* he thought as he picked up the Guardian-shard with caution.

He found himself entranced by the red hue for a moment. *It might work. The shard would temporarily stabilize the Rift, and, technically, I'd gain another Guardian-shard for clearing the Rift again. Not to mention, I'd gain more black-shards and some Experience.*

His eyes shifted back toward the soldiers. One of them was holding two cups of coffee. "If I time it right," he whispered with a smile behind his helmet, "we could clear this Rift as fast as possible and return to Earth during the night. Chances are, those suit-clad vultures would be gone by then, right?"

Don't think . . . Just do.

It was as if he could hear Thomas's voice in his mind, as if an old memory was being brought back to life. It sparked something inside of him, almost daring him to make a move. "Ash, I'm going to need you to tackle us into the Rift like you mean it," Lance said, before giving his friend a deliberate push. He shouted at Ash, making sure everyone at the Rift site could hear him. On cue, Ash rushed at him and tackled him toward the unstable energy. Lance extended his hand toward the Rift, letting the Guardian-shard come into contact with the black energy.

As they disappeared into the Rift, the last thing Lance saw were two cups of coffee falling to the ground and a soldier's face contorted in shock.

With a thud, Lance materialized on the ground, tumbling into the dirt. Ash landed on top of him, but Lance quickly shoved him off, laughing. The sound of his own laughter caught him off guard, as he realized the severity of the situation for both the soldiers and his own party and that he had just made it worse. He reassured himself that, if he was strategic, he could clear this Rift and avoid any repercussions. "We may need to make a run for it once we're out," Lance said as he picked himself up, noticing Ash doing the same.

He examined the familiar terrain, with its dirt, grass, birch trees, and occasional bushes. He observed the remains of his previous camp and evaluated its state. Lance had experience clearing a Rift twice in a row but never so swiftly as this.

Normally, there were several weeks of waiting as the Rift stabilized once again. This meant that a lot more time would've passed within the Rift. During those weeks, the terrain could've changed due to the passage of time. Nature would have attempted to reclaim and overgrow previous camp sites while fortifications might have crumbled due to decay.

[You have combined and retrieved Items 2x]
[You have retrieved an Item 3x]

One by one, his companions appeared beside him. The birds were instantly in the air, scanning the terrain and searching for potential dangers. Both Quill and Viper were in their dull grey overalls. Lance had given Quill a bow and arrows, along with a steel hatchet. Viper now carried several javelins, an iron shield, and the iron sword that Ash had taken from the Rift-guardian.

"Keep this for now," Lance said as he passed the heavy steel mace he had gotten from Dieter to Ash. He also gave him the shadow cloak from his Inventory. "Put this on too." Although Lance had gotten used to how the cloak warped the air around it and gave off a black fog, he knew the monsters would struggle with the Item's distorting effect. He wasn't certain how long it would take for them to reach him, however. *Maybe it'll take longer this time, given that we reentered this Rift so quickly?*

He still remembered the last run and the wave of monsters that had rushed toward them. The two of them had handled it well, but both had had to use their firearms. Lance thought about giving Ash the shotgun again but ultimately decided against it.

"Alright, this is the plan," Lance said as he raised both of his hands and accessed his Inventory. Moments later, several dead Gnolls materialized and fell to the ground. "Before the enemy horde arrives, I want this place fortified. Create a defensive circle of corpses and a small pile in the middle so Quill can have the height advantage while shooting." He then released all the Gnolls from his Inventory and his three companions began dragging corpses around.

Let's see how they handle their first horde without me, Lance thought as he sat on a small pile of dead Gnolls. He opened his status screen and examined his Repair Skill, to see what had changed now that the Skill had reached Level Two.

[Mana/Stamina regeneration] [−5%]
[Restored Durability] [+1]
[Number of Items] [+1]
[Required time per Repair cycle] [−5 seconds]

He read the description thoroughly before testing out his new Skill on an Item. Lance picked one in his Inventory that wasn't 100 percent repaired. *Lower Mana and Stamina recharge rate, but I can repair more items and do it faster. Seems like an overall advantage. I just have to be careful about using it along with my Death Forge Skill unless I want to grind my Mana and Stamina recovery rate to a complete halt.*

He shifted his gaze to the horizon when he heard the crows sounding the alarm, signaling that a threat was near. Lance stood up and climbed on top of the wall of dead Gnolls to get a better view of the horde of monsters approaching. "Fewer compared to last time. Their equipment also looks worse," Lance said as he heard Ash approach. "Ash, I'm placing you in charge of the others. Defend this base and me at all costs. Imagine that I'm an innocent civilian that you must protect."

He then leapt off the wall of corpses and emptied his Inventory of the remaining bear traps, bone knives, and javelins. He wanted his three companions to have as much of an advantage while also having a bit of fun. Lance then sat down on a pile of dead Gnolls as he grabbed his smartphone and selected a song to fit the occasion. A minute later, the horde of Gnolls crashed into the corpse fortification, and the companions forged by Lance's hand were there to meet them with an almost eager determination.

It didn't take long before blood spatters reached Lance as he sat there on his throne of corpses. He remained motionless as he observed his expanding army at work. Droplets of blood ran down the cracked screen of his smartphone, still displaying the names of the songs he was playing at maximum volume.

Status Compendium

Name:	Lance Turner
Level:	35
Class:	Death Smith

Attributes

Endurance:	66	**Agility:**	69	**Wisdom:**	58
Strength:	66	**Perception:**	55	**Luck:**	55
Health:	1850	**Mana:**	375		
Stamina:	575	**Inventory:**	73		

Traits

Taint of death:	Able to use Rift corpses as items	Prolonged use results . . . ~ERROR UNREADABLE!~
Shard instability:	Prolonged use results . . . ~ERROR UNREADABLE!~	Prolonged use results . . . ~ERROR UNREADABLE!~

Skills

Mend Wounds	Lvl 2	Restores minor wounds	+20 Health Stamina	−15 Mana
Death Forge	Lvl 2	Allows (re)forging of death related items	+2 Items	−Raw materials −Black-shards −50% Stamina regeneration −50% Mana regeneration
Repair Item	Lvl 2	Restores durability on items	+2 durability per 2 items per 55 seconds	−Raw materials −Black-shards −30% Stamina regeneration −30% Mana regeneration
Ricochet	Lvl 1	Bounces throwing attacks with greater speed and accuracy	+1 Bounce +5% Speed +5% Accuracy	−25 stamina per bounce
Detonate	Lvl 1	Detonates an item based on its original durability	−50% base Durability	−25 Mana per usage

Retainers

Ash	1x	Human	Rift-glider eye +2 Sight +Heat vision	Centaur-toad muscle +4 Speed +100 Durability
Quill	1x	Human		
Viper	1x	Human		
Icarus	1x	Falcon (hybrid*)	Rift-glider eye +2 Sight +Heat vision	Gnoll bone +1 Defense +120 Durability
Alpha	1x	Crow	Gnoll muscle +2 Speed +40 Durability	Gnoll bone +1 Defense +120 Durability
Bravo	1x	Crow	Gnoll bone +1 Defense +120 Durability	Gnoll muscle +2 Speed +40 Durability

CHAPTER SEVEN

Echo of the Past

A few days later
June, 14 AR
Paris, France

LOUIS

ocus on your breathing . . . keep your mind on the task ahead . . .

Louis Vidal steeled himself as he tuned out the sound of a military plane taking out several airborne monsters that were trying to fly past a portion of the wall that surrounded the city of Paris. He blocked out the sounds of artillery rounds and rockets hitting their targets. Instead, Louis focused his attention on the advancing horde of monsters in the street below him. He could hear the three special forces operatives on the ground floor fighting to stop their advance.

"I repeat, hostiles have overrun our safe house. We have one injured Rifter. We need immediate extraction," the soldier next to Louis said through his radio as he tried to help the injured Rifter by applying pressure to his chest wound.

Echo

Louis activated a Skill and his perception of the world heightened. Ignoring the soldier and the wounded Rifter beside him, he closed his eyes. In that moment, for a split second, he could sense every minor vibration within a small radius. Each felt unique, enabling him to differentiate between human and monster. Even from his position on the roof, he became aware of the situation below.

Barrage
Double Strike
Imbue Wind

As Louis activated three Skills, he felt a portion of his Mana and Stamina burn up. He readied an arrow and drew back on his bow. A second later, the arrow flew upward and disappeared from his sight. When it eventually returned, the arrow had multiplied by five. They landed within the horde of monsters that were rushing toward the building, with each arrow creating two identical, gaping, deep wounds on the monsters. The imbued air-pressure lashed out violently and tore the monsters apart from the inside before the Mana dissipated.

Louis then stored his bow and grabbed a canister from his harness. He pulled out the pin and dropped it downstairs in front of the main entrance. Moments later, he heard the hissing sound of tear gas pouring out. "What's their ETA?" Louis asked as he retrieved his rifle, leaned over the edge, and emptied the first magazine into the monstrous horde.

He could see over three hundred of the Fishmen charging forward, even after he had peppered them with bullets and harassed them with teargas. The monsters were humanoid in build, if lanky, blue-skinned, and hunched over. Their faces resembled those of an anglerfish, their enormous mouths filled with rows of sharp teeth. What made them even more terrifying was that these creatures seemed to hold little regard for their own safety.

"A few minutes . . . hopefully. You know the drill."

"Are the extraction forces Rifters or grunts?" Louis asked the soldier next to him as he crouched down again to change the magazine. A moment later, a large piece of rubble hit the spot where he had been standing.

"Probably grunts," the soldier said as he handed Louis another canister of teargas. "You know how those prima donna shard-polishers can be. Probably too busy rehearsing their next PR moment. No offense."

Louis smiled as he grabbed the canister, pulled out the pin, and chucked it over the edge into the mass of monsters. He could hear the intense fighting as the three soldiers downstairs unleashed a tremendous amount of firepower to keep the hordes at bay. *This is bad. All because this idiot decided to play hero and anger a whole horde.* Louis gazed upon the wounded Rifter. The wound looked severe, and the man was losing a lot of blood. Still, he had seen Rifters survive worse injuries.

He leaned over the edge again. He spotted a few different-looking monsters in the distance. These were large, muscular beasts that were strong enough to flip a car with ease. Dubbed "Minotaurs," these monsters were hard to take down, but explosives and high-caliber rounds could do enough damage if someone knew where to aim. Beyond that, there were wolf-like monsters, and the occasional humanoid that was fully clad in strange metal armor. Those monsters were shorter than the average human but bulkier. "Dammit! We got a little Tin Can up North."

"What the hell! Intel mentioned nothing about Dwarf sightings," the soldier exclaimed. They had heard reports from other soldiers and Rifters about these metal-clad monsters being incredibly tough opponents. Their heavy metal armor featured strange runes that generated a protective barrier. Anything faster than a thrown pebble would lose its momentum because of these runes, neutralizing most modern weapons other than explosives and chemicals. There was a limit to the amount of force that those runes could stop, but they typically took a lot to overcome.

"Since when is intel ever accurate?" Louis said as he dropped his rifle and grabbed a nearby bag. He opened it and carefully pulled out a larger rifle, sliding a fresh magazine into the weapon. Louis had fired a fifty-BMG Hécate sniper rifle a few times when he was in the military before becoming a Rifter. The rifle in his hand was like a bigger brother to that one. *Getting arthritis in my shoulder will be the least of my concerns when using this.*

He took a deep breath and psyched himself up before leaning over the edge again, scanning for a target. He spotted a large Minotaur charging toward the entrance, ignoring the tear gas. A stream of bullets flew from the entrance toward it, but it barely seemed to slow the charging behemoth. Louis pulled the trigger and felt a jolt of pain through his shoulder and spine. At the same time, the Minotaur's skull exploded in a shower of red and black gore as its body fell backwards, crushing several Fishmen behind it.

The second shot blasted a large hole into the chest of another Minotaur, causing it to fall to its knees, thrashing around in what brief moments of life it still had left. The third he aimed at the Dwarf, but the bullet crumpled the moment it hit the strange forcefield that surrounded the monster. Louis's fourth and fifth shots produced a similar effect, slamming into the Dwarf's barrier. "Tin Can over there is ignoring my shots as if I'm throwing croutons at it. We need the extraction now," Louis said as he emptied the rest of his rounds into other powerful monsters before ducking for safety.

"Evac is almost here," the soldier next to Louis exclaimed before several explosions went off in the lower floors of the building they were using for their last stand, indicating that the monsters had broken through.

This is a disaster, Louis thought as he reloaded his massive rifle and aimed it at the concrete surface below him. He closed his eyes, took a deep breath, and braced for what was to come. Despite the three soldiers below being skilled, it was only a matter of time before the monsters would overrun them.

Echo

He could feel the hundreds of vibrations beneath him, painting a mental picture of how the horde of monsters had broken through the barricade on the ground floor and were now flooding inside. Louis could sense the three soldiers rushing up the stairs, barely staying ahead of the enemy. Just as the nearest monster was about to grab one of them, Louis squeezed the trigger. The bullet tore through roof tiles, bypassing several walls before hitting the monster closest to the soldier.

Echo

Echo

Echo

Echo

Four times he fired the rifle with his eyes closed, narrowly missing the soldiers while decimating large groups of monsters that were packed together in the stairwell leading up to the roof. He quickly reloaded and aimed the weapon at the roof's entrance door. A part of him wondered how long they would need to hold out or if they would need to escape on their own.

We can't get away while carrying a wounded Rifter, he thought. The man's wounds were too severe and the amount of gear on the Rifter would make it hard to carry him, even for Louis. The thought lingered in his mind for a moment before he suppressed it. Thoughts like that reminded him of the foul sin he had committed months earlier.

The door flew open as the retreating soldiers rushed onto the roof. Despite the obvious fear on their faces, they immediately turned around and began throwing everything they had into the never-ending wave of monsters. Grenades, teargas, smoke bombs, and every round they had left in their weapons—the three soldiers fired it all into the door opening as they fell back to join Louis and the others. Even now, facing certain death, these men kept a level head.

Louis had already emptied his magazine into the wave of monsters and had switched back to his bow. With his Barrage Skill, he kept pelting the monsters, and his arrows never seemed to lose momentum because of his Imbue Wind Skill. But even with his large Inventory space, he knew he was running out of arrows and burning through his Mana and Stamina.

Still, it wasn't enough to stop the tide, as the monsters finally had enough bodies and momentum to pour through the doorway and onto the roof. Dozens of Fishmen and weird wolves flooded the rooftop as they surrounded the soldiers and Rifters. Even a large, hulking Minotaur joined the swarm, growling and roaring in challenge. It towered over the humans, nearly twice as tall as them and several times bulkier. It whipped the other monsters into a frenzy before they all charged as one.

"Get down!" Louis yelled as he pulled the soldiers down with him the moment his high Perception picked up on something. Moments later, three Gazelle helicopters swooped in with their sides already pointed toward the advancing hordes. The helicopters met the monsters' aggression with their own as their side-mounted mini-guns opened fire, spitting out thousands of rounds per minute.

Louis gripped his bow firmly, ready to take out anything that survived. He stopped when he witnessed the destruction the monsters and the roof itself were enduring. There was nothing in sight that didn't have several holes in it. The Minotaur was hardly recognizable, as a gunner had forced the monster to endure a full minute's worth of fire from one mini-gun.

"Move!" a soldier yelled as they moved toward the first helicopter and helped the wounded Rifter inside, with two soldiers following him in as well. Louis then rushed toward the second helicopter with the rest and climbed in. The helicopters then left the scene while their guns continued to pepper the streets and buildings still packed with monsters. In the distance, Louis could still see the gleam of a Dwarf's rune armor among the monstrous horde.

The trip back to the safety of the wall took practically no time at all. Louis could already see weapon systems on top of the wall tracking their movements. Beyond that, there were helicopters and planes going to and from the walled-off city. It reminded him of a busy beehive. *This seems impossible*, he thought as he realized they had only regained a few streets in the last month.

He heard another loud explosion in the distance, hinting that another strategic location was being targeted by either a missile or bombardment. It wouldn't make a significant dent in the monstrous horde, but it would decrease the strategic advantage that the monsters would have at the start of Operation Bastille.

"How's he doing?" Louis asked through his headset as he felt the helicopter gain altitude to avoid debris that was being flung at them by some monsters in the street below. In response, the gunner at the side squeezed the trigger and sent a few quick bursts of angry metal streaming downward.

"Pressure is holding . . . for now . . . but his chest is all messed up. He needs a proper bandage," a soldier called in from the other helicopter.

Louis bit his tongue in frustration as he closed his eyes. He had disliked the Rifter from the start. The young man was arrogant and thought that a few Levels under his belt were equal to years of combat experience within the special forces. The young man reminded him of Connor Moore. *Hopefully he'll learn from this experience*, Louis thought as he slid his hand in his pocket and let his fingers touch three bullets there. His mood instantly soured when he did so.

"Two minutes," the pilot called in as their helicopter finally reached the wall and flew over it.

Louis took one last glance at the ruined city of Paris. He still remembered how it had looked before the Rift. Old buildings, important historical landmarks, museums, homes, bakeries. Now, there wasn't a building in Paris that didn't show scars from heavy fighting, if it wasn't already reduced to rubble or infested with monsters.

Louis was part of one of the many reconnaissance teams. These teams would map dangerous hotspots and provide vital information that the military would use after July 14th, when Operation Bastille would begin. It was a dangerous job but an important one. Louis, however, had jumped at the chance when the opportunity arose for Rifters to work alongside special forces.

He caught one final glimpse of the ruined city as the helicopter lowered itself and blocked his line of sight. On this side of the wall, he could see the military presence. Hangars, barracks, and other buildings were already in place, with more under construction. There was an airfield in the background, complete with landing zones for helicopters and refueling stations. In the distance, he could see trucks pouring in, carrying more manpower, materials, and ammunition.

Louis remembered a conversation he had overheard between two officers making calculations of just how much actual weight in artillery shells the military would throw at the monsters on the first day. Louis's jaw had nearly dropped when he had realized those numbers were in the metric tons.

He braced himself for a moment as he felt the helicopter land and the engine powering down. Louis and the soldier got out and rushed toward the other helicopter to help carry the wounded Rifter out and into the ambulance on standby.

After shutting the door, Louis and the others watched it drive toward the medical facility in the north. Those left behind realized they had gotten lucky that no one had died and that the helicopters had arrived in time.

"I need a shower."

"You already needed one before we went out."

Louis smiled as he listened to the soldiers chatting while they walked toward the military complex. They were discussing meals and showers, but they all knew they would have to be debriefed first. Louis put most of his gear in his Inventory and followed the soldiers. All the while, he kept his hands in his pockets so that he could feel the bullets there, each of which held an ominous number etched in the casing.

Six . . . five . . . four . . .

CHAPTER EIGHT

Six, Five, Four

LOUIS

As he waited in the corridor with the other soldiers for their debriefing, Louis scratched his chin and observed the other squads. Some had both soldiers and Rifters working together as a combined unit. Sometimes, this proved highly effective. Other times it ended in disaster like what had happened with them. Conflicting personalities and a lack of military training played a role, but the main problem was the differences in their natures. A Rifter couldn't suddenly gain years of specialized training and function perfectly in the military, and trained soldiers couldn't match the resilience, speed, and raw power of Rifters who were in a league of their own.

"Do you want one?" One of his squad members offered him a Carambar, wiggling the caramel-filled candy in front of him.

"Who would say no to such a grand gift?" Louis said as he grabbed the candy and bit off a chunk. The mixture of cacao and caramel rejuvenated his taste buds after his last deployment. It was clear from the other Rifters and soldiers in the room that they had also seen a lot of action.

He felt the urge to slide his hand back in his pocket and trace the lines of the numbers etched on the three bullets there. Louis knew it was bad to fixate on them, but he felt almost compelled to do so. *Six, five, four.* He pushed the rest of the candy into his mouth and forced himself to focus on the sweet taste instead.

To occupy his mind, Louis glanced at the other Rifters, trying to determine their nationalities and assess their Levels. The latter was tough to do unless you had an exceptional Perception or specialized Class. Still, the greater the gap between two Rifters, the more they would feel the difference. Louis was an experienced veteran, with a Level now in the high eighties.

He still remembered meeting Rifters who were of a much higher caliber.

He had met elites with Levels between two and four hundred. They tended to carry a formidable presence. And the time he had met a Master Rifter whose Level was far above the four-hundred mark had been even more unsettling, despite that Rifter being quite friendly. Most powerful Rifters learned to either exploit or suppress the effect they had on others, so they could work with weaker Rifters.

He heard movement before a door opened and several Rifters filed into the room. They were all clad in expensive gear, with a large assortment of Mana stones embedded within it to serve as an external storage. That most of these stones bore large cracks spoke volumes about the amount of overuse and strain these Items had endured. *Most of them are foreigners. They look like Mages or Channelers,* Louis thought as he noticed just how different these men and women were from one another and how specialized their gear was. Either they were all heavy hitters in terms of magical offensive, or these Rifters were all there to act as support for a more powerful individual.

As these Mana-stone-clad Rifters left the waiting room, Louis got up to look out of the window. He was curious to see what guild or organization these men and women belonged to. He had barely gotten out of his seat when he felt his knees buckle due to immense pressure. *I must've been more tired than I realized,* he thought for a moment, yet couldn't shake the feeling that this wasn't true. He wasn't that tired. No, he felt a sense of dread.

The soldiers in the room seemed to be unaffected and were chatting amongst one another or staving off boredom by reading something from the magazine stand. The other Rifters seemed to share Louis's predicament, with many of them clutching the white-shards in their chests as if they were having trouble breathing. *What the hell is going on?*

The door opened once more and a woman in armor stepped in. She had an average build, dull brown hair, and brown eyes. Her skin was sickly and pale. Everything about her seemed average, yet every Rifter in the room found it harder and harder to breathe. Even Louis noticed the pressure in his own white-shard, as if it was reacting to the woman in the room.

"Isn't that Newton?" a soldier whispered as more and more people turned to face the woman.

"Why do they call her that?"

"Why do you think, genius? Haven't you seen footage of her abilities?"

Louis ignored the talk amongst the soldiers as he kept his gaze downward. His chest felt like it was about to explode from some sort of pressure. Any doubt he might've had about the woman's abilities was gone in a second. Just her presence alone was enough to subdue him and make him feel a sense of dread he had never experienced before.

Viviane Beaumanoir, Louis thought as he finally summed up the willpower to raise his head and look directly at her. He knew what she could do. He had heard the stories and seen the camera footage of her exploits. The woman was a powerful Mage and had Skills that could manipulate gravity itself to the point where even most Rift-guardians were powerless to stop her. She was so skilled that other Rifters had dubbed her Newton due to the nature of her Skills. He wasn't ashamed to admit that it took him several minutes after she finally left the room before he felt relaxed again.

Not long after that Louis and the rest of his squad were called in to be debriefed.

Louis left the building with his squad before each of them went their separate ways. All around him he could see trucks delivering equipment or troops or clearing rubble. He could see NATO soldiers in the distance working in unison with the French Foreign Legion, Americans, Australians, and Japanese soldiers.

The sheer logistics behind all of this is insane, Louis thought as he made his way over to a nearby canteen to grab some food. He suppressed the urge to touch the three bullets in his pocket, knowing it would only add to his uncertainty.

He ignored the looks he got as he grabbed some coffee and a hot meal. Louis knew that he stood out with his mixture of chain mail, leather, and modern protective gear. There wasn't a part of him that wasn't broadcasting that he was a Rifter. No doubt most of the soldiers here were wondering why he was eating with them instead of staying in personal compounds designed for the Rifters.

Most of the Rifters had even brought PR teams and personal aides with them. Louis preferred it like this, to stay with the rest of the men. It reminded him of how he had once been before he had sacrificed others to save his own hide.

The debriefing had been alright. The wounded Rifter had been a setback, but the man would no doubt recover in time. Louis had been honest about the wounded Rifter's performance and suggested that the man should take up a different role in the future. One that might better suit his nature.

The intel they had provided had been vital for the next few months. More would be required, seeing as the monstrous threat was both numerous and complex. There were dozens of monster variants out there, ranging from the animalistic feral types to those that showed intelligence and could pull off an ambush.

Louis had seen Rift-guardians lead other monsters down into the sewers or into buildings to take shelter when planes flew overhead. A part of him wondered if the bombardments, artillery strikes, and recon teams the military was already deploying were a bad thing. The idea that the monsters were adapting and beginning to understand the tactics humanity used was frightening.

We need every advantage we can get here, Louis thought as he recalled the way some monsters could shrug off high-caliber rounds and only get angrier because of it. He finished his meal and drink before he decided it was time to get up and take a proper shower. He had become increasingly aware of the fact that he was still dirty from his previous assignment.

He cleaned off his tray before leaving the canteen and making his way over toward a small housing unit to which the GRRO had assigned him. He found the place just as he had previously left it, much to his relief. Just to be sure, he locked the door and propped a chair against it to serve as a barricade. He then checked the locks on the windows before closing the curtains.

"A long shower and a nap will do," he said out loud as he made his way over to his bathroom and stored most of his Rifter equipment in his Inventory. With his gear no longer there, the excess dirt, bits of rock, and dried-up blood all fell on the ground. He then removed his remaining gear and clothing that weren't made from Rift material and placed them in a hamper, making sure to retrieve the three bullets from his pocket before doing so. He placed them in the bathroom sink in such a way that he could see the numbers carved into them.

"Six . . . five . . . four," he said, staring at them for a moment. He wondered what type of psychopath was leaving these things for him. He ran a hand over his stubbly chin. The rough texture helped snap him out of his thoughts as he stepped into the shower and let the warm water wash over him.

He just stood there for a while as he felt the heat of the water easing his tired muscles. He had been going on scouting missions nonstop as of late—both to get away from the psychopath and their countdown and to make a difference in this war for Paris. He truly wanted to help, to get rid of these monsters and hopefully save lives where he could.

He had to. There were monsters out there that even highly trained soldiers were struggling with. He recalled how ineffective the high-caliber sniper rifle had been with the Dwarf. *Just a handful of them could wipe out hundreds of soldiers if they ever broke through the walls.*

In this deployment, the monsters had overrun their position in a matter of minutes when the other Rifters had exposed their position. Despite mines, grenades, and the weapons the soldiers had deployed, the monsters had still broken through. *We might've held them back if all of us had been Rifters. A couple of Warriors to form a chokepoint at the stairwell, with Mage and range support to dish out the damage.*

He didn't like the idea, but this war needed more Rifters. As spoiled and arrogant as some of them might be, the fact that they could go toe-to-toe with these monsters was the only thing that mattered right now.

He recalled what his squad had shared in their debriefing, going over enemy numbers, hotspots, and zones of movement. Even with satellites, drones, and boots on the ground, there still was much that humanity didn't know about these monsters.

The officer and the GRRO official at the briefing had also mentioned a new task force that was to be created—one where skilled Rifters could operate on their own further within Paris. The task was to map out better routes, find high-profile targets, provide more intel on the types of monsters, and establish safe houses throughout the city. All the while remaining unnoticed by the monsters.

"Nothing short of a suicide mission," Louis said out loud as he ran his hands through his hair before turning off the shower. He grabbed a towel and dried himself off as he watched the steam rising in the bathroom. It reminded him of a Rift that he had once been in where visibility had almost been non-existent.

His heart skipped a beat when he caught sight of the bullets in the bathroom sink; where there had previously been three, now there was a fourth. Louis didn't need to look at the number carved in it, seeing as someone had written the same number on the fogged-up mirror: 3.

He could feel his body tense up as it flooded with adrenaline. A blade and a pistol appeared in his hands within an instant as he rushed out of the bathroom to clear the other room. He swept the place twice, having checked all the windows, the steel ceiling, and the floor. There weren't any signs of a break-in, nor was the door unlocked. The chair he had used as a barricade was also still in place.

"Cut it out! Come and face me," Louis roared as loud as he could. He felt his frustration and fear finally get the best of him. This was worse than any Rift or any monster that he had faced before. "I need to get away from here. I—" Louis recalled the offer to join the task force. Suddenly, the suicide mission sounded a lot better. He'd be able to hide within the vastness of the ruined city from this thread.

There's no way this assassin could find me there.

CHAPTER NINE

Luck of the Irish

Several weeks later
The Hag's Attic, Norway

FERGUS

Fergus Murry felt his body struggling for air, but he knew he had to keep fighting. People were counting on him. He saw the devastation around him. Clearly Lance and the silent Ash had failed and were out of commission.

People are counting on you, Fergus. We can't fail now. There's too much at stake. His arms felt like lead, the cramps in his fingers were getting worse, and sweat dripped from his brow. *Fight through it. Ignore the pain.*

He willed his hands to obey his commands, rather than instinctively jerking backwards. He made them hold the object, securing it as gravity and momentum fought against him.

As his body protested, he struggled with the elements and made his will manifest as the object changed shape. Its nature was wild and chaotic, as if constantly shapeshifting through countless possibilities. *Hold it. Contain it.*

"You can do it," Reidar said from his kneeling position next to Fergus. The young man's eyes were just as focused as Fergus's. "Nearly there. Just keep it steady."

"Stop pestering him, Reidar," Eirin chastised her younger brother.

Fergus simply ignored them as he shifted his full attention back to the pottery wheel. The black clay taunted him as it fought against his steady grasp, wobbling left and right. Still, the Irishman held strong against the centrifugal force and the unyielding clay. Seconds later, he pushed his thumbs and index fingers together to close off the cylindrical object. Then he slowly pushed the top inward just a fraction before he stopped the pottery wheel.

"It's . . . done . . ." Fergus said, carefully moving his hands backwards. Just then, Reidar gave him an unexpected bear hug and then backed away to allow the tired Fergus some room to stretch.

The five of them were in an old wooden attic that reeked of old dirt and sweat, mixed with the stink of the old gas heater behind them. All around them were the remnants of Fergus's work. Dozens of hollow spherical constructs that he had made from reddish clay were drying on a nearby shelf. Each of them was as large as a golf ball and shaped to be as thin as possible. Fergus still wasn't sure why Lance had requested they be designed like that. Apparently, he wanted them to be able to break easily.

On the shelf behind it were cylindrical tubes, like the one he had just made. The flat bottom offered enough stability to stand on its own, while the horizontal lines etched in the clay offered a better grip once the clay had dried further and lost most of its plasticity. Compared to the spherical constructs he had made, these cylindrical ones were thicker and would hopefully not shatter as easily.

Fergus paused for a second as he watched Lance get up from his chair. The young man stood surrounded by the works he had made, if one even called them that. Every object either represented some mutated clay monstrosity or was shaped in an elongated manner that would even have startled Sigmund Freud.

The Irishman felt his dry throat go through the motions of swallowing, mostly due to fear, uncertainty, and hope. For the last few weeks, he had been working hard, providing the Rifters with equipment and supplies, and orchestrating logistics. Lately he had been allowed to join the two of them as they received private ceramic lessons from Randi Kristiansen, a bitter old woman who just so happened to be Reidar and Eirin's grandmother.

Despite looking like a senile crone, the woman had been a decent ceramist in the past. Although old age had prevented her from practicing her art, she had taught Lance and Ash before finally shifting her full attention toward Fergus.

Please like it. Please . . . Fergus thought as he watched Lance move closer toward the clay cylinder on the pottery wheel. *I've been at it for days . . . weeks even. I did my best.* At first, he had done so because his boss, Brian, had instructed him to do so. But as of late, he felt a need for Lance's approval.

These people are true Rifters. Fergus watched Lance carefully touching the object with calloused fingers as his hazel gaze inspected it from all angles. *They've cleared five Rifts since they arrived. They've cleared the same Rift back-to-back twice, destroying it entirely.* Fergus still recalled how Brian had reacted to the news that Lance and Ash had first done this back in May. Apparently, it was a big deal because of the speed with which the two men had cleared it.

Fergus didn't really have a reference for what made a Rifter average or great. His most significant achievement in life was surviving his first and only Rift. It had been mostly luck that Rifters had arrived to save him and the other survivors. He hadn't stepped foot in a Rift after that. It was one of the few things that he and Brian shared. The events of the Rift had traumatized them both, although for Brian it had taken a while longer to realize that.

Now, Lance was face-to-face with him. He could feel his piercing gaze on him, weighing him in that moment. Fergus felt a droplet of liquid fear running down his spine as his body instinctively sensed the difference between the two of them. Back in Dublin, he hadn't been able to feel it like this, but now he could. *Just how much stronger have you gotten? Is that growth normal?* That feeling dissipated in a moment, as if the young man were suppressing it again.

"I'm proud of you, Fergus. These are perfect . . . despite what Randi might say when she comes back," Lance said with a reassuring nod before placing a hand on Fergus's shoulder. "The two of us never could've made something as good as this."

"Thanks. But it's nothing special. I'm glad I could help." Fergus lied through his teeth. He had spent every minute of free time he had lately watching pottery instruction videos or going to the old hag for personal lessons. The mere feel of Lance's hand on his shoulder was enough to almost make him cry. *Thank God!* he thought as he met Lance's gaze. For a moment, he felt like they were equals, or at least part of the same team. It surprised him how much he had longed for that.

For years he had gotten by as either muscle for hire or as a fence, using his intimidating size and facial features to scare most people into backing off or thinking he was a Rifter. He knew he wasn't the brightest bulb out there. He had barely passed primary school and later dropping out entirely. But here, now, he felt like he was making a difference.

He had dropped the Rifters at a Rift-site near a town. Ash and Lance had cleared it in four days and destroyed it on the spot. There had been no chance for celebration because the two men had cleared it in the dead of night and had left the site before anyone in town had found out, save for the soldiers that guarded it.

Lance and Ash weren't aware of what their actions had meant for the city, but Fergus knew. He had visited the town the next day for a supply run. He had seen the celebrations. The townspeople had dropped everything that day to make an impromptu festival.

I want to be a part of this. If I can even contribute a little to this, it will be worth it, he thought as his smile widened. "How about we grab a drink to celebrate finishing these bad boys? If we hurry up, we can leave before Grandma gets back. No reason to let this good feeling sour, right?" he asked. Then, all five of them froze on the spot when they heard the creak of the old door behind them. Fergus's face turned the same pale shade as Ash when he noticed that even Lance was afraid. "She's behind me, isn't she?"

Ash and Lance slowly nodded in unison. A tear ran down Fergus's cheek.

A few days had passed since Fergus, Lance, and Ash had finished their ceramic project, most of the pieces having survived the drying process before they had gone into the kiln for heat treatment.

"I don't really feel comfortable doing this," Fergus said as he tore off another piece of duct tape, holding the tablet against his chest. He continued clumsily taping the device against his torso to keep it in place. The small motorhome he was in barely gave him any room to move around in, but the sense of privacy helped calm his nerves.

"Don't be such a baby," Brian said through the speaker. His face could be seen on the screen as he livestreamed. "They'll love it."

Fergus sighed as he tore off and fastened a last piece of tape. He figured the tablet was now anchored firmly. "I look like an idiot, carrying a man on my chest."

"Fergus, you're an idiot. Trust me, it looks cool. We look like Krang."

"What is that?"

"Not what. *Who*! Haven't you seen the Teenage Mutant . . . never mind. What's important is that I make a good impression. And this way I can properly look around the campground and see these 'new companions with the weird names,' as you call them. The pictures you gave me only showed them from a distance."

Fergus paused for a moment. He had a feeling that this was a poor plan. In the last few days, he had made progress with Lance and the others. Ash was still a scary enigma that didn't speak with him, and the two newcomers were similar, although less frightening. Still, Lance had complimented him several times, and he had even convinced him and the two Norwegian siblings to grab a bite to eat at an actual restaurant. "I don't think the Rifters will see it as a good impression. I mean, they either are training, working, or clearing Rifts. You should see the amount of sprinting and weightlifting Lance has been doing, and all the sparring he is doing with the rest of his party in the mornings. All four of them have been working really hard and—"

Brian interrupted him with a snort before he spoke. "Oh? And I haven't?"

"No, you're working hard. I didn't mean it like that, Boss. But you're wearing a Hawaiian shirt and I can see the beach and a tiki bar behind you. I don't think they'll respond positively to that," Fergus said, trying to alleviate the tension that was building up. Brian was a great many things, but he was horrible at being self-reflective.

"Buddy, you're as sharp as a marble. Just leave the thinking to me," Brian said as he shifted his own camera upward so that only his face was visible on the screen taped to Fergus's torso. "But you're positive about the number of Rifts they cleared since then?"

The large Irishmen nodded once before he remembered Brian couldn't see him unless he bent forward to look at his own chest. "Yes, they cleared another Rift last night, so six in total since coming here."

"And the produce?"

"You mean the monsters?" Fergus asked, bemused.

"Yes, I mean the monsters, you bogan. Did you think I was sending them on a grocery errand?"

"Oh, no the monst— um, the produce is good. They brought in four more when they were done. It's on ice and I'll deliver . . . it later today."

"Four more? You're sure?"

Fergus nodded reassuringly before he suddenly stopped. "Yes, I counted them myself."

"Let's just get this over with. Move out, Krang."

"Who?" Fergus asked as he got up and made his way toward the door.

"Don't ruin this for me!"

Five minutes later and Fergus could already feel his mood dropping. Lance was discussing the next items he was ordering while Brian was talking about how the latest shipment of monster corpses had too many arrow holes, thus damaging profits.

Fergus simply kept quiet, occasionally turning around to allow Brian to observe the state of the camp. He aimed the camera at Quill, the pale woman in the back who was using a bow and arrow to shoot at several targets. Like with the others, she wore sunglasses, a hoodie, and a thick coat that hid most of her features, save for her dyed-green hair.

The other newcomer, Viper, was standing next to Ash as they completed their respective tasks. Viper was using old shirts and a barrel to filter wet clay they had brought back from the Rift, removing as much of the impurities as they could. His once-brown hair was now a mess of reddish clay stains. They even covered his sunglasses. The table next to the man contained several of the dried clay orbs and cylinders they had made. Even now, Fergus felt a jolt of pride at how good the finished project looked.

Ash was holding a large metal pot above an improvised gas stove. Occasionally, he used a spoon to swirl the fine sand in the pot, allowing it to heat evenly.

Fergus was at a loss for why these Rifters wanted to heat sand. At first, he figured they were making glass, but he had been told that this wasn't the case. When the sand was hot enough, Lance and Ash would then use a steel funnel and pour the sand into the hollow ceramic orbs before plugging up the hole with a bit of wet clay and glue made from bone. Afterward, Lance would store these items within his Inventory.

"So, have you tested them inside a Rift already?" Brian asked, as he did his best to maintain eye contact with Lance, despite the fact that Fergus was constantly moving around.

"Not yet. We found a decent source of clay and fine sand a while back. I figured it would work better than boiling water or oil," Lance said. He looked annoyed.

"It should stick better, not to mention get underneath and through gaps in the armor. Smart idea. Mass producing them might be hard. But it should work wonders in a pinch," Brian said, doing his best to point at the spherical objects. He then shifted his aim toward the cylindrical ones. One of the Rifters had filled a few of them with wet wood shavings, charcoal, wet grass, and an oily substance, with some dried plant fiber that would function as a wick. "That, however, looks horrendous."

"I don't have many other options, and I don't want to be too reliant on other workshops. Besides, I tested it out, and it produces enough smoke to remain useful," Lance countered as he got more defensive.

"Useful? Sure. I mean, inside a Rift you usually have enough time to light something during combat, and the wick would no doubt have stayed dry throughout your stay there," Brian said sarcastically as he eyed Lance intently. "Your oxidizing agent is horrendous, your fuel source is some weird oil that is no doubt untested, and don't get me started on the moderator."

"And you can do better?"

"Better?" Brian said, leaning closer to the camera while exposing his Hawaiian shirt in the process. "Listen, kid, if there is one thing I know, it's how to abuse substances. I can't conjure saltpeter, lactose, or fancy chemicals out of thin air, but there are alternatives found within a Rift. A chemist can extract those from minerals, animal parts, or plants. It might take time and money, but you can probably get what you need to make your fancy smoke bombs. Or you can find the stuff that you need by chance. You just do your thing and occasionally jump into a Rift that appeared in a supermarket or gardening center. I'll text you a shopping list."

Fergus wasn't sure why, but the arrogant counter from Brian seemed to calm Lance down a bit. Moments later they were discussing proper ways to set up a gas forge, extract and crystalize sugar, ferment Rift-fruit into alcohol, and the benefits of mixing said alcohol with any Styrofoam they might find. The large Irishman still sensed a lot of mistrust between the two of them, but the two men obviously shared a fascination for creative solutions and making things.

"And, kid, if you have any self-respect at all, you get rid of the wicks. I'll send you the schematics for a Mana-fuse. It's made from fragmented Mana stone pieces coated in a red mineral found in a lot of Rifts. It's incredibly stable and dormant until you pour some of your Mana into it. Afterward, it's a lit fuse and it quickly spikes in temperature," Brian explained. Afterward, the man took a generous sip from a cocktail he had just received from a waitress.

"Really?" Lance asked as Brian toyed around with the tiny pink umbrella in his drink.

Brian simply raised an eyebrow. "I'd prefer to be there, right by your side, helping you with your middle school science project, but us grownups have a job to do. I can't help that one of the monster corpse buyers lives around these parts. I'm burdened by fate here. Trust me."

At that, Lance made his way over to Quill and instructed her to help Ash and Viper as he began pulling out arrows from the target he had set up against a tree.

"The new recurve bows I made for you should help . . . and the shields . . . and the short swords . . . and the spears . . . You know, I can't help but notice that you have asked—although 'blackmailed' might be a better choice of word—me to craft you several sets of these. Ten of each. Way more than your current party of four," Brian commented as Fergus stepped closer to Lance again. "Will more of your silent friends join you for the next Rift? Fergus failed to elaborate how the four of you met?"

"I never told Fergus," Lance said, staring at the screen duct taped to Fergus's chest before looking upward, no doubt uncomfortable at the idea of talking about someone that was present and serving as a glorified mobile streaming device.

"Surely you can see why I might have some concerns. Delightful as your new companions might be, I don't know them. You didn't discuss it with me . . . and they're scaring poor Fergus," the fixer said, throwing the Irishman under the bus and destroying what little trust the man had built up with Lance and Ash.

Lance simply flashed an unnervingly pleasant smile as he leaned forward to face Brian. "Like you, I'm also burdened by fate, so you will just have to trust my choices." Afterward, he pressed a finger on the side of the tablet to switch off the device, cutting off Brian's angry response. "Fergus, collect the equipment the drunk promised me. My people are going to need it when we go into another Rift tomorrow."

Fergus just nodded as he stepped backwards to put some distance between them. He quickly tore the tablet from his chest as he made his way over toward his car. *My people . . . Not me . . . I'm right back to Square One. Dammit!* He cursed Brian for talking him into doing this.

Krang . . . They'll love it . . . Right!

CHAPTER TEN

Arabian Dreams

Several days later
Inside Rift 19

LANCE

Fresh blood filled Lance's mouth as foreign memories ravaged his mind. His head was hurting from struggling to make sense of it all.

Don't move, Lance heard himself thinking in a language that wasn't his own. He didn't hear his own mouth uttering those words. They were Iyas's. A soft hand grabbed his own, clutching it tighter by the second. Both instinctively knew that any sound would kill them, even so much as a whisper. *Shahida . . . Don't speak . . . Don't move . . . No matter what we hear.* He simply stood there within the memory, paralyzed by what he was hearing outside of the closet he was huddled in with other family members. He could hear his uncles and aunts being torn apart, his grandmother eaten alive, and his father screaming. The latter was desperately fighting to hold the bedroom door closed to keep at least a portion of his family safe for another few seconds.

Moments later, their father faltered in his task. He watched as the monsters swarmed in and shredded his father until nothing but meat and blood remained. Unnatural fiends, both small and large, grabbed what remained in an effort to satiate themselves.

His sister stayed still, silent, and barely breathing. The two of them simply stood there for hours as the monsters had their fill. If the twins had any doubts where they had learned patience and perseverance, that was it. They stayed there for as long as they could, and longer still. A mere squeeze of their hands was enough to remind the other that both their lives were now linked. This was their life for days until the ground trembled again and something worse than a monster appeared to help them.

Lance then snapped out of the memory. His chest pounded in his chest like it was about to explode. The entire area around his white-shard throbbed painfully. He forced himself to the side as he spat out the liquid in his mouth, savoring the metallic taste.

Mend Wounds
[You have used Mend Wounds Level 3 at the cost of 30 Mana]
[Current Mana 413/495]

The space within his little makeshift shelter lit up in a blue light as the healing energy blinded him. "That's one way to wake up." Twice more, Lance forced the Skill to ease the discomfort and pain he was feeling before some semblance of normality returned. "Shahida," he said out loud, as an echo in his mind reacting to it, while his body warmed. "No," Lance said as he quelled those feelings and hardened himself. *I'm here in an alien world in a Level-Three Rift filled with Goblins.* He closed his eyes for a moment, soothing the beating within his chest.

That was Iyas's sister? And since when can I understand bits of Arabic? His stomach turned as he sifted through what remained of the man, but he suppressed that feeling because of the threat of other assassins out there. *Any bit of information might be an advantage,* he thought before he shifted his attention to the present. "Still alive, Ash?" he called out as he moved into a seated position and retrieved his water canteen from his Inventory. Afterward, he took several generous sips to remove the metallic taste.

"I'm not one . . . of the living," Ash said to him from outside of the tent. The man's deep voice easily made it past the thin layer of fabric that had shielded Lance from the elements. The armored Ash nodded once when Lance threw back the flap of his shelter. Lance had made the walls by stacking empty jerry cans, while a worn-out mattress and some spears made up the roof. He had thrown a large blanket over it all to keep out the wind and sand. It wasn't fancy, but it had provided decent protection thus far.

"It's too early in the morning to play the philosophy card," Lance said as he got out of his shelter, storing the Items again. "So, how are our esteemed party members doing today?" he asked before a blood-stained peregrine falcon landed on his shoulder. "Alright, forget I asked." He patted the bird's head playfully as he admired the creature's unnatural blue gaze.

Ash then rose from his seated position and walked over to Lance, using his spear to point in the distance. "Viper and Quill are finishing up . . . another cycle. Alpha is providing . . . aeri . . . aria . . . *flying* support." The man then pointed up to the sky with his finger following three dots there. Two occasionally fell before they regained altitude again. "Bravo is up there with—"

"Charlie and Delta," Lance commented as he struggled to track the birds properly in the sky due to the blinding nature of the two suns this world was orbiting. "They're doing better," Lance said as he recalled the last few days with his new companions and the almost comical nature with which they occasionally crashed down into the ground. He then took one last sip from his canteen before he stored it and retrieved some roasted meat from his Inventory. He smiled as he felt the heat coming off it. The Inventory system had a lot of perks but keeping your drinks cold and your food hot was certainly at the top of his list.

He had forged Charlie and Delta from white-shards he had gotten after searching the grounds around a Rift-site within a forested area in Norway. Because of the way Norway handled Rifts outside of cities, they usually lost track of debris and animal remains that came out after clearing an Initial Rift. In theory, this was a calculated loss of potentially valuable Items versus expensive construction and maintenance of protective nets and fences. Due to how fast and far the debris could fly out of a Rift, officials and the military rarely found the Items.

Still, Lance had three things the officials lacked: a clear motivation to find white-shards, three avian helpers with amazing eyesight, and three loyal companions that were unbothered by fatigue, rain, or hunger. It had taken them an entire day of searching but they had found three white-shards. One belonged to a large animal, and two had been crows. Lance had created Charlie and Delta from the crows, while he had wasted the last white-shard in trying and failing to get another template.

A few more days of training and those two should be able to fly for longer periods of time. After a few weeks, they'll even be ready to help in combat or with scouting. Lance's mind went over the benefits of having even more aerial vigilance. He tore off the last piece of meat as he made his way over to the edge of the small rocky hill that he had made camp on. He then gazed at the landscape around him.

This world was a strange one, with thousands of smaller islands sprinkled within a sprawling ocean. Some parts of the ocean were waist deep, while others were as deep as the length of a typical bus. The impossibly clear water and numerous islands with their white beaches made the planet almost seem like a tropical paradise. The only thing that stood out was an odd black construct in the distance.

It reminded Lance of an oil rig, being elevated from sea level and supported by pillars of strange black cables. The material seemed almost organic in nature, as if some civilization had somehow spliced together rock and wood. Lance was sure that the Rift-event was located within that structure. Every fiber in his body could feel the pull, pressuring him to move closer toward it.

He shifted his gaze to the left when he became aware of notifications telling him that he had just gained some Experience. In the distance, Quill was shooting at several monsters with her bow, neither hunter nor hunted able to move quickly in the waist-deep water. *More Goblins?* Lance watched Quill land another arrow into the back of one of them. To its credit, it kept walking for a few more paces until its body finally realized that it was dying. *Fools,* he thought as he noticed the obvious trap that Quill was steering the rest of the monsters toward.

By the time the remaining two Goblins reached the nearest island, a spear suddenly slammed into the first one's chest while something rose from the sand to grab the remaining one. Viper had emerged from the sand like his namesake. The man then attacked the monster with several crippling blows that Ash had taught him. Afterward, Viper disarmed and held it down until Quill arrived to aid him. Then, with his hands free, Viper moved forward and sank his fangs into the monster's neck, injecting it with a hefty dose of venom.

Lance smiled. *Good, they're monitoring how long it takes for the venom to take effect. No doubt counting out loud.* An amused smirk crossed his face. He could almost read their lips from this distance. The two fighters had improved a lot during the last few Rifts.

They had evolved faster than Ash had, but that was to be expected due to them having had him to guide and train them every second of the day. Still, certain things such as speech, hand signals, counting, and writing were harder to pick up. It was something that Lance still actively had to teach them, seeing as Ash himself was also still struggling with these things.

After a few minutes, the monster stopped struggling, its body seizing up. *At least we know the venom also works on Goblins.* Lance made a mental note of how long it had taken. His party had experimented with the venom they had retrieved several Rifts ago, testing if it worked well with arrows and blades. It wasn't until Lance had nearly run out of venom that he had considered giving Viper the venom sack upgrade. The venom that Viper could now produce wasn't as potent as the original, but the benefit was that they essentially had a constant supply.

"Icarus, fetch the others," Lance said finally as he shifted his gaze back to the black construct in the distance. He could hear the flapping of wings as Icarus quickly sped off to do as he had commanded. And as Lance worked out a strategy for scaling the large pillars and killing the Rift-guardian without falling to his death, he heard Ash moving up next to him.

"I'm allowed to . . . this time . . . Right?" Ash asked slowly, his unnaturally deep voice showing signs of uncertainty.

Lance knew what Ash was referring to, seeing as the man had been asking for it nonstop during the last few Rifts. *This is a bad idea,* Lance thought, but Ash had proven himself over the repeatedly. Not wanting to say the words, Lance merely nodded as he noticed the shift in Ash's stance. It still surprised him just how similar his companion was to Thomas— yet also completely different.

By the time Viper and Quill had returned, some time had already passed—time that Lance had spent working out in order to psych himself up for what he was about to do. While squeezing out twenty more push-ups, he went over the Retainer screen to inspect his companions' statuses one last time.

Ash	1x	Human	Rift-glider eye +2 Sight +Heat vision	Centaur-toad muscle +4 Speed +100 Durability	Stone walker bone +3 Defense +160 Durability
Quill	1x	Human	Stone walker bone +3 Defense +160 Durability	Goblin muscle +3 Speed +100 Durability	
Viper	1x	Human	Cerint venom +1 Venom strength +15 Durability	Goblin muscle +3 Speed +100 Durability	Stone walker bone +3 Defense +160 Durability
Icarus	1x	Falcon (hybrid*)	Rift-glider eye +2 Sight +Heat vision	Stone walker bone +3 Defense +160 Durability	Goblin muscle +3 Speed +100 Durability
Alpha	1x	Crow	Goblin muscle +3 Speed +100 Durability	Stone walker bone +3 Defense +160 Durability	
Bravo	1x	Crow	Stone walker bone +3 Defense +160 Durability	Goblin muscle +3 Speed +100 Durability	
Charlie	1x	Crow			
Delta	1x	Crow			

The six Rifts they had cleared in Norway had given Lance a lot of black-shards to toy around with, along with several Guardian-shards. Lance had spent a portion of it on repairing Items and forging new ones. Arrows, bone javelins, and spare bone throwing knives were always useful in a Rift, no matter the Level. He also held a decent chunk of black-shards in reserve to repair his companions if an emergency occurred. But most of the shards had gone toward upgrades, with him keeping one Guardian-shard in reserve.

Lance had experimented with monster parts he had harvested throughout the Rifts, upgrading his companions each time he ran into something better or more suitable. Swapping it out destroyed the old Item at the cost of ten black-shards. He had swapped Gnoll parts out for Goblin ones where it made sense. Goblins were agile but lacked the ability to shrug off a lot of blows. In his previous Rift, he had fought slow but durable Stone Walkers. They were as large as big dogs, with rocklike skin. Harvesting their bones had resulted in Lance now having a decent mixture of speed and defensive upgrades for his companions.

Meanwhile, Viper now had venomous fangs. *Even without the upgrades, Ash, Icarus, and Viper could probably clear out this Rift on their own if they took the time to do so, picking off the enemy in smaller chunks,* Lance thought as he pushed himself off the ground and back up on his feet.

"Viper, are you done?" Lance asked as he made his way over toward the tall man who was now hunched over a small steel container. He could see how Viper was nudging the sides of his now-elongated canines against the side of the container, forcing small droplets of white venom into it.

"Yes," Viper said as he stopped the extraction and showed Lance the semi-filled container. That single word was enough to unnerve Lance. His intonation had distinct hints of Iyas within it.

"Good. Put the lid back when you're done. We don't want to waste any of the venom. And speaking of poison . . ." Lance said as he shifted his gaze toward Ash, who was roasting a piece of Goblin muscle over a small fire while sprinkling a bit of salt on it. *No doubt he's been watching cooking shows on the tablet. I should install an ad blocker or something.* Lance then smiled and knelt next to his friend. "Is that for me?"

"Yes. You need your strength," Ash said, handing Lance the half-burned bit of Goblin meat.

"You shouldn't have," Lance said as he gave the meat an exploratory sniff and took a small bite. As weird and disgusting as it might have seemed, he knew from experience that one couldn't be all that picky in a Rift. His stomach still twisted painfully each time he recalled the times where he had had to eat copious amounts of Rirkling meat. *Anything is better than that.*

Lance thought before he took a more determined bite. "Do you remember your assignment for tonight?"

"Secure a foothold as a group . . . break off . . . disrupt the enemy movements . . . destroy their morale," Ash said with determination in his eyes.

"That's my buddy," Lance said, giving Ash a fist bump before the two of them shifted their gaze toward the Rift-event in the distance. A smile formed on his face as he recalled the article that had been circulating around Ireland about what had happened last April in Dublin.

"Tonight, you're going to show them the Demon of Dublin."

CHAPTER ELEVEN

Ninja Pocket Sand

LANCE

A few hours later, Lance was swimming through the cold water. The black construct loomed ahead, casting a massive shadow over him as he slowly drew closer. Closer up, it no longer resembled an oil rig so much as a city on giant stilts. With careful, calculated strokes, Lance moved through the shallow water, trying to stay quiet. His destination was the nearest black pillar, and he was determined to get there without being detected. Lance wasn't sure how many monsters were stationed along the edges of the city, and he wasn't keen on finding out if they could attack him from there. Though he had Icarus, Alpha, and Bravo at his disposal, he had given them instructions to only act if he was in danger.

To avoid detection, Lance would occasionally dive, using the cover of the deep water to hide. How long he could go without air since becoming a Rifter surprised him, as he hadn't properly tested it before now. Lance still remembered the days when he and Thomas used to hang out in the pool, trying to see how long they could hold their breath. His personal record had been around a minute, but he estimated he was now approaching three times as long. While he knew that there were plenty of non-Rifters who could easily surpass his current record, he couldn't ignore the drastic increase in his own abilities.

Holding his breath, Lance dove even deeper as he carefully swam closer to the pillar. He could taste the salty water on his lips, but he ignored it for the moment. He had stripped off all his armor and protective gear, retaining only the dull grey overalls, as he knew their weight would have slowed him down further. He could feel his muscles straining with the effort of swimming. The building seemed to grow taller and more intimidating with every stroke. He kicked his legs and swung his arms, using all his strength to pull himself through the water. As he drew closer, he saw the pillar was rough, with many outcroppings and protrusions. *They look like veins.*

As he approached, Lance reached out and grabbed hold of the pillar, testing his grip. He gritted his teeth as he slowly pulled himself upward. Finally, with a final burst of effort, he was up and over the edge of the ridge.

Now within the city, Lance could see the countless buildings and structures packed tightly together, forming a seemingly endless maze of streets and alleyways. The buildings were of all shapes and sizes, some tall and slender, others short and squat.

[You have stored an Item in your Inventory]
[You have retrieved an Item 2x]

For a moment, he was completely naked, standing in a city filled with monsters. Then, dry overalls covered his body again, and he had a knife in his right hand. He took a few careful steps forward, focusing on staying in the shadows, his eyes fixed on the first building ahead of him. As he drew close to the doorway, he heard faint snoring. His muscles tensed and he held his breath, his mind sharp as he tried to detect any signs of danger. Finally, he peeked around the corner before sliding inside.

He saw a dozen Goblins, all fast asleep. Some were on the floor, while others leaned against the walls or slouched over broken furniture. *This is a terrible idea,* he thought as he snuck closer to the nearest Goblin and aimed the knife above its neck. He could see the monster's leathery green skin and grotesque features, serene in their slumber. Recalling how one of these monsters had killed his best friend, hatred grew within him. He looked at his own knife and felt a sense of purpose.

He moved quickly, muffling the monster's mouth with his left hand before driving the knife into its neck with his right, and dragging it downward, aiming for the lungs, heart, and other vital organs. He glanced around nervously, praying that the commotion hadn't awoken the other monsters.

Like a goddamn ninja, Lance thought, feeling a surge of arrogant pride wash over him. This was the arrogance that had once been his best friend's. He moved on to his next target, silencing its screams with ruthless efficiency, eventually getting each murder down to just four quick stabs.

This would be awesome if I had three other knife-wielding maniacs along with me. Unfortunately, they're still too untrained and loud for this kind of attack. Having killed six of the Goblins, Lance made his way toward the seventh, but his foot slipped on the blood-soaked ground, and he tumbled to the floor with a loud thud.

The room erupted with activity as the remaining monsters awakened to find their fallen comrades lying in puddles of their own blood, not to mention the frenzied human wielding a knife above them. In no time, the entire building turned into a battlefield as the Rifter stabbed and kicked at the monsters, more and more pieces of armor materializing on his body with each passing moment. The screams and fighting eventually drew the attention of the monsters in the neighboring houses.

"This is bad!" Lance shouted, rushing out of the building as quickly as possible and narrowly avoiding another pool of blood at the end. He retrieved the gauntlets from his Inventory and held his arm back as if he were a professional pitcher.

[You have retrieved an Item 3x]

Three ceramic orbs appeared in his gauntleted hand, hissing in the cool air. They were the size of golf balls but filled with sand heated to a thousand degrees. He threw them into the building swarming with Goblins, then retreated from the doorway. When the orbs shattered, they released clouds of the super-heated sand that stuck to the Goblins' skin and armor, and even found its way into their mouths, noses, and eyes, bringing them a personalized form of hell.

"Some ninja I am," Lance said to himself as he heard the city slowly coming to life, filled with the cries of monsters. Within seconds, they emerged from houses all around him, quickly forming a sizable horde. He couldn't help but draw comparisons to the Rift where he had lost Thomas. The major difference now was that he stood at the edge of the city, a steep drop into the sea just a few steps behind him. He heard a bow being drawn before the Goblin had even fully nocked the arrow. He easily dodged it, only to hear the archer's death seconds later as an overprotective Icarus slammed into its neck.

"It's like I'm right back where all of this started," Lance said out loud, turning to face his enemies and letting them see his tall frame covered in layers of cloth, leather, and thick steel. "But this time things are different," he announced, addressing the surrounding threat and aware that he was monologuing like a movie villain. "Because this time . . ."

A shield and short sword materialized in his hands as two pale crows flew down from the sky, circling around him menacingly, and a blood-stained falcon landed on his shoulder. A moment later, three more shield and sword-wielding fighters appeared at his side, the biggest of them draped in shadow. Without a pause, they assumed a defensive position as Lance pointed his sword at the center of the Goblin horde. "I brought my own army."

All four warriors let out a war cry as they suddenly charged to the left, where the enemy horde was thinnest. They crashed into the Goblin line, hacking and stabbing their way through to find more strategic ground.

Hours later, Lance was biting into a blue fruit, struggling with the overpowering sweet and sour taste. It reminded him of a candy he had eaten in the Netherlands when he was a child. He could still recall the way his face contorted after the first bite. He sliced off another chunk with his knife as he glanced around the building that he was in.

Too small to be a proper storage building. Some sort of shed? he speculated, before finishing his meal and wiping the blade on his sleeve.

"You guys are doing great," he said.

Close to him, Viper and Quill were stationed at the door, fending off an enraged horde of Goblins with their spears and shields. Lance had lost track of how long they had been fighting, but it had lasted through the night and both suns were shining brightly in the sky once again. Quill used her shield to block and push back against a Goblin, while Viper swiftly killed it with his spear. He even hit the monster behind it as well.

"Nice, two for one," Lance said, moving closer and getting into position.

[You have combined and retrieved Items]

A recurve materialized in Lance's hand, already loaded with two arrows. It had taken the Inventory system a while to adapt to this specific style. It was generally reliable in knowing what Items Rifters could equip or hold but forcing it to adapt to a particular style or deviate from the norm took more time. Through conditioning, a Rifter could form patterns. According to the GRRO manuals, a higher Wisdom Attribute could help speed up this process.

Detonate
Detonate

As Lance lined up his shot, both arrows began to glow. "Down," he said, and Quill and Viper immediately knelt, interlocking their shields. The arrows flew past the kneeling fighters and into the horde of Goblins, hitting various body parts before exploding into tiny, lethal fragments.

[You have used Detonate Level 1 at the cost of 25 Mana x2]
[Current Mana 251/495]

When he used arrows, the explosions weren't very impressive. The Skill was most effective when used on an Item with high Durability. A throwing dagger would be more potent, as it had larger parts that increased the fragmentation. A javelin would increase the lethality even further. However, there was a downside: if he used the Skill on larger or more complex items, the Mana requirement increased.

Detonate
Detonate

Two more arrows left his bow before exploding into the horde of monsters. "Up," he said as he moved closer, observing the chaos within the Goblin ranks. The arrows had only killed two of them but had wounded twice that many. However, the reason Lance had used his Skill was to demoralize them. He spent another ten minutes taking shots at Goblins who didn't have shields, aiming for the center of their bodies every time. *I need the practice. If Quill keeps up her training, she'll outclass me in no time.*

[You have been awarded with a Level Up]
[You are now Level 48]
[You have 3 unspent Attribute points]

"Perfect timing!" he said as he used up the last arrow in his quiver. He mentally activated his Forging Skill to create some new arrows to replace the ones he had destroyed. *I've gained a lot of Levels in these last few Rifts. The Experience gain here in a Level-Three Rift is really noticeable,* he thought as he considered where to allocate his points. Recently, he had mostly been putting them into Strength, Endurance, and Agility to improve his raw combat abilities. *Maybe I should also increase my Perception? It might help with my ranged attacks.*

[Perception:] [68] (+3)

Quill and Viper had fulfilled their roles as hybrid shield wall and meat grinders. It wasn't until the Goblins retreated that Lance checked them for damage.

"Viper, you're at ninety-three percent. Quill, you're just below eighty. Are you two missing parts?" he asked calmly. They both shook their heads.

He also noticed a white residue on Viper's spear, indicating that during the fight, the man had coated his weapon with venom from his fangs. *He's good under pressure . . . Almost too good.* He decided to leave them as they were, knowing that repairing them would slow his Mana recharge rate even further. *It's better to fix them once it's fully replenished.*

He remembered how brutal the fighting was at the start, with the four of them pushing through the monstrous horde to find a more favorable position. The monsters' aggression and superior numbers had forced Lance and Ash to use their guns at one point to prevent them being overwhelmed.

At least the armor is still holding up. Lance examined the gear the two fighters were wearing. The helmet, cuirass, leg guards, and wrist guards were all still intact, although they bore a lot of scratch marks and cracks in some places. Lance had made them from leather and bone, which offered some protection but was inferior to iron or steel.

He could mass produce them since he had made the initial designs from clay and leather and had gotten the template. The bone he had used was one solid piece, as if he had poured it into a mold before it had solidified. *They look absolutely horrible with all that yellow and white. I need to learn how to use dye at some point.*

He still needed to fine-tune it and learn how to make proper gauntlets, boots, pauldrons, and more, but doing it this way meant that he could create new armor on the go. *At least I don't have to order armor or Brian might get even more suspicious of me.* Despite this, his trust in the armor was growing.

"It will at least absorb a few blows before shattering," he said out loud, feeling a sense of pride forming.

When he saw that he had received more Experience, he smiled. "Ash is clearly having fun. How about we pick up the pace?" Lance grabbed their spears and stored them, then retrieved the short swords for Quill and Viper. He joined them, armed with shield and sword, determined to make his way to the Rift event before Ash could.

CHAPTER TWELVE

Anything You Want

LANCE

Several hours later, Lance slowly walked toward the center of town. He could feel his white-shard reacting to the proximity of the Rift-event. The center was circular and devoid of any houses, except for a single large chamber in the middle. *It's larger than the buildings I have seen thus far. Maybe a town hall or something?* Lance mused as he continued his slow walk, ignoring the forty Goblins that had set up a defensive formation.

Many of the monsters were wearing crude wooden armor, but two of them were noteworthy. They were slightly larger than the others and wore bits of iron. Not much more intimidating than the others, but they were clearly their strongest fighters. *Something feels strange about them.* It reminded him of the stillness of death.

Lance's eyes narrowed on a pale Goblin in the middle of the group. This monster held onto a small cudgel that he was using to nudge and prod the others into formation. Clearly, it was smart enough to recognize a proper threat. *The Rift-guardian and its bodyguards?*

Lance shifted his attention behind him as he heard movement. His heightened Perception picked up on a Goblin that had been stalking him for the last few minutes, no doubt hoping to get to jump on him. But Lance paid it no mind, trusting in the overprotective nature of his companion, Icarus, who was circling above him. He smiled as he slammed his spear against his shield, psyching himself up and rattling the Goblins in front of him. *Clearing a Level-Three Rift and getting payback for Thomas.* He advanced forward. Just then, a single Goblin broke off from the horde and charged at him, but two arrows found their mark within its chest, one piercing its heart.

"Great job," Lance said as he admired Quill's and Viper's handiwork. The two of them were covering his approach from nearby roofs. Lance barely had time to compliment them before he heard an impact from behind him, followed by a notification that he had gained Experience. *So, a distraction and a strike from behind? This Rift-guardian is intelligent and skilled in setting ambushes.*

The failed ambush incited the Rift-guardian to whip its followers into a frenzy and send its armored bodyguards toward Lance. The leader even appeared to sneer as arrows bounced harmlessly off the bodyguards' iron armor; those that found flesh had little effect on their advance.

Ricochet
[You have used Ricochet Level 1 at the cost of 25 Stamina]
[Current Stamina 529/770]

Lance's spear flew from his hand with great speed, slamming into the wall on the left and then bouncing to the right to strike the first armored Goblin bodyguard in the neck. The impact pinned it to the wall, forcing it to remain standing in a brutal display of death. Despite the hole in its neck, the Goblin continued to thrash. *Why won't it die?*

Meanwhile, the other bodyguard continued to charge Lance. It swung a large club at him at a dizzying speed. Lance dodged the strike and lunged forward, guiding his sword through the gaps in the Goblin's armor and into its heart. He felt his wrist strain to keep hold of the weapon as he twisted it. Then he pulled it out in a spurt of blood. He was about to kick the dead Goblin to the ground when two thoughts seemed to slam into his mind, forcing his body to react.

Shield!

Step in closer!

He barely had time to block the Goblin's second blow with his round shield as he stepped in closer to mitigate the weapon's momentum. *What the hell? I tore its heart apart. How is it still standing, let alone taking a swing at me? Are they undead?* Lance thought as his mind went over what he knew about those types of monsters and the abilities that kept them alive. It took him only a moment to understand that these undead probably had similar problems as his own companions.

"It's about time you bastards learn something important!" Lance shouted as he sheathed his sword within the monster's chest, while a wave of strange emotions and thoughts surged up inside his mind. A moment later, four loud, distinct sounds echoed throughout the city. The Goblin bodyguard then fell to its knees, with bloody holes now visible on its knees and shoulders.

Lance slid the pistol back into its holster before a bone dagger materialized in his right hand. It glowed as he activated his Detonation Skill. Afterward, he plunged it into the Goblin's left eye socket as far as he could. Lance then retrieved his sword and left the monster there, continuing his march toward the center. He ignored the minor explosion behind him and the fleshy debris that showered him in its wake.

"You creatures don't seem to understand that you are now among real monsters. And the ones I brought are hungry," Lance said as he stepped into the courtyard, Quill and Viper landing next to him in unison. "Cue the Demon of Dublin," Lance muttered to himself as his gaze shifted to the right, where he could see a demonic-looking figure rushing toward the center. It was a demon holding a shotgun.

Anywhere blood hadn't stained Ash's body, black shadows were pouring out like mist. In a matter of moments, the pale warrior had closed the distance and fired his shotgun several times into the crowd of monsters, causing chaos and a full retreat as the surviving Goblins fled into the town hall.

Ash was about to chase after them when Lance signaled him to stop so he could inspect his friend for any major damage. Compared to the homemade bone armor that Lance had given his other companions, Ash's leather and thick steel armor could withstand quite a bit. Lance didn't doubt that his companion had seen plenty of action ever since he had allowed him to explore on his own. The broken short sword at his hip further cemented this theory.

"Something doesn't add up. You still have over sixty percent of your durability left, despite having been on your own all this time," Lance said as he focused his gaze on him. "Be honest, how often did you use your gun?"

"Yes."

"Yes, isn't an answer," Lance said as he held out his hand, waiting for Ash to hand over his weapon and the remaining ammunition. "Seriously? There are only three shells left. You realize this stuff is expensive, right?"

"Yes," Ash said as he shrugged. "But also fun." His natural blue gaze shifted back and forth between Lance and the building where the monsters were still hiding.

[You have stored several Items in your Inventory]
[You have retrieved an Item 3x]

Lance traded Ash's shotgun and ammunition for Dieter's mace, a smoke bomb, and Thomas's old lighter. He passed the mace to Ash as they stepped closer to the entrance. Every now and then, Goblin spears would appear, thrusting out in an attempt to scare their enemy away. "This is the kind of fun you'll have to get used to for now," Lance said, trying to light the wick of the smoke bomb. It took him four attempts, causing his expression to sour. *I can already picture Brian's self-satisfied grin when I place an order for Mana stone igniters.*

Lance waited until the smoke bomb had created enough smoke before he rolled it inside the building. He could hear the monsters hissing in reaction to the new object. He then handed Ash his smartphone. "It's your turn to make an entrance. I think there's a Necromancer inside. Knock it out and take care of the others. And as a reward, you get to pick a fitting song for this fight."

"Necro—?"

"One of them can prevent the other from dying. Just target the one that looks like it's thinking or one with a red hue in their shard," Lance explained. Ash nodded, but Lance still couldn't shake the feeling that Ash had only heard "Club each of them over the head" instead of his actual advice.

Ash tossed the smartphone back to Lance before he started swinging the mace to get a feel for the weight. As soon as the song came on, he charged into the smoke-filled building and disappeared from sight, but Lance was confident the man's superior eyesight would guide him just fine.

Lance slid down against the wall and took a seat while Quill and Viper started their task of extracting black-shards from the fallen monsters and eliminating the Goblin that he had immobilized with a spear. He could hear Ash replacing the hissing with sounds of terror in the background. Lance smiled as he looked at the name of the inappropriate song that was being displayed on the cracked screen of his smartphone: "Anything You Want" by Guesthouse.

I don't know which is more terrifying, Lance thought as he rested his back against the building. *His new nickname or his choice of music.*

A few hours later, Lance and Ash were on Earth, their bodies adjusting quickly to the sudden change in gravity and climate. "It's good to be back," Lance said as Ash signaled to the soldiers in the distance that they were unharmed. They made their way over and completed the necessary paperwork while Lance texted Fergus and the others to pick them up.

Lance felt the urge to enter the Rift again right away, but he knew he needed to restock on supplies and ammunition. Clearing Rifts back-to-back would draw too much attention. He had already switched to a different Rifter ID to avoid standing out, but he knew camera footage of him and Ash in Rifter gear would be in a database somewhere. Provided they had a reason to check, any observant person could put two and two together. *Maybe I should get several sets of armor or find some civilian clothes made from Rift-materials. That way, I could walk in and out of a Rift in those clothes and equip my armor inside. Maybe that will help me stay off the radar,* he considered, his mind going over the many potential scenarios and variables.

But if I wear civilian clothes, it may also draw attention, and it won't cover my face like the helmet does. Having multiple armor sets would take up too much space in my Inventory, even though I've been gaining more space in there. I've nearly reached a hundred, he thought before he reminded himself that he had Leveled Up again after clearing the Rift. *I'm now Level Forty-Nine. So, that means I've got room for 101 Items . . .*

While he was deep in thought, a soft insistent noise caught Lance's attention, pulling him back to the present. He looked over to see Ash, tapping the side of his helmet as if to check if he was still in there. "Sorry, buddy, I got stuck in my own head for a moment. Let's go grab a shower."

The two of them made their way over to the nearest building, and Lance stepped into his personal booth, closing the door behind him with a soft thud. He heard Ash getting into the one next to him. The booth felt cramped, but it had everything he needed. Lance noticed the shower in the corner, just big enough to turn around in. The locker appeared rusted and squeaky but had kept his belongings secure, and at the moment, the bench next to the sink and mirror looked as comfortable as a lounge chair. He was about to sit down when he heard Ash tapping against the thin wall. "Coming, dear," Lance said as he made his way over to his locker.

Opening the rusty locker revealed a stick of gum, several carbonated drinks, and a package that Lance hoped was black hair dye. He had stored all of it before the Rift, and nothing appeared to be missing. He couldn't help but smile to himself as he imagined Ash walking out of the booth with pink hair. He had tried to pick up Bokmål, but the Norwegian language proved rather difficult for him.

Carefully, he opened the package and prepared the dye as he had done before. Once it was ready, Lance slid the package underneath the thin wall separating the two booths. A second later, Ash slid his dirty clothes and gear under the door. It made sense, as it removed dirt and filth, but it felt like another chore for Lance. "So, this is what my mother had to go through when I was younger."

"What?" Ash asked, his tone unsure.

"Nothing, just clean your hair, apply the dye, and wait a bit before taking a shower," Lance said as he picked up Ash's dirty items and brought them with him into the shower. He turned on the water, letting it run over his gear and clothes. One by one, he stored the Items in his Inventory until the warm water fell directly on his naked frame.

He watched the dirt and blood that had fallen to his feet being carried away by the running water and disappearing down the shower drain. *Ah, what the hell,* he thought to himself as he stepped out of the shower, narrowly avoiding slipping on the tiles as he made his way to his locker.

With a grin, he was back in the water, sipping on a carbonated drink without a care in the world. He knew it was an odd thing to do, but he had earned it. *I deserve this. I just cleared a Level-Three Rift and defeated a Goblin Necromancer.* He then shifted his attention to his status screen and the three Attribute points he could upgrade. "Ash, what should I upgrade? Endurance, Strength . . ."

Without hesitation, Ash interrupted him, "Strength."

A smile spread across Lance's face. It reminded him how Strength-focused his best friend had been. *Yeah, there's still plenty of Thomas in there,* he thought. He looked over the list and assessed his current Attributes. *Endurance, Strength, and Agility are all at ninety-three. Perception and Wisdom are both at seventy-two. Luck is at sixty-nine . . .*

"Nice," he murmured, before realizing he could hear the remnants of his friend echoing the same feeling. With that, Lance made the mental decision to invest the three points into Luck.

[Luck:] [69] (+3)

Seventy minutes later, Lance and Ash were seated in the back of an old white Citroen. Eirin was driving, and Reidar sat in the front passenger seat, fidgeting with the radio. The siblings were bringing Lance up to speed on all the ceramic orbs Fergus had created, as well as the shipment of bear traps that had arrived from Brian, as they made their way back to camp.

Lance knew his lies were getting worse when Reidar questioned him about his other two teammates' whereabouts, and he simply replied that they were busy with another Rift. He realized it was time for him to ask Brian for forged documents for Viper and Quill.

Eirin kept the conversation going, "I mean, Fergus is a natural with clay. You should see the details he can now carve into the edges." She watched the two Rifters in the back of the car through her rearview mirror. Ash had taken off his helmet and was running his fingers through his jet-black hair before he put it back on.

Lance simply nodded as he slipped another piece of gum into his mouth. "Can't wait to see it," he said, his attention returning to his phone. He noticed all the missed calls and text messages, mostly from Daniel. There were also a few emails from Oliver. *Glad to see the little brat is doing alright,* Lance thought as he closed his email and opened his browser, scrolling through the newsfeed that listed anything involving Rifts and Rifters.

He clicked his tongue when he came across an article about Paris that included a growing list of Rifters who had pledged themselves to Operation Bastille. *Just you wait, Louis. I'll kick that pedestal out from underneath you and force you to confess your sins.* He closed the article and scrolled through several others before his eyes suddenly went wide. "Stop the car!"

"What? Why?" Eirin asked, turning her head to see what the problem was. When she saw the shocked expression on Lance's face, she slammed on the brakes, causing the car to skid to a stop. "What's wrong?"

"Svalbard," Lance replied, his eyes scanning the article once more, double-checking the information he had just read.

"What about Svalbard? Is there something-"

"Turn the car around and take me to the nearest airport," Lance said quickly before placing his hand on Reidar's shoulder. "Contact Fergus, tell him he needs to meet us at the airport with tickets in hand. Let him know that if he pulls through, I'll owe him a favor."

The siblings nodded, Reidar nearly dropping his phone while Eirin forced the car into a screeching U-turn. "We'll go to Tromsø first. From there, we can find a plane that will take us to Svalbard. But why do you want to go there?"

Lance smiled knowingly as he kept reading the news article that mentioned an initial Rift that had formed in Svalbard two days ago.

"To find a friend."

CHAPTER THIRTEEN

Oath to Bear

Several hours later
Above Norway.

LANCE

As the airplane flew through the turbulent skies, Lance's eyes were glued to the nearest window. His body was stiff with tension, and his grip on the armrests was so tight that his knuckles turned white with each jolt of the flight from Tromsø to Svalbard. Mentally, he kept telling himself to be mindful of his increased Strength.

He could feel the reassuring pull of avian memories in his mind, as if they were encouraging him to jump out of the plane and experience the wind rushing past him. With great effort, he tore his gaze away from the window and looked over at his pale companion in the seat next to him, unbothered by all of it.

Ash was wearing his glasses, his hoodie pulled tightly over his head as he flipped through a magazine featuring a renowned American Rifter who had just conquered a Level-Twelve Rift with his guild. Lance couldn't help but smirk. *No doubt he's only looking at the pictures.* Lance felt a twinge of envy for his friend's calm demeanor.

The Norwegian siblings explained the island's rich history, from its early days as a whaling destination to its current status as a research center for Arctic studies. As they spoke, Fergus listened intently, his eyes wide with interest. It was clear to Lance that Eirin and Reidar's passion for Svalbard was contagious, as he hung on their every word, eager to learn more about this fascinating place.

And here I thought the man could only follow orders and work with clay, Lance thought sarcastically before correcting himself. He knew he wasn't being fair, as his attitude was based solely on Fergus's ties with Brian. Despite his initial impression of the man, Fergus had proven to be reliable.

Lance shifted his attention back in front of him. He busied himself by tapping his fingers nervously on the armrest, his mind preoccupied with the recent Initial Rift that had opened in Svalbard. Prior to boarding the plane, he had contacted the authorities to request the contract to investigate the Rift.

Lance's mind raced with thoughts of the potential risks and advantages this new Rift presented. So far, he had only explored Rifts that other Rifters had already explored, apart from his first Rift in the hospital. But this time, he was going in blind. The monsters within the Rift could be weak, but there might be no atmosphere, acidic rain, or crushing gravity that would kill him the second he stepped into that world. The chances of encountering such a Rift were low, but it was still a gamble. That was why Rifters typically avoided Initial Rifts unless the pay was incredible, or they had the gear and training necessary to survive in these worlds.

Eirin, in a cheerful tone, confronted Fergus with a peculiar fact. "Did you know that dying or being buried in Svalbard is prohibited?"

With a slight tilt of his head, Lance turned his gaze backward to look at the three people sitting behind him. He raised an eyebrow in surprise as he met their gaze, "Really? You three do realize that I'm going to fight monsters tomorrow, right?" he exclaimed.

Sinking back into his seat, he reached for his earbuds and inserted them into his ears. Lance then pulled out his phone, switching it on before losing himself in the music. He closed his eyes, letting the beat take over and blocking out the apologies from the people behind him. He took a deep breath, trying to mentally prepare himself for what lay ahead: the Rift, the unknown dangers, and the fighting.

A while later, Lance and Ash were back on the ground. They were standing outside in the cold as they waited for Fergus and the others to fetch the car and their luggage. It was June in Svalbard, which meant that the weather was still chilly, with a biting wind blowing through the air. The sky was gray, with low-hanging clouds that threatened to release snow at any moment.

The airport terminal was behind them, its windows illuminating the snow-covered ground with a warm glow. The distant mountains, obscured by thick clouds, were visible in the distance. "It's like we're in a Rift," Lance said.

"Not as cold . . . as with the . . . White Clovers," Ash commented as he looked at the landscape before him.

"Yeah, you are right. Still, that was on top of a mountain ridge," Lance said with a grin as he took it all in. He couldn't help but wonder where the Rift was located, and how long it would take to get there by car or on foot. *Is it even reachable by car?*

"Why this Rift?" Ash asked suddenly as he turned to face Lance.

Lance grinned as he pulled out his phone and typed something. He had been evasive about why he had rushed here. The others had just followed orders, and Fergus was doing everything in his power to earn that favor. Lance had to keep things vague for the others, but he knew he could trust Ash. "The reason we're here is this," he said, as he showed Ash a picture. "Ursus Maritimus."

"Is that . . . a monster? Do I . . . fight it?"

"Good luck with that," Lance grinned as he put his phone away. "They're called polar bears, and they're all taller, stronger, and more agile than you. And a lot heavier." He felt his body tense up at the thought of facing one. From what he had read, he couldn't count on them being easily intimidated by humans. *Would an average Rifter even stand a chance against that?* Suddenly he felt a lot better having Ash's shotgun in his Inventory.

"A large fish, whale, or whatever, washed up on the shoreline there a few days ago," Lance explained. "Its corpse attracted a lot of predators. Even though polar bears usually keep to themselves, many of them gathered there to feast on it, tolerating each other's presence because of the sheer amount of food there. There was footage of this, since researchers had set up cameras around the spot. And, while the bears were there, a new Rift formed. Do you know what that means?"

"Upgrades?" the pale man guessed.

"It's a possibility," Lance said, nodding. "But it also means there will be many white-shards belonging to polar bears. And if our luck holds, we might end up with a template and a spare white-shard. That way, I can train and upgrade a bear companion." Lance playfully jabbed Ash in the shoulder, grinning as he felt more of Thomas's emotions mix with his own. "Can you imagine having a fur-covered cuddle buddy on our team?"

"Yes . . ." Ash said with a fair amount of hesitation, no doubt not yet grasping the full picture.

"Ash," Lance said as he placed a hand on his friend's shoulder and squeezed it gently. "These freaks of nature can sprint faster than a normal person and are incredible swimmers. Sharp claws and fangs, not to mention enough raw muscle to kill or severely injure most animals in a single swipe. The downside to these beasts is mostly stamina, overheating, and their behavior," Lance said as a wicked grin formed on his face.

"We don't have that . . . problem," Ash said as he did his best to contribute. "So, this new friend . . . wouldn't have . . . many downsides?"

"Exactly," Lance said, patting Ash's shoulders and then taking a step forward, breathing in the fresh air. "I'm going to get a fur tank. Bear cavalry that never tires. A submarine with claws. A battering-ram that I can command." He let the words flow out of him into the air, as he imagined the prospect of having such a companion on his team.

Best-case scenario was that he'd have several of them. But even one would be a game changer. Humans were decent combatants, but a polar bear without fatigue issues and who could follow complex orders would be a force to be reckoned with. He knew a bear was just the thing that would help him clear higher-Level Rifts, possibly even Level Six. *An improved apex predator.*

Lance spotted Fergus, Eirin, and Reidar in the distance, making their way over toward them with the luggage. As they approached, Lance could see the satisfaction on their faces as they explained that they had secured lodging and had even gotten an official guide to drive them to the Rift in the morning. "You guys did great. Let's drop our bags and get some dinner. You can find us a place to eat, right, Fergus?"

The man nodded so hard, he nearly dislocated his neck. "No problem. Leave it to me," he said before the five of them started their journey toward their hotel.

Lance sat at the table, listening to the Norwegian siblings sharing stories of their country. They had been going on for about an hour, telling them about famous sites they could take them to if there was a Rift nearby. He couldn't help but smile as he listened. The excitement in their voices was contagious.

"Oh, don't forget about the old copper mines there," Eirin told her brother before waving over to the bar for another round. Fergus sat across from the siblings, his eyes wide with wonder. He seemed fascinated by it all, and with each passing moment, this brute of a man seemed to relax more and more. Fergus already had a few drinks in his system, and it was clear that the alcohol was helping him let go of his inhibitions.

In the middle of the table, there were several empty plates, except for a few crumbs and smears of sauce. Their glasses were half-empty, still holding the remnants of their red wine, beer, and water. Reidar was still determined to finish the half-eaten appetizers while Fergus was particularly protective of the tiramisu that sat in the corner of the table, occasionally glancing over at the others to mark his territory.

Ash, on the other hand, was outside on the balcony, staring out at the sky and the Norwegian landscape. Ash played the silent and withdrawn Rifter role perfectly, but Lance couldn't help but wonder what was going through his mind. "I'm going to see if Ash has regained his appetite," Lance said as he grabbed a few pieces of bread and made his way toward the balcony.

"Any sign of ET yet?" he queried, settling in beside Ash. Lance could almost feel the eyes of the restaurant staff upon them, but he paid them no mind for now. "Not a terrible view from here, huh?"

Ash said nothing, only nodded, his eyes never leaving the panorama in front of them.

"You're awfully quiet tonight," Lance observed, studying Ash's stoic expression. He cocked an eyebrow when no response came. "Still stewing over the fact that I temporarily revoked your shotgun privileges?"

Ash remained silent for a moment longer, then gave a single nod in response. He turned his head to look at Lance, his expression unreadable. "Is this what . . . your friend wanted?"

"What are—"

"Thomas," Ash interrupted, his unnatural voice strained. "Is this what he . . . desired . . ." He paused again and looked as if he was working something out. "Is this what Thomas wanted for you? To clear Rift after Rift . . . to break bones . . . to bleed . . . to dream?"

Ash's words hit home, and Lance was quiet as he processed them. He shook his head slowly. "No, Thomas wouldn't have wanted this for me. He wouldn't have asked me to put myself in danger like this." He closed his eyes, the memory of Thomas dying in his arms still fresh in his mind. This memory was as sharp as the bloodstained knife back then.

I need you to take care of my family . . . Promise me.

Reliving the past had made Lance's blood boil. He had shared some of the details with Ash before but not everything. He knew his companion deserved to know the entire story. Lance stared at this pale reflection of Thomas sitting next to him. He told Ash about his best friend, how he died, the oath he had taken and its significance. "Thomas wouldn't have wanted me to risk my life to get justice. He would have wanted his family to be safe."

Ash's eyes narrowed as he caught sight of Lance's sudden smile. "But?" Ash asked, his tone curious.

"But we rarely take the same path we advise others to take. If the roles were reversed, Thomas would've hunted those three relentlessly, even if it meant jumping into a Rift and dragging them out by himself to get justice. He'd swear an oath to do so." Lance clenched his fist, relishing in the power surging through his body. He could feel the remnants of Thomas echoing in his mind as he did so.

"So, that's your oath to him?" Ash's eyes narrowed while his voice felt heavy with uncertainty.

"Yes, it is."

"But what of the things that he made you promise? To take care of his family?"

Lance's annoyance was palpable as Ash continued to question him. Despite his frustration, he couldn't help but admire the man's constant growth, both in and out of battle. But the topic was hitting too close to home and dredged up memories he'd rather forget. "I've told you before," he explained. "We're training, pushing ourselves harder than ever, to become powerful enough to fend off any threat to Thomas's family. I'll suffer and bleed, or worse, to make sure they're safe."

Ash's confusion was evident as he stared at Lance. "You said Thomas wanted you . . . to protect his family. He made you promise that," he said as he carefully placed a hand on Lance's shoulder. "Did he not see you as family?"

As Ash's words hung in the air, Lance's body tensed up. His jaw clenched, his fists balled at his sides as anger, sorrow, and stubbornness flooded through him, mixed with thoughts of so many others in his mind. He could feel the familiar tightness in his chest, the weight of his past and present bearing down on him. He couldn't deal with this conversation right now, not when the memories of Thomas and his family were so fresh in his mind.

He stood up abruptly, leaving the ledge where they had been sitting. Despite the raging emotions simmering just beneath the surface, Lance suppressed the urge to push Ash off the ledge. *Ash is innocent in all of this.* Without a word, he strode back inside, his frustration evident in every step. He ignored the curious gazes and hushed whispers of the others in the room, his focus solely on getting out of there, away from the memories and questions that were threatening to unravel him. With a push, he flung the door open, the cool night air slapping against his face as he stepped out into the light despite the late hour.

Lance paced back and forth, fists clenched, as he struggled to control his emotions. The echo of his best friend within him was overwhelming, the promise he had made to protect Thomas's family weighing heavily on his mind. He could feel the hatred for those who had abandoned Thomas and him bubbling up again, his rage growing with each step he took. The cool air did little to calm him as he walked, the lack of darkness in the sky making a mockery of his feelings of loss and anger.

Kira.

Louis.

Connor.

Lance slammed his fist against the nearby steel wall, leaving a small dent. Each name fueled his anger and hatred. He turned and walked away into the chilly night, desperate to escape the memories that haunted him. The icy wind whipped through his hair, and he could feel the chill seeping into his bones, but he welcomed it as it helped clear his mind.

CHAPTER FOURTEEN

Stuffed Animal

The next morning
Norway

LANCE

Lance stood in the center of his hotel room in Svalbard, his body shaking from exhaustion as he pushed himself through another one-handed handstand push-up. Sweat covered his bare chest and abs, the muscles straining to maintain the posture. Despite the effort, he pushed through the burn, his determination clear in the set of his jaw. He was only wearing a pair of jeans, his bare feet pointed up to the ceiling. The scars on his body told a story of the many battles he had survived and the monsters that had gotten in a lucky hit along the way.

As he pushed himself to the limit, the adrenaline and endorphins coursing through his veins, Lance couldn't help but feel alive. This was what he was meant to do: to fight and protect, to be the best version of himself for as long as it took to succeed. The sweat on his body glistened under the light, his muscles bulged, and veins popped out as he completed another movement.

As he struggled to lift himself up again, he couldn't help but feel amazed at the increased physical strength he had gained. But even more impressive was the improved control he now had over his body. He'd never been as athletic as Thomas, but the enhanced Agility had vastly improved his motor skills.

With effort, Lance pushed himself up and did one more push-up. "Connor," he said between gritted teeth as he pictured the irritatingly attractive blonde man. He remembered a photo of him and his older brother that had appeared alongside a recent article. He pushed himself up again. "Kira." His whole body was shaking at this point. He activated his Skill and blinded himself in a blue healing light.

"Louis," he said as he gave one last push before finally allowing himself to fall to the floor.

Despite the burning pain, he couldn't help but smile, knowing that he was another step closer to his goal. *Leveling Up is good, but the increased Attributes only multiply what is already there. The harder I push myself physically and mentally, the greater the efficiency,* he thought before he forced another two blasts of blue light through his body. "So, how many did I do?"

"More than . . . ten," Ash said absentmindedly. The man was sitting on the bed next to Lance while watching an MMA fight on the television. Quill and Viper were on the other bed watching a nature documentary about polar bears on Lance's phone.

"Really? You're going with more than ten?" Lance asked as he grabbed a nearby towel to wipe away some of the sweat before throwing the wet cloth at Ash's face. "You not being able to count properly is exactly the reason I took away your shotgun," he said teasingly.

"Pull up your hoods, lads," Lance ordered as his eyes swept over Quill and Viper, who now had black hair like Ash. All three of his companions were wearing hoodies, jeans, sneakers, and sunglasses. The attire wasn't the best for trudging through snow or climbing over rocks, but Lance knew the cold didn't bother his companions. They were content to keep their features hidden for now. "Put these on too."

[You have retrieved an Item 4x]

Four neatly folded brown leather cloaks appeared in his hands with two pairs of leather gloves on top of it. Lance carefully placed them on the bed next to Ash. It took far more time and concentration to retrieve Items from his Inventory folded like that, but Lance was conditioning himself to get better at it. The design of the cloak was from the template he had gotten back in Dublin. It offered only a little protection, but at least it made the four of them appear more uniform, like Rifters.

Lance then went into the bathroom, seeing as he needed a quick shower, his body slick with sweat. He didn't waste any time and quickly stripped off his clothes, stepping under the showerhead. The warm water cascaded over his body, washing away the sweat and grime.

He closed his eyes and let out a sigh of relief as the water hit his sore muscles. Lance stood there for a moment, feeling the tension and fatigue melt away. The steam from the shower filled the bathroom, fogging up the mirror. *This will be my first Initial Rift,* Lance thought as his mind went over all the horrible scenarios that might lurk inside. There were devices that could calculate the Level of a Rift, giving him a better understanding of the monster threat inside. But it wouldn't factor in the atmosphere, gravity, and other potentially lethal aspects.

Fergus and the crew had already made the call to the Norwegian government, informing them of Lance's decision to accept the Rift. *Step one is done,* Lance thought as he tested the limits of his enhanced Endurance, adjusting the shower valves to gauge how much heat and cold he could withstand.

The next step is going to the location itself. After that, we'll wait until specialists can measure the Rift's Level while Brian secures me specialized equipment suited for an Initial Rift. Even with the right gear, the act of stepping through an Initial Rift was still a dangerous gamble. *But I've taken bigger risks before,* he reminded himself.

A loud knock jolted Lance out of his contemplation. He frowned as Ash entered, closing the door with a delicate click. "They are here," Ash informed him, his voice as emotionless as his expression.

Lance stepped out of the shower, steam following him as he grabbed a nearby towel. "It's time to meet our new friend." As he reached for his equipment from the Inventory, he felt his armor wrap around him, encasing him in protection. With a confident smirk, Lance then placed a hand on Ash and watched his gear materialize on him, cladding him in battle gear.

As Lance stepped out of the bathroom, Fergus, Eirin, and Reidar's gazes immediately fell upon him, the three of them stationed near the door like sentries. Lance approached them, his voice carrying a hint of amusement as he noticed them staring at Viper and Quill with confusion. "Did you all sleep well?" he asked, as Ash handed Quill and Viper a shield and spear each.

"Good enough," Fergus replied, his fingers twitching at the back of his neck. "Listen, we gotta talk about—"

Eirin interjected, her tone questioning as she approached Lance, "When exactly did your friends arrive? It's been a while since we were all together. And they refused to talk to us."

Barely had Eirin finished speaking when her brother stepped forward, his voice tense. "Hold up. What's more pressing—will the four of you be enough to tackle this Rift?" Reidar's gaze took in the other Rifters' gear, not to mention their stoic expressions. "Don't Initial Rifts usually require a larger group?" he asked before his eyes went wide. "Sorry, I didn't mean to—"

"It's fine," Lance reassured them, his smile easy. "Quill and Viper arrived a few hours back, fresh off handling other Rifts for the last few days. The four of us can handle securing the Rift site and clearing it." He tried to give them a confident grin but then remembered he had his helmet on. "So, what did you want to tell me, Fergus?" Lance asked, his focus zeroing in on the nervous man.

"Well . . ." Fergus said, his voice wavering as his eyes darted between Lance and Ash. "There's been a development with the Rift. I—"

"An hour ago, the Rift got cleared," Reidar announced, ignorant of Fergus's involuntary twitch. "What's next, Boss?"

Lance was grateful for the helmet concealing his expression as his teeth ground together. *Cleared? Did someone beat me to it?* He pushed the thought aside and stepped toward Fergus. "Which Rifters cleared it?"

Fergus hesitated, his words stumbling as he spoke. "Rifters didn't clear it."

"Time's ticking, let's go," Lance said as a shotgun materialized in his hand. He hefted it onto his shoulder and strode from the room, leaving Fergus behind. Fergus took a moment to collect himself, his nerves jumping. He snatched up his smartphone and snapped several quick pictures of Lance's room before hurrying to catch up.

An hour later, Lance stood at Svalbard's shoreline. It was a rugged and desolate stretch of coast, dotted with jagged rocks and blanketed in patches of snow. The wind howled along the shore, agitating the waves that pounded against the rocks with a deafening roar. It had been worse when the helicopter behind him had still been running. Despite the bleak environment, the sun shone warm and golden, illuminating the glaciers on the nearby peaks. Despite the harsh surroundings, Lance felt excited.

He listened to the siblings talking to the officials in the background, going over the recent developments once again. He didn't need to hear the details to know that something had cleared the Rift. The black Rift in the distance pulsated and thrashed violently, destabilized by recent events. *They did it,* Lance thought with a grin, picturing the monsters inside facing their worst nightmares at the hands of enraged polar bears. *Seeing the Rift scenario reversed like this is pretty funny, to be honest.*

A cluster of snowmobiles lay in the snow, near a tent billowing in the gale. Through the flaps, Lance glimpsed hunters conferring with government officials and scientists, huddled around a heater. The tent served as a temporary base until the army could set up a proper one. Ash, Quill, and Viper stood at Lance's side, weapons at the ready, spears and shields glinting in the light.

Fergus inched forward, struggling to keep his balance on the icy terrain. "It will probably take another day or so before they can bring the army in," he said as he nearly slipped again. "But if you're eager to secure the site, I bet a few of the hunters would—"

"No need," Lance interjected. "Me, Ash, and Viper got this handled. Quill's staying here to keep an eye out for any bear trouble." With a flick of his wrist, his shield and spear appeared, and he pushed them into Fergus's palms. "You can hold the fort for me, right?"

Lance's smile, hidden from view, grew wider as the Irish brute gave an unhesitating nod. *No doubt he's scared out of his wits, but he's loyal. I've got to give him that. With Quill and the hunters there, they should be okay,* Lance thought as he watched Fergus put on the shield properly. *Besides, the polar bears should still only be Level One.* He gave Fergus's shoulder a reassuring pat before turning to Quill. "Help Fergus if things get hairy. Stick to the plan we talked about," he reminded her. Quill simply nodded, taking up a strategic position near the tent, her shield and spear at the ready.

After putting some distance between him and the camp, Lance felt comfortable enough to bring out his five avian companions and instruct them to scout the terrain and find signs of blood or large animals. It took Lance, Ash, and Viper several more minutes of jogging until they reached the Rift itself. Lance noted the unfamiliar rocks, sand, and tufts of grass strewn across the otherwise icy terrain—a clear sign that something had blasted out of the Rift at breakneck speed.

Lance examined the surrounding debris. "Viper," he commanded. "I want you to survey the Rift site. Find any signs of carnage—blood, gore, the works. Don't forget to check the water too. I need a body or a white-shard, understand?" Viper acknowledged the orders and set out, his steps forming a wider and wider circle around the Rift. "Ash, let's go," Lance said, his attention fixed on the birds in the sky.

"And that's another one," Lance said as his fingers closed around the white-shard. He yanked it from the mess of fur and gore, admiring its weight in his blood-covered hand. "It feels heavier than—" He stopped talking, having nearly mentioned how much lighter a human white-shard felt in front of Ash. "This one is quite heavy."

[You have stored an Item in your Inventory x2]
[You have retrieved an Item]

He stored the shard and his bloody gauntlet at once, letting the blood and gore fall to the icy ground. Afterward, he had his gauntlet back on as he walked over toward Ash. "So, how much in total?"

Ash's deep voice held a firm conviction as he replied, "Two."

"Correct," Lance said as he stared up in the air and waited for a bird to return and show the next polar bear corpse. "There were a lot more that survived the Rift than I was expecting," Lance said as he accessed his Inventory screen and started turning the white-shard into a template. He had failed the process once already, which irritated him greatly, but the chance of gaining a template was higher now.

"Apex. . . . . . pret . . . preda . . ." Ash stuttered, his tongue tripping over the unfamiliar word. "Apex bears."

With a grin stretching across his face, Lance exclaimed, "Hell, yeah!" He playfully poked Ash's ribs, feeling Thomas's emotions bubble within him. Despite the excitement, the grisly image of the two corpses—reduced to nothing but gore and bones—lingered. *They must have been far from the Rift-event.* The first white-shard came to mind, smaller than the other. *A cub, maybe?*

[Failure]

Lance let out a disappointed click of the tongue as the template process failed yet again. Ash stepped closer, reading Lance's frustration. "Icarus will find more. There were . . . a lot of white bears."

Ash's sympathetic demeanor provided some comfort, but Lance couldn't ignore the reality that the likelihood of locating another polar bear was low. According to the scientists' records and video evidence, seven bears had feasted on a washed-up whale corpse before the Rift had happened. *Finding two is already a stunning achievement,* Lance reflected. *Maybe I'll get a—*

Lance's head jerked to the right at the sound of a roar in the distance. *I don't need David Attenborough to tell me what that is!* His mood instantly lifted.

"Ash, on me," he yelled, sprinting toward the source of the noise. Scaling another icy, rocky hill with Ash in tow, they reached the top and slid down to see the injured polar bear lying on a fractured rock.

How are you still alive? Lance wondered, clutching his shotgun tightly. Despite his armor and Experience, he knew fighting a bear with just a spear wasn't ideal, even as a Rifter. As he approached, however, he saw the bear was no longer a threat. Its broken limbs and twisted torso were proof that it was near death. "Ash, wait," Lance said as he placed a hand on his companion's spear when he noticed him moving forward as if to end the threat.

Careful as he approached the bear, Lance couldn't help but be impressed by its size, larger than the previous two he had encountered, as evidenced by the size of its white-shard. He placed a hand on the bear's chest. "You went out swinging, didn't you?" Lance asked, marveling at the bloodstained fur, a mixture of red and a strange yellowish tint. "No doubt you tore a bloody path through their num-bers." The fur felt softer than he expected, and he couldn't help but whisper, "Like petting a stuffed animal."

Mend Wounds

"Sorry, man," Lance muttered, a hint of regret lacing his words as Ash took up a position next to the bear. "I don't have the ability to save you. But, hell, you held your own better than I did on my first Rift. Something to be proud of." The bear's massive form seemed to relax under the flow of healing energy.

Mend Wounds

Lance caressed the bear's fur one last time before he gave Ash a nod. "Time to rest, friend. We'll take it from here." He infused the bear with another surge of energy, surrounding it in a brilliant blue aura before Ash mercifully ended its life with a swift spear to the heart. With reverence, Lance unsheathed his knife and carefully removed the white shard. The moment he had freed the item, he stored it and started the destruction process to gain a template.

Lance gave the lifeless body one final pat before he stored it in his Inventory. *With the body and the shard separated, it will count as two unique Items*, he mused, considering the potential of enhancing Ash with part of the bear's remains, if it were a feasible option.

His gaze snapped back to the timer on his status screen, ticking down with each passing moment. His mouth went dry as it hit the single digits, counting down to the inevitable.

[Success]

"You sure about this?" Fergus asked an hour later. The man kept a wary eye on Lance, who was meticulously checking his gear. "It's an Initial Rift, and Brian's still busy getting what you need."

"I'll be fine," Lance said dismissively. "Follow me." He led the nervous man closer to the Rift, past Ash and Quill, who were standing in front of it, ignoring the government officials and hunters trying to talk to them. At that point, Reidar and Eirin swiftly interceded, preventing them from bothering the Rifters. Lance scooped up some dirt that the Rift had spewed out and offered it to Fergus. "What do you see?"

Fergus attempted to make sense of the mound of soil and grass, picking at it, and even bringing it to his nostrils. "It's just dirt and some sort of grass," he concluded, his worries dissipating with Lance's reassuring grin. "So, green stuff means it's safe?"

Lance nodded. "The polar bears cleared the Rift, so there was at least some sort of breathable atmosphere and bearable gravity, no pun intended. And the grass tells me there's vegetation and water. Lower chance of a toxic environment and the possibility of foraging for supplies," he explained as he led them back to Ash and the others. "But there is always a chance of dying the moment we step through a Rift, Fergus," he said, a spear and shield forming in his left hand as he readied himself.

"We'll head in as soon as Viper returns," Lance told the others as he retrieved his helmet from his Inventory. *Today went well,* Lance thought as his eyes scanned over his crafting screen, seeing the new template he had gained. *And if this template works as Thomas's did, it'll be even more useful because of its size.*

With a careful eye, he checked his supplies—water, food, javelins, knives, and arrows—and prepared himself to tackle the Rift. He felt secure enough to clear the Rift at least once before he needed to stock up again. *Perhaps I can ask Brian to find me a white-shard that belonged to a bear? I have the template now. But what kind of attention would that draw? The man's already—* Hushed voices on his right interrupted his thoughts.

Lance cast his gaze to the right and saw what the others were talking about. Viper emerged from the icy water, his shield and spear in one hand, as he dragged the ruined remains of a polar bear with the other. He moved toward Lance, ignoring the spectators, and dumped the bear's remains at his feet. A second later, the soaking wet man knelt down and tore out the bear's white-shard. Then he offered it to Lance as if swearing fealty to him.

Lance's hand trembled as he grasped the white-shard, feeling the weight of the object beyond mere physicality. He was overwhelmed by the barrage of voices and memories that poured into his mind, Thomas's voice ringing the loudest.

Don't think . . . Just do.

Lance yanked Viper to his feet and pulled him into a fierce embrace. It felt like they both needed this moment to wash away the taint of Iyas from Viper.

"Goddammit, Viper, you did good," Lance growled, pride swelling in his chest. He retrieved several of his steel daggers and a Guardian-shard and passed them to Viper. "Take the lead," he said as the four of them strode toward the Rift. Their brown leather cloaks flapped in the wind as they stepped in as one as soon as Viper stabilized the Rift. A moment later, the black energy took hold of them.

The officials bombarded Fergus with questions, but he remained frozen, his eyes fixed on the violent Rift. Within him, loyalties clashed and a burning desire for something more consumed him.

CHAPTER FIFTEEN

Petrifying Presence

Several days later
Norway

LANCE

A few days later, Lance sat on the sturdy branch of a towering pine tree in the Norwegian forest. He inhaled the sweet fragrance of pine and fresh earth as his heightened senses allowed him to pick up on the distant trills of birds. It provided a soothing background for the young man, only for him to drown it all out with the music pouring out of his earbuds. Lance leaned back against the rough bark of the pine tree, the branches creaking under his weight. He shifted his gaze downward to the battle that was going on.

He could see Ash rushing toward the next tree, a patch of red paint smeared on his left shoulder, showing that a practice arrow had hit him. Another arrow hit the position he had just left, and yet another hit his left leg, painting it red.

They've got him on the run, Lance thought as he watched Viper and Quill moving toward Ash, bows at the ready. They occasionally ducked behind cover when Ash returned fire. It was mostly Ash's enhanced speed and power that allowed him to dodge the arrows or put some distance between him and his pursuers.

Lance watched with amusement as practice arrows slammed into the trunk of a large tree that Ash had taken cover behind, effectively pinning him down. The pale man pressed his back against the rough bark as he tried to avoid being hit. Despite that, Lance could see how eager to prove himself Ash was. In terms of physical capability and combat experience, he easily outclassed both Viper and

Quill, but technique-wise, Viper was more capable while Quill was beyond even Lance's skills.

Viper circled around the tree, a blank expression on his face as he closed in on his prey. But when he reached the tree, Ash was nowhere to be found. Confusion flashed across Viper's face as he spun around, searching for any sign of the man he was hunting. That's when he looked up. Ash was in the trees, bow at the ready, arrow already nocked. The hunted man took aim and let the arrow fly. Viper barely had time to react as it slammed into his chest with enough force to cause actual damage. The red paint from the tip of the practice arrow marked a red smear on Viper's chest, marking him as dead in their game.

Lance watched as Viper stumbled back, a look of confusion on his face. "Ouch, that has got to hurt," Lance said as Viper held the bow above his head to signal his defeat. Five birds flew to the ground to locate the stray arrows, making it easier for Viper to collect them. Meanwhile, Lance could hear something heavy slamming into the ground. "Keep trying, buddy."

Ash jumped down from the tree branches next to Viper, landing with a loud thud while shrugging off the kinetic force of the fall like it was nothing. His triumph was short-lived, however, as a second later he caught an arrow out of the air that would have otherwise hit him in the face. Quill walked out of the nearby bushes, holding not one but three arrows placed between her fingers. Her eyes were cold and calculating as she advanced on Ash. She fired the arrows one after the other in rapid succession.

Ash was quick, blocking the first arrow with his bow. But the second and third hit him center mass, marking his chest with two large red smears. To his credit, he even threw himself on the floor, landing on his back to play dead.

Lance's sarcastic slow clap echoed through the forest, his amused grin widening by the second. "Bravo, Ash," he called down, his voice filled with mock admiration. "You should get an Oscar for that performance." He then gave Viper some pointers for his special awareness and complimented Quill for her recent improvements. *The Saracen archery style suits her well. No doubt it will take her a long while to master it, but the increased firing rate is incredibly helpful. I don't want her to be a typical archer who just stands and fires. I want her to be quick and able to use the bow both at long range and close-up.*

"Alright, shield and spears!" Lance declared, clapping his hands together to signal the start of the next phase.

Ash, Quill, and Viper quickly grabbed their steel shields and their spears, the tips of which were wrapped in cloth to prevent any fatal injuries. The cloth held fresh paint, ready to leave a mark on a successful hit.

Quill and Viper circled around Ash, their spears at the ready. With quick thrusts and jabs, they tried to find an opening in Ash's defenses, probing for weakness. But Ash was faster and stronger, blocking their attacks and shrugging off any damage. With each shield-bash from Ash, the other two stumbled back, the force of his strikes overpowering theirs. But Quill and Viper didn't give up. They worked together; their movements coordinated as they tried to find a way through Ash's guard.

It's like watching robots with unlimited batteries fighting, Lance thought as he sat up a bit. Even Rifters would've gotten tired after swinging and stabbing constantly, yet his companions did not. If they kept it up, they would lose durability over time, but by the way Ash was overpowering them with a flurry of quick strikes, it clearly did not bother him. Quill was the first to fall when Ash landed a perfect strike against her abdomen with enough force to send the woman back a few paces. After that, it became a one-on-one between the stronger, more experienced Ash and the graceful, unpredictable Viper.

Ash and Viper faced each other with steely determination, their eyes fiercely locked as they sized each other up. They shifted into a fighting stance, their spears held tight, and their shields raised, ready for the next exchange. And then, like a thunderbolt, the two warriors clashed. Ash attacked with the relentless force of a raging storm, his spear crashing against Viper's shield in a series of powerful blows. Viper was quick and agile, his expert footwork allowing him to evade most strikes while deflecting the others.

After taking too many smaller hits, Viper dropped his shield and grabbed the spear with both hands, allowing for greater speed and power in his strikes. He fought back with all his might, each blow slamming against Ash's shield before returning at a different angle. The two clashed in a whirlwind of steel, neither giving an inch.

In one final explosive clash, Viper dived underneath Ash's spear thrust and rushed in, countering with his own spear to strike his opponent. Had they been equal in speed, the thrust would have been a lethal one, but Ash twisted his body to the side, taking the blow to his right shoulder instead. At the same time, Ash forced every bit of power into his left shoulder as he propelled the edge of his shield toward Viper's skull. "Enough!" Lance's voice boomed out, freezing Ash's killing blow. The two warriors stepped back, calm and composed but still eager for more.

"Superhero landing time," Lance muttered to himself as he wiggled forward and let himself fall out of the tall tree, hitting the ground with one knee bent hard. *Nailed it.* In the past he would've snapped an ankle at the very least, but because of his high Endurance Attribute, it only stung a little. His companions merely looked at him, clearly not impressed. *Tough crowd,* he thought as he went over toward them and inspected them for damage.

Lance issued the order as he finished mending his companions' injuries. "One more hour of training. Fergus and the crew should be back in four," he said as he gave Ash a fist bump, letting him know he was in charge. Lance then ventured deeper into the forest, the sound of his own footsteps barely audible above the cacophony of nature.

Lance walked through the forest with a spring in his step. He reveled in the feel of solid rock beneath his feet, and from time to time, he launched himself from one large rock to another, grinning as he felt the wind rushing through his hair. His increased Strength allowed him to pull off jumps like these with ease. A short distance behind him, the sound of rustling leaves and snapping twigs echoed through the trees.

As he approached a small river, he spotted a fallen log and used it as a bridge. However, seconds later, the sound of something heavy slipping off the log behind him filled the air. He turned around and laughed in amusement as he saw his brand-new bear companion on her back struggling in the shallow water.

"No worries. We'll keep it simple for now," Lance said as he pointed to a nearby rock where the bear could maneuver her way back to him. "You are doing great. Even the birds needed a lot of time to learn how to fly properly. Not that I'll expect you to fly." He placed a hand on the creature to check for damage while giving her a moment to get her bearings again.

Baloo over here still has a ways to go before I can trust her enough in the field, Lance thought as he watched the imposing creature settle into a normal stride again. He had found out that she was female after he had cleared the Rift twice in a row, annihilating it completely. During that time, the researchers had examined the body and had determined its gender. Lance had taken their word for it, seeing as they all looked alike to him, beyond their sizes. *Still, she's a lot bigger now than her original body.*

He had gotten the template from an adult male pushing three meters in height. She wasn't an exact copy in terms of height, weight, and muscle mass, but it was an amazing improvement. "It's somewhat similar to what happened when I made Quill. More height and muscle. Now, the big question is . . . what do I name you?"

He had several possibilities already in mind, but most were immature to say the least. "White Fang? Ice Breaker?" Lance knelt in front of the massive polar bear, his eyes fixed on her face. Like with most of his companions, the bear was a monochromatic gray. Her eyes, teeth, nose, and tongue—all lacked color. Its eyes were the lightest shade of gray, nearly white, and they watched Lance with a curious intelligence. Her face was devoid of any hint of warmth or life, a cold, hard mask that hinted at the deadly predator hiding within.

From a distance, it was hard to notice, because of the fur resembling that of an actual polar bear, yet the absence of color in its eyes and snout was a dead giveaway that something wasn't right. "I don't think I'll be able to slap some fresh paint on that face of yours between Rifts. Not that having a polar bear following me around all the time isn't weird regardless," Lance said with a smile. "Still, the fact that I can conjure you out of thin air whenever I want is just awesome. Any threat I face will suddenly have to deal with a monster of my own.

"Alright, let's practice riding again," Lance said as he ran his hand through her thick fur. Lance clambered onto the polar bear's back, his heart pounding with excitement. He gripped the fur tightly, feeling the animal's muscles shift beneath him. The bear stood still for a moment, as if uncertain of her next step, before taking a hesitant one forward.

As they moved through the forest, Lance's grin widened with each stumble and awkward step the bear took. There was little grace in her movements, yet she was moving. They gradually picked up speed, with the bear's clumsiness making the journey bumpy and uncertain.

Lance gently patted the bear's neck. "You did well." He pointed toward the clearing on the left and said, "Let's go over there." Despite dedicating much of his free time inside the Rift training the bear, Lance understood it would take much more work before she could understand the difference between right and left.

Dismounting with ease, Lance beamed as he scratched the bear behind its ears. He guessed it wouldn't feel anything from it, like how Ash was numb to most emotions and pain, but he couldn't resist petting an animal that would've other-wise mauled a human. "All we need now is to slap some proper armor on you," he said. "I'd love to see you in thick steel plating, but I have a feeling I'll have trouble explaining that to that fixer." Lance then guided the bear to a spot in the clearing that contained just two trees.

[You have retrieved an Item 2x]

With two bone javelins materializing in his grasp, Lance strode up to a tree and plunged them into the bark with all his might. He examined his handiwork to make sure he had buried the tips of the javelins as deep as he could. *Still, if a massive polar bear and my other silent companions don't send Brian's alarms ringing, then my freakish growth in Levels and conquered Rifts will definitely do the trick.*

[You have retrieved an Item 2x]

He buried the next two javelins into the second tree with ease. *Less than a year of being a Rifter and I've already hit Level Fifty-Three,* he reflected. *I remember when me and Thomas became Rifters last year back in August. We had spent months slowly climbing the ranks to even get close to Level Ten. And now, since March, I've been going at it alone and my Level has jumped by over forty in just four months. Even powerful guilds dedicated to Leveling Up their members would be hard-pressed to match that.*

[You have retrieved an Item 2x]

Two dead monsters hit the ground beside Lance. The bipedal beasts had bright red fur and two heads, the spoils of his fight in Svalbard's Rift. Despite these monsters not being especially fast or strong, the sheer number of them had been annoying. He grabbed a body and pressed it against a tree, securing its wrists to a javelin with leather strips and suspending it upright. He repeated the process with the second monster.

"Alright, time to see what you can do," he said to the bear when he was done. He then turned his gaze back to the monster and raised his hand. "Kill." The grey polar bear obeyed, lunging forward and attacking the corpse. Her powerful claws ripped through the monster's flesh, breaking bones, and scattering its remains all over the ground. Lance watched in silence as the polar bear went through several more swipes, painting its front paws red in blood and gore. There was little left of the monster after that. None of it had been graceful or precise, but it would do for now.

"Not half-bad," Lance said, gesturing to the monster lying on the ground. "Now, let's see if you can sink your teeth into the right places." He pointed to various points on his own body. "Vitals, that's where it counts. Got it?" The polar bear just stared at him, not reacting. "Alright, I'll take it. Now show me what you've got."

The bear lumbered forward as its jaws locked onto the monster's thigh. Lance winced as he watched the bear take its first bite, not quite the target Lance had in mind, but it was a vital area. *I'd prefer to get shot in the head than let a bear bite or eat me there.* The bear corrected its aim for the next attack, sinking its teeth into the monster's neck. "That's more like it," Lance said with a chuckle.

Lance's smartphone vibrated in his pocket, the sensation jolting him out of his focus. He watched as the polar bear continued its training, ferociously tearing into the monster's corpse. Satisfied that the bear had plenty to do, Lance turned his back on the scene and fished out his phone.

He swiped to answer the call, holding the phone to his ear. "Fergus, what's the problem?" he asked, his voice all business. "Yes, I know it's a big order, but I need those items. I don't care about the cost." He listened, his eyes sweeping the forest as he spoke. "Just get me the extra supplies, the steel jerry cans with water, a sturdy tent, a folding chair, and some grooming supplies. A razor and scissors. Yeah, that is it. Thanks." He disconnected the call and slipped the phone into his pocket, his thoughts already shifting to his next move.

Lance let out a deep sigh, struggling to keep his frustration in check. He could comprehend Fergus's apprehension, considering he'd sent him on a shopping trip to Norway's largest market for Rifters, shelling out tens of thousands of kroner. Still, with Fergus always came the aftertaste of Brian, the fixer. "Alright. We've trained with monster corpses. Fergus will hand over the supplies today. The only thing left for now is to give you a proper name," Lance said as he turned around to see how his bear was doing.

When he did, he was suddenly faced with the towering monstrosity, feeling small and insignificant. The bear's once-gray fur was now stained with blood, nearly all of her body drenched in crimson. The sight of the blood dripping from her jaws sent Lance's heart racing. Fear took hold, gripping him with an icy fist and weighing down his limbs as if made of stone. The bear's gray eyes, cold and merciless, locked onto him.

"Damm," Lance breathed, feeling his chest heave. He took a step back, regaining control of his body as his mind cleared. He walked toward the bear once more, a grin appearing on his face. "Just one glimpse of you was enough to freeze a Level Fifty-Three Rifter. I've got just the name for you," he told her with a smile as he stored the polar bear in his Inventory and opened his status screen.

[You have named this Item "Medusa"]

Status Compendium

Name:	Lance Turner
Level:	53
Class:	Death Smith

Attributes

Endurance:	100	**Agility:**	100	**Wisdom:**	77
Strength:	100	**Perception:**	77	**Luck:**	77
Health:	2750	**Mana:**	555		
Stamina:	845	**Inventory:**	109		

Traits

Taint of death:	Able to use Rift corpses as items	Prolonged use results . . . ~ERROR UNREADABLE!~
Shard instability:	~ERROR UNREADABLE!~	Prolonged use results . . . ~ERROR UNREADABLE!~

Skills

Mend Wounds	Lvl 2	Restores minor wounds	+20 Health +8 Stamina	−15 Mana
Death Forge	Lvl 2	Allows (re)forging of death related items	+2 Items	−Raw materials −Black-shards −50% Stamina regeneration −50% Mana regeneration
Repair Item	Lvl 2	Restores durability on items	+2 durability per 2 items per 55 seconds	−Raw materials −Black-shards −30% Stamina regeneration −30% Mana regeneration
Ricochet	Lvl 1	Bounces throwing attacks with greater speed and accuracy	+1 Bounce +5% Speed +5% Accuracy	−25 stamina per bounce
Detonate	Lvl 1	Detonates an item based on its original durability	−50% base Durability	−25 mana per usage

Retainers

Ash	1x	Human	Rift Glider eye +2 Sight +Heat vision	Centaur-toad muscle +4 Speed +100 Durability	Stone Walker bone +3 Defense +160 Durability
Quill	1x	Human	Stone Walker bone +3 Defense +160 Durability	Goblin muscle +3 Speed +100 Durability	
Viper	1x	Human	Cerint venom +1 Venom strength +15 Durability	Goblin muscle +3 Speed +100 Durability	Stone Walker bone +3 Defense +160 Durability
Icarus	1x	Falcon (hybrid*)	Rift Glider eye +2 Sight +Heat vision	Stone Walker bone +3 Defense +160 Durability	Goblin muscle +3 Speed +100 Durability
Medusa	1x	Bear			
Alpha - Delta	4x	Crow	Goblin muscle +3 Speed +100 Durability	Stone Walker bone +3 Defense +160 Durability	

CHAPTER SIXTEEN

Five Hours

One week later
July, 14 AR
Bergen, Norway

PETER

Standing in line at the chaotic Bergen mall, Peter Nenonen fiddled with his wedding ring, sliding it on and off his right hand with the remaining three fingers of his mangled left. Through his Bluetooth earpiece, he muttered in broken Swedish to his ex-wife, irritation evident in his tone, "I don't understand, Thea. We're divorced now." The muscular man stepped forward, placing his item on the checkout belt. "The knife is already in my back. Why twist the handle at this point? Look, just tell me what you want."

Minus the missing fingers, Peter was a nondescript man, with unremarkable features except for the jagged scar that ran across his nose. His dull blue eyes and thinning blonde hair were forgettable, but the disfigurement gave him an air of menace he didn't always appreciate. It helped him prevent fights, but most of the time, it only served to isolate him further.

As he stood in line, Peter's gaze flicked to the pack of gum sliding along the belt. But it stalled behind an older woman's pile of groceries. "Thea, I'm not a monster," he murmured into his earpiece. "I just want to see him for a few days next month. A boy needs his father. Thea? Thea!" He scowled as the other end went silent, clicking his tongue in annoyance and pulling the earpiece out.

"You're being quite rude and unnecessarily loud," a person behind him suddenly called out in Norwegian.

Peter spun around to face the source of the voice, only to be forced to look down at a scrawny teenager with messy brown hair and a crestfallen expression that was partially hidden underneath a red hoodie. "What?" he asked in Norwegian.

The young man's finger jabbed toward Peter, as if branding him with an accusation. "Your phone conversation is invasive and disrespectful. And talking about monsters for all to hear. Don't you know how triggering that word can be for some? Especially after everything that's happened to some of us?"

Peter chuckled menacingly as he ceased fiddling with his ring and closed in on the young man, looming over him. Still, the teen didn't back down. *Not an ounce of fear in him. Either brave or stupid. Probably both*, Peter mused, respecting the teen a bit more. He then shoved his disfigured hand in the young man's face before pulling down the collar of his shirt to reveal the white shard beneath. "Save your pity for someone else. I've been through the wringer already and lived through it. How about you get your own acne issues in order before you try to police someone else?"

"Well, you made us live through something far worse, seeing how you managed to butcher both the Norwegian and Swedish languages within the last five minutes," the teen countered.

"You know what, boy? You remind me of my son," Peter said, turning his head to look back at him.

"Handsome, intelligent, charismatic?"

Peter's grin broadened as he opened his mouth to speak. "Nah, it's the fact that you two both are proper little—" His words were cut off suddenly as a strange sensation rippled through his body, making him feel as if the world had tilted slightly off-kilter. The lights overhead flickered and the checkout belt ground to a halt.

"Rift!" Peter's cry rang out across the store as he yanked the young man and the old lady to the ground. With one swift motion, he shoved them both under the checkout belt and shouted, "Take cover! Stay low!" A sudden wave of dizziness washed over them all, and the world trembled around them.

Everything shifted in an instant, as if someone had knocked the world off its axis. The mall twisted and turned, buckling and groaning as if it were alive. Peter's stomach churned as he stumbled forward, his enhanced Strength doing little to help him keep his footing. The sound of screams and shattering glass filled his ears, and he saw people flung about like rag dolls by the sudden upheaval. Anything that wasn't bolted down became a projectile.

Products and debris flew in every direction, shelves collapsing and walls splintering. The supermarket shook and groaned under the weight of the earthquake. The screams of shoppers were drowned out by the sound of metal and concrete tearing apart, filling the air. After what felt like an eternity, the tremors ceased, and the chaos subsided.

"Are you two alright?" Peter asked as he got back to his feet and searched underneath the checkout belt for the old lady and teen, yet sadly only found the latter. *Dammit,* he thought, as he carefully helped the boy to his feet, ensuring he didn't slide down and injure himself. He didn't see what happened to the older woman, but he doubted she had survived what they had just been through.

The young man's eyes widened as he noticed the splotch of red on Peter's shoulder. "Blood . . . You're bleeding," he said, gesturing to the spot.

"I'm fine. Just focus on getting down safely," Peter said as he surveyed the numerous fractures in the walls and ceiling of the shop. They had survived the initial plummet into the Rift, but he knew better than to let his guard down, seeing as this place could fall apart any second now. It had been six years since he'd last been inside of a Rift, and the memories flooded back: the hardships, the fear, the desperation. He had tried to be a proper Rifter once, but the cost had been too high. Two missing fingers, a jacked-up knee, and a permanent scar on his nose were all he had to show for his efforts.

"My name's Peter," he said, his voice low and steady. He helped the young man over the last obstacle, before quickly steering him to the right to avoid the sight of the dead body crumpled beneath a steel shelf. "What's your name?"

"Finn," the teen said, his eyes darting nervously around the ruined landscape. "This is real, right? We're really in a Rift?" His voice cracked with fear.

Peter didn't answer. Instead, he grabbed Finn's shoulder and steered him toward the sounds of other people. What could he say that would make the kid feel better? Nothing. They needed action now, not words. As he reached for his Inventory and donned his old gambeson and iron helmet, a steel sword appeared at his hip. They rounded the corner and spotted several other survivors.

"Listen up, people! If you want to make it out of this hellhole, follow my lead."

Five hours later, the scent of dust and blood hung heavy in the air as Peter pressed his hand over Finn's mouth, their bodies huddled between rolls of toilet paper. Peter had carefully arranged them in stacks to create a barrier, hiding them from the monsters that had overtaken the mall.

Did we truly only manage to survive for four hours? The sounds of chaos echoed around them, screams and shouts punctuated by the hissing of creatures too terrible to imagine. Peter's heart pounded in his chest as he strained to listen, his mind filling with images of what was happening outside their hiding place. And then the laughter began. Unnerving, high-pitched, and deeply unsettling, it came from the monstrous elves that now ruled this place.

The ruined shop had no natural hiding places. Finn knew it, and so did Peter. Danger surrounded them as the monsters were closing in. Every breath was a risk, every movement a gamble. Peter's mind raced as he searched for a way out, but nothing presented itself. For now, all they could do was stay still and pray that they wouldn't be discovered. The waiting was torture, but they had no other choice.

Five hours. Five hours of leading these people, and now it was all for nothing. Peter bit down hard on his sleeve, fighting to keep his breathing quiet. It had started out well enough, with him gathering survivors and leading them to a more secure location. They had looted a nearby hardware store for weapons and supplies, and Peter had divided them into teams. Some worked on defenses, others on scavenging for food and medicine, and the rest on finding more survivors. He had motivated them all, letting them know that this was a Rift near a major city. The chances of the government sending a large group of Rifters would be incredibly high.

Finn's contributions had also been a great help. Despite his youth, the young man's intelligence and creativity proved invaluable, as many of the traps that formed their last line of defense were of his design. Simple materials like string, elastic, electric lighters, and hairspray were transformed into flamethrower traps. Soap and a row of sharpened broom handles became a deadly, slippery corridor of spikes, while cleaning agents had been mixed to form acidic traps. The survivors had repurposed shelves as walls, turned alcohol bottles into Molotov cocktails, and torn spare clothes into bandages. Peter had been confident in their readiness, but it was clear that he had underestimated the task at hand.

The monsters descended upon them with frightening speed, decimating the survivors' defenses in a matter of minutes. The initial wave consisted of large, four-legged beasts that resembled a cross between a horse and a wolf, their thick black fur bristling as they charged forward with ferocious abandon. Though the survivors were able to hold them at bay with fire, things quickly took a turn for the worse when the Elves arrived.

Riding atop the monstrous creatures, these slender humanoids wore armor and wielded weapons, some choosing bows while others opted for spears. Their arrival marked a turning point in the battle, as the monstrous mounts lost all fear of the flames and charged recklessly through chokeholds, determined to kill at all costs. The hours of preparation were undone in mere moments.

Peter's heart leapt into his throat as a heavy thud echoed from nearby, signaling the arrival of one of the monsters. The creature sniffed the air, searching for its next victim, and Peter knew that even with a group of fighters, taking it down would be no easy feat. This wasn't like the Level One and Two Rifts he'd faced before; it was harder, more dangerous. *Don't move, don't breathe,* Peter thought frantically, praying that Finn was both quick-witted and telepathic.

He had dragged Finn and several others with him during the commotion when the monsters had broken through. Eventually, he found a hiding spot behind the toilet paper in a corner of the store. Finn's experiments with all the chemicals in the last few hours still clung to him, hopefully masking their scent.

Peter surveyed their surroundings, taking in the rolls of toilet paper and the terrified teenager next to him. *Is this how it ends?* he wondered, his mind racing for a way out. A plan formed in his mind. *I could draw the monsters away. Give Finn a chance to escape, or at least a few more seconds to live.* He wrapped his arm around Finn, pulling him close as he imagined himself with his own son, saying goodbye.

Peter nodded to himself with a resigned look on his face, ready to sacrifice himself as bait for the monsters that were closing in on them. But just as he was about to take a step forward, the entire ruined mall suddenly shook. At first, he thought it was the monsters causing the tremors, but then the sound of fighting started. It was different this time, no longer a one-sided slaughter. The sounds of explosions going off, gunfire, and the sound of Skills being used to rip monsters apart echoed through the mall.

Peter's heart raced with excitement and terror as he realized that this was their one chance. He grabbed Finn and burst out of their hiding spot in an explosion of toilet paper as he rushed through the shop as fast as a Level-Eleven Rifter could. Monstrous creatures lunged for them, but Peter ducked underneath one and jumped to the side to evade another, hearing it slam into a cabinet behind him. In the distance, he could hear the screams of dying monsters, mixed with the battle cries of the fighters who had come to their rescue.

Peter's eyes widened in amazement as he saw a group of heavily armed soldiers fighting against the horde of monsters. Their weapons glinted in the dim light, and their Skills sparked with deadly force. It was a sight to behold, and Peter felt a surge of hope. They were no longer alone.

"Survivors!" he roared as he reached the end of the shop itself and made a beeline toward the exit. He could hear Finn's ragged breathing and knew that the boy was exhausted and scared out of his mind. But they had to keep moving. *Please, just let me save this boy.* Peter knew that their only chance of survival was to get out of the shop and reach the Rifters.

Peter's heart pounded in his chest as he and Finn rushed forward. At the last moment, a monstrous creature and its rider sprinted to the entrance, blocking their escape. The Elf atop the beast had a maniacal grin, as if relishing in the terror it caused. Its four-fingered hand gripped its spear with lethal grace.

"Elf!" A voice called out as a few Rifters broke off from the major force and rushed toward the entrance of the shop while one of them activated a powerful Skill without looking further than the direct threat ahead of them.

"Friendlies!" Peter shouted, but it was too late as the Rifter's ice attack engulfed the shop, slamming them all backwards. The building groaned and collapsed in on itself, burying everything beneath a mountain of rubble. Peter scrambled to push Finn out of the way, doing so just before a huge chunk of debris smashed into his head, knocking Peter unconscious.

Peter woke later, accompanied by a wave of agony. He realized he was on his back and pinned down, unable to move. "What the hell happened?" he muttered as he tried to shake off the haze. His breathing was shallow and labored, something heavy crushing his chest and lower body. *How long was I out cold?* Peter attempted to shift his arms, but his right one was broken—he could feel it. His left was thankfully intact, and he flexed what remained of his fingers to reassure himself. *No! What happened to the boy?* Scanning his surroundings, he searched for any sign of him. Only rubble greeted him. "Finn! Are you alive?"

He groaned as he fought to push himself up, his body protesting every movement. When he managed to raise his head, he saw the culprit: a huge piece of concrete had entombed him with twisted rebar poking into his flesh. "Alright, I didn't want to see that," he wheezed, feeling the pain radiating through his chest and arm. "And my legs—I can't feel them." Fear gripped him as he realized the gravity of the situation. "Nope. Not good at all."

Peter's survival instincts kicked in, despite the many years it had been since his last Rift. He took a deep breath and shut his eyes, trying to slow his racing heart. He concentrated on the task at hand, summoning his strength to move his broken arm despite the agony. He knew step one was to minimize his bleeding and prevent further injuries. "Finn, are you okay?" he called out, but the only response was silence. Then, from behind him, he heard shifting rubble. His heart lifted for a moment before he saw what was approaching: a massive, black-furred monster, ridden by a grinning Elf with a spear.

"Finn, if you're there, you need to run! Now!" Peter's cry was a guttural, desperate sound as the creature closed in. Its jaws widened, its hot breath washing over Peter's face as his screams left his throat. The monster's saliva dripped onto his face, each drop a cruel reminder of his impending doom. He squeezed his eyes shut, waiting for the inevitable.

But the sound of a large object crashing into something, followed by a wild roar, jolted Peter from his inevitable death. As he opened his eyes, he saw a massive polar bear standing over him, having just tackled the monster and its rider into a pile of rubble. It stood on its hind legs, towering over both him and the two monsters as it let out an unnatural roar again. Then the bear suddenly charged at the black-furred monster with a ferocity that left Peter shaking in awe. Teeth and claws tore into flesh with savage strength. "What the hell?" he gasped, still struggling to make sense of the chaos.

The monstrous Elf's gaze flicked back and forth between his mount and Peter, before he charged at the wounded, pinned-down Rifter, spear raised to strike. Just as the Elf was about to deliver the fatal blow, another Rifter charged at the monster, brandishing a shield and short sword. The Elf altered his course and struck first, plunging his spear through the newcomer's shield, piercing the man's torso as well. Despite the fatal wound, the Rifter kept charging, roaring as he slid further up the spear shaft until he was within stabbing range of the Elf.

Peter bore witness to the brutal battle between the Elf and the Rifter, his heart pounding in his chest as the sound of clashing steel filled the air. He could do nothing but watch as they clawed and stabbed at each other with savage abandon, each one fighting on through sheer rage. In the end, it was three precise arrows that brought the Elf down, piercing his chest, neck, and eye socket. As Peter looked up, he saw three hooded figures approaching, one wearing steel armor and the other two in some strange, gray material. *Reinforcements?* he wondered, his mind racing as he tried to make sense of the situation.

With a few well-placed arrows and throwing daggers, the two Rifters rushed to help the polar bear finish off the monstrous creature before securing the site. The third, clad in steel armor, pulled out the spear from his impaled ally. Peter watched in confusion as the injured Rifter then just took up his position in the group without a second glance.

A voice, certain and composed, pulled Peter back from his shock. "Are you still with us?"

Peter heard the man's words in fluent Finnish, but he was certain that the man wasn't speaking Finnish. *Is he English?* he thought as he concentrated on the man's voice, forcefully suppressing the innate ability of the Rifters to understand each other. "Yes. Yes, I'm still alive," Peter said, finally letting out the breath he didn't realize he was holding. "There were dozens of others with me in the beginning, including a boy. I tried to save them, but . . . Are you—"

Without a word, the man suddenly placed a hand on Peter's shoulder, and a warm, blinding light flowed from his palm. The wounded Peter gasped in surprise and then relief as the pain melted away. "You did everything you could," the man said, his voice suddenly soft. "We'll take care of the rest."

CHAPTER SEVENTEEN

Sucker-Punching Elsa

Ten minutes later
Inside Rift 22

LANCE

The injured man let out a deep sigh of relief as Lance's Healing Skill once again coursed through his battered form. "I can't thank you guys enough," Peter said. "I was practically at first base with that mutt." He gave Lance a weak smile.

Mend Wounds

Lance placed a comforting hand on Peter's shoulder and spoke softly. "Just focus on your breathing." He closed his eyes and channeled more of his Skill into the man's body, as he had been doing for the last ten minutes. As he looked at the rebar piercing through Peter and the weight of concrete crushing him, Lance knew he was fighting a losing battle. *He's not going to make it,* he thought with a heavy heart. *There's no way I can remove all of that without killing him. The bleeding will finish him off in minutes, if not seconds. And even if I could save him, he'd have to endure crush syndrome, infections, and days of grueling travel to reach the Rift-event. Our party doesn't have a skilled, dedicated healer who could fix this.*

"It's that bad, huh?" Peter said, his face suddenly a shade paler.

Lance's heart ached as he nodded. "I'm sorry," he began, his voice heavy with regret. "There's no way to remove the rebar without killing you, and you'll die in a few hours if we do nothing."

Peter's face twisted in pain, and he uttered a quiet curse before looking up at the destroyed ceiling. "Will I suffer?" he asked, his voice barely above a whisper.

Lance hesitated before answering, unsure of what to tell Peter. "It's hard to say for certain," he said slowly, choosing his words carefully. "But if we don't do anything, things will get worse over time. Severe cramps, aches . . . more pain. Bleeding out is quicker, but . . ." Lance stopped at that, his mind recalling the bloody knife and Thomas's pale face. "I'm sorry."

"Don't be," Peter said with a forced smile, wiping away the evidence of his lies with the back of his hand. "I got myself into this mess by running into danger. I just wanted to save the kid."

"I know," Lance said, pouring another stream of energy into the man's body. He had spent the last ten minutes stabilizing him and patching him up as best he could. During that time, Peter had shared the details of his time inside the Rift and how he'd tried to protect his fellow survivors, but ultimately the monsters had overwhelmed them.

The wounded Rifter had tried to save Finn, a teenager in a red hoodie, but lost sight of him when they got hit by the ice attack. "I'll see if the others found anything. The two Rifters here will keep you safe," Lance said, patting Peter's shoulder before getting up. The moment Lance walked away, he heard Quill and Viper move toward the trapped man, taking up a protective position.

Leaving the man behind, Lance struggled with his emotions as he surveyed the wreckage. He had dispatched Ash and Medusa to search for survivors, but he wasn't optimistic about their chances. By the time he had found Peter, an hour had already passed. The other Rifters had scoured the area, but the buildings had mostly crumbled, burying the living and the dead. No one had expected to find any more survivors.

A few seconds later, Lance encountered Ash and the polar bear, who were laboring to move a large concrete slab. "Did you find anything?" Lance asked, bracing himself for the answer. He let out a muffled curse when Ash nodded in affirmation.

"A male . . . young," Ash said, his deep voice making the message sound even more depressing.

After swapping places with Ash, Lance descended into the opening they had made. The dust and rubble made it difficult to see, but he could make out the mangled form of a human, crushed by the falling debris. *Dammit.* Lance's heart sank as he recognized the red hoodie that Peter had described. "I'm sorry, Finn," he murmured softly, his hand gently touching the mangled body.

[Would you like to store this Item?]
[Yes] [No]

The notification hit Lance like a punch in the gut, and he recoiled from the young man's remains as if burned. A deluge of conflicting emotions overwhelmed him as he grappled with the realization that he had nearly accepted it. It had almost been instinctual, to store the body and turn it into a companion. *This is wrong on so many levels,* Lance thought as he gazed at the broken teenager. Memories of Thomas, Mira, and Iyas bubbled up like a toxic brew, but he pushed them down and left Finn's body there.

He instructed Ash and Medusa to keep searching for other survivors before returning to Peter's side. The man was looking worse by the minute. "How are you holding up?" he asked, concern etched on his face as he knelt beside him. Placing a hand on Peter's chest, Lance closed his eyes and focused on sending another healing surge of energy through the man's body.

"Living the dream. Any luck finding the boy?" Peter's weak voice struggled to form the words, despite Lance's attempts to ease his pain.

"The others are still looking for survivors. We'll keep looking," Lance assured the dying man, choosing his words carefully to avoid any falsehoods.

"Yeah," Peter said as he strained his voice. He sounded tired at that moment. "No doubt the little runt got away in time—" He stopped talking when a jolt of pain assaulted him again. "I don't think you were right about me having a few hours."

"Just hold still," Lance said as he forced another wave of energy into the man, illuminating Peter's body in a blue glow for a few seconds. *My Mana reserves won't last forever.*

"I'm sorry to spring this on you," Peter said, three fingers digging into his palm as he suppressed another jolt of pain. "I know it's a dirty move, but I can only play the dying card once in my life. I figured a dying man might ask for three favors." He paused, took a deep breath. "Please."

"Whatever you need Peter. Just let me know."

"The first one is about Finn. He's an annoying little brat, but he's smart. If he's out there, could you protect him? I don't want this Rift to swallow up a young kid like that. It isn't right," Peter implored, his smile faltering at the thought of what could happen to Finn.

"The second one is about my son. I want him to have a message from his old man. Something to remember me by beyond an official casualty report," Peter said, his face contorted with pain. "I'm not a number in a report. I'm his dad. Paper and pen will do, or if you've got a phone, I'd like to leave a voice recording," Peter said as he shifted his gaze toward Lance.

"Sure, I can do that for you," Lance said as he retrieved his smartphone from his Inventory and unlocked it, seconds later handing it to Peter. "What was the last thing?"

"Let me borrow your gun."

The minutes dragged on as Lance sat on a piece of concrete, his eyes unfocused. Quill was making another security sweep at the entrance, while Viper worked on dissecting a monster, trying to figure out how it functioned. "Elves," Lance muttered as he watched Viper carefully remove the black-shard from the creature's torso.

Those Elves are a tough foe to face. Even Ash had struggled with them, ending up impaled. *I doubt I would've survived this Rift if it wasn't for the others.* Nearly thirty other Rifters had answered the call to secure the Initial Rift that had occurred in Bergen. A lot of Rifters had done it to potentially save a few or even hundreds of people that the Rift had swallowed up. But Lance figured the majority had done so for the chance of getting valuable resources.

I'm not one bit better than those scavengers. Lance recalled how eager he had been to join up with this massive rescue operation. To save lives, yes, but also to get his hands on a lot of things Brian had put on a shopping list for him. His Inventory was now crammed with spare clothes, chemicals, fertilizer, batteries, Styrofoam, sugar, two large speakers, and more. Lance sighed as Ash approached him, Lance's smartphone clutched in his hand.

"He's ready," Ash said as he passed it to him. "Are you alright?"

"I'm fine," Lance lied through gritted teeth as he turned his gaze to the ruined mall. Bits of debris still tumbled around him, a constant reminder of the destruction. *Focus on why I'm here,* he reminded himself. *Justice for Thomas. And if I can save lives along the way, I will*—The loud bang behind him shattered his train of thought, reminding that he had just failed in the latter. Clenching his jaw, Lance shifted his gaze to his smartphone, his cracked screen displaying Peter's recorded audio message. "That makes two favors," Lance muttered as he got up and made his way toward Peter's body.

Kneeling beside Peter's still frame, Lance retrieved his pistol and picked up the empty casing. "I'll get the message to your son, I promise," he said, placing a hand on the body and making a mental note to have Brian transfer a sizable donation to ensure Peter's son would be taken care of.

Lance stood up. "You did your best, Peter. You tried to save people," he remarked. He knew it was futile, but he wanted to pay his respects. *I wish I could've done more for you.*

[You have stored an Item in your Inventory]

Lance stowed away his phone as he followed the same route he had taken before, stopping at the spot where Ash and Medusa had been digging. With care, he lowered himself into the pit until he saw the blood-stained hoodie. "Now for your last favor," he whispered as he cautiously stretched out his hand.

[You have stored an Item in your Inventory]

Several days had passed since the Rifters had entered Bergen's Rift and the air was still thick with tension and the sounds of fighting. The Rifters had split into two teams, the higher-Leveled and Damage dealers venturing closer toward the Rift-event to fight the Guardian while others remained behind to protect the wounded survivors. Lance and his companions had offered to help with guard duty, keeping a watchful eye on the surroundings to ensure that no monsters snuck up on them.

This is at least a Level Five Rift, maybe Six, he mused, recalling the difficulty his companions faced while battling a handful of monsters on their own. He had spent a lot of time and black-shards repairing them over the last few days. Even Ash was barely keeping up, despite having proper armor. He currently had Quill and Viper in his Inventory again, getting them repaired. Luckily, there were a lot of skilled Rifters present, some with Levels in the Two Hundred range.

Lance cast a backward glance at the group of survivors, his attention drawn to Ash and the other Rifters' efforts of carrying the wounded and children. With nimble movements, they carefully traversed the uneven ground and waded through streams, their precious cargo held securely. Despite the inherent danger, Lance felt a fleeting sense of relief, knowing that they were safe—at least for the moment.

The environment of this world had a familiar feel to it, reminiscent of Earth, albeit with subtle variations—the vast expanse of freshwater lakes, abundant foliage, rolling hills. Lance couldn't help but notice the unusual tinge of the trees—a blend of orange and yellow—but their branches and leaves still offered solace from the heat of the sun.

As they drew nearer to the battle, Lance couldn't help but feel the unnatural pull of the Rift-event itself. Its energy radiated out, beckoning him and the other Rifters closer. Though he knew he should focus on protecting the survivors, his attention kept darting toward the horizon, where the fighting raged on. There, amidst the chaos and destruction, he searched for a glimpse of the blue fabric that had plagued his mind for days, filled with foreign and fragmented memories. *Just a little longer.*

As they crested the small hill, the location of the Rift-event came into view, and Lance's eyes widened in amazement. An enormous, ruined temple lay at the center of the valley, infested by hordes of monstrous creatures, and Elves mounted on their backs like knights of old. The Rifters that were fighting them were a flurry of motion, their Skills unleashing deadly attacks as they darted in and out of battle with overwhelming force. Amidst the cacophony of clashing swords and spells, Lance could hear the unmistakable sound of automatic weapons firing in the distance.

Lance was focusing on the center, where an immense fireball suddenly went off, causing him to avert his gaze several times. As the brightness dissipated, a powerful gust of ice followed, freezing swaths of monsters. Just as he was about to step closer to the spectacle, Lance noticed several Elves and their mounts breaking off from the main force and rushing toward him.

"Incoming enemy!" Lance heard another Rifter shout. He fell into position with his fellow Rifters, readying his weapons and activating Skills as the monsters approached. Lance charged forward, hurling a javelin toward an Elf, only to miss as it deftly dodged.

Lance's momentum carried him between two towering mounts, where he swiftly retrieved throwing knives from the sheaths on his gauntlet. The blades flew true, piercing the creatures' throats, but instead of remaining lodged in flesh, the knives ricocheted back toward the other mount, striking it a second time.

Lance skidded to a stop as two explosions ruptured the air behind him. The throwing knives had splintered into a thousand deadly shards, creating a chain reaction of lacerations that took out two of the mounts in one fell swoop. He spun around to face the Elven riders, only to find one hacked to pieces by a short Rifter with a vicious axe. Meanwhile, Ash had the other Elf pinned to the ground, his foot crushing its chest as he aimed a shotgun at its face. Lance averted his gaze but heard the gunshot a second later.

The group barely had time to check for injuries when the ground trembled, announcing the death of the Rift-guardian and the instability of the Rift-event. "We need to move quickly," barked one of the Rifters as everyone sprang into action.

Lance hollered at Ash to carry one of the children while he assisted with a wounded woman, then bolted toward the Rift-event.

Lance emerged from the Rift, fighting off disorientation as he slid across the ground. The wounded woman in his arms cried in fear and absolute terror. "You're safe," he reassured her softly, easing her down to the ground as he knelt beside her. "We made it. You're back on Earth."

The aftermath of the Rift clearing was pandemonium. Lance observed Rifters rushing to assist wounded survivors and transport crates of resources. Most of the survivors appeared bewildered, like the woman he held. To his right, he saw Ash, still cradling the injured child in his arms. Despite his imposing frame and dirty armor, Ash was gentle and caring.

The arrival of military personnel and government officials brought a sense of order to the chaotic scene. Lance observed as they helped the injured survivors, carefully placing them on stretchers for transport to nearby hospitals. He knew that soon the location would be teeming with ambulances and trauma helicopters and possibly double that number of reporters.

Lance gently assisted the wounded woman onto the stretcher, offering a reassuring smile and holding her hand for a few moments longer. "Don't think about all the chaos around us," he said, hoping she would find comfort in his words.

"These people here will take care of you until you get to the hospital. Just focus on your breathing and try to stay calm."

The woman held onto Lance for a few seconds longer, tears streaking her face. "Thank you so much," she said, her voice choked with emotion. The soldiers eventually pried her away and carried her to a safer location. Lance turned to Ash and gave him a nod as soldiers approached him, letting him know he could trust them with the child he was holding.

Despite the good they had just done, anger kept bubbling up to the surface in Lance's mind. Ash had been amazing, a bastion of safety for those who needed it. Seeing him covered in dirt and dust, Lance couldn't help but think how similar he was now to Daniel and Dieter. He wanted to hug the pale man and tell him how proud he was, but his anger prevented him.

Lance shifted his gaze to the side and fixed his attention on a Rifter draped in blue fabric and chain mail. The man was engaged in a relaxed conversation with his party members, their laughter filling the air as they celebrated yet another successful run. A surge of anger pulsed through Lance's veins, the residue of Finn and Peter's emotions still lingering in his mind. Fragmented memories of their last moments had tormented Lance's dreams throughout the Rift, revealing the gruesome reality of what had occurred.

The muscles in Lance's jaw clenched as he fought against the urge to grind his teeth together. His fingers dug into his palm, a physical reminder to hold himself back. *Don't!* he shouted internally, trying to block out the torrent of emotions flooding his mind. Finn's pain and fear were a tangible presence, the memory of the rubble tearing into his small frame haunting Lance.

He also felt Peter's desperation, his valiant efforts to protect Finn undone by a reckless Rifter wearing blue fabric and wielding Ice Skills. *Don't!* he thought, although it wasn't his own thoughts that were screaming at him to control himself. He could hear traces of Mira in his head, almost begging him to stay his hand, for the sake of the traumatized survivors around him. *Don't do this!*

All else faded away as Lance's rage consumed him. He stalked toward the Rifter without a word, his fury threatening to boil over. "Oi, Elsa!" he bellowed, his voice ringing out sharply before he lunged forward with a sucker-punch to the man's face. Lance's anger melded with Thomas's technique and Iyas's lethal instinct, fueling the explosive power behind the punch, which transformed from a powerful straight to a devastating cross, the force behind it fed by Lance's pent-up rage.

The Rifter hurtled backward through the air for a moment, slamming into the ground with a loud crash, denting the man's helmet. *Consider this my fourth favor, Peter.*

Lance stood there, his chest heaving as he stared down at the unconscious man. "That's for the two people you killed," Lance snarled, ignoring the Rifters converging on him, some even drawing their weapons.

CHAPTER EIGHTEEN

Boomerang Burger

Five minutes earlier
Bergen, Norway, Bergen
Near Rift 22

BRIAN

Brian's fingers drummed on the steering wheel of the motorhome as he peered out the window, his eyes fixated on the ruined mall ahead. The site was a stark contrast to what it used to be, with large nets and barricades surrounding the area, keeping people out. The Rift had devoured most of the mall, only remnants left standing. In the center of the destruction lay a menacing black orb of energy, pulsating ominously.

He watched as military personnel continued securing the area, setting up mobile barracks and fortifying the barricades. Government officials were also on site, taking readings and measurements of the Rift itself. Brian couldn't help but feel uneasy as he watched them work, wondering what fresh horrors the Rift would unleash. Despite being a Rifter and dealing mostly with his kind, he disliked being near Rifts, especially after the incident that still haunted him to this day.

He averted his gaze to the side, past the empty chip bags, and picked up a tabloid paper, the cover plastered with the image of a Hollywood A-lister caught in a whirlwind romance with a Spanish Rifter. Brian flipped through some of the glossy pages, seeking distraction from the ominous presence of the Rift. Despite his efforts, an unshakable feeling of impending doom clung to him. *Don't stress, mate,* he chided himself. *Picture yourself lounging in a massive pile of cash, sipping on an ice-cold beer, or soaking up the sun on a private island.*

Brian recoiled from the magazines, his gaze darting toward the door as it scraped open. Fergus, his massive frame weighed down by a heaping pile of fast food and chips, barged in. The scene was almost comical as the hefty man deposited his armful onto the dashboard, unleashing a tidal wave of snacks before thrusting a burger toward Brian.

"What's with the 'no bag' approach?" Brian asked, unable to suppress his curiosity.

Fergus paused for a moment, as if pondering something. "It wasn't on the list?"

Brian let out a sigh of exasperation, pressing his forehead against the steering wheel. "Mate, I don't have the time nor the crayons to explain just how much of an idiot you are," he groaned, shaking his head.

Fergus wiped his mouth with the back of his hand, smearing ketchup on his cheek. "So, did I miss anything?"

Brian gestured toward the ominous black vortex looming in the distance. "Take a wild guess," he sighed, his voice laced with irritation. "It's still there, and—" He fell silent as the Rift suddenly flared up, unleashing a violent shockwave that sent debris flying in every direction. Most of it hit the protective nets surrounding it.

As the blast faded, Brian and Fergus dashed out of the motorhome, tripping over the mess of pizza boxes and bottles. They sprinted toward the Rift-site entrance, and Brian wrestled with his jacket, trying to appear somewhat put-together. Amongst the chaos of townsfolk, panicked families, and journalists, they elbowed their way to the gate, only to meet the stern gaze of guards who barred their path.

"We're here on guild business," Brian declared, as he and Fergus adjusted their shirts and displayed their white-shards. It took a few more seconds of waggling his silver tongue and Fergus emphasizing his large build before one guard finally nodded and allowed them access to the site.

Upon entering, they witnessed soldiers and officials racing toward the Rift, hauling medical supplies and stretchers. Brian couldn't help but notice the masses of wounded survivors and all the Rifters congregating near the Rift. There wasn't a single piece of the Rifters' armor that wasn't caked in grime or stained with blood. "Relax, you're not going in there," he murmured to himself, taking a deep breath as he approached the Rift, his throat constricting with anxiety.

Brian scanned the crowd, searching for "his" Rifters. He saw Ash helping a young boy on a stretcher and Lance moving away from a wounded woman, but Quill and Viper were missing. *Okay, this is it. Showtime,* he thought, feeling the swirling thoughts in his head. He saw Lance's armor, dirty and bearing fresh scratches and dents. *He's definitely exhausted, bruised, and battered. Loving it!* Brian mentally weighed the items in his Inventory. *Sure, the kid will be upset, but I have gifts for him. And he's already in a good mood, having just saved lives. Happy, tired people are easier to manipulate.*

As if proving the man wrong, Brian saw Lance making his way over to another group of Rifters. Before he could understand what was happening, Lance had knocked out another Rifter, denting the man's helmet and sending him flying. Rifters drew their weapons and soldiers rushed to the scene, wanting to prevent any bloodshed. Ash was already walking up to the Rifters surrounding Lance, drawing a nasty-looking mace of his own.

No, no, no! He was supposed to be happy! Brian hurried forward, Fergus hot on his heels, seeking to untangle the mess caused by Lance "Honey Badger" Turner.

A few minutes later, Brian sat across from Lance in the motorhome, his eyes darting between the young man and the window as he shifted the curtains to peek outside. Lance remained seated on a bench at the back of the vehicle, his armor still on and his helmet resting beside him. His face was stoic, and Brian couldn't tell if he was thinking or simply exhausted. *Well, at least he's angry at someone else. That's good, right?*

Between them sat a small, foldable table that held a small bowl of chips and two carbonated drinks he had poured for them but which remained ignored by Lance. The silence between them was suffocating, broken only by the occasional rustle of fabric as Brian shifted in his seat, his eyes glued to the window. Outside, Fergus was in deep conversation with a group of soldiers and Rifters, trying to undo the mess that Lance had caused. Ash stood guard beside him, his gaze scanning the crowd for any sign of trouble.

Despite not being able to hear the conversation outside, Brian could sense the tension from Fergus and the other Rifters' body language. He knew this incident would warrant an official investigation, and he mentally added new passports and Rifter credentials to his to-do list. He let the curtain fall back into place and leaned back in his seat, running his hand through his curls, twirling the ends. "I heard you speaking Norwegian to one of the soldiers. I didn't know that you picked it up."

"I didn't," Lance responded, his gaze focused on the helmet next to him.

"Alright," Brian said, having no idea what Lance meant. "So . . . anything special about the bloke you hit? Chakras not lining up?" he asked, trying to lighten the mood.

"He messed up." Lance's hazel gaze abruptly shifted toward Brian, his voice like ice. "His actions led to two people's deaths."

"Ah, so the guy was a proper—"

Lance's gaze pierced Brian as he leaned toward the sofa. "Why are you here, Brian?"

Well, this is going great so far. Brian took a deep breath, preparing for the fallout. "Listen up," he began, his voice tinged with a hint of self-assurance. "I've got a few things to say, some you'll find endearing—because, let's face it, I'm a likeable guy—and others might rub you the wrong way." He let his hand hover over the table. Moments later, two Mana stone fuses materialized. He snatched the first one out of the air with ease but fumbled the second, sending it careening into the bowl of chips. Swearing under his breath, he lunged after the runaway fuse as it bounced across the table and fell to the ground.

Brian retrieved it from the floor, dusting it off with a quick swipe of his sleeve. He let out a self-deprecating chuckle, trying to ease the tension in the room. "Good thing it was just a fuse, huh?" he quipped, flashing a wry grin at Lance. But the stoic expression on Lance's face made his grin falter, forcing him to shift his focus back to the matter at hand. *Here goes.*

"I know what you did to Thomas."

Brian steeled himself for the worst as he spoke, his mind replaying the brutal beating Lance had unleashed on his crew in Dublin. He expected a similar response from the young man, or something even worse now that Lance had gained even more Levels. But instead of a physical assault, Lance remained motionless, his eyes drilling into Brian with a predator's focus.

Brian's fingers moved over the bowl, slowly gathering chips into his hand as he attached names to each one. "Thomas Walker," he said, setting one down with a soft clink. "Mira Rose O'Molony," he added, placing another. "And then there's Iyas Al-Jabri. One of a dozen names tied to this assassin. First two dead, the latter presumed alive. That's according to my sources within the GRRO."

Brian's smile twisted into a smirk as he watched Lance's expression carefully. "I don't know about you, but I find it a little suspicious that your buddies look like carbon copies of people that are supposed to be dead," he said, his voice low and dangerous. "Don't you think that's interesting?" He was almost daring Lance to refute it.

He had pictures to back it up, GRRO files, and several suspicious observations that Fergus had made for him, each more damning than the next. With a slow, deliberate movement, Brian pressed his finger onto the first chip, crushing it. "You had the upper hand last time. Now it's reversed. We're going to renegotiate our deal." he said, his voice low and dangerous.

Brian pressed his finger down, crushing another chip. "You don't want your family or Thomas's knowing about this," he said, eyeing Lance. "And you don't want to explain to the GRRO why you're running around with creepy, shoddy, printer-run-out-of-ink lookalikes in your squad." He leaned in, hovering over the third chip. "But that's not why you're going to renegotiate with me." He teased the last chip, sweat beading on his forehead. "No, you're going to do it because of this." He snapped the chip in half, the sound echoing in the tense silence.

"I figured out who hired Iyas in the first place . . . Kir—" Suddenly something violently slammed Brian into the wall. His chair clattered to the ground, and he gasped for air, a dagger pressed against his throat and the tip of a short-sword pressing against his chest. It took him a moment to realize what was happening—out of thin air, two warriors had materialized into existence, both deadly and ready to strike.

Brian's heart thundered in his chest as he stared into their emotionless eyes. Their lifeless gray irises locked onto him, making his skin crawl. Their sharp steel pressed against his skin. He knew he had to keep his cool if he wanted to survive and negotiate with Lance. Brian steadied his shaking hands and took a deep breath, trying to focus on Lance, who remained seated calmly at the table, watching him with cold detachment.

"T-that . . . explains how you're able to store and retrieve corpses," Brian stammered as he addressed Lance. His eyes darted nervously between the two warriors. "But blades and the undead won't change anything. I came here to negotiate."

"They're not undead," Lance corrected, his gaze unwavering as he signaled to Quill and Viper to lower their weapons. "I tire of your games and theatrics, Fixer. What do you want?"

Brian's hand trembled as he lifted his chair and sat back down, ignoring the pale figures that still hovered nearby. Despite his efforts to calm his nerves, his mind raced with questions. *What kind of Class does this kid have? I've never heard of someone able to make sentient minions out of dead Rifters. What else did he have hidden up his sleeve?*

Brian knew he couldn't let Lance see his fear. So he plastered on a smile and leaned back in his chair. He then pointed at the bowl of chips. "That," he said, his voice still a bit shaken. "That's what I want."

"More food?"

Brian slid the bowl toward Lance with a strained smile, his finger lingering on the rim. "What I want is the whole bloody bowl," he said, his tone bordering on desperation. He then held his hands above the table and retrieved several more Mana stone fuses, entrenching tools, and other Items that Lance had requested. "You're an anomaly, kid. A freak of nature able to repurpose the dead and clear Rifts like nobody's business. I want to be more than just a coerced merchant pawn in your game."

He then produced two more Items in his hands as he slowly opened them, letting Lance see two Skill-shards resting in his palms. "One Skill-shard to imbue items with lightning, the other able to extract moisture from things or the air itself. A gift of offense and survival. You don't even want to know how much this has cost me," Brian said as he slowly placed them on the table and carefully slid them forward.

"Kid, you're on a path that's as perilous as they come. I can hardly fathom the dangers you face," Brian said, his voice tinged with concern. "The GRRO has a file on you the size of my father's hemorrhoids, and there's a task force investigating the Dublin incident. And if that wasn't enough, you've ruffled the feathers of an assassin so deadly that my sources are unwilling to divulge any information. You have enemies, but what you need is a friend who isn't bound by any laws and who will stand by your side no matter what."

Brian then retrieved and opened a box from his Inventory. "A friend who won't ask questions when you request a weapon forged from the broken shield of your dead friend." Brian slowly slid the box toward Lance. "Or when you ask for a weapon that can take down a Rifter."

Lance's gaze fixed on the Item in the box as if it held some profound significance that Brian couldn't possibly fathom.

"And in return?" he asked, his voice laced with suspicion.

"You clue me in on this path of yours, where it came from and where it is leading you," Brian said before a smug grin appeared on his face. "That and I want to be filthy rich. Despite your feral nature, you are still a golden goose."

"Alright, Brian," Lance said as he traced his fingers over the Item inside the box, feeling the cylindrical shape and the pointed tips. "On two conditions."

"Sure, kid. Just name it," Brian said, his voice eager.

"The first is non-negotiable. Fergus is on my team now, and you will treat him accordingly. I won't tolerate you having your talons in him, so find another informant. Understood?"

Lance's request caught Brian off-guard. "Fergus? But he's a brute. I swear Fergus is the reason shampoo bottles come with instructions." The tension in Lance's eyes made Brian pause. "Alright, Fergus is off-limits to me if he chooses to join you. I won't interfere. I swear on my honor."

"You don't have any. Which brings me to my last condition," Lance replied as he leaned forward and placed a hand each on Quill and Viper, seconds later letting the two warriors blink out of existence. Lance then smiled as he pointed at the fixer. "I'll bring you into the fold, and I'll keep you stocked with plenty of monster corpses. You can even keep most of the profits as long as it doesn't slow me down."

"I'm sensing a 'but' here, kid," Brian said nervously.

"If you sell me out to anyone, if you endanger those that are close to me, or if you prevent me from getting what I want, I'll let Medusa tear you limb from limb," Lance said, raising his hand up as if making room for something.

"What the hell is a medu—" Brian asked before something massive and gray materialized in front of him, slamming him into the ground as a high-pitched scream escaped his lips, his bladder also betraying his trust.

A while later, Brian stood alone in the middle of the road with his eyes fixed on the receding motorhome. His heart was pounding in his chest, his pants soggy and his palms slick with sweat. He gave the vehicle's occupants a polite wave, praying to whatever deity that could hear him that the motorhome wouldn't turn back.

As it faded into the distance, Brian let out a deep sigh of relief. But his sense of security was short-lived. A sudden bout of nausea overtook him, and he staggered to the side of the road, hunching over as he violently threw up the burger he'd eaten earlier. His left hand shook as it clung to a tree trunk for support, and his mind raced with thoughts of the menacing young man who had terrified him to his core.

"Why did I think it was a good idea to poke the hornets' nest?" Brian muttered to himself, recalling Lance's icy stare and unnerving presence. *I could barely breathe around that psychopath.*

Despite his previous hesitation toward Lance in Dublin, Brian's fear of the young man had reached a new level. Lance exuded an aura of dominance, commanding an army of unnatural, undying companions. Brian had heard of Necromancer Rifters, but he had never heard of what Lance was capable of. He took a deep breath to calm his nerves and straightened himself. *I know he's been clearing Rift after Rift, but after being in the same room with him, I can see he's gained a lot of Levels in a short time. The air around him feels heavier. And who in their right mind pulls out a polar bear as a trump card?*

Brian wiped his mouth, the sleeve of his shirt stained with bile. His hands shook as he tried to steady himself, recalling all the things Lance had shared with him. The idea of working closely with the man filled him with a mix of terror and excitement. The benefits of being part of Lance's inner circle were too tempting to ignore, even if it meant dealing with assassins, the GRRO, and other government agencies—not to mention one of America's most powerful guilds.

Brian couldn't shake the sense of anticipation that filled him as he smiled like an idiot. Despite the looming threats hanging over Lance like the sword of Damocles, Brian couldn't resist the urge to see how far the young man could go. Witnessing the emergence of such a unique individual was a once-in-a-lifetime opportunity, and Brian didn't want to miss out. Besides, the bonus of even more monster corpses to sell made the opportunity even more enticing.

Brian's attention snapped back to reality as his phone started ringing. He fished it out of his pocket with practiced ease, taking a steadying breath before checking the screen. The caller was a broker he had sold a handful of monster corpses to several weeks ago.

Brian brought the phone to his ear, shaking off the tumultuous thoughts and emotions he had been struggling with. The faint sounds of a busy city street filled his ear as he listened to the voice on the other end. "I can acquire more," he replied calmly, a small smile forming on his lips. "Your client wants fifty?"

Brian's heart skipped a beat. He had expected the call to be related to business, but the sudden and sizable demand caught him off-guard. It was a large order, and he knew it would be a challenge to fulfill, especially after the way things had ended with Lance. Still, the prospect of another big payday was too tempting to ignore.

"No problem. I'll get you the corpses. As for Japan? I'll make it happen," Brian replied, his voice dripping with confidence despite the fear still churning in his gut. "It might take me a bit longer this time, though." As the call came to an end, Brian felt a rush of excitement and relief wash over him. *This will impress even the kid,* he thought, striding down the road toward the nearest town, his mind already consumed with the details of the deal he had just made and the demands that Lance had placed upon him.

Tropical island, here I come!

CHAPTER NINETEEN

Starting Off with a Spark

Three days later
Near Ålesund, Norway

LANCE

Lance stood in front of the massive black Rift, his hazel eyes taking in the malevolence of the black energy in front of him. He put on his new armor, a mix of leather and strengthened steel plates. His new gear was less durable than his previous, but it allowed him to move around more freely, something that was critical in a fight. The black leather was soft, yet sturdy, while the steel plates offered additional protection against enemy attacks. The armor was also less reflective, which was a plus, as it made it harder for enemies to spot him in the dark. Completing the ensemble was Daniel's keffiyeh, tucked neatly between his helmet and breastplate.

His current location had a protective fence built around it, surrounded by a sea of trees and vegetation. The thin steel wall was a poor testament to the danger that lay within. As with most Rift-sites in Norway, there was a mobile housing unit near the entrance, with several soldiers guarding the grounds. Lance had driven there with his team, just a short drive east of Ålesund, prepared to face what lay within.

Double-checking the information on his phone, Lance went over the types of monsters that lurked inside, and the last strength reading of the Rift. It was currently a Level-Three Rift, which meant that he could handle most of the monsters inside it. In terms of Experience gain, it would only be modest, but he was tackling this Rift for a different reason.

To Lance's right, Quill and Viper stood armed with spears, javelins, and shields. Their cloaks concealed most of their features, but glimpses of leather armor showed when the wind blew. They said nothing, but Lance sensed their eagerness to battle the horrors of the Rift the moment they entered.

Lance shifted his attention to his left, seeing Ash limbering up and stretching his muscles. Lance raised an eyebrow at that, although it remained hidden behind his helmet. "Really? Warming up?" he asked incredulously. Ash simply shrugged and continued to stretch, his muscular frame clad in thick leather and steel, with a cloak covering most of it.

Lance turned as the sound of footsteps grew louder. Fergus emerged from the trees, his steel breastplate, greaves, and gloves clanging together as he walked. He held his helmet in one hand and wiped his mouth with the other. It was clear to Lance that Fergus had just vomited, and the fear in his eyes was palpable.

"Feeling better?" Lance asked with a hint of amusement and concern. He knew it was no small feat for a Level-One Rifter like Fergus to venture into a Level-Three Rift, especially for someone who was terrified of them. Despite Fergus's affirmative nod, Lance could see the fear in his eyes as the man fumbled with the helmet. With a deep breath, Fergus took up position beside Lance, his fists clenched tight.

Lance placed a hand on his shoulder and spoke softly, "Just focus on your breathing. You don't have to go in there if you don't want to. There are other ways to help me on the outside." He paused for a moment before adding, "But if you go in with me today, you'll have my word that I'll get you out safely." Fergus nodded while his attention was still fixed on the black energy in front of him.

[You have retrieved an Item]

Lance's hand curled into a loose fist, and a bone cylinder materialized in his grasp. At its tip, a small blue cap, crafted from metal and Mana stone, shimmered in the dim light. "Smoke grenade, version two," he murmured, testing its weight and balance. No longer made from crude things like wet grass but actual decent chemicals that he had brought back from his last Rift. Lance slid the canister into his pocket before he held up his hand again.

[You have retrieved an Item 2x]

Two small blue mechanisms made from Mana stone flashed into existence. He examined them closely, testing their complexity and wondering how people manufactured them. *Mana-fuses and mana-sparks. The fuse types are dormant and need to be infused with Mana. The more poured into it, the longer the delay before it triggers. So, they are perfect for grenades.* A mischievous grin spread across Lance's face as he imagined how much Thomas would have loved to get his hands on a few of these.

Mana-sparks need to be primed with Mana but can hold a large amount. These function more like pressure plates or mines. More expensive, but could work wonders in terms of defensive strategies or ambushes. Lance stored the Items back in his Inventory, making a mental note to test them out in the field. *I've got about ten smoke grenades and four explosive grenades to mess around with now.* With a sense of excitement and anticipation, Lance stepped closer to the Rift, ready to face whatever lay ahead.

"We leave in ten," Lance said as he stepped closer to Fergus, inspecting his gear one last time. He heard Ash, Viper, and Quill gearing up for battle, their weapons at the ready. "Whatever you decide to do next is fine," Lance added, calmly patting Fergus's shoulder. He then retrieved a shield and spear from his Inventory. "Just remember, once I step inside, the Rift will turn unstable after a minute or so. All right?"

Fergus nodded before flinching when Lance shoved the spear and shield into his hands. The man was clearly terrified, but instincts kicked in as he recognized the value of having steel in his grasp for protection.

"Three . . . two . . . one . . ." Lance counted down before he and his three pale companions stepped forward in unison, disappearing into the massive black vortex.

Lance stood amidst the spruce trees, the ground below him damp and the air heavy with the scent of pine. Broken tree trunks lay scattered about, while others stood unscathed. He fiddled with the single Skill-shard that he had left, tracing its jagged edges with his fingers. In the distance, the unmistakable clash of steel-on-steel echoed through the air.

The Norwegian pine forest gave way to a vast expanse of mossy flatland, the likes of which he had never seen. There were no mountains or bodies of water, just an endless stretch of terrain that seemed to go on forever. It was strange being on this massive flatland, seeing as he had been used to more treacherous terrain during his time as a Rifter.

Lance waited patiently, his eyes scanning the forest for any sign of movement. Five minutes had already passed here, but he figured only a few seconds had passed on Earth. "I don't blame him for not—" Fergus suddenly popped into existence, his body shooting forward with an explosive force, as if he had launched himself into the Rift. Lance sprang into action with lightning reflexes, his enhanced physical abilities allowing him to catch Fergus in midair and prevent a disastrous fall onto the rough terrain or a nearby pine tree.

"I got you," Lance said, his voice calm and reassuring. He helped Fergus onto his feet, holding onto his breastplate to help steady him. "Deep slow breaths now. And focus on the rock in front of you. Don't look at anything else."

Fergus nodded weakly. His eyes were unfocused because of the strain of traveling through the Rift. Lance felt the man's body tremble with shock while holding onto him, keeping him steady until his disorientation subsided. He looked up at Lance, his eyes still wide as if he was slowly realizing that he was indeed inside of a Rift for the second time in his life. "Thank you," he said, his voice hoarse. "I . . . I'm here."

"That you are," Lance said with a chuckle, clapping Fergus on the back. "Didn't even drop your gear," he remarked, nodding toward the shield and spear still firmly in Fergus's grip. "Follow me. The others are this way."

Lance led him toward the fighting, toying with the Skill-shard by flicking it in the air now and then. Fergus followed close behind, shield raised and spear at the ready, wary of any lurking danger. As they approached the front lines, the two men could see Ash, Viper, and Quill holding off the monsters near a chokepoint, with fissures at their sides. The three of them were wielding spears and shields, their faces set in grim determination. The screeching of diving birds filled the air as they descended upon the monsters, knocking them off-balance or drawing their attention away long enough for a well-aimed spear to strike.

Lance's companions battled peculiar monsters with two legs and four arms, their bodies covered in fur. The creatures' mouths gaped with flat teeth, and they had four eyes that gleamed with an eerie purple tint. Although Lance had never encountered such monsters before, he sensed their threat level was low. They lacked intelligence, didn't use tools, and only charged in like feral beasts.

Medusa, Lance's massive polar bear, sat stoically as the fight unfolded before her, ready to pounce on any monsters that dared to sneak past their defensive line. Lance had ordered her to stay back until necessary, and she seemed to be heeding his command, her eyes scanning the battlefield for any potential threats. Lance was quick to approach her, his hand sliding over her fur and patting her back playfully, aware that Fergus watched the entire scene with a hint of awe and fear.

After his conversation with Brian, Lance had brought Fergus into the fold, revealing the secrets of his Class, Skills, and companions. He told him that his goal was to get justice for Thomas and do as much good as he could along the way. Fergus had handled the situation surprisingly well, despite the initial freak-out from the whole assassins threat thing.

"Let's get a closer look," Lance said, motioning toward the front line. Piles of dead monsters were everywhere, with more joining the scene every few seconds as they kept running into the mobile meat grinder that was Ash, Quill, and Viper. After observing the battle for a few minutes, he turned to Fergus, his voice low. "What should we call these things?"

The monsters surged forward, hurling themselves at the shield wall with reckless abandon as they died in droves. Fergus scowled, his eyes tracing their violent descent. "How about Devil Apes?"

"That's a horrible name," Lance said, his lips curling into a smile as he saw Fergus deflate. "But I love it." He reached into his pocket and pulled out his brand-new smoke grenade, tossing it over to Fergus. The other man stumbled for a moment before catching it while fumbling with his spear and shield. "Let's have some fun."

Lance then walked toward Ash and the others with a confident grin hidden underneath his helmet. "Ash, smoke coming in. Maintain position," he called out before turning to Fergus. "Throw the smoke near Ash. And please don't miss. If it falls into the fissure, you're going down after it to collect it."

Fergus nodded in response before placing his spear on the ground and walking closer to the frontline. With a smooth motion, he infused the smoke grenade with Mana, twisted the cap, and rolled it toward Ash. The container hit the ground and a thick cloud of smoke erupted from it, quickly spreading throughout the area.

Lance observed the smoke with a satisfied smirk. *Much stronger than my previous version,* he mused. As the haze thickened, it swallowed up Ash, Quill, Viper, and a decent chunk of the monstrous horde in a matter of seconds. *Of course, Ash won't have trouble inside of the smoke because of his thermal vision.*

Lance stood back and watched the monsters become disoriented, their coughs and hisses joining the sounds of the dying. The smoke was thick and suffocating, and many of the creatures stumbled into fissures, either injuring themselves or dying. "This is some potent stuff. Imagine what it could do in a building or confined space," Lance said as he stepped back a few paces with Fergus. He watched the man staring at the smoke and the faint outlines of three spear-wielding fighters, as if wondering how they could endure all of it.

"Ash and the others don't need to breathe. And they don't respond to pain or irritation in the eyes as much as we do," Lance explained as he watched the smoke linger for a few more minutes before it finally cleared up, revealing even more bodies piled up near the shield wall.

"All three of them are so strong," Fergus said, his wide eyes visible despite the sturdy helmet he was wearing. "They're like proper Rifters."

[You have retrieved an Item 3x]

Lance retrieved Thomas's old lighter and two slender bone containers that resembled beer bottles and handed one to Fergus, taking extra care this time. As he swirled the liquid inside and fiddled with the bit of cloth that was stuffed in the neck of the bottle, he said, "In a way, Ash and the others are stronger than Rifters . . . but also weaker. Keep clearing Rifts with me and you'll become just as strong as them, if not stronger."

Lance used Thomas's lighter to set fire to the cloth. He watched with satisfaction as the flame spread to the alcoholic contents inside. "Shield up!" he commanded Ash and the rest of the group, alerting them to the imminent danger before tossing the homemade weapon into the heart of the monstrous horde. The bottle shattered on impact, unleashing a cascade of liquid fire that coated the creatures in a blaze of terror and pain. *Almost as if I'm a Fire Mage.*

Panic-stricken, some monsters scrambled to avoid the spreading flames, only to plunge to their doom in the nearby fissures or inadvertently cause others to ignite while slamming into them. The sharp tang of burning fur filled the air as the intense heat fueled by the alcohol content of the makeshift Molotov cocktail consumed things in its path.

With a smirk on his face, Lance tossed the lighter to Fergus. "You're up," he said. "If you hit a large group, you might even Level Up when they finish burning."

"Alright," Fergus muttered, his hands trembling. With a flicker of flame, he managed to set the bottle ablaze before lobbing it over the shield wall with a shaky toss. The bottle shattered amidst the monsters, unleashing a torrent of chaos and destruction. "Nailed it!" he said excitedly.

Even with the destruction wrought by the flames, the monsters persisted. More of them rushed in, quadruple eyes filled with fury and hunger as they thundered toward the shield wall. Taking a deep breath, Lance braced himself for what would come next. *It's good for Fergus to experience a one-sided fight like this,* Lance thought, recalling his own experience when Daniel had guided him and Thomas through their second Rift.

[You have retrieved an Item 3x]

Two short-swords and his smartphone manifested before him as he quickly snatched them out of the air. He stepped back, feeling the weight of the blades in his hands. "Ash!" Lance barked from a distance. The man gave a quick nod and slammed his shield and spear, acknowledging that he heard. "Medusa incoming. Ten seconds. Give her some space."

Lance strode over to the polar bear, his gaze flickering toward the mass of monsters in the distance before pointing at them. "I need you to break those things over there," he explained, his voice soft and reassuring. The bear rose to her feet, letting out a rumbling growl from deep within her massive body. Lance then turned to Fergus, motioning for him to clear out and make way for Medusa.

"Rip and tear, Medusa!" he shouted, as the polar bear suddenly shot forward, accelerating at a frightening speed.

Ash leapt aside, letting Medusa charge into the fray. The bear's powerful bulk bulldozed past the shield wall and into the mass of monsters, her immense strength and weight effortlessly pushing back dozens of monsters. With each swipe of her paw, she sent them flying, her jaws and claws crushing through their flesh and bone with ease.

The battle raged on in front of him, but Lance kept his attention focused on Medusa. It was like watching an angry child play with their dolls, tossing them around as if they weighed nothing, or pulling off limbs out of boredom. The monsters couldn't mount an effective defense against her, barely able to claw into her flesh. It was a stunning display of power, and Lance couldn't help but feel proud of his fur-covered death machine.

Lance's voice was barely audible over the sounds of dying monsters as he shouted his commands. "Ash, fall back! Viper, Quill, hold the line!" Ash hesitated for a moment, his blue gaze lingering on the chaos before finally retreating. Viper and Quill remained at the chokepoint, their spears and shields at the ready.

Lance didn't waste any time as soon as Ash reached his side. "You're on Fergus duty. I don't want to see a scratch on him." Ash nodded, his eyes scanning the battlefield for any potential threats. He moved closer to Fergus, a silent sentinel, ready to fend off any attackers.

Fergus's nervous voice was barely audible over the sounds of battle. "What are you going to do?" he asked, his eyes darting around the battlefield.

Lance's words were laced with sarcasm as he readied his swords. "Just picking up my end of the sofa," he quipped. With a flick of his wrist, he sent arcs of blue energy crackling along the blades. He took a few practice swings, the swords humming with power as he approached the shield wall. He paused for a moment to select a song on his phone. *Let's hope Medusa saved some for me.*

He sighed as he felt Thomas's influence inside of his mind as he scrolled through the list of songs until the cracked screen displayed "Thunderstruck" by AC/DC. Stuffing the phone into his pocket, he forced more of his Mana into his weapons, causing a shower of blue sparks to burst forth from the blades.

"Icarus!" Lance bellowed as he suddenly rushed forward, speeding past the shield wall and several monsters as he started carving his way through several others in order to reach Medusa.

By then, the only thing Fergus could see were the sparks of lightning going off, several bodies being thrown in the air by something massive, and monsters' throats suddenly exploding in a gory mess as something fast shot through it.

CHAPTER TWENTY

Finishing with a Bang

A few hours later

LANCE

Lance stood at the ledge of the nearby fissure. He peered down into the depths of the chasm, taking in the gruesome sight of the monster corpses that littered the bottom. Most of them were missing their black-shards, bloody wounds now marring their chests. *My shard collection is steadily growing,* he thought as he mentally catalogued how many he had in his possession and how many more he'd need for all the upgrades he wanted to implement.

Lance's gaze flicked upward, his expression relaxing as he scanned the skies for any sign of movement. Three gray shapes caught his eye, soaring high above the flatland. He knew that his avian companions were keeping watch, alert for any new threats that might appear on the horizon.

With a sharp cry, one of the dots abruptly veered off from the others, swooping toward Lance at a dizzying pace. But as it drew near, he recognized the form of his peregrine falcon, its sleek body glimmering in the sunlight. In a flash, the bird had alighted on his shoulder, its talons finding purchase on the sturdy material of his armor.

A gentle smile played on Lance's lips as he reached up to stroke its beak, his fingers tracing the sharp curve of its bill. He gazed out across the endless expanse of mossy flatland, taking in the serene quiet that enveloped him.

Lance's thoughts turned to his companions as he mused aloud, "I wonder how far Quill and Viper have gotten by now." He had dispatched them several hours ago to scout ahead, each accompanied by their own avian ally in case of danger or if they became disoriented. This wasn't the first time Lance had sent them out on such a quest. They were well-versed in this kind of mission, mapping out the landscape, checking for hostile monster groups and recording any new monster variants.

The Rift-event beckoned to Lance, and he felt its insistent tug in the depths of his consciousness. It was a reminder that time was of the essence, and they needed to press on if they were to reach their destination before they ran out of supplies. He shifted his attention to his gauntleted right hand; the leather and steel equipment suddenly began giving off sparks of bright blue lightning.

[Imbue Lightning: Level 1]
[Cost per usage: −5 Mana per second]
[Allows the user to imbue an Item with deadly electrical energy without harming the user]

Well, Goal One for this Rift has been a big success. A grin spread across his face as he remembered the devastating effectiveness of his new Skill. He had used it on both his armor and weapons, the former turning into a sort of electrical cloak that damaged enemies when they got too close to him, while the latter tore and boiled enemies from the inside. His satisfaction was palpable, but he couldn't ignore the drain on his Mana reserves. "Still," he muttered, "it comes at a hefty cost."

With a deep breath, Lance deactivated his Skill and turned to make his way back to the makeshift camp. He felt his Mana levels stabilize again shortly afterward. The sun was just dipping below the horizon, and the rocky terrain was awash in deep shadows. As he approached, he noticed Fergus seated in front of two figures. One was large and broad of shoulder, while the other was a small, equally pale figure. Both were wearing bland, gray overalls.

Lance studied the figures before him, noting how they were different than his memories of them as well as the nightmares that had plagued him over the last few days. *Just mere echoes of who they were before. Thomas's template is quite noticeable in Peter. He looks built for frontline combat. Like a brick house.* He examined Peter's robust physique and intact fingers. Finn, on the other hand, had grown taller, yet still exuded a youthful energy that pained Lance to witness. *I'll keep my promise, Peter. I'll keep the lad out of harm's way.*

Then, Fergus picked up an empty smoke canister. He then turned to the two others. The younger one watched intently as Peter clumsily attempted to replicate the motion, struggling to keep hold of the canister and dropping it repeatedly. Fergus remained patient, placing the empty canister in front of Peter again while nodding reassuringly. "You'll get it," he said in a gruff voice. "Just keep practicing."

"General, what's the verdict on our new recruits?" Lance asked, joining Fergus at his side.

Scratching his bald head uneasily, Fergus said, "They're faring better than we anticipated. The biggest challenge is keeping them on their feet, but Peter is proving to be quite promising."

"And what about the little one?"

Fergus shifted his weight for a moment, avoiding Lance's gaze. "He's a strange one, but it's only been a little while since they started training," he said as he glanced at Finn, who was simply watching him and Lance. "He just . . . *watches* It's a little—"

"Unsettling?" Lance said, a small chuckle escaping him. "I get it. I explained my abilities and Class to you and Brian, but seeing it firsthand is another story." He lowered himself to Fergus's level and looked him in the eye. "How are you holding up, Fergus? It must be tough being back in a Rift."

"I'm . . ." Fergus paused, as if searching for the right way to phrase it. "I'm scared, and I'll probably have to wash these pants several times when we return to Earth," he said with a reassuring smile. "But I'm relieved that I'm scared and not *terrified*. The horde of monsters that just charged us was overwhelming, but so was our one-sided slaughter."

"Yeah, it took me some time to get used to that too. Not all Rifts have a monstrous charge in the beginning, and if they do, it's usually the weaker foes and cannon fodder that attack first. The stronger enemies are typically found closer to the Rift-event. I think it has to do with the concentration of Rift-energy in that area."

Peter struggled to pick up the canister again. After a few clumsy attempts, however, Peter finally managed to hold on to it as he presented it to Fergus. Lance had read about Peter's background in construction before his first Rift encounter, and while it might not help much in combat, Lance figured this affinity could be useful when building fortifications or digging trenches. "Fergus, we're going to say goodbye to Peter," Lance announced, "and welcome our newest member, Brick."

[You have named this item "Brick"]

Fergus's eyebrows rose in surprise. "Brick?" he repeated, clearly confused by the nickname.

Lance stood up and gave a slight nod, as if he needed to confirm to himself that he had made the correct decision. "Large build and a perfect frontline soldier," Lance said as he leaned forward slightly.

"What about the little runt?"

"I'm not sure," Lance said, his gaze switching over to Finn, who was watching him intently. "I've promised Peter that I'd keep Finn safe," he said slowly, weighing his words carefully. "And I don't think he'd make a good frontline fighter, but perhaps he could be an archer." There was something unnerving about Finn. Even now, mere hours into his new life, the pale young man was already different than any of Lance's other companions. *Quill was also a bit different, more alert. But Finn is an enigma. Perhaps it has something to do with a high intellect?*

Fergus got up as well, looking around at the group. "Alright. So, when are we going to give them some proper armor?" he asked.

Lance let out a weary sigh before replying, "We'll hold off on the armor for now. They need to get used to fighting without it, and I don't have any spare sets lying around. And I'm not that handy in making my own."

"I have noticed that," Fergus said carefully, having seen the state of Quill and Viper's shoddy leather and bone armor.

"I had to keep a low profile for a while, but now that Brian and you are in the fold, I can order some decent gear for the others. It might slow down the progression a bit because Brian would also need to do any upgrades I want for the armor."

"You're a Crafter too, right?" Fergus posed the question to Lance, his hand absentmindedly running over his own armor. "So why do you have to rely on Brian's ability?"

"Unfortunately, my Class has its limitations," Lance admitted. "I can only manipulate dead materials," he explained.

"I've got an idea," Fergus said, his mind already racing. "Until Brian is done with the gear, I can sculpt a temporary set from clay, and you can swap it out with other materials like bone, leather, or scales. Remember how we made the grenades? Sort of like that!" He then gestured around him. "We'll have plenty of replacement parts out here. And perhaps there is a stronger type of bone out there? And that way I could prove my worth."

Lance raised an eyebrow at Fergus's words. "Prove your worth?"

Fergus glanced down at his hands, clenching them into fists. "Yes. I want to help however I can," he said, his voice laced with hesitation. "But let's be real, I'm not exactly frontline material. I ain't a seasoned warrior. Can't promise I won't get myself killed out there."

Lance wordlessly summoned a mace from his Inventory and thrust it into Fergus's hands. "Quit overthinking it. You're not here to be a grunt," he said firmly. "Try infusing the weapon with your Mana."

Fergus grasped the hefty mace, examining the metal for a moment before giving a nod of approval. With closed eyes, he concentrated on channeling his Mana, struggling with his low level. After a tense moment, he felt the metal grow increasingly warm under his fingertips until the tip of the mace blazed with an intense red glow. Fergus opened his eyes in surprise, feeling the surge of power emanating from the weapon. He shot Lance a wide grin and nodded in appreciation.

"Ash and the others are skilled fighters, and I'm uncertain how to classify Medusa, but they all have their limitations. Mana happens to be one of them," Lance said as he stored the weapon in his Inventory again. Finn's intense gaze bore into him as he did so. "Fergus, you'll find your own way of contributing. You don't have to fight on the front lines unless you want to." He reassured Fergus with a nod before pointing to the spot from which they had emerged from just a few hours ago and gestured toward the tree line. "But I do have a task for you."

Lance patted the man's shoulder, his confident stride leading them toward the trees.

A few hours later, Lance finished the last few knots on Fergus and his improvised sled, his calloused hands pulling on the leather straps to tighten it in place. He stepped back, inspecting his work of art with a critical eye. The sled was a crude board made from branches and leather, covered in moss and smaller branches. They strapped Lance's old mattress on top of it to serve as a cushion.

Lance snorted to himself as he took in its sorry state. It was a jumbled mess of things, but it was the best they could manage, given the circumstances. Then, he shifted his focus to the rest of the group with a sigh. Ash was busy checking his gear while giving Finn and Brick a crash course in what was what.

His polar bear, Medusa, stood a few feet away, her massive form shifting restlessly from side to side. Fergus was hesitantly trying to place the ends of the leather straps inside the bear's mouth, securing it in place. Lance walked over to Fergus and Medusa, offering an amused smile.

"She won't bite, will she?" Fergus asked nervously.

Lance's shoulders lifted in a casual shrug as he spoke. "Your guess is as good as mine," he said, his fingers idly petting Medusa's fur. "My companions have never hurt me before, unless it was in training."

Fergus just nodded, sweat beading on his forehead as he worked on securing the sled to the massive bear. They had spent quite some time working on several designs and discussing it during lunch before deciding on this one. The whole idea was to make a mobile bed to rest on as Medusa dragged it across the flatland, with his companions providing protection.

"I think it's done," Fergus said as he tied the last knot and stepped backwards to inspect it. "It looks—"

"Absolutely atrocious," Lance interrupted.

Fergus offered a simple nod before cautiously settling onto the sled. "Well, it's comfortable enough."

The sound of a bird's cry yanked Lance's attention to the right. He caught sight of Viper and Quill on the horizon, making their way back toward the group. "Medusa, try walking around slowly to test out the sled for us."

The polar bear pulled the improvised sled carefully, hauling Fergus along with it. Lance watched as Fergus's face lit up with childlike glee, and he couldn't help but grin himself. *No doubt it will cave in on itself within an hour.*

Upon Quill and Viper's arrival, Lance turned to face them as they stood beside him, their voices speaking in haunting unison: "We have returned." They then nodded respectfully.

As he took in the bloody boots and gloves, Lance raised an eyebrow. "Did you run into trouble?" he asked, his tone curious.

"None that remain," Quill replied in a calm tone, prompting a single nod of approval from Lance.

Fergus hopped off the sled. The man's face was a mix of curiosity and discomfort as he listened to their unnatural speech.

"Are you alright?" Lance asked, concerned.

"Yeah. It's still a bit weird hearing them talk. I was so used to their silence," Fergus replied, taking up a position next to Lance. "But I think I am slowly getting used to it."

Lance nodded. He had forgotten how strange it must be for someone who had never heard his companions speak before. "It's good that you are getting used to it, because it only gets weirder from here," Lance said as he held up his hand and accessed his Inventory screen.

[You have retrieved an Item 2x]

A partial polar bear corpse and a severed Elven arm materialized in front of him. "Quill, go for the tendons," Lance instructed, pointing at the arm. "Ash, go for the polar bear muscle."

Ash and Quill acknowledged Lance with a nod before kneeling down in front of him. They picked up the remains before eagerly sinking their teeth into them. The sound of ripping flesh and the crunching of bones filled the air, and Lance couldn't help but take pity on Fergus. He knew it was a lot to take in, but this was their current reality. He placed his hands on his companions before accessing his status screen again.

[Do you wish to reforge this Item?]
[Yes] [No]

I can't wait to see how this turns out, Lance thought as he accepted the reforging, carefully selecting which previous upgrade to sacrifice. The kneeling figures before him shook violently, as if experiencing an enormous change.

Moments later, Ash and Quill started retching up a mass of gray flesh from a previous monster. He had to take a step back to avoid the projectile vomiting. Their bodies twisted and contorted in inexplicable ways, as if they were shedding their former selves to emerge anew.

After what felt like an eternity, Quill and Ash's convulsions finally came to a halt, and they rose to their feet as one. Lance could see that they looked the same, yet something about them felt different. He sensed a newfound power and speed emanating from them, even before glancing at the status screen.

[Item upgraded x2]

"Twist me sideways," Fergus muttered under his breath as he watched the ghastly aftermath of the scene. "That was seriously messed up."

"Let's put those upgrades to the test," Lance said, running a hand through his hair. "How about a sparring match? Shields and spears should—"

"Brick, showtime," Fergus suddenly interrupted. "Spear! The large pointy thing. Let's prove our worth, just like we've practiced. Take it to Quill," he instructed, his eyes lit up with enthusiasm.

At that, Brick slowly got to his feet, his pale form wobbling unsteadily as he fumbled through the nearby supplies. Eventually, he picked up a steel shield and clutched it tightly. "Close enough," Fergus said, his grin encouraging as Brick tottered over to Quill, almost falling a couple of times before finally handing over the equipment. "Well done, Brick. Now, get Ash a shield."

Brick wobbled his way back to Finn, his movements uncertain as he rummaged through the supplies. "Don't worry, Lance. I'll whip Brick and Finn into shape," Fergus declared, his tone determined. His confidence wavered as Brick returned with a grenade that he almost dropped a few seconds later. "Alright, so he needs a little more work. But what is important is the fact that he's got heart."

Lance's eyes darted toward a sudden blue glint, and he reacted instinctively, pulling Fergus backwards, and materializing his shield. "Ash, grenade!" he yelled, positioning himself firmly in front of Fergus while Quill and Viper took up a defensive stance in front of them, shielding them further. Lance could hear Ash's mad rush toward Brick like lightning.

The noise was overwhelming. Ash's body slammed into Brick with a sickening thud, followed by the explosion that Lance could feel in his chest before his ears registered the sound. His shield and his companions took the brunt of the impact, absorbing the force of shrapnel and flesh crashing against it. Lance grunted, struggling to maintain his balance as the concussive force slammed into him.

"You okay, Fergus?" Lance asked once the ringing in his ears had subsided. Quill and Viper slowly backed away from him, bloodied and battered. Much of their gear was torn and ruined.

"Yeah," Fergus said as he took a seat on the ground. His hand instinctively went to his chest, rubbing it in discomfort. "What the hell just happened?"

With a heavy heart, Lance stood up and looked around at the devastation that had been wrought upon their camp. Ash was slowly getting up as well, his right arm missing and gray blood pouring from the wound. Miraculously, Ash was still standing. What remained of Brick's body lay broken and lifeless beneath Ash.

"Lance, what the hell happened?" Fergus asked again, also looking around at the sight of the explosion.

"Something incredible," Lance said, his wary expression slowly giving way to excitement as he helped Fergus back on his feet.

"One of my companions just wielded Mana!"

CHAPTER TWENTY-ONE

Oath Keeper

An hour later

LANCE

Lance's ears perked up as the clicking sounds continued going off one by one by him. However, he kept his focus on Ash as his bone, flesh, and skin slowly re-formed in front of his eyes until the last of Ash's pale fingers finally regrew.

He could feel the decreased Mana flow within his system, but he still had plenty to spare now that he had reached Level Sixty. "Just a minute left, buddy," Lance said, reassuring Ash when only his thumb remained.

[Repair Item has reached Level 3]

"Nice, we Leveled Up the Repair Skill," Lance shared with Ash, while keeping the Skill active. He watched as it finished repairing the last bit of skin and nail before he pulled away from Ash and inspected the finished product. "There, back in one piece."

Most of the armor on Ash's right arm was in a horrible state and would require a lot of mending, but Lance figured the rest was in decent shape for now. "I'll fix the rest of your damage when I can, alright?" Lance asked and Ash gave a single nod in response. He then shifted his attention to the status update regarding his Repair Skill.

[Repair Item: Level 3]
[Cost per usage: −35% Stamina/Mana regeneration (Temporary)]
[Effects: Allows the user to repair Items]
[At Level 3, restores 4 Durability per 50 seconds on 4 Items]

So, a 5 percent larger drain, while doubling the number of Items and how much Durability I can repair. And it's even faster now. Nice. Lance closed the menu and patted Ash on the back before shifting his attention back to the source of the clicking noise.

He could see Quill, Viper, Brick, and Finn sitting on the ground in a semicircle, each holding onto a Mana fuse. The fuses glowed with a faint blue light, and Lance could see the intense concentration on their faces. Slowly, with what little Mana they could produce, they began setting off the fuses again, each creating a small blue spark. Each time it happened, Fergus would grab the device and reset it again.

"We can use . . . Mana?" Ash asked, as he flexed his newly formed shoulder, tensing the muscles for a moment before he shifted his attention back to Lance. "How will this . . . change us?"

"Yeah, there is Mana inside of you. We just never noticed it because of the meager amount available," Lance said as he recalled all the times that he had tried to get Ash to wield Dieter's old mace, hoping he could use it like a Rifter could. "As for how it will change you guys, just watch."

He then moved to the side and picked up a Mana fuse before placing it on the ground. "Alpha, touch the device," Lance said. Seconds later, the gray crow landed on the ground and slowly touched the device. "Keep touching it and focus on the object." Seconds passed, yet nothing happened. Lance could hear Fergus moving away from the others and joining him and Ash. "Bravo, Charlie. Help your brother."

One by one, each bird landed and touched the fuse. It wasn't until the fourth had joined in that it finally went off. *That proves that they all can produce Mana, but the amount might be different . . .* Lance then picked up the fuse and threw it up in an arc, allowing Ash to catch it. "Apparently all of you can produce Mana. It's only a trickle compared to what Fergus and I can produce, but it will add up over time."

Lance then gave Fergus and Ash a reassuring smile. "As for what this might mean in the future. I don't know. But at the very least, some of you will be able to place mines and throw grenades on your own. Just the versatility of that is enormous."

"What about Mana stones?" Fergus asked.

Lance nodded. "Good point. My companions might be able to store enough Mana inside of those stones over time. Sort of like having sentient batteries to draw upon." Lance then pointed at Brick and Finn, who were still sitting there, staring at their fuses. "Fergus, I want them on their feet and ready to move out."

Lance clapped his hands. "Viper, Quill, bows at the ready on our flanks. Ash, you guard the rear," he said before making his way over to the polar bear and fastening a rig to her mouth that would allow her to drag the sled behind her. "Just head in that direction at a constant pace," he instructed before gently pushing her rear to get her moving toward the Rift-event. At that, the party slowly started moving, forming a weird-looking caravan of sorts.

Let's see how quickly we can take on this Rift.

Lance and his companions trudged through the flatlands as they had been doing for the last two days. The seemingly endless stretch of land spread out before them, with no end in sight. Still, Lance could feel them getting closer to the Rift-event. *Just a bit further,* he thought as he forced himself to keep going.

The twin moons were casting a pale light over the mossy terrain, but it was the bioluminescent moss that caught Lance's attention. It gave off a red glow, illuminating their path in a soft, otherworldly light.

[You have retrieved an Item]

Lance let the Skill-shard materialize in his hand as he gripped it tightly, feeling the weight of it beyond the material aspect. *I could give it to Fergus. Guide him into more of a support role?* Lance debated his options. From what he could learn of the Skill, it was something that could pull moisture from the air or objects. It wouldn't help him in combat, but the ability to essentially always have water on hand would be an incredible boon.

With a flick of his wrist, Lance threw the Skill-shard into the air and deftly caught it a few times as he continued walking, his footsteps echoing in the red glow behind him. He stole a quick glance at Fergus, who was sound asleep on the sled next to Finn.

As he pondered, Finn remained fixated on Lance, his eyes tracing every movement with a borderline obsessive intensity. Lance couldn't help but feel a little uncomfortable under the weight of his unwavering gaze. *Creepy little bugger.* Lance threw the Skill-shard up in the air as high as he could, his heightened senses able to track it in the dark air before he quickly snatched it at the last moment again.

Afterward, Lance picked up the pace and moved closer to Finn, holding out the Skill-shard. "Keep it safe for me," he instructed firmly, watching as the boy's slender, pale fingers gripped it with surprising strength. Finn's eyes never left Lance's face as he nodded, his features devoid of emotion.

A sound behind him drew Lance's attention away. He turned to see Ash bending down to pick up Brick, who had stumbled and fallen to the ground once again. Ash lifted him with ease, setting him back on his feet before continuing on, without missing a beat. *Just how much stronger has Ash gotten?* Lance had seen Ash's status increase, but reading a number on a screen couldn't compare to seeing it in person.

Brick struggled to keep up with the group, his movements slow and labored. Lance couldn't help but feel a twinge of guilt at the sight, remembering Brick's state after the explosion that had left him battered and broken.

I feel like I'm being too harsh with Brick compared to the others. But I can't argue with the results. He's already moving much better and improving faster compared to the time I spent with Ash, Viper, and Quill. He watched as Brick stumbled again but this time managed to steady himself before falling.

[You have retrieved an Item]

Lance retrieved a steel shield as he positioned himself next to Ash and Brick. "Good job with him, Ash," Lance said, patting him on the shoulder. "And Brick, I'm proud of you. Keep it up." He passed the shield over to Brick, pointing toward Finn. "The reason you are working so hard is due to a promise that I made. I swore to protect the young man over there. Do you understand?"

Brick's eyes flickered between Lance and Finn, his expression contemplative as he tried to make sense of Lance's words. After a few moments of silence, he finally nodded in understanding.

Lance smiled briefly before he slowed down and finally stopped moving altogether, staring at the moss on his feet. His mind pondered what was causing the red glow and he couldn't help but wonder if there was something like it back on Earth and if he could use the moss for something useful. He knelt and inspected it closely, trying to piece together any clues that might explain its unusual properties.

Then he pulled out a knife from his belt and carefully scooped up a few large chunks of it, storing it in his Inventory afterward. As he stood up and looked around, he noticed Ash up ahead, looking back at him with a curious expression, as if to ask him what was taking so long. Lance chuckled to himself and quickly caught up with Ash, tucking his knife away as he did so.

Fergus was snoring on the sled nearby. Lance couldn't help but grin at the sound. *That's practically loud enough to wake up the whole Rift!* He knew Fergus was going to be in for a rude awakening when he realized what was planned for him.

"Alright, let's move a bit faster," Lance called out to his companions, and they all picked up the pace.

The following morning, Fergus, Brick, and Viper were holding off two wounded monsters with their tight shield wall, their spears slicing forward as they fought to keep the monsters at bay. "Keep up the pressure," Lance shouted as he watched Fergus and Brick struggling to finish the monsters off.

The creatures hissed and roared at their opponents, unbothered by the many cuts and bruises that they had already sustained from the countless spear thrusts and shield bashes. "Brick, keep up the momentum. Fergus, you're wrapped in steel. Act like it," Lance bellowed as he followed the back-and-forth between the two sides.

Quill stood at the sidelines, her bow trained at the monsters, just in case they managed to overwhelm the others. She watched the creatures closely, waiting for the perfect moment to strike. It was probably overkill, seeing as Viper alone was skilled and fast enough to take them out within seconds. But he was mostly there to block and counter any attacks from the enemy that might otherwise overwhelm Brick and Fergus.

Meanwhile, Lance picked up and stored more moss, his gaze still fixed on the fight in front of him. *Just a few of these controlled fights should help Fergus out with both his Levels and with any lingering doubts that he might still have about these Rifts.*

"Can I help them?" Ash asked, as he sidled up to Lance, his tone indicating his eagerness.

Lance shook his head. "No way in hell," he replied sternly. "You're usually too motivated to finish off your opponents, and your recent upgrade isn't helping. Besides, they've got it under control." The two of them looked on as Fergus, Brick, and Viper battled the two wounded monsters with fierce determination.

Viper was using his shield to hit one of the monsters repeatedly. He moved with surprising speed, dodging limbs, and bashing ribs with his spear. Fergus and Brick, worked together, each taking turns to land blows on the other monster with their spears. Fergus managed to strike a vital hit, piercing the monster's chest, while Brick followed up with a stab to its leg, after which it quickly bled out.

The remaining monster turned its attention to Viper, who continued to shield-bash it relentlessly. The monster tried to strike back, but Viper was too fast, dodging its attacks and landing hits of his own. As the creature stumbled, Fergus seized the opportunity to strike, delivering a powerful blow to its side that sent it crashing to the ground. Fergus followed up with a final strike, plunging his spear into the monster's neck and killing it instantly.

Ash watched the fight with a critical eye, his expression unreadable. Lance could see the tension in his muscles, the way he held himself ready to leap into action at a moment's notice. *He's conditioned for war,* Lance thought as he clapped his hands to signal the end of the fight. "Well done, all three of you."

Panting, Fergus made his way over to Lance while removing his helmet, wearing a proud smile. "Two kills! And I even Leveled Up again."

"Great! I'd suggest spending your points on either Agility or Endurance at the beginning. It's better to be able to tank a hit and evade it, rather than being a glass cannon. Besides, you're strong enough at this Level," Lance said, patting the man on his back before nodding to Ash and Quill to go out and find another group of monsters. *Just a few more Levels like this and we should be ready to take on the Rift-guardian.*

Lance knew that letting Fergus kill the two monsters was detrimental to his own Experience gain, but he wanted Fergus to Level Up quickly and get his Class. With that and additional Skills, he wouldn't have to worry so much about Fergus in the future.

A few more Rifts like this and Fergus will be able to clear them with just the help of Quill and Viper. When that happens, we'll be able to clear two Rifts at the same time, Lance thought as he accessed his Inventory and found the icon of the weapon that he had tasked Brian to forge. He hadn't used it yet. A part of him wanted to, but a larger part was also hesitant and worried about wielding it.

He recalled the promise that he had made to Thomas and the words he had written on his friend's coffin. *Soon, Thomas. Just a few more Rifts and I'll be strong enough to get justice for you.*

[You have named this item "Oath Keeper"]

Status Compendium

Name: Lance Turner
Level: 60
Class: Death Smith

Attributes

Endurance:	115	**Agility:**	116	**Wisdom:**	85
Strength:	109	**Perception:**	85	**Luck:**	84
Health:	3100	**Mana:**	625		
Stamina:	950	**Inventory:**	123		

Traits

Taint of death:	Able to use Rift corpses as Items	Prolonged use results . . . ~ERROR UNREADABLE!~
Shard instability:	~ERROR UNREADABLE!~	Prolonged use results . . . ~ERROR UNREADABLE!~

Skills

Mend Wounds	Lvl 2	Restores minor wounds	+20 Health +8 Stamina	−15 Mana
Death Forge	Lvl 2	Allows (re)forging of death-related Items	+2 Items	−Raw materials −Black-shards −50% Stamina regeneration −50% Mana regeneration
Repair Item	Lvl 3	Restores Durability on Items	+4 Durability per 4 Items per 50 seconds	−Raw materials −Black-shards −35% Stamina regeneration −35% Mana regeneration
Ricochet	Lvl 1	Bounces throwing attacks with greater speed and accuracy	+1 Bounce +5% Speed +5% Accuracy	−25 Stamina per bounce

Detonate	Lvl 1	Detonates an Item based on its original Durability	−50% base Durability	−25 Mana per usage
Imbue Lightning	Lvl 1	Imbues Items with electrical energy without harming the user		−5 Mana per usage

Retainers

Ash	1x	Human	Rift-glider eye +2 Sight +Heat vision	Polar bear muscle +3 Speed +6 Power +300 Durability	Stone Walker bone +3 Defense +160 Durability
Quill	1x	Human	Stone Walker bone +3 Defense +160 Durability	Elf muscle +5 Speed +120 Durability	Elf Sinew +2 Speed +2Defense +110 Durability
Viper	1x	Human	Cerint venom +1 Venom strength +15 Durability	Elf muscle +5 Speed +120 Durability	Stone Walker bone +3 Defense +160 Durability
Brick	1x	Human			
Finn	1x	Human			
Icarus	1x	Falcon (hybrid*)	Rift-glider eye +2 Sight +Heat vision	Stone Walker bone +3 Defense +160 Durability	Goblin muscle +3 Speed +100 Durability
Medusa	1x	Bear			
Alpha - Delta	4x	Crow	Goblin muscle +3 Speed +100 Durability	Stone Walker bone +3 Defense +160 Durability	

CHAPTER TWENTY-TWO

Black Reaper

The next day

LANCE

Lance shook his head, trying to clear the ringing in his ears, and pushed himself back to his feet. He could taste the metallic tang of his own blood in his mouth, and he swallowed it down quickly before the creature in front of him made another move. The being resembled rocks fused together into a humanoid shape both massive and menacing.

It's slow, but it hits like a truck. Lance glanced at his dented helmet, which lay discarded to the side. All around him was fighting. He could hear steel slicing through flesh and monsters hissing as they died. Nearby, Ash was dealing with a similar humanoid creature made of dirt and clay. Despite his best efforts, his spear seemed to sink into the soft, pliable mass with little resistance before getting stuck.

Meanwhile, Quill, Brick, and Fergus were holding their own against a group of Devil Apes, using their shields to block incoming attacks and impaling the monsters on their swords and spears. Finn remained safely protected in the center of their tight formation as the group fought valiantly against the onslaught of monstrous creatures.

I could've stored Finn inside my Inventory but having him around incentivizes both Brick and Fergus. Lance circled his stony adversary once more. He hoped that having someone weaker around Fergus would inspire some bravery into the man, or at least a sense of purpose.

With lightning-fast reflexes, Lance suddenly launched himself forward, sliding effortlessly beneath the monster's relentless swipes. He sprung upward in a graceful flip, manifesting a bone javelin in midair. With a fierce grunt, he hurled the weapon downward, plunging it deep into the crevice between the rocks.

The bone javelin detonated on impact, sending a small concussive force rippling through the air. Pebbles and bits of rock sprayed in every direction, pummeling the surrounding terrain. Lance landed in a crouch, his boots skidding backward as he faced down the monstrous creature. His muscles tensed, ready to spring into action at a moment's notice.

As the dust cleared, Lance watched in irritation as the monster's fragments stirred. Stones and rocks shifted and swirled around its core, and its broken torso and face stretched and knit themselves back together. Soon, the monster was whole again, and it continued its advance.

Lance's frustration boiled over as the monster finished regenerating. He couldn't believe how tough it was. "Are you kidding me?"

Lance clenched his jaw as he realized what he had to do next. *I'm going to hate myself for this.* At that, a massive revolver materialized in his right hand, the cylinder already slid to the side, ready to receive ammunition. The weapon was more akin to a hand cannon, a thick, lengthy cylinder capable of holding three rounds. The black metal gleamed in the light with hints of Mana stone worked into the metal.

[You have retrieved an Item]

Lance's fingers moved with practiced ease as he summoned a single round of an absurdly large caliber. The round hovered in front of him for a moment before he snatched it out of the air with his left hand. He glanced at the bullet for a moment, admiring its size, the Black-shard tip and the intricate lines carved alongside it. *Black Reaper rounds,* Lance thought as he recalled the ammunition specs Brian had given him. Instead of gunpowder, it relied on energized Black-shard powder with an unstable Mana core.

Brian had warned him against using it at a lower Level, saying it would either break his arm or worse. *Time to find out.* Lance deftly slid the Black Reaper round into the cylinder. With a flick of his wrist, it slid back into place with a satisfying click. Lance took a deep breath and braced himself for what was to come.

He gritted his teeth and glared at the monster, his mind already made up. He drew in a deep breath and aimed Oath Keeper at the creature's torso. He planted his feet in a solid stance, his grip steady as he squeezed the trigger.

The massive revolver roared to life, unleashing a thunderous blast that sent him stumbling backwards several paces. A sharp crack echoed through his wrist and shoulder, but he ignored the pain, his attention focused on the monster.

The round sped toward the Rock-monster with incredible speed and force, tearing through the air like a comet. The bullet slammed into its target, unleashing a powerful burst of unstable Mana that completely obliterated the creature in a blinding explosion of stone and dust. Lance shielded his eyes with his arm, feeling the intense heat of the blast wash over him. When the dust settled, he lowered his arm and surveyed the area. The monster was gone, reduced to nothing but a pile of rubble.

Lance's teeth clenched as he hissed through them, feeling the burn in his wrist and shoulder. "Bloody hell," he muttered, realizing that he had hairline fractures in several places. The pain, however, was the least of his concerns; he watched in horror as the pebbles started to shift and gather once more. "Aw, come on!" he exclaimed in frustration.

With a frustrated sigh, Lance's hand went to his belt to grab a grenade, but he froze as the Rock-monster suddenly crumbled away into nothingness, leaving him standing amidst a pile of debris.

As Lance's gaze darted to the side, he caught sight of Ash's mud and dirt monster, also crumbling into dust. The realization hit him like a sack of bricks as he processed what had just happened. *Viper found and killed the Rift-guardian.* A violent tremble shook the ground beneath him, as if to confirm his thoughts. Lance then sifted through the debris and noticed the lack of a shard there. *So not actual monsters but summoned creatures? Golems?*

"Rout the stragglers, Ash!" Lance barked, gesturing toward the remaining Devil Apes. He then quickly joined Brick, Fergus, and Quill as they battled the last of their foes while Medusa's destructive rampage was still going strong in the distance.

Lance called out to Finn and Medusa, motioning for them to follow him as he returned them to his Inventory. He quickly stored his birds too, glancing over at Fergus as he spoke. "You okay to move, Fergus?" he asked in a concerned tone. Fergus was covered in blood, and it was hard to make out how much was his own and what belonged to the monsters.

"Yeah, I can still go," Fergus declared, before the two of them took off toward the Rift-event. Ash and the others dawdled for a moment longer, ripping out the black-shards from the fallen monsters and surrendering them to Lance afterward.

A few moments later, Viper finally reached them, dragging a hacked-up monster carcass by its legs and clutching its Guardian-shard in his other hand. "It kept itself well . . . hidden . . . Apologies."

Lance secured the Guardian-shard, and the monster remains, then examined Quill and Viper, noticing how their leather and bone armor had endured the battle. Lance recalled how Fergus had tinkered with their leather armor during rare moments of leisure. The man had made clay plates and attached them strategically on their armor. After that, Lance had destroyed several copies of them before gaining a template he could re-create with leather and bone.

"Alright, no one died or is missing a limb. Everyone! Huddle up near the Rift-event and get ready," Lance said as he nudged Ash toward Fergus and grabbed onto Brick and the others, repairing them while they waited. A short while later, the Rift-event exploded as black energy expanded outward and swallowed them whole.

With a sudden burst of light, Lance and the others materialized back on Earth, skidding to a halt on the rough terrain and kicking up a cloud of dust. Fergus lost his footing and would have hit the ground if not for Ash's quick thinking. He grabbed his shoulder and hauled him upright, preventing a potentially nasty fall.

"I'll never get used to that sickening feeling," Fergus said as he steadied himself for a moment, his gaze fixed on the ground below him.

"You will," Lance confidently, as he took a few steps away from the Rift so the soldiers on the site could see them. He gave a reassuring wave to let them know that everything was alright before accessing his status screen.

Level Sixty-Two. One from clearing the Rift and one because I killed the Rift-guardian, Lance pondered how to spend his six free Attribute points. His mind shifted to the powerful hand cannon Brian had made him and its painful kickback. *I need either more Strength to be able to wield the bloody thing, or Endurance to deal with the pain.*

[Endurance:] [117] (+3)
[Strength:] [111] (+3)

As he allocated the points evenly, he also activated his Healing Skill, feeling the blinding energy envelop him before sinking further into the bones of his right arm. *No doubt I'll do plenty of healing the next few hours to lessen the damage. It could be a decent way to Level Up the Skill further?* Lance flexed his arm for a few moments before turning his gaze toward Fergus. "Are you good?"

"I'm alright," Fergus said, his voice steady despite the blood smeared across his armor. He flexed his fingers, testing for any lingering pain. "Just some bruises. Nothing too bad. But look at their armor—it's held up pretty damn well." He motioned to Brick, Quill, and Viper's leather and bone armor; the plates were still intact despite the beating they had just endured.

Lance approached Fergus, his gaze flicking briefly over his companions' armor before settling on Fergus. "Your design held up well," he said, his voice neutral. "But what's your Level now?"

Fergus cocked his head, his expression puzzled. "You mean now?" he asked, his tone skeptical. Then, as Lance nodded, he let out a low whistle. "I'm Level . . . Five? I totally forgot Rifters get a Level when clearing a Rift."

Lance looked at Fergus with a measured gaze, considering his options. "Put the points in Agility or Endurance for now," he said. Fergus raised an eyebrow at the instruction but complied nonetheless as he allocated his newfound points.

He's Leveling Up quickly because of his low Level and the fact that I've instructed the others to wound most of the monsters he's facing, providing Fergus with easy kills. Still, at Level Five, Fergus should have around thirteen storage slots, Lance thought to himself as he watched how Fergus dealt with the minor changes happening to his body. "In your next Rift, you'll see a sharp decline in Experience gain because the others will be too busy fighting and clearing the Rift."

"Next Rift?" Fergus watched as Lance retrieved large jerry cans filled with water and containers filled with dried food from his Inventory. This only heightened Fergus's growing confusion. "Lance . . . when is the next Rift?" he asked, his voice tinged with uncertainty.

"Right now," Lance said, grabbing a Guardian-shard and placing it in Fergus's hands. Lance then patted the confused man on the shoulder before turning to Brick, Quill, and Viper. "The three of you will keep Fergus safe," he commanded, and the trio moved to flank him. Lance checked their gear one last time before handing Viper and Quill a crow each and telling them to release the birds when they were back inside the Rift.

"You don't have to go too fast. Don't focus too much on Experience gains or black-shards. Just get the job done with as little risk as possible. I can trust you two with this, right?" Lance asked. Viper and Quill nodded in agreement.

Fergus furrowed his brows, clearly confused by the suddenness of the mission. "Wait, so soon? Don't we have to wait until the Rift stabilizes again?" His voice was tinged with nervousness as he realized the weight of the task Lance was assigning him. "And what about you and Ash? What will you two be doing inside the Rift?" he asked, his eyes flickering between Lance and Ash.

"Well, that's the neat part . . . we won't join you," Lance said as he handed the first container to Fergus and nodded. "You cleared the Rift already, back when it was a Level Three. It's Level Two now. You know the monsters, the terrain, and you are now far more capable then before," Lance explained as he watched Fergus store all the water and rations one by one with trembling hands.

"Listen, Fergus," Lance said, placing a reassuring hand on his shoulder. "Quill and Viper can handle this Rift with ease. You and Brick are just there to enjoy the ride. Take your time, have faith in my team, and if you get scared, you can always fall back to the first camp and let the others do the work. Alright?" Lance asked as he slowly steered Fergus toward the hissing black Rift.

[You have retrieved an Item 3x]

Lance materialized his pistol and two spare magazines, then presented them to Fergus. "Take it. It won't be as effective against the higher-Level monsters in other Rifts, but it should work fine against the weaker ones in this one." He squeezed Fergus's shoulder to reassure him before stepping back.

Fergus secured the pistol and spare magazines behind his belt and grasped his shield and spear in one hand, keeping the Guardian-shard firmly in the other. "Alright . . . I've got this, Lance. Just you wait and see." He took a few hesitant strides toward the Rift, holding the shard out in front of him as he went. It glowed a brilliant red hue as soon as it contacted the unstable gateway. A sudden explosion of light filled the area as the shard disintegrated into tiny particles, the energy releasing in a powerful burst that caused the Rift to ripple and warp. Slowly, the Rift stabilized and formed a secure pathway.

With a solemn expression, Fergus tightened his hold on his shield and spear and looked back at Lance. "I'll be going now," he said before they shared a nod of understanding. Afterward, Fergus and his three companions slowly advanced toward the Rift, disappearing from view as they stepped through.

Lance stood watching the Rift for a few moments, the black sphere of energy lashing out chaotically around itself. *Don't overthink it,* he reminded himself, taking a deep breath and trying to remain calm. *Fergus will be fine.*

Ash moved up next to Lance, his gaze fixed on Lance. "Do you want me to go in and help?" he asked, his features unreadable.

"No," Lance said firmly, turning away from the Rift, gesturing for Ash to follow. "We need to resupply and deliver a few monster corpses to the drop-off point first." As he made his way toward the entrance, his mind was already focused on the next task. "After that, we'll tackle a tougher Rift. Maybe Level Five or Six."

"Can we manage a Six . . . on our own?" Ash asked, cracking his neck as if eager to discover for himself.

"Only one way to find out," Lance stated as he retrieved his things from the locker in his cubicle before making his way outside, past the soldiers that were on duty. "Half our party is going to clear the Rift again. They'll be out in a few days," Lance explained to them before heading out, all the while still wearing their blood-covered gear.

The white Citroen came into view, and Ash strode toward the car, opening the right-side door and placing their gear in the backseat. Lance followed, taking out his smartphone from his Inventory and waiting as it connected to the cell tower. A flood of missed calls, mails, and text messages came pouring in.

Lance shook his head in disbelief as he scrolled through the notifications on his phone. "Fifty missed calls from Daniel. That's got to be a new record," he muttered to himself. He hesitated for a moment, contemplating whether to respond, knowing that his friends would only try to talk him out of his mission. He couldn't risk that, not when so much was at stake.

Still, I should give them a sign of life. I owe them so much for all that they've done for Thomas and me.

DIETER

Meanwhile, across the sea in Ireland, Dieter was scratching Little Hans behind his ears, calming the large hound while trying to ignore the commotion coming from inside the building he was leaning against. "It's alright, boy. Daniel's just a little upset," he explained, hoping the dog would pick up on his peaceful vibe. He glanced down at the smartphone still displaying the text message he had just gotten from Lance.

Dieter, I'm doing alright here. Hope you and Daniel are as well.
I'm still busy with the thing I need to take care of.
Until then, I'll need to have some distance. I hope that you'll understand.
PS . . . take care of Daniel for me —Lance

Dieter heard Daniel's voice ringing through the walls of the building. "Are you going to give me a name or what?" he demanded of the two men they had tracked down. "We know you've been in contact with the fixer who deals with the Demon of Dublin. Refusing to cooperate will only make this harder for you two."

"We don't know anything!" one of the men protested, sweat beading on his forehead. "We never saw that damn Demon, we swear! We were in the hospital when it all went down."

"Yeah, we were out of the count after a Rifter beat the—"

"Stop lying," Daniel growled, his voice low and menacing. "We know you've had contact with them. Give us the fixer's name, or things are going to get very unpleasant for you both."

"We already told you; we don't know. He goes by different names each time, never a surname," the other man said, his voice crackling out of fear.

Dieter let out a long, tired sigh as he re-entered the room. The two men were trembling in the corner, their faces streaked with tears and snot as they cowered before the Rifter who had tracked them down. He approached Daniel and tried to offer a friendly pat on his shoulder, but Daniel brushed him off with an irritated shake of his head. "I'm fine."

"Clearly," Dieter said, his tone bored. "But you've been sitting here for a quarter of an hour, and you're starting to look less like a GRRO employee and more like you're ready to don a cape and cowl. Let me handle this. I don't have to worry about all the bureaucratic red tape." He grinned and shoved his phone into Daniel's hand. "Oh, by the way, the kid sent a message."

Dieter crouched before the two frightened men as his face twisted into a cruel smile. "Look, I'm actually on my day off, so I'll make this easy for you," he said, his thick German accent dripping with malice. "Give me the name of the fixer, or I'll let Daniel call the authorities. And just for fun, I'll let you spend a little quality time with my buddy over there." He nodded toward the massive Rift-hound, which growled low in its throat. "Hopefully, at least one of you will last."

As the massive Rift-hound lumbered closer, one of the men let out a terrified whimper and lost control of his bladder. The other paled visibly, his eyes darting around the room as if searching for a way out. They backed away further into the corner, one trying to pull the other in front of him. "Please," he begged, his voice shaking. "We don't know his name. We were just hired muscle."

"Tick tock, gentlemen," Dieter said, tapping his foot impatiently. Little Hans padded forward, his jaws open in a silent snarl.

One of the men trembled as he spoke, his voice barely above a whisper. "Fergus . . . Fergus Murry," he repeated, his eyes fixed on the Rift-hound. "I think he's the fixer's right-hand man. That's all I know, I swear!"

CHAPTER TWENTY-THREE

Impact

Twenty hours later

LANCE

The muddy water had enveloped Lance completely, leaving him suspended in a world of liquid darkness. He focused on his breathing, in and out, in and out, through the steady rhythm of his oxygen mask. Above him, he could see the outlines of massive figures, their bodies rippling and distorted by the water's movement. Some lingered near him, while others passed by without a second glance, their paths leading them along the murky depths.

As he quietly observed the monsters, notifications would occasionally pop up, showing that he was gaining Experience even though none of his companions were currently fighting inside this Rift. *At least I know Quill and Viper are still active.*

He shifted his attention to his side; Medusa and Ash were in the water next to him. Both companions kept their focus on what was happening on the surface, waiting for the right moment to strike. Suddenly, a massive figure above them slammed into the water, sending ripples through the murk. Lance watched as the figure sank to the bottom. His peregrine falcon was still stuck to the monster's ruined neck, twisting violently to free itself. *These Orcs are a lot more durable compared to the Elves I've fought before. Luckily, they aren't as quick.*

As if on cue, Ash slowly swam upward through the murky water before suddenly lunging out and grabbing the nearest two Orcs, dragging them back into the water with him. The Orcs thrashed around violently in the water, their attempts to break free of Ash's grasp futile. One Orc was unfortunate enough to be the target of Ash's blade, and it suffered repeated stabs as Ash dragged it down. Meanwhile, the other Orc's lungs filled up with water, unable to break free of Ash's iron grip until it stopped moving all together. *The bear muscle upgrade really makes all the difference.*

[You have been awarded with a Level Up]

Watching the figures above him panic and stab at the water, Lance allowed himself a small smile. *I've only been here a day, and I've already gained several levels. Still, I need to be careful. I can hold my own against a single opponent, but if I'm surrounded, I'm toast.* Lance, Ash, and Medusa had already taken down several smaller groups like this, using the birds to locate Orc patrols and set up devastating ambushes.

After taking one last deep breath, Lance stored his oxygen gear back in his Inventory, and prepared to leap. He exploded upward, his powerful legs providing the momentum that he needed to break the surface of the water. As he breached it, two glinting knives materialized in his hands. He slammed into the nearest Orc, his blades slicing through its neck and armpit with ease. Not trusting just two hits, Lance quickly twisted and stabbed the knives several more times before kicking the Orc down to the floor near its brethren.

Lance's sudden appearance caught the remaining three Orcs off-guard, and they jumped back in alarm. But their surprise was short-lived, and they quickly regained their composure, their eyes narrowing with suspicion as they prepared for battle.

He eyed the three Orcs warily as they closed in on him. They were massive, their skin a dark shade of greenish brown and their bodies covered in a mishmash of fur and iron armor. Jagged teeth jutted out from their mouths, and they held clubs and axes with deadly ease. The Orcs barked orders to one another in their guttural language, their voices deep and menacing. They circled Lance slowly, eyeing him with suspicion and hostility. Growls rumbled in their throats as they communicated their plans, their weapons at the ready.

The Orc in the back suddenly let out a piercing howl as a sword impaled its chest from behind, causing it to stumble forward onto its knees. Ash emerged from behind the creature, his face set with determination as he yanked his sword free from the Orc's body. The dying Orc gurgled and thrashed but quickly grew still as its life drained away. Ash glared at the remaining Orcs, daring them to take another step closer to Lance.

"Formation Odin!" Lance shouted as he stretched his arms to the side, his mind channeling his Imbue Lightning Skill. After several agonizing seconds, four ashen crows descended from the sky, diving toward him before abruptly altering their course. As they swept past, their feathers brushed against Lance's outstretched hands, becoming engulfed in a potent surge of electric energy, casting an iridescent glow across the sky. The crackling of electricity filled the air, like the sound of a thousand small explosions going off, one after another.

The birds slammed into the Orcs with brutal force, their wings enfolding their victims' heads, forming a cloak of lightning as the energy leaped into the Orcs like a raging storm. The creatures howled in agony, their muscles contracting and convulsing under the immense power of the lightning as they boiled from within. Then they fell to the ground, lifeless.

Ash moved forward, cutting out the black-shards embedded in the Orcs' bodies while Lance took in their surroundings: a sprawling city of smooth granite paths and towering walls that stretched up into the gloomy sky. *It's almost as if it's designed as a labyrinth of sorts.* Lance then repaired his birds before sending them out in the air again to scout the terrain.

"Done," Ash said, presenting Lance with a handful of black-shards dripping with orc blood. Without another word, he slipped back into the murky water. The labyrinthine city teemed with Orc patrols, making travel by land treacherous. But the many interconnected waterways offered a path of relative safety.

We've been making a lot of progress already. Not to mention farming Levels, Lance thought as he stored his gear and reequipped his oxygen mask, following Ash back into the water moments later as he heard sounds of screaming and horns being blown, indicating that a nearby Orc party had picked up the scent of freshly spilled blood.

The cold water enveloped Lance, his eyes struggling to adjust to the dark depths. He could just make out Ash and the shimmering form of Medusa in the distance, waiting for him. They nodded at each other in silent agreement and grasped onto the polar bear, whose enormous size dwarfed them. Lance pointed toward the Rift-event and the bear obeyed, swimming toward it while effortlessly dragging the two men along with her.

Just a few more hours and we'll reach the Rift-event. Then we'll find a place to rest there before making a surgical strike on the Rift-guardian.

Lance slowly opened his eyes, feeling Ash's hand gently shaking his shoulder. "Lance . . . it's time." Yawning, Lance sat up, his legs hanging over the edge of the stone ledge. He surveyed the desolate world in front of him. Black clouds hung overhead, casting a gloomy pall over the ashen landscape.

The endless labyrinthian city sprawled out before him, a twisted maze of death and destruction. The water that had overtaken much of the city reeked of decay, adding to the sense of hopelessness and despair. The city's most prominent feature was the towering spire of black metal and granite that dominated its center. Having stealthily scaled that structure with Ash earlier that night, he now surveyed the state of this death-world from the spire's lofty summit.

In the far-off distance, two towering columns of smoke rose into the sky, evidence of the chaos they had sown. Groups of hulking creatures raced toward the source of the disturbance. "Looks like they took the bait," Lance noted, pulling a strange, purple fruit from his Inventory and biting into it.

In the distance, an explosion lit up the eastern horizon, followed by a third plume of smoke rising into the sky. "I hope this is enough," Lance muttered to Ash, finishing the last of his fruit and quickly donning his gear. He had prepared a handful of grenades earlier, imbuing them with a large dose of Mana that would give them a longer fuse. His crows had carried those grenades to different spots in the city.

Lance crept along the roof, careful not to make a sound. As he approached the center, he spotted Finn and his enormous polar bear companion huddled together, peering down through the glass dome that was missing bits here and there. "Do you understand what I need you to do?" Lance asked as he peered down as well, seeing the hundreds of Orcs at the lower level.

"Yes . . ." Finn's word came out clumsy and unpracticed, but the conviction in his voice was clear. "Smoke . . . Death," he said, pulling several canisters of smoke bombs from his overalls and holding them up for Lance to see.

Lance then retrieved the remaining Skill-shard and handed it to Finn, cautioning him to keep it close. He wasn't entirely certain why, but Finn seemed to perform better with more responsibility, as though eager to prove himself. It was a risk, entrusting the untested youth with such an important task, but in this dangerous plan, every move was a gamble.

He stayed still for a while, the sounds of horns and screaming Orc patrols gradually increasing in volume as he waited for the perfect moment to strike. Eventually, the commotion grew large enough and Lance could hear a sizable group of Orcs storming out of the spire and rushing out into the city, toward the three plumes of smoke. *Only seven of them left, including the Guardian. Showtime.*

Lance slid further down the spire with the grace of someone not wanting to fall to his death. Once he was close enough to Ash, he grabbed onto the man's hand before sliding off the edge of the ledge. He let the momentum of his drop swing him toward the nearest balcony of the spire, storing Ash in his Inventory at the last second and dropping onto the balcony like a seasoned thief. *That could've gone far worse,* Lance thought as he glanced backwards, seeing the large drop to the ground floor.

He then went inside the spire itself and made his way toward the stairs, his eyes fixed on the remaining six Orcs and the massive Rift-guardian. *Some sort of Orc-chieftain?* Lance stuck to the shadows, his movements silent. Step by step, he made his way down the winding staircase, his heart pounding in his chest.

Peering over the edge, Lance positioned his hand carefully. He waited for the right moment when the nearest Orc was directly beneath him. Suddenly, an Orc corpse appeared underneath his hand as he activated his Detonate Skill. The corpse fell, hitting the Orc below with a sickening thud. The explosion that followed was deafening, and Lance had to duck to avoid the flying debris of bone and flesh.

He then leapt over the railing and retrieved a spear from his Inventory. In one fluid motion, he thrust it through the neck of another Orc, using his momentum to drive the weapon all the way through the creature's body. With a sickening squelch, the spearhead emerged from the other side. *Five left*, Lance thought grimly as he watched the other Orcs eyeing him warily before rushing in.

Four Orcs rushed at Lance, their weapons at the ready. The Orc chieftain sat on a broken granite throne, observing the fight with amusement. Lance backed off, his eyes darting between the attackers, searching for an opening. The Orcs charged at him with a roar, swinging their weapons wildly. Lance dodged the blows with practiced ease, his movements just a hair's breadth faster than the Orcs'. He retreated slowly, inching toward the massive open door that led to the ruined city.

[You have combined and retrieved Items 2x]

As the four Orcs reached him, a shotgun suddenly materialized in Lance's hand, and Ash appeared at his side, shield and sword at the ready. "Door!" he bellowed as he squeezed the trigger, sending metal spitting toward the nearest Orc and hitting it square in the face. The monsters in a Level-Six Rift were durable enough to endure standard weaponry for a while, but even they felt the force of a shotgun round hitting them at close range.

Lance quickly switched targets and kept firing until his weapon was out of ammunition. The Orcs continued to advance.

The deafening sound of two massive doors closing reached Lance's ears, followed by the metallic sliding of a heavy crossbar; Ash had finished his task. As if on cue, a cacophony of screeches and shattering glass filled the air as four crows and a peregrine falcon crashed through the glass dome of the spire. Each bird carried a smoke bomb as they hurled themselves toward Lance and Ash. Within seconds, parts of the chamber became engulfed in a thick cloud of smoke, making it almost impossible to see.

"Now, Ash."

[You have retrieved an Item]

Lance crouched down and pulled Daniel's keffiyeh tightly over his nose, filtering out the thick smoke that filled the chamber. He stepped back cautiously, listening to the sounds of his birds as they swooped and collided with the Orcs' eyes and ears. Ash was in the thick of it, hacking and stabbing with deadly precision, aided by his ability to see through the smoke. As the smoke cleared, Lance could see the lifeless bodies of the Orcs scattered around the chamber, as well as Ash snapping the neck of the last one while making eye-contact with the Rift-guardian.

[You have been awarded with a Level Up]

Slowly rising from his throne, the Orc chieftain's lips twisted into a cruel smile as he gazed at the bloody aftermath. Lance lunged forward, hurling a dagger at the chieftain's neck, but the weapon merely bounced off its thick hide, leaving no trace of a scratch. To make matters worse, Lance could hear banging on the door behind him, meaning that reinforcements were now mere moments away.

The Orc chieftain advanced toward Lance and Ash, its speech a jumble of grunts and snarls. Its wide smile bared sharp, yellowed teeth as it flexed its massive arm. Just as it took its fifth step, a hail of glass shattered, peppering it from above. Then, with a force that shook the earth, a polar bear plummeted from above, smashing into the chieftain and crushing it into the ground. Finn was still sitting astride the bear, a mixture of confusion and curiosity visible in his gray eyes.

Ash and Lance charged forward without hesitation, plunging their weapons into the fallen Orc with a fury that bordered on the fanatical. They targeted every vulnerable spot they could find: the throat, eyes, armpits, and inner thighs. Still clutching the Skill-shard, Finn, as well as the severely crippled Medusa, joined in the attack, biting and kicking the chieftain with all their might. The onslaught continued without pause, until it seemed that the very world itself began to shake and tremble beneath them.

[You have been awarded with a Level Up]

"It's dead!" Lance exclaimed, his excitement palpable as he rose to his feet and swiftly stowed the polar bear in his Inventory. "Ash, gather our gear and start collecting shards. Finn, find my knife and stay by my side," he ordered, watching as the young man hurried off, Skill-shard still clutched in his hand. "Birds, gather the empty cannisters." After that, he turned the Rift-guardian on his side and used his knife to cut the Guardian-shard out before storing it and the corpse itself in his Inventory.

Several tense minutes passed as he and his companions scrambled to collect their gear and any valuables they could find, all the while listening to the deafening sound of monsters pounding on the other side of the door. "Enough. Let's fall back," Lance ordered, leading Finn and Ash toward the throne that lay shattered in front of the Rift-event. They took up position there as the pounding on the door grew louder and more frenzied. Finally, with a deafening crash, the door burst open, revealing a horde of snarling Orcs that came pouring inside.

[You have retrieved an Item 2x]

He snatched up two of the Orc corpses he had just looted and activated his Detonate Skill, the strain of it eating away at what little Mana he had left. "Ash!" he shouted as the two of them flung the heavy corpses toward the oncoming horde before they erupted in a sickening blast of blood, gore, and bone. Before Lance could even assess the damage, the ground shook violently as a surge of black energy burst forth from the Rift-event, engulfing everything in its path.

[You have been awarded with a Level Up]
[You are now Level 69]

Lance could feel the dirt beneath his skin as he inhaled deeply. He slowly opened his eyes to the sight of a clear blue sky, confirming that he was back on Earth. After a moment, Ash appeared, hovering above him. *No doubt checking to see if I'm still alive and kicking,* Lance thought with a smile while undoing the straps on his helmet.

Lance slowly got into a sitting position, his body feeling heavy and uncooperative after the lengthy battle. Finn was a few paces away, slowly rising to his feet, brushing off dirt and grass from his face. The Skill-shard glinted in the young man's hand, with gray blood dripping down his fingers. *Must've been clutching it so tight that he hurt himself.*

Ash helped Lance up, his expression unreadable. "That plan was . . . reckless," he said, his voice deep and unnatural.

Lance got to his feet, dusting off his gear and running a hand through his hair. "I know," he said with a grin. "But you have to admit, it worked." Then he studied the messages on his status screen, reminding him that he had several Attribute points left to spend.

[You have retrieved an Item]

Lance's damaged smartphone materialized in his hand and he waited for it to connect to the nearest cell tower. In no time at all, it vibrated several times, hinting at missed calls, but he ignored them all. He selected Fergus from his Contacts and initiated a video call. *I'm sure he's fine.*

A few seconds later, Fergus's shiny bald head appeared on the screen before the man adjusted the camera. "Lance! Finally. You had me worried. When the three of us came out of the Rift, I couldn't contact you. And the car was missing as well. What happened?"

"Yeah, sorry. Ash and I tackled another Rift while you were busy," Lance said as he held up his hand, preventing Fergus from asking the next flurry of questions. "Are Quill and Viper there?" As if on cue, they stepped into frame, still wearing their bone and leather armor. "How did it go?"

"It went as commanded, . . . sir," Quill said, her tone as rough as Ash's, if not slightly less demonic. "We cleared the Rift . . . without Fergus dying. Brick is also fine . . . mostly."

"Sir?" Lance asked, an eyebrow raised in the process.

"Yeah, sorry about that," Fergus said with a nervous laugh as he elbowed his way back in front of the camera. "In the Rift, I tried to help them with their speech and mannerisms. I figured they needed a proper way to address you, since you are the leader of this group."

"Lance will do fine. I don't need a fancy title," he said.

"Quill, Viper, are you well enough to clear the Rift on your end one last time?" Lance asked. They both nodded. "Fergus, hand them the Guardian-shard and let them clear the Rift over there. You and Brick will stay put and wait for me, all right?"

Lance's resolve was clear in his eyes, and Fergus knew better than to argue with him. "Alright, we'll handle it," Fergus said with a shrug. "Brick and I will just kick back in the barracks for a bit longer. We've already turned enough heads here by clearing the Rift twice in a row. What's one more go, right?"

Lance acknowledged Fergus with a nod before he disconnected the call. *Fergus did great. He's earned the spare Skill-shard.* Lance slid the phone into his pocket and shifted his attention to Ash. "I'm going to hit the showers and change into something less Rift-y. After that, we'll find the nearest store and grab some food for me and Fergus. Want some?" Lance grinned when Ash shook his head, remembering the countless times he'd tried to expand his pale friend's culinary horizons.

"Why just two companions? Fergus and Brick could help?" Ash mused, eyeing Lance as if confused.

"Faster, perhaps," Lance admitted. "But I still don't know the limits of my Class. I know you guys can freely enter and exit a Rift with me, or with another Rifter like Fergus. But I need to know if you guys can fully clear a Rift without anyone else entering it." Gesturing toward the site entrance, he instructed Ash to head over and show the soldiers that they were safe.

Lance picked up and donned his helmet as he mulled over the potential risks of his plan. *The worst-case scenario is losing Quill and Viper,* he thought, shuddering at the thought. *It would set me back, but I can recover. And if it works, the rewards would be worth it. More shards, more Experience. It's a risk I have to take.*

He finished with the straps of his helmet as he took a few steps to the side of the Rift itself, seeing Ash calmly walking toward the soldiers there. "It's not like I haven't taken risks before. Besides, I'm feeling optimistic," he thought aloud as he shifted his attention toward Finn, intent on storing him and the Skill-shard for now.

As if Finn could understand what Lance wanted to do, the young man's eyes widened and he shoved the Skill-shard into the back of his mouth, swallowing it, before Lance had the chance to reach him or command him to stop. The Skill-shard now rested inside of Finn.

"What the hell did you do?" Lance angrily barked. Lance's hand gripped Finn by the overalls and he had to struggle to not give in to the urge to lift him up in the air out of frustration. "Do you have any—" Lance suddenly stopped and his eyes widened when he became aware of the notification screen.

[Do you wish to re-forge this Item?]

CHAPTER TWENTY-FOUR

Pinning a Favor

Near Ålesund, Norway

LANCE

A few hours later, Lance and Fergus reclined in the front seats of the small car, which was parked just outside of the Rift that Viper and Quill were in. Both men had their feet up on the dashboard. They had changed out of their Rifter gear and donned civilian clothes after taking well-deserved showers. Lance wore a hoodie that kept him warm and hid most of his features. A pizza box and other snacks sat between them, and Fergus dipped each slice into a container of garlic sauce before taking a bite. Lance took a bite of his own, enjoying the gooey cheese and crispy crust.

Lance gazed ahead past his feet and saw Ash and Brick standing outside. Ash was holding Dieter's mace like a baseball bat, while Brick was stooping to pick up another rock. Fergus leaned in with a pizza-crusted smile and placed his last two fries into the empty cup in front of him before speaking. "I'll bet you my last two fries for your last donut that Ash will miss at least once in the next minute," he stated, gesturing toward the men outside.

Brick hurled rock after rock at Ash as fast as he could, but Ash was up for the challenge, slamming the bits of rock away with the mace. Some rocks flew upward at an incredible speed, while others simply shattered upon contact. "Easiest fries I've ever won. It'll take more to beat my boy," Lance said proudly before snatching the first fry, savoring his victory treat.

"Alright, how about your boy has to hit left-handed?"

Lance smiled and grabbed another slice of pizza before turning to Fergus. "And what might be the prize of this gentlemen's wager?" he asked, playfully adopting a posh accent.

"I'll wager your last fry and a favor for my soda," Fergus declared, holding up the Norwegian soda can with a mischievous twinkle in his eye. "But bear in mind, we don't know what's in it. It could be good, it could be bad," he added, wiggling the can as if to increase its value. "Mystery soda sounds tempting, doesn't it?"

Lance raised an eyebrow as he scanned the can. "It's cherry-flavored. And what favor?"

Fergus squinted at the soda can, his eyes scanning the strange, foreign letters as if it could help him magically decipher their meaning. "No pictures of cherries," he murmured disappointedly, turning the can around in his hands. "Since when can you speak and read Norwegian? And don't worry about the favor."

"That's Bokmål," Lance corrected him, "and no, I don't speak it." He could feel the presence of Finn and Peter in his mind, lending their knowledge to his own, allowing him to decipher the words. He still felt uneasy relying on their foreign memories, but he couldn't deny their usefulness. "But you have got yourself a deal."

As Lance looked on, Fergus nodded in agreement and deftly rolled down the car window. "Left-handed swing," Fergus directed Ash, his voice ringing out with an authority that didn't really suit him. With Fergus's order fresh in his mind, Ash shifted the mace to his left hand and prepared to swing.

Despite his best efforts, Ash missed all three of the rocks Brick threw. Fergus's grin widened with each failed attempt. In the end, he snatched the donut and fry away from Lance as if his life depended on it.

"Soda was never my thing anyway," Lance lied nonchalantly before he grabbed an empty cup and turned around in his seat, spotting the pale Finn in the back seat staring back at him. "Time to earn your worth," Lance instructed as he handed Finn the cup.

Finn's eyes narrowed in concentration as he held his other hand over the empty cup. For a moment, nothing happened, but then a soft blue light began to emanate from his palm. Soon, water droplets formed in the air underneath his hand. They fell like raindrops into the cup, slowly pooling at the bottom. "Come on, Finn, we don't have all day," Lance said sternly. "You wanted that Skill-shard, so let's see what you've got."

Lance struggled with his mixed emotions. He knew Finn's actions regarding the Skill-shard needed to be addressed, but he also couldn't help but feel a sense of excitement because Finn's actions had resulted in him learning more about upgrading his companions. Mentally he opened his status screen to check out his companion's upgrades.

Finn	1x	Human	Skill-shard: Moisture Extraction
			+1 Skill
			+15% Mana regeneration
			+1000 Mana
			+200 Durability

The increase in Mana regeneration and storage will be useful in a Rift, Lance thought as he placed his finger on Finn's hand, seconds later pouring some of his own Mana into the pale youth. *A walking efficient Mana battery that can also pull moisture out of the air or other things. I'll never need to worry about water again.*

Fergus glanced at Lance with a furrowed brow. "Don't you think you're being a bit harsh on him?" he asked, gesturing to Finn as he filled Lance's cup halfway.

"Probably," Lance said as he grabbed it and drank all the water before wiping his mouth on his sleeve. "He's a handful, as you've seen yourself. I mean, lightning is more predictable. I don't know if it has to do with his intellect or his youth, but he's harder to guide. He's . . ."

"Different?" Fergus asked, to which Lance nodded in agreement. "But that doesn't have to be a bad thing, right? Maybe his independence is a strength. He's the only one who can use a Skill, and he's also learned to use it in a matter of hours. I'd say that's pretty special, like a fledgling Mage or something."

Lance's lips quirked up in amusement as he glanced over at Fergus. "Mage, eh?" he said, his tone lightly teasing. "I've seen better water tricks from a toddler with a cup and a puddle. But you are right about him being the only one on my team able to use a Skill." Lance then handed Finn the empty cup and seized his wrist as he opened his status screen.

[You have named this item "Magnus"]

"There. Your new name is Magnus. Do you understand?" Lance inquired. The young, pale man stared back at him before giving a single nod of comprehension.

"Magnus?" Fergus arched an eyebrow at Lance. "That seems a bit grandiose, don't you think?"

"Hey, you said he was a Mage," Lance said with an amused grin. Then, without warning, a hard object struck the hood of the car with a resounding thud. Lance and Fergus whipped around in their seats to find a dent where it had impacted. Ash stood a few paces to the side, carefully sliding his mace behind his back, hiding it.

Fergus leaned out of the window, his face twisted in shock and worry as he glared down at Ash and Brick. "What the hell, lads?" he shouted. "This isn't going to buff out!" Ash's shoulders lifted in a dismissive shrug. Then he pointed at Brick, who was sheepishly holding a rock in his hand. "Didn't you teach them to be careful around vintage—" Fergus halted in mid-sentence, his eyes drawn to the intensity of Lance's focused expression. "What's wrong?"

[You have been awarded with a Level Up]
[You are now Level 70]

"I think Viper and Quill are nearly done," Lance said as he shifted his gaze toward the Rift in the distance. "I'm guessing they just killed the Rift-guardian, since I just Leveled Up."

Lance's prediction proved true as the Rift exploded with an ear-splitting roar that sent a shockwave of dirt, dust, and rubble in every direction.

Lance's mind raced with the urgency of their situation as he and Fergus burst out of the car and hurtled toward the gate, with Ash, Brick, and Magnus close behind. "Come on, come on," he pleaded out loud, hoping that Viper and Quill had made it out. They reached the site of the Rift, unbothered by the guards' half-hearted attempts to secure the site. Lance observed the soldiers' expressions for a moment, noting the confusion etched on their faces. "We've been drawing too much attention," Lance muttered under his breath. "We need to go somewhere else and switch up our IDs again."

The cloud of dust hung thick in the air, obscuring Lance's sight. He felt his throat dry up as he waited, his eyes scanning the haze for any sign of movement. Slowly, two shapes formed, striding out of the swirling chaos with a clear purpose. Their bone and leather armor, drenched in blood and grime, was mostly still intact. Lance could feel his body relaxing at the sight, although his mind raced with what this meant. He hadn't gotten a Level Up after Quill and Viper cleared the Rift, only gaining Experience from killing.

The bloody pair walked straight past the others and came to a stop in front of Lance, each sinking to one knee as a sign of respect. "Sir, we have finished our task," they said as one, their voices unnatural, but focused. Without a word, Quill offered Lance a Guardian-shard, while Viper presented him with a sack filled with black-shards. Both companions then looked upward, meeting Lance's gaze. "What is your next command, sir?"

Then Brick and Magnus also slowly sank down on one knee, facing him. Lance studied them all, wondering what could have caused them to show such deference. Before Ash could follow suit, Lance's hand shot out and grabbed him by the shoulder, stopping him in his tracks. "Don't. Please, don't." he pleaded, his voice a fragmented whisper. With a gentle pull, he brought Ash back up to his feet. "Not you, Ash. You'll never kneel."

Ash's eyes locked with Lance's, a flicker of recognition passing between them. Without a word, Ash straightened his back and took up a position next to him. "What do you need us to do, sir?" he asked, his voice deep and resolute.

Without warning, Fergus darted in between Lance and Ash, his arms wrapping around their necks in a bone-crushing embrace. "What do you think? Lance, I'm calling in that favor because we're hitting the lanes tonight," he bellowed, a mischievous twinkle in his eye.

"We're going bowling, lads!"

A few hours later, Lance was looking down at his feet, his eyes settling on the hideous bowling shoes he was wearing. The color was a putrid shade of green, almost like vomit. He shifted his weight, feeling the hard plastic against the soles of his feet. It was uncomfortable, to say the least. He couldn't help but think how ridiculous he looked.

He sank back into his seat, feeling a reassuring shoulder pat from Reidar while his sister got up to pick up a bowling ball. "I'm sure next time will be better," the young Norwegian man comforted before shifting his attention back to his sister, Eirin, who was lining up at the bowling lane. The woman near Ash was competing for first place while Reidar and Fergus were fighting for third.

Lance's hand closed around his glass, bringing it to his mouth as his gaze wandered around the place. While doing so, he did his best to ignore the throbbing sensation in his chest. Fergus and Reidar were causing a ruckus, shouting profanities at Eirin in an effort to distract her. Meanwhile, Ash held onto his own bowling ball fiercely, as if it were the most valuable thing in the world to him.

Brick, Quill, Viper, and Magnus occupied the seats in front of him, their eyes trained on different targets around them. Each one of them held a glass of water, attempting to blend in with the crowd. Their efforts fell short, however, due to their peculiar pale looks—not to mention the hoodies and sunglasses which only drew people's attention.

At first, the addition of Magnus and Brick to the group had piqued Reidar and Eirin's curiosity, but before long, they fit in seamlessly with the rest of the team. It was no surprise, given that the Norwegian siblings had already grown accustomed to Lance's other pale, enigmatic companions.

"Strike!"

"You are way too lucky for your own good, sis," Reidar said with a wide grin. "Come on, Ash, you can beat her!"

Ash merely nodded before getting up, cradling his lucky bowling ball before getting in position. *He's so similar to Thomas, even beyond mere appearances,* Lance thought as his pale friend released the ball, which slammed into the pins seconds later. *Combining Thomas's natural gift for sports with Ash's recent polar bear muscle upgrade is practically cheating by this point.*

One by one, the rest of Lance's group took their turns in the lane, and each one seemed to throw the ball with more skill and finesse than Lance. The sound of strikes and spares echoed through the alley, and Lance could only watch as everyone racked up points while his were still in the single digits. Even Brick and Magnus were at least able to hit a few pins with each throw, despite the two of them barely being able to walk several days ago. Magnus seemed to be studying the lane, adjusting his approach with each throw and fine-tuning his technique to improve his score.

Lance knew they were just teasing him, but it still frustrated him how his boons as a Rifter hadn't made him any better at this. *I might as well throw blindfolded. I bet even Medusa could beat me at this.* He tried to keep a positive attitude and even pictured a polar bear hitting a strike, but his first throw only knocked down a single pin. On his second attempt, he accidentally rolled his ball onto a neighboring lane, much to the amusement of the others.

"Well, I'm just a natural," he said, rolling his eyes before giving Ash—who was already cradling his "lucky" ball again—a pat on the shoulder. "I'm going to the toilet." He walked away from the group, making a beeline for it. On his way, he caught sight of Fergus and Eirin in the midst of a heated argument over which snacks to get.

Lance was eager to escape the noise of the bowling alley. He turned on the faucet, intending to wash his hands, when another jolt of pain shot through his chest. He tried to ignore it but ended up clutching his chest as a burning sensation spread through his lungs. Lance coughed, the sound harsh and ragged. Blood splattered into the sink; his weakened state starkly reflected in the deep red color. He knew suppressing it would only make it worse, so he let go, coughing even more violently until it subsided.

Lance washed his hands and mouth, the water running red with blood. He looked up at his reflection in the mirror, his face pale and drained. He wiped away a droplet of blood from his chin, feeling the weight of his condition bearing down on him. Lance knew that every new companion he forged made his condition worse, but he couldn't stop himself. He had sworn an oath. He had to keep going, no matter the cost.

More Endurance points seem to help lessen the effect a bit. And I think a higher Wisdom count makes the nightmares and memories less frequent and chaotic. He took a swig of water and swished it around his mouth before spitting it out. Then he opened his status screen again. *I still need to spend the three points I got from Quill and Viper.*

[Endurance:] [131] (+2)
[Wisdom:] [101] (+1)

"Level Seventy," Lance said to himself, feeling the weight of the number. His rise in Levels had been swift, a product of his unique Class and willingness to take risks. As he contemplated the possible gap that still separated him from Louis's Level, he considered the benefits that his companions could bring to the table in bridging the Level gap.

His voice was low and steady as he straightened up and looked at his own reflection. "We can do this," he said, while a flash of blue healing light surrounded him, his Skill negating some of the lingering damage inside of him and restoring some of his color. "Medusa . . . Icarus . . . the crows . . . Magnus . . . Brick . . . Quill . . . Viper . . . Oath Keeper . . ." he whispered. Each name was punctuated by another flash of blue light as he sought strength in them.

"Ash," he whispered the last name. Memories and emotions that didn't belong to him swirled up to the surface as he did so. He allowed the intrusion, for a moment feeling as if Thomas stood next to him, urging him to make the right choice. "Paris," Lance said, his voice quiet but firm. "I'm heading to Paris."

The sight of his group gathered around the table, snacking and chatting, brought a small smile to Lance's face as he left the bathroom. Across the room, Eirin jumped up to grab another ball, her unnaturally lucky movements drawing Magnus's attention. He was studying her like a hawk. Fergus lingered to the side, conversing on his phone while Viper stabbed a little wooden toothpick through an olive.

In contrast, amidst the carefree ambiance, Ash held a steady gaze on Lance, as if sensing a change in him that the others had missed. Lance merely nodded, trusting that his friend would understand.

Fergus remained on his phone for a few more minutes before rejoining the group and taking a seat opposite Lance. "Brian just called," he shared, a hint of eagerness in his voice. "He's got some fresh IDs lined up for us and he's currently working on new credentials for our guild. He wants our input on the name."

Lance snatched an olive and twirled it between his fingers, his mind a whirl of suspicion. *That fixer's just trying to look cooperative,* he thought wryly. "Why don't you pick?"

"I'm sorry?" Fergus furrowed his brow, his confusion evident.

Lance scratched his head sheepishly. "I'm not the greatest with names," he admitted before eating his olive and accessing his Inventory. A moment later, he retrieved Dieter's mace from his Inventory, the weapon materializing in his hand, much to the surprise of the Norwegian siblings. "You've earned the right to pick the next guild name, as well as have this. I did owe you a favor, right?"

Fergus gingerly took the mace, as if afraid it might break in his hands. He marveled at its weight and craftsmanship, his eyes growing wide with wonder. He attempted to say something, to offer the mace back to Lance, but didn't know what to say each time he looked into his determined eyes.

A few seconds later, Fergus suddenly sprang from his seat, his eyes shining with excitement. He dashed toward the bar like a man possessed. Shortly after that, he returned to the group carrying a tray of frosty beers with a waitress right on his heels, carrying a Polaroid camera.

"Fergus—"

"Relax, it's not digital," he interrupted Lance, handing him a cold beer before distributing the rest of them around. "Four Rifts cleared in a matter of days—a feat that only larger guilds have been able to pull off before now. And we did it without any casualties! And I've gotten the best gift I can imagine, and I don't mean the weapon you just gave me."

Fergus smiled at the others as he stood up straight, his beer glass slowly raised upward. "I've helped clear a Rift, permanently. I'd say that deserves a toast!"

Reidar rose from his seat, clinking his glass against Fergus's. "To the bravest Rifters I know," he said with a twinkle in his eyes.

"And the only ones we know," Eirin stated, elbowing her brother in the ribs before joining her glass with the others.

Lance and his companions rose from the table one by one, each adding their glass to the growing collection. With a reassuring nod to Fergus, Lance spoke up. "Alright Fergus, go ahead. To what name are we toasting?"

Fergus gave a quick nod to the waitress before slinging his arm around Lance and Ash, tugging them close so that they stood side-by-side. "Just two," he called out, grinning as the waitress readied her camera and started counting down for them.

"The Sentinels."

CHAPTER TWENTY-FIVE

Putrid Plunge

Three weeks later
August, 14 AR
Paris, France

LANCE

Lance's fingers fumbled with the oxygen mask, tugging at the straps until it fit snugly against his face again. Blood spatters coated the visor, obscuring his vision until he wiped them away with his sleeve. The dim light revealed the filth and grime of the sewer, and the stench of decay lingered in the air due to all the broken pipes and pooled-up filth. The water sloshed around his boots. "Let's keep going. Ash, go scout ahead," Lance said, the words garbled by the apparatus on his face. He paused, waiting for Ash's nod.

Ash stepped forward, his movements slow and cautious as he made his way deeper into the smoke-filled sewers. The fact that his bone and leather armor had been dyed black made him even harder to spot. Over the last three weeks, Fergus had steadily been making armor improvements. The current design was a work of art that covered nearly every inch of a person's body in overlapping bone plates. Although not as durable as proper steel, Lance had upgraded each piece with additional bone upgrades, improving their overall effectiveness.

While Ash led the way, Lance could hear Brick and Viper next to him, slowly stepping forward, shields out in front, along with their short swords. Although both men were skilled fighters up close, inside the sewers, with little to no light, Ash and his unnatural blue eyes were king.

Every one of Lance's companions, along with himself, were now equipped with the bone and leather armor, making them all look uniform and difficult to distinguish. Still, he recognized them by their height and build alone. As he looked back, he caught sight of the polar bear, her massive form guarding their rear.

With his spear in hand, Lance joined his shield brothers as they slowly advanced, relying on the faint light provided by his torch. As they made their way forward, the group stepped over the butchered remains of large insectoid monsters, their lifeless eyes staring up at them from their grotesque, mangled bodies. *We're getting closer,* Lance thought as he stepped over another corpse, noticing the missing black-shard in its chest. *Ash is overdoing it again.* Ash and his steel axe had hacked apart most of the monsters, or simply tore off limbs by brute force alone.

As they crept forward through the murky sewer, occasional heaps of rubble or filth impeded their progress. *Don't think too much about what's sticking to your skin,* Lance thought as he waded onward. He and his companions were on tunnel duty. It was a job mostly done by Rifters, to clear out underground monster hotspots or even hives that littered the sewers of Paris. Most soldiers struggled in the tight corridors with monsters that either shrugged off most projectiles or were either feral or zealous enough to simply not care about any damage or casualties.

Tunnel duty had been one of the many jobs Lance and the Sentinels had taken over the last few weeks. Each new job he took brought him closer to tracking down Louis, while also farming more and more Experience. Three weeks of constant fighting, keeping up appearances, and gathering intel.

A sudden hiss shattered the silence as a swarm of insectoids charged at them in a frenzied fury. Brick and Viper raised their shields to deflect the assault, the sound of metal clashing against chitin ringing out in the darkness. Their swords flashed and darted with practiced speed, stabbing and slicing into the monsters again and again.

Lance's spear moved with lethal precision, impaling the insects one after another with swift jabs to their torsos and heads as he stood behind his companions. Behind him, Medusa roared in rage as she clashed with another group of insect monsters, signaling that the monsters had tried to flank them. Lance gritted his teeth, cursing the monster's intelligence as he pulled his spear back and thrust it into another torso.

"Lightning," Lance bellowed as he placed his hands on Brick and Viper while stretching one of his legs backwards, pressing it against Medusa's rear.

Imbue Lightning

Lightning crackled around his three companions, illuminating the dark sewer and casting sharp shadows around them. Lance felt the strain on his Mana, the powerful surge of energy being expended through his body. Trails of sparks leapt across the bodies of his companions, and with a sudden burst of ferocity, all three charged into the enemy ranks, unleashing a brutal assault of fur, steel, and lightning.

Lance followed Brick and Viper as they pushed forward, slaughtering the monsters until those that remained turned around and scampered away. "Form up," Lance instructed as he watched all three companions return to formation before they moved onward like a team again. They continued through the tunnel, picking their way over the fresh corpses and searching for black-shards. When they reached the branching paths, Lance hesitated, sensing something was watching him. And then he saw them: a pair of bright blue eyes, staring back at him from the darkness.

Lance's eyes widened as Ash came into view, his armor battered and torn. "What the hell, man?" Lance exclaimed, taking in the extent of the damage. "What the hell happened to you? I said scout, not try to get yourself killed." Even Ash's helmet was missing large chunks.

Pointing toward the tunnel behind him, Ash gave a nonchalant shrug. "Ran into a big one down there . . . A queen, I think," he said. "Eggs as well."

Lance just exhaled deeply as he pointed at the tunnel. "Viper, Brick, take the lead. Medusa, rear guard," he instructed while grabbing Ash by the shoulder and following the others. As they walked, Lance started repairing Ash and his equipment. He also started crafting a few more bone javelins and throwing daggers, seeing as he was running low. Then, just as he climbed over a bit of debris, he spotted a notification.

[Death Forge has reached Level 3]

Perfect timing, Lance thought as he jumped down from the debris and landed in a puddle of filth hard enough for some of the water to splash upward and hit him right underneath his helmet. *Gross.* To distract himself from the smell, he quickly opened his status screen and started to check the improvements of his Skill.

[Death Forge: Level 3]
[Additional −50% Stamina and Mana regeneration per forge]
[Forging items: +1 item in total]
[Re-forging slots available] [+1 slots]

He quickly put it to the test and ordered another throwing weapon to be forged and indeed, saw that three Items were being crafted at the same time, although his Stamina and Mana recovery had crawled to a halt. *This will do just fine. I'll be able to resupply my companions far more quickly at this rate. But the extra re-forging slot is even better.* Lance then went over Ash's three slots that he had already filled. *Just how much more powerful could Ash get now?*

He quickly began to do the math and felt his enthusiasm snuffed out when he realized that a fourth upgrade would mean at least ten thousand black-shards, or ten Guardian-shards. *That's way too much. Even now, after all this time of constant Rift clearing and fighting in France, I only have eight of them. And I was saving them up to upgrade Medusa and the crows.* Lance finished crafting a few more weapons and ordered up three more. *I'll deal with that later. For now, let's clear this nest.*

The sewer tunnel terminated in a narrow, winding path, its walls marred by the marks of the insectoids who had carved it out with their sharp, deadly claws. Step by cautious step, Lance and his companions descended further into the bowels of the earth, finally breaching a large, cavernous chamber. The walls were a mixture of dirt and organic tissue that contained weird eggs that seemed to pulsate with a sickly glow.

The chamber's centerpiece was a colossal insectoid queen, her massive chitinous frame glittering in the light. Several hulking bodyguards lurked at her side, their claws and jaws poised to strike. As Lance scanned the room, his eyes fell on the gruesome remains of unlucky soldiers, their flesh and bones partially consumed. Among them, he found a semi-dissolved Rifter, the breastplate and chain mail their only remnants.

Lance and his team readied themselves for battle, their eyes fixed on the swarm of massive insects before them. "Viper, Brick, flank them. Ash, stay close," Lance commanded as he noticed the queen and her guards pause, likely sensing the threat to their eggs. Before he could even register it himself, he plunged his spear into the eggs, triggering an angry hiss from the queen. *Don't think.* The phrase echoed in his mind as he reacted instinctively, calling forth a surge of lightning and letting it flow across the tip of his spear, destroying the eggs in an instant. The furious queen charged, with her guards right behind her. "Medusa, take care of mum."

With a fierce roar, Medusa charged forward, Lance right on her heels. The gray bundle of angry fur barreled toward the insectoid queen, who raised her spindly arms to strike. The queen and Medusa clashed, claws digging into one another as they struggled for dominance. The polar bear pushed forward with all her might, her heavy frame outweighing the queen despite the monster's larger size. With a huge shove, Medusa forced the queen backwards, chitinous limbs scraping against the rocky ground before two of her guards charged into Medusa.

Just do, Thomas called out in Lance's mind while steering his actions as he hurled his spear toward the nearest wall while activating his Ricochet Skill. As the weapon rebounded faster, he sprinted toward the nearest insectoid guard and grabbed it by its neck, angling it toward his oncoming spear, while slamming the weapon through the monster's head with brutal force until it stuck out halfway.

Lance retrieved his spear with a quick flick of his wrist, booting the lifeless body out of his path. As he pivoted to confront the next danger, the queen slammed one of its large limbs into him, propelling him into the fray between Brick and another monster. After a dizzying few seconds, Lance scrambled back to his feet while Brick continued to cover him with his steel shield, wielding his sword to fend off the next wave of attacks.

It didn't take Lance and Brick long to kill the monster, the former keeping it pinned down while the latter went in for the finishing strike with his sword. As they turned to face their next foe, they saw that Viper and Ash had already taken care of business and were now standing amidst a heap of torn and hacked-apart corpses. In the background, Medusa remained focused on clawing her way further inside the queen's skull and finally killing her.

[You have been awarded with a Level Up]
[You are now Level 79]

Making their way toward the others, Lance audibly groaned as his hand traced the fractured breastplate, revealing the numerous cracks in the bone. "I'm going to feel that in the morning," Lance said before he encased his body in a bright blue light for a few seconds in an attempt to heal some of the damage that he had sustained. Even blinded, Lance was able to access his status screen and go over the Level Up notification.

"You were slow," Ash remarked dryly as he walked over to the queen's torso and began tugging on a Guardian-shard embedded there. "Another red one."

"Alright, first off . . . I was busy fighting," Lance retorted as the blue light faded. Ash nonchalantly tossed the Guardian-shard to him and he caught it in an easy motion. "And secondly, I didn't see you offering any assistance back then."

With a dismissive shrug of his shoulders, Ash turned away from Lance, his bright blue eyes scanning the carnage for valuable black-shards. "I was busy as well," he said emotionlessly as he plucked them out one by one.

Lance snorted, a mixture of irritation and amusement coursing through him at Ash's remark. He shot him a sideways glance before turning his attention to the grim task at hand: searching the human corpses for any form of identification.

His hand moved carefully over what remained of them as he looked for anything that could identify the fallen, anything that might bring them a step closer to closure. After he had finished with the human corpses, he made his way over to the Rifter's body. With a solemn reverence, he placed his hand upon the lifeless form, a gesture of respect for a fallen enemy. *Female,* Lance thought before shifting his attention to her gear, clocking its sturdy nature. *Perhaps a warrior?*

[You have stored an Item in your Inventory]

Another white-shard pressed down on Lance's soul, offering him a choice he was reluctant to make. Paris had yielded two of these so far, each one presenting him with the opportunity to gain another companion. He wasn't ready to make that decision yet. Instead, he turned his attention to the task at hand, directing the others to destroy the eggs as he carefully gathered up the monster corpses to store in his Inventory.

"Ash, burn this place down."

The journey out of the tunnels was a dirty one, Lance and his party moving at a snail's pace to avoid falling in filth or running into a monster that they had missed. Lance had one hand placed on Ash's shoulder as he repaired his friend and his gear. Just when Lance began to wonder if they had taken the wrong route, he spotted the familiar sewer entrance they had used before. The sight of light ahead was like a beacon, a promise of freedom and fresh air after what felt like an eternity in the dark.

"Friendlies," Lance called out in French as he gestured to his companions to move ahead while he retrieved Medusa. "Coming up!" he yelled once more after he had pulled off his oxygen mask, hoping the soldiers above them weren't on edge and could hear him. With the massive polar bear safely stored away in his Inventory, he climbed up the steel bars leading him to the surface. Not long after, he could feel several hands reaching for him and carefully hoisting him up to safety.

As Lance adjusted to the bright sunlight, he noticed three soldiers backing away from him as his sewer perfume wafted toward them. "You reek," their squad leader commented bluntly. "Are you doing okay?"

"I will be after a shower," Lance replied as the two of them stepped toward Ash, Brick, and Viper. "We cleared the nest and the guardian. There might be a few weaker stragglers left, but for now, it should be fine."

The squad leader nodded toward two soldiers who were rigging explosives near the entrance in case the remaining monsters resurfaced in that spot. "I'll inform the higher-ups," he said to Lance. "Do you want to head back to base or are you ready to move on?"

Lance retrieved a flask of water from his Inventory as a surge of Thomas's emotions and bravado coursed through him. "That depends, do you lads have enough bullets to keep up with us?" he asked the squad leader, a smirk playing at the corners of his mouth.

The man grinned, respect shining in his eyes. "You Rifters are something else," he chuckled before turning away to confer with his soldiers. "Private Lucroy, let HQ know we're heading to the next point. Jacquinot, your vehicle takes point."

As the soldiers organized, Lance simply brushed off most of the filth from his equipment before clambering into the back of the truck, followed by Ash and the rest of his team. "You all did well," Lance said as he retrieved some food from his Inventory and quickly took a few bites, knowing he needed to restore his energy. "We'll do another run, then meet back up with Fergus and the others."

"Nest clearing?" Ash asked quietly, making sure only Lance could hear him.

"Probably. The military has driven out most of the monsters here and created another potential secure zone, but there's still work to be done," Lance said, food in hand. He felt the truck lurch forward as the engine started, followed by the sounds of three other vehicles. "We'll have to clear out the remaining pockets of activity before this ring is secure."

The convoy of military vehicles drove through the ruins of Paris, the city a haunting reflection of its former glory. Rubble and debris, bombed-out buildings, and burned-out tanks and vehicles painted the streets. The smell of death and destruction hung heavy in the air, as the remnants of monster corpses lay scattered about. Lance could see smoke plumes rising in the distance, a constant reminder of the danger that still lurked around every corner.

To his left stood the first wall, an enormous, fortified structure that encircled the entire city, erected shortly after the first outbreak. To his right, temporary structures marked the second and third walls, hastily constructed in areas where the military had managed to push the monsters back. Lance shook his head. *I can't even begin to fathom how much blood has been spilled to move that wall closer to the Rift. Thousands? Tens of thousands?*

As Lance took a bite, his eyes flicked toward Viper, who had moved to the front of the vehicle. With his bow and arrows in hand, Viper climbed onto the hood and kept a watchful eye on their surroundings. Despite soldiers manning the turrets in the other vehicles in their convoy, Viper remained alert, knowing that danger could strike at any moment.

He spotted another few notifications appearing, stating that he had received more Experience. *Glad to see the others are keeping themselves busy,* Lance thought as he opened his status screen and glanced over his Attributes, wondering where he'd spent his three points. *Paris has been a nonstop battlefield for me. Three weeks in and I've already gained nine Levels.*

[Endurance:] [151] (+1)
[Strength:] [144] (+1)
[Agility:] [151] (+1)

Lance distributed his points evenly and leaned back against the metal railing, gazing up at the sky. His thoughts drifted to Louis, and he wondered how much more powerful the man had become since they last met. *Could I even defeat him and bring him to justice?*

As Lance's gaze wandered, he noticed Ash sitting across from him. Despite the bone helmet, Lance could see his bright blue eyes peering through the slits. Without a word, Lance held out his fist in front of him, and he responded with a fist bump. They both understood each other without saying a word.

I'm almost there, Thomas.

Headfirst

Two hours later
Paris, France

LANCE

Lance stood near a doorway in the ruined apartment complex, his hand tightly gripping the hilt of his knife, already wet from a mixture of Goblin blood and Viper's poison. He could hear gunfire in the background and the occasional rocket hitting another building somewhere else in Paris.

On the opposite side of the doorway, Ash stood with a similar expression of intensity etched across his face. They nodded to each other in silent readiness. Instead of being clad in bone armor, both were wearing just their leather gear, decreasing the amount of noise they would make. They had been clearing the old building they were in bit by bit, while Viper had taken a different route.

As they waited, Lance's mind raced with thoughts of the task ahead. The apartment building was one of the many locations suspected of still being infested with monsters. Lance felt comfortable in taking it on by force, sending all his companions in fully equipped and ready. But clearing it out by stealth was something his companions needed to work on. Even after all his Leveling and clearing of Rifts, Lance's current Level was pathetic compared to those of some monsters closer to the Rift-event itself.

Suddenly, the sound of shuffling footsteps echoed through the room next to them and Lance tensed. He readied his knife as two Goblins entered the room, each clad in crude iron armor and wielding sharp spears. They were like the Goblins he and Thomas had faced before, although these had scorch marks covering their skin and armor.

Without hesitation, Lance sprang into action. He darted toward the first Goblin, closing the distance between them in an instant. Before the creature could react, Lance placed a hand around its mouth and swiftly slit its throat with his knife. Afterward, he stabbed it repeatedly in the chest before lowering the lifeless corpse to the ground, careful not to make a sound.

Meanwhile, Ash was busy with the other Goblin, grabbing it in a chokehold with so much force that he snapped its neck with a sickening crack almost instantly. The Goblin's limp body fell to the ground with a thud. Lance just shook his head, mouthing the words "Really?" to his companion in disbelief.

They froze for a moment as the sharp sound of gunshots coming from outside increased, along with the commotion of battle below them. Lance knew that Brick and the soldiers were drawing attention away from them, providing a distraction that would allow them to move forward unnoticed.

Afterward, both men ripped out the black-shards from the monsters like pulling out teeth. Lance then stored them in his Inventory. Gripping his knife again, Lance then moved forward, peering into the next room. He could see three more Goblins lurking near the windows and looking outside. The room they were in was cluttered and the floor itself was a mess of holes and rotten wood. He held up three fingers to Ash, who nodded in understanding. Without a word, they rushed into the room, weapons at the ready.

Activating his Skill, Lance threw his knife at the nearby wall, causing it to ricochet toward the furthest Goblin at an increased speed. The blade hit the creature in the throat, forcing it to fall to its knees in agony as it scratched at its own throat. The other Goblins spun around, surprised by the sudden attack.

[Ricochet has reached Level 2]

Lance's focus was on the enemy to his left, a Goblin with a rusty sword and crude armor. He ignored the notification of his Skill increase, knowing that his priority was to take down the threat that was still in front of him.

Closing the distance as fast as he could, he slammed into the Goblin, his fist connecting with a sickening thud as he punched it in the throat with enough force to crack something. The Goblin tried to wheeze and cough, but it couldn't. While doing so, its grip on the rusty sword loosened momentarily. Lance seized the opportunity, pulling the monster's arm to the side before slamming his knee against the elbow with a sharp crack. The Goblin's eyes widened in pain and at the state of its injured arm.

Without skipping a beat, Lance grabbed the rusty sword and rammed it through the Goblin's chest with enough force to be embedded in the wall behind it. The creature convulsed briefly before it grew still, while pinned to the wall.

Lance was about to check on Ash's progress when he heard a terrible sound: the tearing of flesh and the snapping of bones.

Lance turned around just in time to see a Goblin's head rolling across the floor, blood spraying in its wake. Ash was standing nearby, dropping the dead, headless monster that he had been holding with a look of guilt. "It was an . . . accident," Ash said, while Lance watched in horror as the Goblin's head rolled further away from them toward a rotten section of the floor before falling into the gap there, leaving a trail of blood in its wake.

They listened as the Goblin's head crashed into something on the floor below them, causing a loud bang that echoed through the building. Several other sounds followed, as if dozens of pots and pans were clattering to the ground. Lance winced with each sound, his eyes darting to Ash, who looked even guiltier than before. Despite his usual emotionless posture, Ash's body language betrayed his sense of responsibility for what had just happened.

For a moment, the silence that followed was so deafening that Lance almost believed they had gotten away with it. "Perhaps they didn't notice?" Ash suggested. But before Lance could even shrug in response, they heard a terrifying roar coming from upstairs, shaking the very foundations of the building. Ash's eyes widened, and Lance shot him a withering look that seemed to say, *Why did you have to jinx it?*

"Alright, suit up," Lance ordered as he grabbed Ash's arm while accessing his Inventory. A moment later, both were decked out in bone armor and wielding shield and sword, with Ash having several javelins clipped to the inside of his shield. "Viper, back us up! Brick, keep the entrance blocked," Lance bellowed, no longer caring if monsters could hear them or not.

"Bear time?" Ash asked while taking up a defensive position and eying the doorway.

"No. The soldiers might see her, and I want to keep that a secret for now," Lance said, thinking of Louis for a moment. "We'll stop the monsters here. If not, we'll jump out through the window behind us and hopefully not break anything when we land." Lance then retrieved several bear traps and mines from his Inventory, while Ash began placing them.

Tense seconds passed as Lance and Ash prepared for the approaching onslaught. Above them, they could hear the unmistakable sound of numerous footsteps running across the floors, some going up, others going down. The hissing of monsters mixed with the clattering of weapons and the sounds of infighting. Lance kept his focus trained on the doorway, feeling surprisingly calm and composed. A drop of blood splattered onto his shield, coming from the ceiling above them.

As the sounds of fighting intensified above them, Lance retrieved several bear traps and mines from his Inventory and placed them strategically while Ash threw a smoke grenade through the doorway, filling the opposite room with a thick haze to disorientate the approaching horde. They then took up position next to one another, waiting for the inevitable while Lance took a quick glance at his upgraded Skill.

[Ricochet: Level 2]
[Stamina cost per Bounce] [+5]
[Additional Bounce] [+1]
[Additional Speed] [+5%]
[Additional Accuracy] [+5%]

It's a bit more draining, but the extra bounce and speed will no doubt be helpful, Lance thought as he transferred his sword to his shield hand while retrieving a bone-throwing dagger from his Inventory. He carefully aimed it near the edge of the entrance, intent on bouncing it onto the floor toward him. It surprised him how much clearer the trajectory line in his mind became compared to the previous Level.

With a flick of his wrist, he released the dagger. It bounced precisely along the intended path, hitting the doorway, then the ceiling, before slamming into the ground right in front of his feet. He wanted to smile, but stopped as he picked up on the sounds of monsters closing in. Seconds later, four Goblins rushed into the room, hissing and fuming, their partially burned skin and armor drenched in the blood of their brethren.

Lance quickly stepped back a few paces, activating his Skill and launching the dagger toward the first Goblin's stomach. The blade tore through flesh before bouncing off and hit another one in the chest, then bouncing again and hitting the last one in the eye. The first two Goblins fell to the ground immediately, while the last one sank to its knees, trembling, its one remaining eye staring in shock, as the dagger hilt stuck out of where its other one used to be, before finally dying.

Meanwhile, the fourth Goblin stood frozen in fear while Ash calmly retrieved a javelin from his shield. Without hesitation, he threw the javelin, impaling the creature against the wall. Its body hung limply as blood trickled down the brickwork. "You missed one," Ash said flatly before grabbing his sword again.

It didn't take long before the sound of a larger group of monsters echoed through the hallway as the horde arrived, composed of Goblins, Lizardlings, and other smaller monsters. They poured in like an angry tide. Lance and Ash stood their ground, their weapons at the ready.

The monsters rushed forward, some falling into the bear traps scattered across the floor, while others triggered mines that exploded in a hail of shrapnel that took out dozens of them at once. Still, the horde kept coming.

Lance swung his sword in a wide arc, cleaving through three of the monsters before using his shield to block an arrow that flew toward him. He barely had time to register the Goblin archer when he felt daggers and claws slamming into his back. The bone armor held up, but the force of the blows made him stumble forward.

It didn't take long before Ash appeared by his side, pulling a Lizardling away from his back and crushing its skull in one swift motion. With blood and gore still clinging to his hand, Ash hurled the remains into the horde, blinding some of the monsters before grabbing a javelin and killing one of the Goblin archers.

Lance took the opportunity to strike, thrusting his sword forward and piercing the chest of a blinded Goblin. As he pulled the sword free, he felt a sharp pain in his leg and saw a Lizardling biting into the back of his knee where the armor didn't offer as much protection. He shook it off, using his shield to bash its skull in before quickly dispatching a nearby wolf-like monster with a downward strike of his sword, cleaving through its neck.

A mere second later, two Lizardlings jumped onto his back, their claws scrabbling at his helmet and chest. With a quick, fierce movement, Lance thrust his blade over his shoulder, killing one of them as blood sprayed all over him. The other continued to scratch at his face plate, its nails scraping against the metal, creeping closer toward the gap for his eyes. Suddenly, the Goblin gurgled, a bone throwing dagger sticking out of its throat. It fell to the floor, thrashing and bleeding out before Lance crushed its face with his boot.

[You have been awarded with a Level Up]

Shifting his gaze to his side, he spotted his other companion moving toward him and Ash, covered in wounds and only wearing leather armor. Viper rushed in as fast as he could, wielding a short sword and daggers. The pale man sidestepped most of the monsters' attacks or shrugged them off, then countered with quick and efficient strikes, aimed at vital organs or places rich in veins and nerves. The monsters fell one by one, cut down by Viper's deadly precision or the generous coating of poison on his blades.

As Viper reached them, Lance quickly grabbed him by the shoulder while accessing his Inventory, before covering Viper's body in thick bone armor as well. The three of them then stood back-to-back, hacking and slashing at anything that came near, but the monsters kept swarming around them like a sea of rage and hatred. The sound of steel clashing against scales and bone echoed through the room as the horde relentlessly pushed forward until the entire building shook.

What's stopping them? Lance thought as he eyed the nearby window again, wondering if it was time to make their escape.

A deafening roar that crashed through the building ended the trio's momentary respite. Lance's eyes widened in horror as the ceiling above them began to crack and crumble. Before they could react, a portion of the ceiling gave way, collapsing in a shower of dust and debris as a massive creature burst through the rubble.

The beast was a terrifying sight to behold, with its towering size and hulking muscles. Its body was covered in tough scales that shimmered in the dim light, and its large leathery wings with spikes at the end beat powerfully, sending gusts of hot wind that threatened to knock the trio off their feet. Despite the room being spacious, its wings were large enough to reach the opposite sides of the room. As it landed on the ground with a thunderous impact, the creature opened its mouth, unleashing a torrent of scorching flames upward, setting the room above them on fire.

Lance could feel the heat of the flames on his face and knew it was time to go. *Perhaps with Medusa? No, that thing feels way too strong for me to kill on my own. Did the other Rifters miss such a high-Level monster when they cleared this sector, or had it been hiding here with the weaker monsters?* Lance thought as he watched the winged demon kill several other monsters that stood too close to it. "We need support from other Rifters. Let's retreat for now. Jump out of the window on three," Lance said as he placed his foot on several monster corpses, storing them in his Inventory. "One . . . two . . . three."

Lance's heart pounded in his chest as the three of them rushed forward, weapons at the ready. They hurled javelins and daggers at the massive, winged monster, hoping to distract it long enough for their escape. As they dashed past the creature, Lance conjured monster corpses from his Inventory that glowed for a moment as he activated his Detonate Skill.

Without looking back, the trio crashed through the nearby window, shattering the glass while leaping out into the open air. They fell toward the ground with explosions devastating the old building behind them in a shower of death and fury. Just as Lance was about to crash into a military vehicle parked below, he felt himself violently yanked backwards and thrown upward at great speed to the point of him blacking out.

A few seconds had passed before he regained consciousness, although he was still struggling with his sense of direction, not knowing which way was up or down. He soon realized that the winged monster had grabbed him and was now climbing upward, its powerful wings beating the air as it ascended higher and higher. Lance was being swung around violently as he caught glimpses of the military vehicles and his companions down below, slowly shrinking in size as they grew increasingly distant.

As the creature climbed further up in the air, Lance knew that he had to act fast. He drew his sword and began hacking at the beast's scaly hide, hoping to weaken it enough to break free. But it was like trying to cut through a wall of solid rock, and his efforts seemed to have little effect. Still, he tried again, slamming the blade into the monster as hard as he could.

Lance gritted his teeth in frustration as his sword shattered on impact with the creature's tough scales. He materialized another sword from his Inventory, but before he could strike again, the monster landed a heavy punch to his chest, cracking his bone armor in that area. Lance gasped in pain, struggling to breathe as he felt his ribs crack under the force of the blow, forcing him to drop his weapon.

The monster let out a triumphant roar while dropping Lance; he began to plummet through the air. Just then, Lance barely managed to catch the monster's leg in a desperate bid to save himself, hugging it tightly as he struggled to regain his bearings.

But the respite was short-lived as the monster kicked him in the face again and again, drawing blood and even destroying his helmet. Lance endured the blows, ignoring the pain while using all his strength to climb up the monster's leg and onto its back.

The monster continued to ascend, its massive wings beating the air with powerful strokes. Lance clung to the monster's back, desperately searching for a weak point as the beast's scorching breath singed the hairs on the back of his neck. Eventually he just resorted to grabbing the monster's wings as he activated his Imbue Lightning Skill on his gloves, sending arcs of deadly energy through the monster's wings and into its torso, eliciting a deafening roar of pain from the beast.

In retaliation, the monster grabbed Lance and pulled him off its back. He then held the Rifter in front of it and readied itself to breathe fire. Lance struggled against the creature's grip, trying to break free as he saw the flames building in its throat.

Desperate, Lance punched the monster in the throat before slamming his hand further into its mouth, as deep as he could. He could feel the hot flames licking at his arm and the monster's teeth biting down hard, but he didn't let go. Instead, he activated his Lightning Skill. Lance felt the monster convulse around his arm as he electrocuted it from within, its gurgles worsening as Lance continued to pour more Mana into his Skill, determined to finish the creature off.

Still, the monster endured it all as it started clawing at Lance's chest, breaking his bone armor further and occasionally digging past it to rip into flesh. Lance clenched his jaw and focused on his task, ignoring the pain as he continued to electrocute the monster.

Higher they climbed, reaching the clouds ahead as they disappeared from sight in a trail of lightning and desperate roars. He could feel the monster's strength fading, its movements becoming sluggish as it struggled to stay airborne. Lance then slammed his other hand into the creature's eye socket, feeling his fingers sink deep into its flesh. And then, with a burst of lightning, Lance depleted the last of his Mana, boiling the monster's head from within.

As Lance's assault ended, the monster began to slowly pull him off its body and out of its throat while its remaining eye stayed fixed on its prey with pure hatred. Lance's eyes widened in fear as he was now out of Mana and his Stamina was running dangerously low. He could feel the monster's grip on his arm, nearly breaking his bones, forcing him to realize that he was about to be killed.

Because of that, he felt something snap in his mind as a memory of Thomas suddenly came to life, recalling how his friend had roared in defiance against overwhelming odds. Lance's mind fused with that memory as he yelled out with all his might, breathing life into his friend's determination.

[You have combined and retrieved Items]

A large revolver materialized in his hand, wedged inside the monster's throat aimed downward. Lance's howl intensified as he squeezed the trigger. The resulting explosive shot tore apart most of the monster from the inside out in a gruesome display of flesh and blood. As the monster died, Lance tumbled back down to earth again.

[You have been awarded with a Level Up x2]

As Lance plummeted, his arm throbbed with pain and discomfort from the burns, the bite wounds, and the kickback of his revolver, Oath Keeper. He gritted his teeth and tried to focus, his eyes darting around to assess his situation. With parts of the monster still wrapped around his arm, he knew he had to act fast.

With a grimace, Lance stored the weapon and the monster remains in his Inventory, wincing at the pain in his arm. He glanced downward, seeing the ground rush toward him with alarming speed. Lance's mind raced as he remembered how he had arrived in Norway, illegally jumping out of the back of a plane with a parachute.

Accessing his Inventory once again, Lance materialized a parachute and strapped it to his back. He pulled the chute with a sharp and painful tug, and his heart leapt as the parachute unfolded above him, slowing his descent. He let out a sigh of relief as he felt the wind rushing past him, and his eyes flickered down to the ground below.

Despite the relief of the parachute, Lance's arm and ribs continued to ache, and he winced with every movement. He steered his chute as best as he could, aiming toward the street near his companions and the military vehicles while trying to land on his feet while running. However, his descent was too fast, and he slammed into one of the vehicles with a loud thud before falling backwards and landing on his back with a groan.

Lance lay there for a moment, breathing heavily as his body protested the pain. He could see his companions and soldiers rushing toward him, concern etched on the soldiers' faces.

"Are you alright?" Ash asked, his deep voice drowning out the other voices and clearly unbothered by the fact that the soldiers could hear his unnatural voice.

"That was incredible," a soldier said as he knelt next to Lance, helping him undo the parachute harness.

"You Rifters are nuts!"

Slowly, the squad captain came into view, leaning over him with a mixture of respect and amusement. "Sir, Rifter, my boys still have plenty of ammunition left. Do you want to move on or return to base?" he asked, his grin widening by the moment. Lance let out a painful chuckle before matching his grin.

"I think I'm ready to return to base now."

CHAPTER TWENTY-SEVEN

Permanent Marks

Four hours later
Military Hospital
Paris, France

LANCE

After a lengthy ride back to the main base, Lance was standing in a dimly lit examination room, his chest exposed. A hint of unease lingered in the air. The technician's thick French accent crackled through the intercom, breaking the silence. "Could you raise your arms a bit higher?"

Lance obliged, his movements slow and cautious, wincing as the sharp ache in his ribs protested the motion. He adjusted his stance, shifting slightly to find a more suitable position in front of the X-ray machine. It didn't take long for the machine to come alive, producing clicking and buzzing sounds.

The Frenchman's voice flared up now and again, guiding Lance through the process. "Breathe in . . . hold . . . and release," he directed, synchronizing with the machine.

Finally, the machine fell silent, signaling the completion of its task. Lance released a pent-up breath he didn't realize he had been holding, his chest relaxing with relief. "Alright, we're done. You can get dressed again. The doctor will see you in a few minutes," the man said, giving him a thumbs-up, before leaving his little cubicle with a folder.

Lance slowly stepped away from the machine while retrieving his civilian clothes from his Inventory, his hoodie and jeans materializing on him. *It beats having to put it on myself,* Lance thought as he winced at the state of the burned skin on his arm. Just as he was about to head toward the door to meet the doctor, however, it swung open, revealing a woman clasping a familiar folder in her hands.

She was tall, nearly his height. Her dark skin stood out in the faint light that spilled into the room. Her hair, braided intricately with shaved sides, had small Mana stones woven into it; her attire was a striking blend of chain mail, supple leather, and sturdy linen. Embedded within the fabric were more Mana stones secured around the sleeves.

As Lance looked past her into the next room, he caught a glimpse of the technician behind her, his expression flustered. It was evident that she had taken charge. *A Rifter? She's dressed as a Mage.* The mysterious woman closed the door behind her with a smile, giving them some privacy.

"So, you're the Rifter with wings," the woman remarked, a smirk playing at the corners of her lips, as she playfully made her way toward a nearby desk and settled into the chair. Her eyes held a glint of amusement. "It's not an easy task taking down a Baelsworn, let alone one in the air."

Lance's eyebrow arched in curiosity. "Baelsworn?" he inquired, his tone laced with hesitation.

"The winged monster you killed. Nasty creatures. They're usually found in Level-Nine-to-Eleven Rifts. No doubt the main force had missed one when they made their push to establish another secure zone. It's an impressive feat . . ." Her words trailed off as she opened the folder before her, scanning the information contained within. "John Smith? Hmm, you don't look like a John."

Lance's gaze flickered toward the folder and the woman holding it. He knew she was reading the false credentials Brian had procured for him. "I don't look like a lot of things," he remarked, a hint of wryness coloring his words. "And you don't look like a real doctor."

A flicker of an amused chuckle escaped her as she glanced at another page. "It's been a few years since I was a proper doctor. Back before all these troubles with Rifts started," she explained, leaning against the back of her chair. "I'm Nerriah Aguda, a former-doctor-now-Rifter from South Africa, here to help France do the impossible."

Flipping through pages, Nerriah located Lance's X-rays. "I'm a Healer Class. Most of the time, I deal with life-threatening emergencies, regrowing bits and whatnot," she explained, her voice tinged with a mixture of boredom and fatigue. "But I was on a break when I heard the story of a 'mere' Veteran-ranked Rifter killing a Baelsworn on his own, in the air. Hearing that, I just had to take a look."

"Well, you've had a look," Lance replied, his voice carrying a hint of weariness, as he began to make his way toward the door.

Nerriah, still engrossed in the contents of the folder, nodded absentmindedly. "Three broken ribs, several hairline fractures in the arm, and second- and third-degree burns," she recited, her tone shifting into that of a seasoned doctor. Propping her legs against the table, she effortlessly pushed herself and the chair toward him. "One of the ribs is pressing against your lung. You have been busy."

The chair gradually came to a halt, stopping in front of Lance. Nerriah rose from her seat, placing the folder on the chair's surface. "They suggest surgery and at least a month of rest, or in Rifter terms . . . you're out for a week or so. Lucky for you, I am a skilled Healer," she declared, her words overflowing with confidence. "I can pop those ribs back into place and mend most of the damage. It'll hurt like hell, but John the Baelsworn Rider isn't a stranger to pain, right?"

"Fine," Lance responded, his voice measured, as he carefully pulled up his hoodie, granting her easier access to his ribs. "You're a strange person."

Nerriah leaned forward, her eyes scanning the myriad of scars that adorned his body. "Says the one falling out of the sky," she retorted, running a finger across his ribs, inspecting the area. "I think the ribs and the burns are doable in one session. I should have enough Mana left for that. But the scars and older injuries will require follow-ups."

Lance interrupted her, his voice firm. "Just fix the ribs and the burns. The rest isn't important."

Raising an eyebrow, Nerriah regarded him with curiosity. "Oh, I'm sorry, I didn't know you were collecting scars. You know, hoarding stamps and old coins is also an option, right?" she asked sarcastically as her hand began to emit a vibrant blue glow, matching the luminescence that now enveloped her eyes. "Want something for the pain?"

"I'm good," Lance replied as he activated his own Healing Skill, a radiant light spreading throughout his body, dulling the pain for a moment.

"So, you're an airborne suicidal fighter with a Healing Skill?" Nerriah mused aloud, her voice filled with equal parts amusement and disbelief, and placed her glowing hand on Lance's ribs.

In an instant, the effects of her Skill surged to life, slamming into Lance like a sledgehammer. Agony wracked his body as the bones were yanked back into place and forcefully fused together, mending the damage that would have taken days or longer to heal naturally within mere seconds. Lance clenched his teeth while beads of sweat trickled down his back.

Nerriah's attention then shifted to Lance's injured arm, her firm grip encircling the burn wounds. With a determined hold, she eradicated the damaged skin, causing Lance to wince in torment. Then, her Skill meticulously knitted the raw flesh back together, subjecting him to a renewed wave of pain. Moments later, she withdrew her touch, leaving Lance with a lingering ache in his limb.

As the woman settled back in the chair, Lance inspected his newly healed arm. "You good?" she inquired, shifting slightly to the side so that she could retrieve the folder from beneath her.

Lance pulled his hoodie down, his hand sweeping across his forehead to wipe away the perspiration clinging to his brow. "That is one nasty way of healing," he remarked, his tone mixed with a blend of admiration and discomfort.

A casual shrug rolled through Nerriah's shoulders, a faint smile curving her lips. "Hey, it worked, right? Besides, every Skill is different. And mine is a bit more potent compared to that Band-Aid of a Skill you've got going on."

Lance's gaze lingered on her. He grappled with conflicting thoughts, torn between the twin impulses of saying thanks and leaving the room, or learning more about Nerriah. The true source of these thoughts eluded him; he couldn't discern if they were his own or somehow influenced by Thomas and the remnants. "Thanks for the fix. I appreciate it," he finally said.

As he made his way toward the door, his hand firmly grasping the handle, a sudden question from the woman cut through the air, freezing him on the spot: "So why the lies?"

Lance slowly turned around. His mind raced, wondering if Nerriah had uncovered the fact that his credentials were fake. The walls of the military hospital suddenly felt like they were closing in on him. *What should I do?* he pondered, his thoughts swirling with uncertainty. He knew that he had to tread carefully. The rest of his team had already returned to Fergus, meaning he was on his own, save for the polar bear in his Inventory.

Despite the rising tension, Lance maintained his composure, calmly meeting Nerriah's gaze as he weighed his options in the face of a complex situation that was threatening to unravel.

"Why pretend you're below Level One Hundred?" Nerriah questioned, a playful smile dancing on her lips. When Lance remained unresponsive, she grabbed Lance's X-ray before making her way over to the desk to retrieve a marker. She quickly removed its cap using her teeth. "Come on, you can be honest with me. Why fake a lower Level? Normally, Rifters do so to avoid the dangerous jobs, but you falling from the sky kind of defeats that point," she stated as her hand drew a few arrows pointing at the center of the X-ray.

"Who says I'm a higher level?" he retorted, his voice steady despite what he was feeling inside.

"I do," Nerriah said as she moved closer to Lance and handed him the X-ray. "That and the tell-tale signs on your X-ray." As he peered at the image, his eyes spotted the signs of the former fractures traversing his ribs. Moreover, a distortion marred the center of his chest, emanating from the white-shard within.

"Normally, the higher a Rifter's Level, the more energy the white-shard emits, thus ruining these sorts of scans," she explained, her touch gentle as she grasped Lance's left arm and began drawing numbers onto his skin. "Judging by the distortion on the X-ray, I'd estimate you're around Level 150, perhaps 200?" Her words mirrored the numbers written on his arm.

Lance simply stood there as he glanced at the numbers on his arm and what they meant. Inwardly, relief washed over him, recalling how Nerriah hadn't mentioned his falsified identification. Yet, he remained perplexed as to why his white-shard emitted more energy than normal. *Does it have something to do with my Class?* Lance wondered, his thoughts drifting momentarily before he focused on the woman again. "You do realize that is permanent marker, right?" he stated, a tinge of dry humor coloring his words.

"Says the man who's collecting scars," the woman countered, her voice carrying a playful undertone. Without hesitation, she reached for Lance's other hand, gently coaxing it away from the door handle. Her fingers glided skillfully across his skin, leaving behind a trail of written numbers.

Lance watched her actions, his brow furrowed. "The X-ray could've been faulty, for all you know," he reasoned, his gaze fixed on the long series of numbers taking form under her touch.

A mischievous smile curved Nerriah's lips, her eyes sparkling with a hint of amusement. "Could be, but I haven't been suppressing the energy in my white-shard for the last five minutes, and you're not struggling around me like weaker Rifters usually do," she said, her words laced with a subtle challenge. She maintained unbroken eye contact with Lance as she finished writing and handed him the marker.

Lance felt a lingering wariness, unsure of Nerriah's true intentions. "But your secret is safe with me, John," she assured him, her tone holding a note of playful finality. With those words, she opened the door and stepped past Lance.

"Just like that, you heal my injuries and keep a secret? What do you want in return?" Lance's voice held a cautious tone as he voiced his lingering doubts.

"Well, you've got my personal number now, Skyboy. I'll let you figure it out," she responded cryptically before striding away, leaving Lance alone in a state of confusion. His gaze fell upon the numbers written on his arm, mentally connecting the dots and realizing it was a cell phone number.

Just as Lance was beginning to process the situation, her head suddenly popped back into view, peeking into the room. She made a soft *pssst* noise, capturing his attention. "You're weird. I like that," she whispered with a mischievous grin before vanishing once more, leaving Lance feeling even more bewildered.

Shaking his head awkwardly, Lance struggled to make sense of the encounter. With a sigh, he decided to leave the room as well, tucking the medical folder and the X-rays securely under his arm.

After a short walk back to the outer wall, Lance ascended the ladder to a nearby tower that he and Fergus frequently used as a meeting point. The sound of gunshots reverberated through the air, echoing the chaos that engulfed the vicinity. Amid the commotion, notifications occasionally flashed across Lance's vision, indicating that he had just gained Experience. But he paid them no mind, his attention fixed on the task at hand.

Climbing higher, Lance reached the top and spotted Fergus and his companions. Ever resourceful, Fergus had set up a small stove and was heating a meal. Ash sat nearby, engrossed in watching a martial arts fight on his tablet, intently studying the fighters' movements.

Off to the side were Magnus and Quill, scanning the ruined city of Paris for any signs of monsters and taking turns trying to shoot it with a sniper rifle. Brick and Viper were standing behind Fergus, Viper grabbing pieces of sculpted clay armor and placing them on Brick's frame. *I see Fergus has made another new prototype,* Lance thought as he noticed the thicker layers around the chest and pauldrons. "The new threads look amazing."

Lance's sudden arrival did not go unnoticed. Fergus, caught off-guard, nearly dropped his food as his eyes met Lance's. In an instant, he abandoned the stove and rushed over, his worry palpable. "Hey!" he exclaimed, his voice filled with relief as he enveloped Lance in a tight hug, before quickly backing off as if realizing the state he was in. "Are you alright? Ash mentioned you got hurt and needed treatment, but . . ." Fergus glanced over his shoulder to observe Ash for a moment. "Well, you know how Ash is—not the talkative type. But seriously, are you alright?" The concern in Fergus's voice was genuine, his gaze searching Lance's face for any signs of distress.

"Yeah, we ran into a tougher monster during the last run And I got overconfident, that's all. Cracked a few ribs, but a Healer fixed it right up. Good as new," Lance explained, his hand nudging his own ribs to emphasize his swift recovery.

Fergus raised an eyebrow at that. "Ash said something about a parachute?"

Lance offered the bald man a reassuring pat on the shoulder while guiding him back closer to the others. "I'll tell you later." The two of them settled on the edge of the tower, allowing their legs to dangle over the side. The clamor of another loud bang filled the air as Quill dispatched a nearby monster.

"How goes the progress?" Lance asked, his fingers unconsciously rubbing his arm, the presence of the woman's number on his skin suddenly making him feel self-conscious.

Shaking his head, Fergus sighed. "No solid leads yet, but we'll get there. I didn't hear any new coordinates mentioned on the radio, and three of your scouts have already returned," Fergus replied while pointing at the three gray spots circling in the air above them. Afterward he reached into his pocket and retrieved a map of Paris. Fergus unfolded it, revealing a black spot marking the Rift itself, surrounded by smaller circles representing potential locations where Louis could be. They had crossed out most of the circles, indicating previous searches that had yielded no results.

Lance stared off into the distance, observing the construction of the new walls gradually encroaching closer to the Rift. Each section of Paris reclaimed by humanity stirred a mix of emotions within him. There was a sense of loss as he surveyed the bombed, ruined city, fully aware that even if they managed to destroy the outbreak, the task of eliminating the remaining hidden monsters or those who had sought refuge underground would take months, if not years.

Lance reached for the map, his eyes scanning the marked spots. Realization dawned on him that finding Louis was just the first step. Getting to the man was an entirely different challenge. *There are monsters there that can wipe out entire guilds. If I'm going to do this, I'll need to be surgical in my approach.*

Thus far, Lance had fought monsters in the area between the main wall and the outer walls, tackling the weaker monsters that the primary Rifter assault force couldn't spare the time or manpower in cleaning up. Weaker Rifters or smaller guilds were usually tasked with clearing out these remaining pockets of monster activity.

It was still dangerous work, but Lance was picking up a lot of Levels—even more so with all the sniping Quill and Magnus were managing from the tower, with Fergus there to provide ammunition and deal with any onlookers.

Rising from his seat, Fergus collected the cooked food and divided it onto two plates, offering one to Lance. "You should eat. You've been out all day," he said, handing over the plate.

"Thanks for this. So, did I miss anything while I was out?" Lance asked between bites, savoring the nourishment.

"The same horrors as always. I heard on the radio that a monster wiped out an entire squad in the east. So, that's bad. But there are reports of the walls in the north holding up, so at least some things are going smoothly," Fergus replied, taking a bite and nearly burning his mouth in the process. "I also heard Newton is planning another push for the Rift in a few days."

"Really?" Lance glanced at the Rift, able to discern the swirling vortex of unnatural black energy and the faint white shimmer overlaying it. *Trying to break down the barrier again?* Lance mused to himself. "How many attempts has she made thus far?" he asked. Fergus raised four fingers in response while continuing to stuff his mouth.

Lance's thoughts turned to the barrier itself. It acted as a protective dome, encasing the Rift, preventing bombardments or reinforcements by air. It was the reason the military couldn't deploy their experimental weapon against the Rift.

Newton's guild had been carving a perilous path toward the Rift, their objective to eliminate the Rift-guardians who maintained the barrier. However, their efforts had resulted in heavy losses, and the situation was growing increasingly desperate.

Lance's gaze shifted to the right, catching a glimpse of movement. His peregrine falcon came into view as it descended from the sky, gracefully landing on the edge near them. It cocked its head, waiting on Fergus.

Without hesitation, Fergus yanked the map out of Lance's hands, a playful glint in his eyes. "I believe I was placed in charge of gathering intel," he remarked, planting the map next to him and tapping his finger on it.

The falcon inched closer, as if understanding what came next. With several small hops, it approached the map, tapping its beak lightly on several spots, each touch deliberate and purposeful. Fergus studied the markings, going over them again before taking a pen and crossing out those spots on the map. "Sorry, Lance. No luck," he announced, a hint of disappointment in his voice.

Lance leaned backward, his gaze fixed on the sky as he exhaled deeply. Icarus hopped toward him, finding a perch on his chest, its unnatural blue eyes meeting Lance's own.

"But even if we knew the location, how on earth would you get there, subdue Louis, and escape without being killed by him or torn apart by countless monsters?" Fergus asked.

"I'll think of something," Lance replied flatly, his voice tinged with exhaustion.

"I could help," Fergus pitched, offering his assistance. "I've been helping Magnus and Quill with shooting, so I've Leveled Up a few times already."

"So we can both either die or potentially face criminal charges?" Lance retorted with a sigh, his weariness evident.

Fergus paused for a moment, scratching the back of his bald head in contemplation. "How about a distraction?" he suggested.

"A distraction?"

"Yeah, I can create a massive distraction to lure the monsters away from Louis so you can swoop in and confront him," Fergus explained, nudging Lance playfully. "Smart, right?"

"Very," Lance said sarcastically. "Just one problem with this plan of yours. This distraction will end up pulling an ungodly amount of monsters toward you. So, you'll probably die." Lance opened one eye and glanced at Fergus. "You itching to take one for the team?"

Before Fergus could respond, Lance suddenly felt a jolt in his stomach, as if someone had punched him. Startled, he sat upright, only to find a wounded gray crow on its back next to Icarus. "Alpha?" Lance uttered, seeing the crow's missing leg and the evident damage caused by some sort of acid attack.

"He's barely in one piece," Fergus remarked as he carefully picked up the injured crow. Meanwhile, Lance rose to his feet and reached out, his instinct to heal the bird kicking in, but the crow struggled in Fergus's grasp, slipping from his hands before landing hard on the ground. Limping awkwardly, the bird made its way toward the map and pressed its beak against one of the circles, maintaining contact.

"Is that what I think it is?" Lance asked, his throat suddenly feeling parched. He glanced at Fergus, who only nodded. "Did Alpha locate him?"

Fergus knelt next to the creature, carefully sliding it slightly to the side. "Alpha, where is Louis?" he asked, his voice filled with anticipation. The injured bird limped back to the spot on the map and placed its beak in the exact same spot. On seeing that, Fergus slammed his fist on the ground and let out a joyful yelp. "Alpha did it! He's there."

Lance's companions joined them, Ash taking up a position next to Lance. "What do we do now?" he asked, his deep and unnatural voice demanding Lance's attention.

"I . . ." Lance paused, pondering his next move. He glanced at the map, calculating the proximity of Louis's recent position to the Rift. "Fergus, you said Newton was going to make another push for the Rift, right?"

"Yeah, why?" Fergus replied, curious about Lance's train of thought.

"I'll need you to find out exactly when that is," Lance said before turning his attention to the rest of his companions. "The rest of you, I want to farm as much Experience as we can until we make our move. That means continuous sniper duty or going on raids with me. Not you, Magnus. You'll help me out with this." Lance held his hands to the side, and two large speakers materialized underneath them, landing on the ground with a small thud. The same speakers he had recovered from the Rift in Norway where he had also encountered Peter and Finn. "You're going to be in charge of crafting something for me. I'll explain later." Magnus simply nodded as Lance retrieved his smartphone.

He opened a recent email that he had received from Thomas's brother, Oliver, and scrolled through several music files before finding the desired one: Warcub—*My World*.

Well, it's a bit much, but it will be one hell of a statement, Lance thought, a wicked grin forming as he shifted his gaze toward the clay prototype armor that Fergus had been tinkering with. "Fergus, I need you to make me one more armor. A big one this time."

Fergus raised an eyebrow, slightly confused. "Sure . . . but what is this all for?"

Lance pointed directly at the Rift looming in the distance. "I'm going to take a page out of your book," he declared boldly while retrieving the mutilated Baelsworn corpse from his Inventory. It immediately fell to the ground, producing a sickening wet thud.

There was scarcely anything left of the creature's remains; its head and wings were mangled, and it only had a single arm left. What remained of its chest were mere strands of flesh and a Guardian-shard that Lance quickly ripped out.

He then shifted his gaze toward Ash, who acted without needing a single word. He just removed his helmet and sank his teeth into the corpse, tearing off chunks of flesh and swallowing them whole. Fergus, witnessing this gruesome sight, nearly succumbed to the urge to vomit while Lance just grabbed Ash's shoulder and mentally accepted the loss of all his Guardian-shards as he went for a fourth upgrade.

[Do you wish to re-forge this item?]
[Yes]

Locking eyes with the sickened Fergus, Lance exuded a presence of unwavering conviction as he explained what his plan was.

"We're going to create a distraction."

CHAPTER TWENTY-EIGHT

Aegis

Several days later
Near the Rift
Paris, France

LOUIS

Louis positioned himself carefully amidst the rubble, his body blending seamlessly with the debris. He brought the cold metal scope of his sniper rifle near his eye, his trained gaze searching for any signs of movement within the ruins.

Through his earpiece, a voice interrupted the crackle of static. "Target Orc-chieftain spotted at grid reference Alpha-Four. Threat Level: Red, over." Louis's senses heightened in anticipation of the imminent confrontation. Adjusting his rifle, Louis ensured the alignment was spot-on. His gloved finger hovered over the trigger, ready at a moment's notice.

A large group of Orcs emerged around the corner, their hulking figures intimidating even from a distance. In the center of the horde stood a heavily armored monstrosity, radiating an aura of brutality. Within its chest, Louis spotted a glimmer: a Guardian-shard.

"Copy. Lynx Four has eyes on," Louis relayed in a hushed tone, his voice barely a whisper against the backdrop of the war being raged within Paris. He observed the Orc leader and considered the best approach to neutralize the imminent threat.

The radio crackled once more, voices overlapping in a flurry of urgency. Amongst the chaos, Lynx Two called out Louis's call sign, giving instructions and counting down from three. Each digit served as a reminder of the gravity of the situation, fueling Louis's focus. They were also an uncomfortable reminder of the bullets in his back pocket with numbers etched in them. *Don't think about it, just focus.*

Zero arrived, a moment frozen in time. Louis squeezed the trigger, his finger releasing a fraction of the force that lay coiled within him. The projectile streaked through the air, hurtling toward their intended target.

Seconds later, the hulking Orc's eyes exploded in a grotesque shower of goo as the projectile found its mark. Louis watched with grim satisfaction as the monster went on an enraged blind rampage, hitting the other creatures next to it as it clawed at its face.

"Lynx Four, confirmed hit," Louis reported, his voice tinged with a mix of relief. *Those Guardians are too durable to kill with these weapons. Still, we can maim and blind them just fine.* Louis scanned the battlefield, noting the Rifters in the distance, slowly making their way closer toward the Rift itself. "Lynx Four has eyes on Aegis."

"Lynx Five has eyes on Aegis and the procession," a crackling voice resounded in Louis's earpiece.

His gaze narrowed in on the Rifters' steady advance, the armored figures gradually closing in on the Rift. Louis marveled at how they moved as one, a collective force dressed in a fusion of modern protective gear and heavy plate armor. Most of them carried a weighty backpack, pulsating with an ethereal blue glow.

Among the throng, a figure stood out to Louis. Clad in minimal armor, the Rifter had donned a flowing black robe with shimmering red Mana stones woven into it. His eyes locked onto the plain-looking woman. *Viviane Newton Beaumanoir,* Louis thought, recalling his past encounter with her. He still remembered the weight of her presence, the very air growing thin in her proximity.

Louis understood the significance of this moment. The group's collective attention fixed on the nearby Rift, guarded by a protective barrier. He observed the woman's unwavering focus, as if her gaze alone could shatter that barrier.

While the Rifters moved, artillery cleared the route in front of them, and attack helicopters provided cover from above. However, the group of Rifters stood as the primary defense on the ground. Any additional ground-based force accompanying them would succumb to the overwhelming monstrous horde within minutes, as they had witnessed in the previous failed attempts to reach the Rift. The remnants of shredded, burned-out tanks and personnel carriers scattered alongside the route served as grim reminders.

The group's reliance rested solely on aerial support and the aid of snipers. The daunting odds and the absence of substantial ground reinforcements emphasized the magnitude of the challenge Newton's group faced. Still, the weight of France's military was fighting at different fronts, gaining ground and reclaiming parts of the city while drawing the attention of the majority of the monsters within Paris.

As Louis scanned the route that the Rifters were taking, he turned his gaze toward a nearby dilapidated building. He picked up movements near an open window before identifying several Goblins. The vile creatures wielded bows, preparing to unleash an ambush.

Without hesitation, Louis swiftly calculated distance, wind, and the best course of action. Whispering, he transmitted his findings over the radio, his tone devoid of emotions. "Lynx Four, engaging with hostile ambush. Threat Level: Yellow. Two clicks north of Aegis. Building with the red and green tiles, second floor," he relayed, the words resonating through the crackling airwaves, echoed by the responses of his comrades.

Positioning himself better, Louis raised his weapon, aligning his sight properly before he began. Shot after shot, he unleashed a barrage of deadly precision upon the Goblin assailants, his bullets finding their mark with ruthless accuracy, penetrating torsos, ripping apart organs, and painting the walls red.

Even as panic seized the remaining Goblins, their feeble attempts to escape proved futile. He tracked their movements, calculating their speed and height as they fled away from the windows. Walls posed little resistance as angry metal slammed through it and the monsters hiding behind them. After a while, he couldn't detect any further movement, causing him to relax for a moment.

Soon afterward, Louis picked up an urgent message resonating through his radio, intermingling with the metallic click of a weapon being reloaded. "Lynx Three sees multiple targets heading toward Aegis. Threat Level: Orange." As Louis absorbed the information, his gaze instinctively shifted toward a small horde rushing toward the Rifters, their numbers an amalgamation of Orcs, Minotaurs, Elves, and Lizardmen.

But before Louis could even squeeze the trigger for a single shot, an invisible force surged forth, driving the monstrous adversaries to the ground. A wave of awe swept through Louis as he witnessed the overwhelming power that seemed to crush the monsters' advance with ease. The force intensified, its grip tightening like a vice, causing the very ground beneath the monsters to tremble and crack.

In a concentrated area around Newton's party, gravity itself seemed to warp and magnify, as if an invisible hand had increased its pull tenfold. The consequences unfolded with horrifying clarity. The monsters that were caught within this localized gravitational anomaly bore the weight of unimaginable force upon their bodies.

The scene played out in excruciating detail—a macabre symphony of shattered bones, crushed flesh, and agonized cries. The merciless pressure continued, exacting a ruthless toll on its foes. Louis just watched, transfixed, until nothing except red smears remained of the monsters. "Threat negated by Aegis," Louis finally called in, his gaze shifting toward Newton. The woman calmly continued walking, her hand still raised upward in a fist.

"Lynx Four relocating to new vantage point. Current location hot. Over," Louis called in as he backed off from his position while storing the sniper rifle inside his Inventory. As he did so, he heard attack helicopters lay down another barrage of devastating fire as Newton's group advanced further.

"Lynx Four, nearly in position," Louis whispered through his radio, his voice a mere breath amidst the stale air of the room. He edged closer, his footsteps silent as he approached a trio of Orcs feasting upon a lifeless Goblin. They tore at its limbs, their savage hunger on full display. In an instant, a bow materialized within Louis's hands with an arrow already nocked.

Imbue Wind

Upon activating his Skill, an invisible force formed around the arrowhead, imbuing it with heightened destructive potential. Louis released the arrow, the fletching whispering against the air. The projectile found its mark, piercing the nearest Orc's flesh with brutal force. The wound it left behind was a gaping hole; much of the monster's innards had been ripped apart.

The remaining Orcs, enraged by the sudden assault, lunged toward Louis when they spotted him. Their clubs swung with malicious intent, but the French Rifter proved to be no easy prey to take down. He danced with death, his body relying on both experience and instinct. He evaded their initial strikes before rushing forward and sliding beneath the outstretched arm of one Orc, while never ceasing his relentless barrage of arrows.

The projectiles flew from his bow, each one finding its mark—piercing eyes, exposed throats, and vulnerable spots upon their monstrous frames. One Orc stumbled, falling to the ground in a gurgling mess of blood, its life slipping away. Yet, undeterred, the remaining Orc charged once more, fury fueling its every move despite its wounds.

Barrage!

Louis activated his Skills as he nocked three arrows on his bow; immediately afterward, they sliced through the air with deadly precision. At the last second, each projectile multiplied, becoming fifteen arrows in a blink of an eye. The Orc's chest was a canvas of puncture wounds and embedded arrows. It sank to its knees. With an air of calm resolution, Louis approached, his bow drawn taut. "Get out of my city," he whispered. The final arrow, charged with purpose, tore through the monster's skull, extinguishing the last remnants of its grotesque existence.

Silence settled in the room after that, broken only by the fading echoes of combat. Louis stood amidst the carnage, his breath steady, the remnants of his adversaries strewn about him. The city—*his* city—would bear witness to France's unwavering resolve.

He felt the change in weight as his bow vanished from his grip, replaced moments later by his sniper rifle. He positioned himself near the broken window, his eyes scanning the scene outside. The main party of Rifters was slowly advancing toward the Rift in a straight line, drawing dangerously close to the barrier.

His gaze locked on the nightmarish scene that unfolded before him. Countless monsters, numbering in the thousands, swarmed around the Rift, underneath the safety of the barrier. Among them loomed massive behemoths, towering like menacing sentinels, their size rivalling entire buildings. More of the monstrous horde poured in from other streets, threatening to surround the vulnerable Rifters, repeating the tragic fate of the previous attempts.

Without hesitation, Newton unleashed her offensive Skills. Dozens, if not hundreds, of the monsters crashed into the ground, their bodies reduced to gruesome pools of red gore. The display of power offered a momentary respite to the besieged group, as gravity itself wreaked havoc on their foes.

Louis swiftly shifted his focus, providing crucial backup to his comrades. From his vantage point, he targeted ranged units from a distance, ensuring their projectiles never reached their intended targets. He also looked out for winged monsters, preventing any surprise attacks from the sky with well-placed shots.

A sudden interruption shattered the chaos. "Lynx Six, position compromised," a voice crackled through the communication device. "Multiple Orange threats swarming my location. Relocating to—" The transmission abruptly cut off, leaving a haunting silence.

"Lynx Six, respond!" someone called out urgently. Louis just waited for a response, yet none came. In a moment of grim acceptance, he steeled himself for the reality they all faced. With anger etched on his face, he resumed his relentless assault on the monstrous horde.

With that, more and more of the monsters met their gruesome fate under Newton's offensive gravity Skills. However, Louis's attention was drawn to the glowing backpacks adorning the Rifters near Newton. They seemed dimmer, as if being drained of their Mana charge. Worry gripped his thoughts. *This is bad. It's going to end up like last time,* he contemplated grimly.

Knowing the direness of the situation, Louis reached into his backpack and retrieved a detonator. With steady hands, he primed the explosive charges that he had painstakingly placed over the last few days. "Lynx Four, activating explosive charges in ten . . . nine . . . eight," he counted down. Seconds later, a series of thunderous explosions reverberated through the air, their impact shaking the surroundings. Parts of the monstrous horde instinctively veered away, drawn toward the distant sounds.

A few seconds later, the radio flared up again. "Lynx Two, activating explosive charges in— . . ." The voice halted abruptly, leaving a brief moment of silence before resuming with a touch of disbelief. "I'm picking up on something . . . Is that *music*?"

The sudden change in tone caught Louis's attention, along with the others. He could hear the radio flare up as someone else spoke. "What's wrong? Lynx Two, what's happening?"

Before the man could respond, another sniper suddenly called in through the radio. "What the hell was that? I think a Rifter just sped past my position, riding something while blasting music?"

Confusion clouded Louis's mind as a distant melody caught his attention. The music grew louder and louder, nearly drowning out the sound of fighting as English lyrics dominated the chaos. "Reinforcements?" he murmured, a flicker of hope igniting within him.

As the monstrous horde fragmented, their attention diverted toward a focal point, Louis brought his scope to his eye, searching for the source of the commotion. His gaze settled upon a trail of vibrant red smoke streaking through the battlefield at great speed. Intrigued, he followed the smoke's path, his eyes widening with disbelief as he did so.

There, amidst the chaos, he spotted something that defied conventional explanation: a heavily armored Rifter perched atop a polar bear clad from head to claw in thick armor. The Rifter had strapped two large speakers to the bear's armor, belting out music at maximum volume.

The bear and its rider charged through the gaps in the monstrous hordes with practically zealous conviction, seemingly unfazed by the blows they received. Leaving a trail of crimson smoke in their wake, the rider and mount drew a significant portion of the monstrous horde behind them, as they raced away from the Rift and the barrier once again.

"Lynx Four has eyes on . . . I don't know what I just saw . . . A Rifter riding a bear, blasting music," Louis uttered, his words laden with a mixture of disbelief and uncertainty. He struggled to comprehend the situation unfolding before him, barely registering the request for more information from the other snipers and people at HQ. *Does that Rifter have a death wish?* he wondered, his mind grappling to make sense of the weird spectacle he had just witnessed.

Despite the urge to watch what the strange Rifter was doing, Louis forced himself to pay attention to Newton's group, knowing he had a job to do. He couldn't afford to lose sight of the woman as she pressed on, her party's unwavering resolve evident in every step they took. He witnessed the astounding gravitational effects she, the sheer power of her abilities crushing the monstrous adversaries that dared to cross their path, reducing them to mere fragments within a matter of seconds.

The route led them closer and closer to their goal, arriving at the strange barrier that shimmered above the Rift, a tangible manifestation of the unseen forces at play. Louis marveled at the sight of the Rifters moving with caution toward the barrier, knowing that no form of reinforcements could reach them there.

As they pressed forward, several towering behemoths thundered toward Newton's group, their tremendous size causing the very ground to quake beneath their weight. To Louis's astonishment, the behemoths seemed almost impervious to Newton's Skill, their large frames shrugging off the force of gravity itself. These monstrous entities were a grotesque blend of muscle and thick scales, with crystalline protrusions on their spines, poised to unleash unimaginable devastation upon the group.

Louis could only watch from the sidelines, his rifle useless from his current position and the barrier in front of him. In that moment, Louis realized that the fate of Paris hung precariously in the balance, with the possibility that the main assault force was about to get wiped out.

Louis's eyes widened as he watched the other Rifters falling into a tighter formation around Newton, their bodies forming a protective shield around her. She stood tall, her hands once again extended in front of her, fingers splayed wide as if channeling something.

Just as two towering behemoth monsters closed in on her group, something horrible unfolded. The beasts contorted in horrifying spirals, their flesh tearing and ripping as they twisted into grotesque shapes. Blood sprayed in every direction, wrung from their flesh, which compressed into smaller and smaller spirals until the twisted masses of flesh that dropped lifelessly to the ground. Newton's power had reduced them to nothing but macabre fleshballs.

With each behemoth dispatched, the protective barrier encasing the Rift shimmered, its potency diminishing before their very eyes. But there was no respite for Newton and her companions. Three more behemoths came storming toward her from a distance, accompanied by another wave of smaller monsters. The other Rifters readied themselves, forming a stalwart shield wall while their comrades unleashed offensive spells. Soon, fire, ice, and projectiles rained down upon the relentless wave of enemies, creating a deadly storm that pushed back the encroaching darkness.

Louis observed the relentless struggle unfolding before him. The Rifters held their ground, but Newton's focus was now solely on the behemoths in front of her. She could no longer keep up with the ceaseless onslaught of smaller monsters that swarmed them. There were moments of heart-wrenching loss as some Rifters fell, dragged away by the ravenous creatures and torn apart in mere seconds.

Louis could see the exhaustion etched on Newton's face as she gazed at the last three behemoths, her fingers now slowly intertwining. An unseen force began to draw the creatures and countless smaller monsters toward a central point.

Monsters of all sizes and shapes converged, pressed together in an ever-narrowing space. It was a horrifying spectacle, reminiscent of the power of a black hole. Louis stood frozen in awe, his sight fixed on the cataclysmic destruction unfolding before him.

The glowing backpacks carried by the other Rifters lost their glow, their power drained. Some even shattered. Newton dropped to her knees, exhausted, her Mana reserves now depleted. As the effects of her Skill subsided, the monsters dropped to the ground. The aftermath revealed hundreds of mutilated monster corpses strewn everywhere. Some were still vaguely recognizable, while others had been pressed and folded into incomprehensible piles of gore.

The remaining Rifters fought on desperately amidst the gruesome aftermath. Newton had her gaze fixed on the dissipating barrier, watching as its shimmer slowly faded away, a smile slowly forming on her lips.

"They did it," Louis whispered to himself, his mind slowly coming to accept what his heart was already feeling. His radio crackled to life, interrupting the moment of victory. Other soldiers reported what he was seeing, their voices filled with barely contained triumph, confirming the destruction of the barrier.

Mere moments later, dozens of attack helicopters surged forward. Now unhindered by the protective shield, these aerial machines became instruments of vengeance, raining down punishing firepower upon the encroaching enemy, inflicting devastating losses.

Again supported, the Rifters fought valiantly, blades and axes slashing through the air with precision, their Skills tearing through the ranks of adversaries. Amidst the chaos, one of the Mages conjured a shimmering reflective sphere. It expanded gradually, enveloping the beleaguered group of fighters, until, in the blink of an eye, they vanished from sight, transported to another location through arcane means.

Louis's radio crackled to life, reporting that Aegis had completed its mission and had successfully withdrawn. Not long after that, a message came in from headquarters, instructing the remaining ground forces to initiate a withdrawal toward their predetermined extraction sites. "Repeat. Rift-Breaker is inbound. All remaining assets near the Rift are to evacuate immediately."

Aware that time was of the essence, Louis swiftly reached for his things, preparing to move out before the area around the Rift was completely leveled. Before he could turn around to leave, a thunderous crash shattered the silence, and a heavily armored figure crashed through the boarded-up window nearby, hurtling toward Louis with astonishing force. In an instant, Louis found himself pinned to the ground beneath the weight of this unknown assailant, who now had a short sword to his throat.

The figure pressing down on him was clad in black armor and wearing a cloak of shadows that distorted the very air around his imposing form. Pressing the blade more firmly against Louis's throat, he spoke, his deep voice sending shivers down his spine. He sounded like a demon. "Louis Vidal . . . I'm here to repay you for your sins . . . and the blood on your hands." His chilling words hung in the air.

"Who the hell—" Louis attempted to speak, but his words trailed off as someone materialized beside him in the shadows, a female presence solidifying within mere seconds.

Before Louis or his demonic assailant could process the sudden arrival, the newcomer swiftly pressed a pistol against the armored man's helmet and fired, the sound of the gunshot echoing through the air. The armored man collapsed backward, his helmet partially shattering under the impact.

In a display of remarkable dexterity, the woman caught the expelled shell casing out of the air, a smile gracing her features as she turned to face Louis. Her black hair and sun-kissed skin added an air of mystery to her presence.

"My, my, Louis. You're a popular man today," she spoke, presenting the casing for him to see. The number one was carved into it. "Sadly, I had to spend my last gift for you on your new friend over there. But we'll just have to pretend the next one was intended for you, all right?"

Reacting instinctively, Louis spun around and lunged toward his rifle, taking a shot at the woman. However, his bullets found only black smoke, dissolving into nothingness. The woman warped into existence again, appearing beside Louis in an instant. With lightning speed, she pistol-whipped him, sending him crashing into the ground with enough force to fracture the floorboards. "Good," the woman said with a smile as she stepped toward him. "I like it when they struggle."

Louis tasted the metallic tang of blood in his mouth. "Who the hell are you?"

Her gun pressed against his leg. "How rude of me! I'm Shahida, your personal assassin," the woman said with an innocent smile. "That's spelled with an S . . ." Her weapon discharged, a bullet hitting Louis. "h . . ." Another shot pierced through his upper leg. "a . . ." A third bullet struck him in the stomach. "And another lovely h—" Shahida fired once more, this time hitting Louis in a higher region before stopping.

Flinching, Louis awaited the onslaught of more crippling pain, but to his surprise, nothing followed. Opening his eyes, he found Shahida staring at something in a mix of shock and confusion. Louis followed her gaze and saw the supposedly dead armored man rising to his feet. The two of them remained frozen, as the man tore off his helmet, revealing a pale face adorned with a bullet hole oozing white blood.

The pale man dropped his broken helmet, his unnaturally blue eyes shifting toward the others in the room. Louis's eyes widened in disbelief and recognition as he felt a cold chill settle in him. "No . . . You're supposed to be dead!"

At that, the pale man let out a deep and deafening roar before charging toward them.

CHAPTER TWENTY-NINE

Grey Puppets

LANCE

Lance ascended the worn-out stairs with meticulous care, his gloved hand carefully grasping the railing as he tested his weight on each step before daring to ascend further. Each creaking plank beneath his sturdy boots sent a shiver of caution up his spine. The air itself felt heavy with anticipation, mingled with the scent of aged wood and musty decay that clung to the old staircase. *Just a few more steps, Thomas. Just a few more and I'll drag Louis out of this hole and get you a third of the justice that you deserve.*

He could hear Brick, Quill, and Viper follow in his stead, their heavily clad forms filling the narrow passageway behind him. They all had coated their armor as dark as night, each set nearly indistinguishable from one another. Each warrior bore an array of weapons, gleaming and sharp, ready to be unleashed upon any foe that dared to challenge them, with Lance holding onto a shotgun.

As they neared the door, Lance's gauntlet-clad hand rose in a fist in silent command for his comrades to halt. The tension in the air was palpable, their eyes scanning the surroundings for any signs of danger. He then held up five fingers, four, then three. The tension grew with each passing second, building like a coiled spring, ready to be released.

But just as Lance's count reached his final digit, the door exploded open with a resounding crash. Startled, he instinctively leaped backward, his heart pounding in his chest. Out of the rubble and splintered remains of the door, a figure emerged, disheveled and wounded. It was Ash, his helmet missing, revealing a bloodied face twisted in confusion, along with a gunshot wound.

"Engage," Lance hissed, his voice a low growl as he propelled himself toward Ash. He quickly grabbed hold of him as he activated his Repair Skill. The energy surged through his fingertips, flowing into Ash's battered form, slowly mending the damage, the bullet hole slowly closing. *Did Louis do this?* Lance thought as he opened Ash's status.

Ash 1x	Human	Rift-glider eye	Polar bear muscle	Orc chieftain bone	Baelsworn wing
		+2 Sight	+3 Speed	+7 Defense	+3 Speed
		+Heat vision	+6 Power	+700	+2 Power
			+300	Durability	+100
			Durability		Durability
					+30% Heat
					resistance

Even with a fourth upgrade, he still got messed up. Just how much stronger is Louis? Has he gained a lot more Levels since I last met him? Lance heard his comrades rushing past him, their footsteps echoing as they stormed into the room. Not long after that, a symphony of battle filled the air—a cacophony of clashing metal against wood, the thunderous boom of gunfire, and the resounding thud of bodies colliding with walls.

Turning his attention back to Ash, Lance saw his friend slowly rise to his feet. "Are you alright?" Lance asked, as he activated his Inventory screen and stored the shadow cloak that Ash was wearing.

Ash just nodded before slowly placing his hand on Lance's shotgun, his fingers curling around the weapon before claiming it for himself. "Yes . . . another Rifter hit me," Ash murmured, his tone devoid of emotion. "Female . . . called herself Shahida," he explained as he checked the weapon's readiness. "Iyas's twin?"

Lance's brow furrowed beneath the sturdy bone armor, his expression a mixture of confusion and irritation that he fought to conceal. After a moment's pause, he nodded slowly, his voice carrying a weight of foreign memories and pain. "Yes," he confirmed, the haunting specter of Iyas's thoughts vivid in his mind as he did so.

A steely resolve settled over Ash's features when he observed Lance, afterward gripping the shotgun more firmly. "We'll deal with her," his deep voice declared as he stepped away from Lance before charging into the room, weapon at the ready. Lance followed closely behind, the shimmer of a shield and a short sword materializing in his hands, drawn from his Inventory.

The two of them rushed into the room, the air thick with tension and the stench of conflict. Lance's gaze swept the room, taking in the chaos unfolding before him. His attention honed in on a woman, agile and elusive, effortlessly evading the strikes of multiple sword-wielding assailants and the occasional arrow or thrown javelin. Shahida bore a strange expression, as if puzzled by the futility of her own actions as she attempted to choke Brick, her grip seemingly ineffectual. She was wearing basic leather armor with sturdy chainmail underneath, much of it covered in a blend of red and gray blood.

Lance's mind raced, analyzing the situation, seeking an advantage. He caught a glimpse of Louis in the background, blood staining his clothes and a trail of crimson marking his path. The wounded man limped desperately, a frantic attempt to escape the combat. The man's eyes widened in disbelief when he caught sight of Ash again, unscathed and with no trace of the bullet wound that had previously marked him.

Despite Lance's desire to rush toward Louis, he forced himself to shift his attention toward the woman who had now disarmed and was kicking Brick with astonishing force, sending him crashing through a nearby pillar. The stone shattered upon impact, dust and debris filling the air. Quickly, Shahida's attention shifted to the other combatants as she dodged an arrow from Quill. The assassin retaliated by aiming her pistol and firing three times, hitting Quill in the neck and chest in quick succession, only for Quill to stumble backwards but remain standing.

Seeing Shahida's confused expression, Viper seized the opportunity, his body a blur of motion as he threw his shield toward her face, only to dash to her side as she blocked the projectile. With a well-timed strike, he slammed the gun out of her hand, disarming her with a resounding crash. Viper then evaded her retaliatory punches with ease, despite Shahida being faster than he was. It was as if he was familiar with her patterns. After avoiding one of her large swings, he ducked down while pulling out his poisoned knife. Then he shot forward and slammed the weapon into her thigh, piercing through her armor and layers of flesh and twisting it to maximize the wound.

Shahida's eyes gleaming with malicious intent, she closed in on Viper in a split second, her fingers finding purchase on his bone chest plate. With a surge of unearthly strength, she effortlessly lifted him off the ground, his body suspended in midair before she slammed her free hand into his torso hard enough to punch a hole into his armor. A grim smile curled her lips as she swiftly withdrew the knife from her thigh, her gaze briefly flickering to the substance staining its blade.

"Really? You call that poison?" she mocked, a hint of disdain in her voice. With a sadistic flourish, she launched a relentless assault upon Viper's stomach, the knife becoming a blur of deadly steel. The ferocity of her attack reached its zenith as she nearly gutted Viper before dropping him, his body now left to sprawl upon the ground.

Gray blood pooled around Viper as he struggled to keep his innards inside of him. "What the hell *are* you people?" Shahida asked, her eyes on the colorless blood and organs on display. Before the assassin could learn more, she suddenly had to move sideways, dodging several more arrows, javelins, and a shotgun blast from Ash, as he and Lance quickly closed the distance.

Ash brought his shotgun to bear again, the deafening blasts filling the air as he discharged the weapon at close range, hitting the assassin a few times before she momentarily disappeared, engulfed in a puff of shadowy smoke.

Her vanishing act was short-lived, however, as she materialized next to Ash in an unsettling display of speed and cunning. In one swift motion, she snatched the shotgun from his grasp, her fingers deftly manipulating the weapon with fluid familiarity. The assassin spun it around, a malevolent grin adorning her face. "Too slow," she teased before she unleashed the remaining ammunition upon Ash.

The force of the blast shattered the protective shell of Ash's armor, rending bone and leather alike. The impact sent him hurtling backward, his form crumpling onto the unforgiving floor. Compared to the many wounds now adorning Ash's frame, Shahida had only suffered minor cuts and bruising, hinting at the amount of Endurance the female Rifter had.

What the hell? She's durable enough to shrug off a shotgun blast?! Lance glanced at Ash's still frame before catching the sounds of shifting bricks behind him. "Brick, back me up. Quill, go for the kill!" Lance's bellow cut through the chaos, his voice commanding as he closed the distance between himself and the assassin. He moved swiftly with his shield raised protectively, charging at her from the side, sword at the ready.

The clash erupted like a tempest, a dance of steel and flesh. Lance and the assassin were locked in a deadly duel, their movements a blur of sharp strikes and last-second dodges. Unarmed, Shahida relied on her unnatural strength and speed, her strikes slamming into Lance's shield with a force that left dents on its surface with each blow.

When Brick arrived, he threw himself into the fight but couldn't match the assassin's prowess. His movements were slower, and when he did manage to score a hit, it barely seemed to faze her. Arrows flew past, grazing or narrowly missing the relentless woman each time she threatened to overwhelm Lance or Brick. The two warriors worked in tandem, a symbiotic and desperate dance against a much more powerful adversary.

And then, like a phantom, Shahida vanished once again, dissipating into a shroud of shadowy smoke. A split second later, she reappeared behind Brick, her fist tearing through his chest with terrifying force, emerging from the other side, clutching bits of gray organs and rib fragments. With a powerful kick, she then sent Brick hurtling toward Ash's crumpled form.

Turning her attention back to Lance, Shahida's lips curled into a cruel smile that made her dark features more pronounced. A macabre satisfaction gleamed in her eyes as she licked the pale blood and remnants of organs from her fingers. "All of you look human, but you don't taste like it," she taunted, her voice a chilling melody. With swift, predatory grace, she closed the distance and continued her assault.

Lance fought with every ounce of his being, his sword slashing and hacking as fast as he could. But the assassin seemed to speed up even more, as if she had activated a Skill. She suddenly came at him from all angles, delivering bone-rattling blows to his sides and chest, stealing his breath and fragmenting most of his thick bone plating before the woman grabbed his shield, intent on ripping it out of Lance's hands.

In a moment of defiance, desperation and fear, Lance activated his Detonation Skill before letting go of the shield and jumping backwards. The item exploded in her hands in a hail of steel fragments, severely damaging her left hand and stunning her for a split second. Seizing the opportunity, Lance charged at her, swinging his sword as fast as he could. He landed a cutting blow across her cheek, drawing blood and eliciting another snarl of pain from her.

Backing off, Shahida cradled her wounded left hand, the sight of countless lacerations and steel fragments embedded in her palm now reflected in her gaze— a gaze filled with simmering malice. She extended her right hand before him.

In the blink of an eye, a ball of fire ignited within her palm, growing rapidly in size and velocity. The searing sphere hurtled toward Lance with alarming speed, intent on incinerating its target. Lance's instincts screamed at him to escape the impending doom. Yet, before he could react, Shahida vanished into the shadows again.

A heartbeat later, a forceful impact struck Lance's back, the grip of an iron hand seizing his neck with absurd strength. The weight of her presence pressed against him as she materialized, her hold unyielding. With a satisfied grin, Shahida forced Lance headfirst into the fiery orb, his body subjected to its scorching heat. The intensity of the flames seared his senses for a moment before he felt himself being slammed against the nearby wall.

After that, he felt her grind his head across the wall, shattering stone tiles with his bone helmet, while even the brickwork crumbled beneath the brutal assault, leaving a trail of destruction in its wake. The only respite that he got was when the woman had to stop and dodge several arrows and then retaliated by throwing a piece of brickwork at Quill's head with enough force to send her flying backwards with a cracked helmet.

With a vice-like grip, Shahida then seized Lance's throat, nearly crushing his windpipe. Blood trickled from his mouth, dripping out through the slits in his helmet. Through the pain, he could hear her mocking words, a venomous taunt hanging in the air. "Red? So, we find the puppeteer amongst his puppets?" Slowly she drew closer, her tongue darting out to taste his blood, savoring it. "Much better than your friends," she whispered while her clenched fist drew back, poised to deliver the finishing blow.

But before her strike could land, a blur of motion intercepted Shahida. Ash and Brick barreled toward her as one, quickly closing the distance. The assassin spun around to face the incoming threat, only to lose sight of her assailants as a blinding blue light enveloped her entire being, briefly lessening the pain of her injured hand.

Blinded by Lance's intervention, Ash and Brick slammed into her, hurtling her body away from Lance while ramming through two sturdy stone pillars, lifting her up as high as they could. Acting as one, they drove her downward, the force powerful enough that it shattered the floorboards beneath them, plunging the trio through several floors of debris and crumbling infrastructure.

Dust billowed upward, obscuring the battlefield in a haze. Lance, leaning against the wall, seized the moment to catch his breath, the taste of blood lingering in his mouth as it continued to drip from his numerous wounds and lacerations.

Mend Wound

In response, his body emanated a blue light as well, a soothing glow that enveloped him for a fleeting moment. Minor injuries ceased to bleed, and the throbbing ache in his body dulled slightly, granting him a respite for a few seconds. *That was close,* he thought as he struggled to breathe through his bruised throat.

Quill, still bleeding from her chest and neck, approached Lance, offering a helping hand. Lance accepted it for a moment while scanning the area for danger, as well as to find Louis, but only spotted a trail of the man's blood leading toward stairs that led upward.

Turning his attention to Viper, Lance observed the pale man on his knees, his body badly damaged and organs exposed. *He's in bad shape. It'll take me a long time to repair him,* Lance thought as he limped over toward Viper.

[You have retrieved an Item 5x]

Kneeling beside Viper, Lance retrieved several grenades from his Inventory, their cylindrical forms materializing within his grasp. Carefully he placed the grenades next to Viper as he spoke. "I'll fix you properly afterward. For now, hold on tight and use these if you catch her off guard. Understand?" Lance's hand rested on Viper's shoulder, briefly activating his Repair Skill to restore a bit of his durability. Viper nodded in acknowledgement; his gaze fixed on the grenade closest to him.

Lance then got up and joined Quill as they moved toward the gaping hole in the floor, leading down several floors. He swiftly discarded his broken bone armor, storing it, and in an instant, his previous steel gear enveloped his form, reinforcing his Defense alongside his large revolver, Oath Keeper. *Let's see her try and brush off a Black Reaper round.*

With their weapons gripped firmly, Quill and Lance leaped into the unknown depths, poised for what awaited them below.

CHAPTER THIRTY

Arm for an Arm

LANCE

Quill and Lance fell through the air, ultimately landing on the floor several levels below, their landing punctuated by the shattering of rubble and the splintering of broken floorboards. As they regained their footing, Lance's hazel gaze took in their surroundings—a dilapidated kitchen, reduced to ruins.

The remnants of a fierce struggle lay scattered before them, evident in spatters of gray blood and shattered fragments of bone and leather armor. Beyond that, Lance could also see old filth and chewed-up bones in a corner, hinting at monsters that might have used the building as a lair at one point.

With a cautious step, Lance and Quill maneuvered their way out of the kitchen into the adjoining living room. There, they encountered further destruction—crumbling walls, swirls of dust, remnants of shattered furniture, and holes marring the floor and walls. Lance also noticed an empty gas canister abandoned in a corner, a tell-tale sign that Ash had resorted to blinding his foes and exploiting his unique ocular abilities.

A thought flickered in Lance's mind: *Which way did they go?* Yet, before he could dwell on the question, the unmistakable clamor of combat resonated through the air, followed by a building-shaking explosion of a grenade. *That was one of ours.* This development spurred Lance forward. Rounding the corner, his heart pounding with adrenaline, Lance surged ahead, his actions mirrored by Quill, who had her bow partially drawn, ready to unleash her lethal arrows at a moment's notice.

Lance's breath caught in his throat, his grip on the gun tightening as he came to an abrupt halt. Dread washed over him as he bore witness to the nightmarish scene unfolding in front of him. Shahida had impaled Ash against a wall with several of his bone javelins. His right leg was severed, his left ravaged as if it had endured an explosive force, and nearly every part of his body was covered in lacerations. From the wounds, sickly gray blood trickled down and stained the floor in a morbid display. Lance's gaze shifted to Brick, slumped lifelessly over a mound of rubble, his head ripped from his body. It lay a few paces away, staring blankly at a spot on the wall, devoid of all emotion.

She took out Brick and Ash, just like that? There's no way for us to beat her. We need to retreat. His mind raced as he took a step back.

Shahida's gaze swiftly shifted toward Lance and Quill, her eyes sharp and calculating, as if dissecting their every move. "Fancy steel armor won't conceal you . . . nor will it spare you my pleasure . . . Puppeteer," she said teasingly, turning to face Lance. Her hands were stained with pale blood, as if she had inflicted Ash's lacerations with her own fingers. "I can almost taste the fear from here. There's no place to run—"

"Quill, barrage!" Lance shouted, interrupting the assassin's chilling words. In a seamless motion, he swept his hand across the four arrows held by Quill.

Detonate

Detonate

Detonate

Detonate

The arrows glowed for a split second before Quill unleashed them toward Shahida. Each arrow detonated upon impact, either upon the assassin herself or the surrounding room, destroying the building further. Shahida's equipment took the brunt of the damage; the attacks had only bruised her.

Undeterred, she charged toward them, closing the distance with alarming speed. "I'm going to enjoy tearing you and your puppets apart!" she hissed, venom dripping from her words as she lunged forward.

Desperate, Lance aimed his large revolver, squeezing the trigger at the last second. The Black Reaper round collided with the woman's hand in a gruesome display. Bones shattered and flesh was torn asunder, reducing the appendage to a blood-soaked mess. Struggling with the immense recoil, the second round found its mark in her left leg, tearing away a substantial chunk of flesh, and the third round missed its target entirely as Shahida abruptly vanished into a shadowy plume of smoke.

Lance and Quill stood frozen for a moment, their hands quickly reaching for additional ammunition. *She's much stronger than Iyas was. Not to mention brutal and* bloodthirsty, Lance thought as he shifted his gaze toward Ash, who was desperately struggling to free himself from the javelins that were impaling him.

As seconds turned into minutes, nothing happened. Slowly reaching Brick's body, Lance placed his foot on the still corpse.

[You have stored several Items in your Inventory]

Brick's body and ruined gear vanished from the room, now safely stored inside Lance's Inventory, while he quickly activated his Repair Skill to undo the damage Brick had sustained in combat, along with the severed head. *It'll be a while until Brick's combat-ready again,* Lance thought as he shifted his attention back to Ash. But just as he took a step closer toward his pale friend, the assassin materialized beside him, wielding a colossal war hammer, her frame encased in thick blood-red armor.

With a menacing swing, the woman nearly decapitated Lance in her initial strike. Instinctively, he evaded the deadly blow and retaliated, firing several shots in rapid succession before she vanished once more. Two of his rounds had missed and had slammed through a nearby wall, leaving sizable holes as the surrounding structure began to crumble.

"Run!" Ash howled when Lance froze up, looking at his trapped companion. The desperate scream forced Lance and Quill into action as they sprinted away, the cacophony of collapsing debris accompanying their frenzied escape, while Ash got buried behind them. They darted into a hole in the wall and ran into the adjacent building and nearly threw themselves down a nearby staircase. At the foot of the stairs, Shahida materialized, poised to strike Lance with her war hammer. In a selfless act, Quill pushed him out of harm's way, bearing the full brunt of it on her shoulder before vanishing amidst a shower of splintered wood and debris.

[You have retrieved an Item 2x]

Lance's adrenaline spiked when two fireballs *just* missed him while he was retrieving two daggers from his Inventory. He quickly activated his Detonation Skill before propelling them behind him. Parts of the building quaked and crumbled as the daggers exploded, causing a violent collapse. Bursting through a nearby boarded-up door frame, Lance slid to a halt inside the next room, his breaths coming in rapid bursts as he readied his revolver with trembling hands. His arm was still aching from the last time he had used the weapon.

Lance's heart pounded in his chest as he realized he was alone. Thoughts raced through his mind as he replayed the fight. *She's a proper monster,* he acknowledged, his brow furrowing in concern. *Power, fire manipulation, and teleportation abilities . . . I can't match them. But there must be a cost to using such powers, right? She only employs them sporadically. Perhaps—* Before he could finish his train of thought, the woman materialized in a billowing cloud of shadowy smoke, her back turned to him. In the moment before she noticed his presence, Lance recalled what Daniel had once taught him about Skills and their potential downsides.

Lance's voice boomed, "Iyas!" The abruptness of his shout and the familiar name caught the woman off-guard, providing Lance with the perfect opportunity to act. Without hesitation, he squeezed the trigger, unleashing a Black Reaper round that collided with her torso. The impact tore through parts of her armor, followed by a small explosion. Two more detonations came on its heels, striking the woman at close range and ripping off more layers of armor and flesh. After the third shot, Lance's weapon vanished into his Inventory as he charged at her.

Thomas . . . Iyas . . . I need you . . . now! Lance's thoughts echoed in the depths of his mind as he slammed into the woman, ramming her head against a nearby wall. For a fleeting moment, Lance closed his eyes, allowing the remnants of his best friend to resurface, almost overwhelming his senses. Like an additional hand on the steering wheel, Thomas's consciousness intertwined with his own, followed closely by the influx of Iyas's memories of Shahida, filling Lance's mind further.

Lance's eyes snapped open, catching sight of the woman nearly elbowing him in the face as she spun around. He barely evaded the attack, narrowly escaping its impact. Shahida, driven by the pain and damage she had endured, relentlessly lunged at Lance, seeking to repay him in kind. Lance just observed her movements, adapting to her rhythm and combat style as if he was familiar with it. Three times in a row, he countered her attacks before she had even started them, delivering swift strikes to her vulnerable ribs in between the gaps of her armor. She was faster and stronger, but at that moment, Lance knew her as well as a twin.

Frustration and confusion clouded Shahida's mind, escalating her fury to a point where she surged forward with an almost supernatural speed, her hand rushing toward Lance's neck. "How do you know that name?" she hissed angrily.

Her prey just stepped in and executed a flawless counter at the last moment by turning her momentum against her. A powerful uppercut landed squarely underneath her chin, accompanied by a surge of crackling lightning that traveled across her face. The impact split open her lower lip, jolting her with the sheer force of the blow, causing her helmet to fly off her head. Then two more fast blows followed, bloodying her nose and chipping two of her front teeth before Lance stepped back, feeling the damage he himself had sustained. He had hit her as hard as he could, but it had felt like striking solid concrete, leaving his fists swollen while blood trickled down inside his gloves.

Lance darted away from the wounded woman, his heart pounding in his chest as he heard her catch up to him. She paused for a second when he retrieved the first monster corpse from his Inventory, followed by dozens of others, until they created a grisly improvised wall composed of dead Orcs, Goblins, Insectoids, and

Lizardmen. Lance's hand quickly slid across their motionless bodies, causing a few to shimmer briefly in his wake.

Detonate
Detonate
Detonate

With his Mana nearly depleted, Lance sprinted with all his might, his feet pounding against the wooden floor as he hastily retrieved a steel shield from his Inventory. With a firm grip, he held it behind him, hoping to lessen some of the shrapnel that might hit him. He nearly reached the end of the hallway when the corpses detonated with a thunderous blast. The force propelled him forward as he crashed through a nearby window and out of the building. Gravity instantly took its toll, yanking him down until he slammed into a burnt-out car. His world instantly went dark.

Lance slowly regained consciousness. Groaning in agony and clutching his right shoulder, he felt disoriented and battered. *Please, just let her be dead,* Lance thought as he forced himself upright before sliding off the car, realizing that his shoulder was dislocated. *Scratch that . . . I wish I was dead.* He observed the building he had just been forcefully evicted from, witnessing its weary surrender as additional floors succumbed to the strain, shrouding the street in a billowing cloud of suffocating dust. Parts of it were on fire, either from the earlier fireballs or one of the many explosions it had endured.

"Icarus!" Lance's voice rang out, a desperate call to his avian companion to back him up. Wincing through the searing pain, Lance then activated his Healing Skill while preparing himself. He clenched his teeth and gripped his injured arm just above the elbow. He applied steady pressure, carefully aligning the dislocated joint. Through the searing pain, he adjusted the angle until, with a sudden pop, the joint slid back into place. The relief was immediate, though the ache remained.

Lance fought to steady himself, his breath catching in his chest as he regained his composure. He hissed as he retrieved his shield, swiftly stowing it in his Inventory. Taking deliberate steps toward the partially collapsed building, he noticed the neighboring structures still standing strong. *No way that she survived that,* he tried to convince himself before his thoughts turned to his companions. His gaze shifted to the building next to the collapsed one, a flicker of hope in his eyes as he imagined Viper and Louis safe within its mostly intact sections. He then checked his Inventory screen to see how Brick's repairs were going. *80 percent. Just a little while longer until—*

A sudden thunderous crash reverberated as an unseen force slammed into the burnt-out car behind him, causing him to freeze in place for a split second before pivoting. His eyes widened at the sight of Shahida, barely clad in ruined armor and marred by a coating of dust and blood, her body a ruin of lacerations and bruises. She inhaled deeply, as if for the first time. "Nowhere to run," she spat at him before vanishing into smoke, only to reappear behind him, gripping his right arm before slamming his face into the unforgiving metal of the car, arm bent backwards. The force was powerful enough to tear apart the leather strip that kept his helmet in place.

"You're going to tell me how it is you know the name Iyas. More importantly, you ruined my arm. Do you know how costly it's going to be to get this healed?" She pressed her tortured limb against the front of his helmet, crimson droplets now dripping on Lance. "I think it's only fitting that I return the favor, starting with those nasty fingers of yo—" Her words came to a halt as she noticed the revolver materializing in Lance's left hand, aimed right at her. Before he could squeeze the trigger, however, she executed a swift kick, knocking the weapon out of his grasp, causing it to skid across the pavement.

"Those tricks and that weapon of yours are getting old. Now, like I said, fingers first." Her grip then tightened around Lance's fingers as she methodically applied pressure, deliberately fracturing each bone, subjecting him to unbearable torment. He was trapped, unable to escape the pain she was inflicting. Drawing closer, she uttered in a chilling whisper, "Now, the wrist." In one swift movement, she snapped it, causing Lance to emit a gut-wrenching howl that echoed in the air. "Oh? Still conscious? Very good. Now, let's move on to the next section," she said as her hand slowly moved upward.

"Icarus!" Lance yelled before his voice transformed into agonized screams as she broke the bones in his lower arm. The sound of something swift approached, causing her to release Lance's arm to protect herself. This granted him a momentary reprieve to scramble away. His helmet slipped off as he clutched his mangled arm, pain coursing through his body. Casting a desperate glance backward, he witnessed Shahida, with a perplexed expression on her face, clutching a feathery, gray object in her hands that she had just snatched from the sky.

"First puppets, now birds? What's . . ." Shahida stopped talking when she spotted Lance without his helmet on. Her expression suddenly shifted, her eyes widening in a mixture of realization and anger. "You!" she spat, her hand clenching until the bird exploded in a macabre shower of meat and feathers. "You were supposed to be dead! Why are you here?"

Lance kicked himself backward, his eyes locked on her as she drew nearer. "What happened to Iyas?" Her war hammer once again materialized, its metallic grind underscoring her vile intent as she closed the gap. "Where is my brother?"

Lance kept moving backwards until the debris of the building behind him was pressed against his back. A sense of his impending death gripped him, while a peculiar emotion coursed through his veins. It was as if Thomas's will was commanding Lance to defy his fears and meet his end head-on like he himself had done. "Would you like me to arrange a meeting?" Lance said, slowly raising his left arm and provocatively extending his middle finger. "Here you go." He even gave her an amused smile as he watched her lift the war hammer with one arm.

The partially collapsed building behind Lance rumbled; several bricks and fragments of wood were dislodged before sliding downward, stirring up a billow of dust. From within the swirling haze, a deep and unnatural voice resonated: "Don't . . ." Accompanying it was a scraping noise growing ever louder as the ominous presence inched closer to the building's edge. The figure materialized slowly, its crippled silhouette emerging through the murky shroud. "Touch . . . Him . . ."

With an amused grin ruined by two missing teeth and a split lip, Shahida lowered her weapon. "Seems like one of your puppets still has some strings attached," she jeered, taking deliberate steps forward before viciously planting her foot onto Lance's chest. "You there, Pinocchio! Why don't you crawl over here and make me?" Her voice dripping with cruelty, she increased the pressure on Lance's chest, drawing a painful groan out of him.

"If you . . . touch . . . him . . ." Ash hissed. His pale figure partially emerged from within the shroud of dust, covered by a layer of gray blood and dirt. Bit by agonizing bit, he dragged himself toward the edge, exposing more of his broken body, shredded chunks of flesh, and his missing left eye. His back contorted grotesquely, swelling unnaturally until it burst open in a spray of gore and swirling dust. Two massive leather wings unfurled with a power that sent a torrent of particles in all directions, nearly engulfing Lance and Shahida in the blinding chaos.

Ash's wings carved a path of destruction, their pointed tips scraping against the jagged remnants of the ruined building before slamming into the broken floor. With an eerie grace, Ash lifted himself from the ground, his wings extending. The scene exuded both a demonic and angelic aura as Ash hung suspended in the air, supported solely by his wings. His missing legs were a macabre reminder of Shahida's malice. Gray blood continued to drip from his wounds, anointing the ground with his resolve. ". . . I'll rip your shard out," Ash threatened, his deep voice eerily calm in that moment.

Silence settled between Shahida and Ash, their eyes locked in a quiet exchange. The weight of the impending clash hung heavy in the air, Ash's towering figure perched atop the mountain of rubble. After a moment, Shahida made her choice, evident in the click of her tongue, followed by movement. Several of Lance's ribs crumpled beneath the violent pressure of her leg, sending waves of agony through his body while robbing him of his ability to scream.

Unleashing his rage, Ash shot forward, his enormous wings crashing into the rubble and propelling him forward, straight into Shahida, with enough force to disarm her. One of Ash's wings pierced her shoulder as they hurtled toward the opposing building complex, slamming through the wall before the entire building became a symphony of battle, reverberating with primal roars and further destruction.

Lance lay motionless amidst the chaos, his breaths shallow and pained. A faint blue glow emanated from him whenever his Mana surged back, lessening a fragment of his pain before it returned just as sharp. After a while, a gray figure materialized by Lance's side before immediately dropping to a knee to help, its head only partially restored.

"Brick, help me . . . Get me to Viper . . . and the others," Lance uttered through gritted teeth, each word an immense struggle. With a single nod, Brick swiftly retrieved Lance and Shahida's weapons, gear, and Icarus's shard before helping Lance get back on his feet and supporting his limping frame toward the partially destroyed building where Viper and Louis were.

CHAPTER THIRTY-ONE

Reunion

Five minutes later

LANCE

As Lance's jaw clenched, a blinding blue flash robbed him of his sight, followed swiftly by a constricting sensation around his right arm. Support was being applied. The piercing agony made him grit his teeth as he felt improvised leather straps being tightened.

Biting through the agony, Lance blinked away tears as his vision gradually returned, the healing effect of his Mend Wounds Skill slowly fading. His gaze fell upon Brick, who was diligently securing another leather strap around the makeshift splint fashioned from rebar and wood. "Good," Lance acknowledged, sensing the completion of the knot. *Just loose enough to maintain circulation*, he thought as his pain-riddled mind desperately clung to what he could recall of his previous career as a nurse that might help him stabilize the arm further.

With a deep inhalation, Lance nodded at Brick. "Now, the sling. Let's finish this." Brick promptly elevated Lance's injured arm and secured it against his chest with an improvised sling. A groan escaped Lance's lips, and he shifted his weight, stomping his legs in an attempt to dull the pain. A nearby wall became the target of a few frustrated kicks, offering him some momentary release.

"Done?" Brick inquired, holding a few stray straps awkwardly, unsure of what to do with them now.

Lance responded with a nod, then rested his left arm on his companion's shoulder while accessing his Inventory. Within seconds, Brick found himself encased in a spare set of bone armor, armed with a steel sword and shield instead of the leather straps. "You did well," Lance commended, patting him on the shoulder.

Lance winced as he took a painful first step toward the nearest visible stairs, feeling the burn in his ribs and right arm. "Help me get back to Viper and protect me along the way, alright?" Brick positioned himself beside Lance, carefully offering support as they embarked on their climb, the aged floorboards groaning beneath their shared weight.

A few minutes and several ruined rooms later, Lance noticed a few familiar elements that reminded him of the corridor where he and Quill had fought the assassin before losing one another. Still, it was hard to tell with all the damage the building had sustained in the last hour alone and a layer of smoke slowly forming.

"Brick, I'll need you to remember this spot," Lance said as he made a vague gesture around him that did little to narrow it all down. "I think I lost sight of Quill somewhere around here. Let's find Viper first and tend to his damage, then we'll locate Quill," he said while weighing several options in his mind. Lance felt torn between searching for Quill or Viper, while at the same time also deciding between repairing Icarus or settling for faster Mana regeneration in order to heal himself sooner.

The two of them rounded the corner, navigating past a collapsed section of the building. The resounding echo of artillery fire hitting a nearby area could be heard, which intensified their sense of urgency. Brick frequently had to grab Lance more firmly when the building trembled or a section of the floor started to break apart underneath them. *We need to hurry this up,* Lance thought, their footsteps quickening as they arrived at the spot where he had encountered Louis and Shahida earlier, coinciding with another explosion that shook the entire building. He pondered whether it resulted from artillery or relentless aerial bombardment.

He fixed his gaze on the remnants of a shattered door where Ash had previously landed. *I hope you're all right, buddy,* Lance thought as he clenched his left hand, not feeling whole without him. Thousands of thoughts were swirling in his mind about what had happened to Ash and what had caused the physical transformations that had led to his wings. *Even now, after all this time, I don't know anything about my Class or my companions.*

He limped into the next room, the aftermath of the intense battle rendering it nearly unrecognizable. Amongst the debris, he spotted Viper sitting in a corner near a shattered window. Viper weakly raised his hand, stained with his own gray blood. Despite his condition, the man was able to muster a polite wave before pressing his hand back against his gutted stomach, desperately forcing some of his organs back inside.

Hobbling closer to Viper, Lance's ears caught the distant echoes of explosions, while he spotted plumes of smoke near the Rift's vicinity. Even from their position, he could see that more and more deadly pressure was being applied on the area around the Rift. "How are you holding up?" he asked, his voice tinged with concern.

"Fine," Viper replied confidently. Lance couldn't tell if Viper was genuinely failing to grasp the severity of his injuries or if he was purposely downplaying it to ease his worries.

"Fine? Right . . . and I'm just resting my right arm," Lance said with a sigh as he feared his companions might be picking up on some of his bad habits, or those of Fergus. He accessed his Status screen and checked the state of his Stamina and Mana reserves.

[Stamina:] [176/1340]
[Mana:] [11/885]

Just a little more and I'll be able to use the Mend Wounds Skill again. Lance sat down next to Viper, pressing his knee against Viper's and activating his Repair Skill. He knew that he didn't have much time, and that staying in this place wasn't smart, but he didn't have any other options.

Either Ash kills her, or she'll take him down. Either way, I can't leave here on my own just yet, Lance thought, knowing full well that he'd be dead in a matter of minutes if he tried to traverse the monster-infested city on his own with broken ribs and one functioning arm. Even with just Brick and Viper, he didn't like his chances. The fact that they hadn't been swarmed by monsters yet was a testament to the success of his polar bear distraction and the intensity of the fighting done by France's main attack force comprised of high-Level Rifters.

"I wonder how Medusa and Magnus are doing," Lance muttered as he leaned back against the wall, feeling the building shake as another artillery barrage hit the city somewhere. *I had to use them as a distraction, but right about now, I'd love to have a polar bear to back me up.* A pained smile formed on his face as he imagined Medusa beating Shahida to death with her own war hammer. *Not that it would've made a difference. Ash is about as strong as Medusa, if not more skilled, and he got taken down a few times. She'd probably also be able to handle Medusa as well.*

Lance exhaled and directed his gaze to a specific spot on the wall before nudging Viper in the side. "You realize your sister is absolutely unhinged, right? I always assumed assassins were meant to be stealthy."

Viper just responded with a casual shrug while Lance retrieved his robust revolver, revealing two rounds inside. His mind raced as he contemplated the dwindling supply. "Only two Black Reaper rounds left," he mused, wondering whether he should resort to using his other type of ammunition. Four other rounds were in his Inventory—steel Vindicator rounds that Brian had expertly fashioned, using the remnants of Thomas's old shield.

Lance's thoughts drifted, questioning the effectiveness of the Vindicator rounds since the Reaper rounds had failed to eliminate their target. The Vindicator rounds carried an important meaning but lacked the destructive force of the Black Reaper ones. As he grappled with this dilemma, he realized that his Mana had regenerated sufficiently for another healing burst.

Activating his Skill, a soothing blue light enveloped him, accompanied by the distant cacophony of Paris under even more bombardment. After riding out the healing wave, Lance activated his Inventory again, seeing Shahida's war hammer within. He had claimed it for himself, though he realized it was useless with his banged-up ribs and arm, and him being down to one and a half companions.

The building quivered again, as if struck forcefully from the side, followed by distant explosions and the hum of passing airplanes. Lance felt an urge to peek out of the window to see what was going on, but before he could act on it, an enormous impact rocked the building above. Moments later, Ash and Shahida fell through the ceiling, crashing to the floor below amidst a tempest of violence, dust, and splintered wood. Their collision reverberated through the building, a cloud of dust slowly settling around the impact site.

Lance could see Shahida, standing triumphantly atop a bloodied Ash and letting out a roaring cry. Her rage was palpable as she viciously tore off one of Ash's wings, then drove her fist through his chest, ripping out his heart. Afterward, the woman rose slowly, her breaths rapid, betraying signs of exhaustion. Then she clenched her hand, crushing the colorless heart within, before running her stained fingers through her hair, smearing the gray gore and blood through it.

Her gaze swept across the room with the predatory intensity of a seasoned hunter, her eyes locking onto Viper, Brick, and Lance, who were all bearing the wounds of battle. With an accusatory point of her finger, she singled out Brick, as if she could identify him by his stance alone. "Didn't I kill you already?" she sneered as she watched Brick assuming a protective stance in front of Lance and Viper, his shield and sword at the ready. "Adorable . . . really, but your feeble puppet won't save you today." As she closed the distance quickly, Lance suddenly confronted her by aiming his revolver at her in an instant.

Lance pulled the trigger twice, but she evaded the bullets as if now familiar with their trajectory and speed. The rounds sped past her and demolished sizable portions of the wall behind her. "Too slow," she hissed, her eyes fixed warily on the weapon in his grasp, anticipating a third and final shot.

So, she just stood there, a momentary pause stretching into eternity, her gaze fixed upon Lance's trembling left hand. Each passing second seemed to linger, pregnant with anticipation, before she took a purposeful step forward. As she did so, a faint smile formed on her lips when nothing happened. "I'm going to take that vile weapon of yours and beat you to death with it," she said teasingly as she flexed her hand, slowly balling it in a fist. "But first you are going to give me back my weapon and tell me where my brother—"

"Sister."

A soft, unnatural voice resonated abruptly, spoken in Arabic. It was enough to halt her in her tracks, her gaze shifting to its source as Viper struggled to rise from the ground, clutching his wounded stomach. "Shahida," Viper whispered, taking uncertain steps toward her, passing by Brick and Lance.

Viper's hand slowly moved upward, fumbling with the straps of his damaged helmet before removing it and dropping it to the floor. The shock in Shahida's eyes was palpable as she watched the gray variant of her brother reveal himself, his voice calling out to her once again. "Sister, is that you?"

She recoiled from Viper and the others, fear coursing through her. "Iyas?" Her back nearly collided with a wall before her widened eyes narrowed once more. Her gaze fixated on Lance and Brick cautiously inching toward Ash, before her gaze shifted back to the revenant before her. "Brother, is that really you? What happened to you?"

A torrent of gray tears streamed down Viper's face as he staggered forward, his movements unsteady, almost on the verge of collapsing to his knees. "I can't remember . . . Lance . . . he did this . . ." His bloodied left hand trembled, rising slowly as he reached out to her, attempting to touch her face. She flinched and recoiled. "Sister," he uttered once more, his gaze fixed upon her while his trembling hand moved toward her again, finally cupping her cheek.

"Don't leave me," he pleaded, revealing his wounded stomach, his right hand pressed firmly against it as gray blood seeped out. "I don't want to die," Viper said as he fell to his knees, his left hand sliding across Shahida's battered frame, gripping fragments of her torn garments while pulling her closer to him.

"You!" Shahida hissed suddenly, shifting her gaze to the side, her eyes filled with pure venom as she stared at Lance and the others. "You're going to undo what you've done to my brother. Now!" She hissed, feeling her brother's arms wrapping around her waist.

A steely resolve settled upon her as what remained of her brother clung to her with desperation. "Lance Turner, I will personally hunt down every person you've ever held dear and subject them to unspeakable agony," she swore, her gaze piercing Lance like daggers. "I will destroy any trace of your existence through excruciating torment and—"

As she spoke, something hard fell onto the floor beneath her, interrupting her words. Her attention shifted to the object slowly rolling away from her and Viper. She recognized the gray cylinder—a grenade similar to the one Ash had attempted to use against her before but had failed.

"I'm sorry for this, sister," Viper's voice sounded soft and remorseful. A sudden realization washed over Shahida, causing her eyes to widen as she felt Viper's grip tighten as his fangs pierced her side, injecting her with a stream of venom. Simultaneously, four dim lights glimmered within Viper's stomach, hinting at the activation of something violent he had previously hidden there amidst his guts.

With an earth-shaking roar, she exerted all her strength, forcefully tearing her brother away from her grasp. But in that fleeting moment, before she could take another action, an immense explosion erupted within Viper in a cataclysmic burst, engulfing both siblings in an instant.

Wooden debris and stone splintered and soared through the air like deadly projectiles propelled by the explosive force. Dust billowed in thick clouds, instantly obscuring the once-familiar surroundings. The resounding boom reverberated through the very core of the building, drowning out all other sounds except for the deafening cacophony of destruction.

The passing minutes felt like an eternity before the dust settled and the building stopped groaning and collapsing in on parts of itself. After a while, Lance opened his eyes and could see Brick standing in front of him, acting like a protective shield against the devastating blast. Cocooned around the two of them was a partially destroyed, leathery membrane. Lance's mind raced with a mixture of dread and relief as he caught sight of Ash's enormous wing gradually retracting from its embrace, the wing and Ash having absorbed the brunt of the explosion.

The room lay in ruins, bearing witness to the destructive force unleashed. Among the wreckage, Lance could see the assassin's broken body, devoid of legs and one arm, as she lay bleeding out on the floor. The left side of her face was ruined, her left eye a horrible hollow socket, most of her torso shredded. Even now, she clung to life tenaciously, dragging herself toward them with a venomous tongue. "I'll kill . . . you . . . Kira will . . . kill you."

Lance rose to his unsteady feet, aided by Brick. He groaned as his protesting ribs sent waves of pain through his body. He slid his revolver, Oath Keeper, into his belt, as he moved toward the horrible gray smear on the floor that marked Viper's remains. With a painful groan and a horrible wet sound, he retrieved Viper's gray-shard, his fingers clutching the nearly indestructible object.

To the side, he could hear Ash crawling toward the assassin, the sound of his remaining wing occasionally thudding against the ground, aiding his movement. "Don't worry about Kira," Lance said, suppressing the desire to cough up blood, his voice strained by his battered body. "I'll handle her when the time comes." From a distance he showed her Viper's gray-shard while Ash forcefully flipped the assassin onto her back, pinning her down.

The pointed edge of Ash's wing slammed through her shoulder, anchoring her to the floor in a violent thrust. The assassin howled and cursed, yet she kept her eyes fixed on Lance the whole time, as if her hatred for him was stronger than any pain she felt. Over time, her howls turned into sadistic laughter. "You fool . . . You don't even know how to find her . . . let alone be able to stop Kira . . ." she taunted, her remaining limb pointing at him before Ash pinned that down as well.

"She's an enigma . . . a specter . . ." Shahida said, before pausing for a moment to catch her breath. "Only a handful of people know . . . how to contact her . . . Fewer can find her. If you kill me . . . you'll never find Kira . . . You'll be forced to wait . . . until she finds you."

[You have retrieved an Item]

The massive war hammer materialized in Lance's hand and he slammed it into the ground with a resounding bang. "I don't care, Shahida," Lance said, his voice a tired whisper, yet resolute. He handed the large weapon to Brick before he limped toward Shahida.

"Why should I waste my time on your web of lies? . . ." Lance said in her native tongue and dialect, channeling Iyas's vile memories. ". . . when I know you will soon show it to me within my nightmares?" A faint smile graced Lance's lips, woven with the understanding that it would come at a personal cost. The woman's eyes widened as a sudden realization hit her harder than any weapon ever could.

"Now . . . I made a promise to reunite you with your brother," Lance stated, disregarding the woman's howls and threats as he hurled Viper's shard toward Ash. His wounded friend then slammed it in the woman's bloody left eye socket. Nodding to Brick, Lance turned his back and limped a few steps away before leaning against a nearby wall for more than physical support.

The massive war hammer glided ominously along the broken floor, its crooked path accompanied by a foreboding grinding sound. Abruptly, it stopped as Brick hoisted the weapon above his head, eliciting a last defiant howl from the assassin. "At least have the gall to do the act yourself, you spineless coward!"

Lance clenched his jaw, his resolve hardening as Brick roared, bringing the war hammer down with every ounce of raw power he had in him. The sickening sound of thick steel meeting an unbreakable object followed, accompanied by the destruction of bone and flesh. Simultaneously, Lance's body radiated a blinding, blue healing light, shielding him from the sight of Shahida debris hitting the surrounding area. Even blinded, the sudden notifications on his status screen were enough for him to accept what had happened.

[You have been awarded with a Level Up]
[You have been awarded with a Level Up]
[You have been awarded with a Level Up]
[You have been awarded with a Level Up]
[You are now Level 90]

Lance closed his eyes as he shifted his focus on his breathing, determined to remain focused and suppressing the urge to retch. The room fell into an eerie stillness, occasionally punctuated by distant explosions or the reverberations of artillery. It seemed hours before Ash's voice broke the silence. "Lance, are you—"

"Brick, retrieve Quill or her shard, then join Ash," Lance interjected, his cold gaze shifting to the trail of blood Louis left behind, which was leading to a set of stairs. He heard Ash dragging himself closer to him, wanting to reach him. "Ash, retrieve Viper and Shahida's shard. Check for a Skill-shard while you're at it. When you're done, gather any gear or Items we might have lost on this floor. I'll repair you when I get back."

Concern laced Ash's unnatural deep voice. "What are you planning to do?" His eyes fixed on the shadowy cloak suddenly materializing around Lance's shoulders, mirroring his dark mood.

Lance withdrew Oath Keeper from its holster, his hand seamlessly accessing his Inventory as a single Vindicator round materialized within the weapon. Pausing for a moment, Lance felt the weight of the steel round, an indescribable heaviness settling upon him. After steeling himself, Lance pulled the shadow cloak over his head to obscure his features as he began his slow journey following Louis's blood trail.

[Strength:] [162] (+12)

"What Thomas would've done."

Status Compendium

Name: Lance Turner
Level: 90
Class: Death Smith

Attributes

Endurance:	159	**Agility:**	164	**Wisdom:**	129
Strength:	174	**Perception:**	124	**Luck:**	114
Health:	4600	**Mana:**	925		
Stamina:	1400	**Inventory:**	183		

Traits

Taint of death:	Able to use Rift corpses as items	Prolonged use results . . . ~ERROR UNREADABLE!~
Shard instability:	~ERROR UNREADABLE!~	Prolonged use results . . . ~ERROR UNREADABLE!~

Skills

Mend Wounds	Level 2	Restores minor wounds	+20 Health +8. Stamina	−15 Mana
Death Forge	Level 3	Allows (re)forging of death related items	+3 Items	−Raw materials −Black-shards −50% Stamina regeneration −50% Mana regeneration
Repair Item	Level 3	Restores Durability on Items	+4 Durability per 4 Items per 50 seconds	−Raw materials −Black-shards −35% Stamina regeneration −35% Mana regeneration
Ricochet	Level 2	Bounces throwing attacks with greater speed and accuracy	+2 Bounce +10% Speed +10% Accuracy	−30 Stamina per bounce

| **Detonate** | Level 1 | Detonates an Item based on its original durability | −50% base Durability | −25 Mana per usage |
| **Imbue Lightning** | Level 1 | Imbues Items with electrical energy without harming the user | | −5 Mana per usage |

Retainers

Ash	1x Human	Rift-glider eye +2 Sight +Heat vision	Polar bear muscle +3 Speed +6 Power +300 Durability	Orc chieftain bone +7 Defense +700 Durability	Baelsworn wing +3 Speed +2 Power +100 Durability +30% Heat resistance
Quill	1x Human	Orc bone +5 Defense +500 Durability	Elf muscle +5 Speed +120 Durability	Elf Sinew +2 Speed +2 Defense +110 Durability	
Viper	1x Human	Cerint venom +1 Venom strength +15 Durability	Elf muscle +5 Speed +120 Durability	Orc bone +5 Defense +500 Durability	
Brick	1x Human	Orc bone +5 Defense +500 Durability	Orc Muscle +2 Speed +4 Power +100 Durability		

Magnus	1x	Human	Skill shard: Moisture Extraction +1 Skill +15% Mana regeneration +1000 Mana +200 Durability		
Icarus	1x	Falcon (hybrid*)	Rift-glider eye +2 Sight +Heat vision	Orc bone +5 Defense +500 Durability	Elf muscle +5 Speed +120 Durability
Medusa	1x	Bear	Orc bone +5 Defense +500 Durability	Orc Muscle +2 Speed +4 Power +100 Durability	
Alpha - Delta	4x	Crow	Orc Muscle +2 Speed +4 Power +100 Durability	Orc bone +5 Defense +500 Durability	

CHAPTER THIRTY-TWO

Vindication

LANCE

Lance ascended the creaking wooden steps with painstaking slowness, awkwardly maneuvering around the holes. His left hand occasionally reached out to touch the nearby wall for support whenever necessary, navigating the unsteady ground beneath his feet. A trail of blood snaked its way ahead, beckoning him further up, toward an inevitable rendezvous.

His body protested against his efforts in climbing the stairs, causing his wounds to worsen and the swelling in his right arm to flare up further. He longed to employ his healing Skill, to mend even a sliver of the damage his battered body had sustained. But Lance knew all too well that his Mana reserves had been depleted, leaving him devoid of the necessary energy for several more painful minutes.

Midway up the stairs, he paused, gasping for breath. His chest burned, his ribs throbbing with the dull ache of bruises and fractures. He leaned against the dirty wall for a minute, gaze vacant as he collected himself. *Stop complaining. It's only pain,* he told himself as he shifted his attention to his broken arm. A part of him wanted to call Nerriah, the female Rifter who had previously fixed his ribs previously. He still recalled the number that had adorned his arm a while back.

I'll need to clean the wounds soon, to prevent infection. When I'm done here, I'll grab some spare cloth and immobilize my fingers and arm further. He interrupted his train of thought as a pained smile formed. "Even now . . . still thinking like a nurse," he said as his smile widened, remembering a recent past that now felt like a lifetime ago. *Sometimes it feels like I haven't changed all that much since the day I became a nurse.*

He recalled first putting on the hospital uniform and starting his first shift with Thomas, both of them equally terrified and optimistic. The memory shattered as he shifted his gaze toward the large steel revolver in his hand, forged from his best friend's broken shield. *But I have changed.* He slowly turned his sights back toward the end of the staircase, as though an unseen force was luring him forward, urging him toward his destination.

Amidst the backdrop of explosions and artillery fire, Lance's footsteps echoed through the decrepit building. The structure groaned in protest, teetering on the verge of collapse, adding to the heavy atmosphere of unease.

Lance finally reached the top of the stairs, his gaze fixed on the trail of blood that led him toward a rusted steel door. As he drew closer, his eyes caught sight of the bloodstained handle, a grim reminder that Louis had passed through this very entrance not that long ago.

Lance's gaze lingered on the blood, his thoughts swirling in a mixture of conflicting emotions and desires that did not belong to him. The yearning to flee and escape this place battled with an overwhelming urge to charge forward, consumed by a bestial rage. Simultaneously, Lance felt the pull to both kill and protect. At his very core, he felt torn. Yet, above all, the thirst for justice burned within him, strengthened by the memory of Thomas sacrificing his own life to save him.

Fueled by the memory of that knife, Lance's hand closed around the door handle, feeling the blood stick to his hand. Resolute, he turned it, slowly pushing the door open and stepping out onto the rooftop.

The rusty steel door slammed shut behind Lance, although the sound was drowned out by the escalating chorus of artillery strikes devastating a portion of Paris. Glimpsing skyward, he observed a swarm of airplanes converging upon their destination and unloading their volatile payload. In the distance, he could just see the Rift's outline, its true form clearly visible now that the protective barrier had been destroyed.

They did it! Lance thought, a flicker of pride igniting within as he accepted what humanity had pulled off here in Paris. This even though his own actions had endangered parts of that plan by going after Louis and causing the musical distraction.

Tracing the blood trail across the rooftop, Lance soon found Louis near the corner. The man was clutching his stomach, his left hand fighting to keep what little blood he still had left inside of him. His other hand was holding a pistol against his own temple, trembling as he did so. Their eyes met, and Louis instinctively reacted to the peculiar shadow cloak adorning Lance, his features hardening. As the wind tugged at Lance's garments, his hood lifted momentarily, exposing a face that evoked a sense of recognition within Louis.

In a fleeting instant, Louis's countenance fractured, a maelstrom of emotions dancing across his features before settling into an exhausted calm. With a sluggish and wearied gesture, his right hand fell to his side, as though accepting an unavoidable truth. "It's been a while, Lance," he finally uttered, his voice frail and exhausted as he let go of the weapon.

Lance advanced slowly as he ignored the pain in his body, refusing to show his limp or reveal any signs of weakness. His left hand tightened around the grip of his large revolver, while his wounded right arm remained concealed beneath the protective shroud of his shadow cloak.

Louis groaned, his voice strained with a mixture of relief and surprise, his eyes fixed on Lance's approaching figure. "I'm glad it's you . . . The woman . . . and I didn't get along from the start . . . Is she . . . is she dead?"

As Lance paused just in front of Louis, he studied the Frenchman for a while, noting the many bullet wounds, his ashen look, and the copious amount of blood he had already lost. "She's dead," Lance finally responded, his cold voice carrying the weight of buried emotions. He pushed down the memories of the gruesome scene he had witnessed, the sound of Shahida's body being smashed apart. Placing his foot on Louis's pistol, he carefully nudged it aside, out of reach.

A heavy silence descended upon them, broken only by the distant echoes of explosions reverberating through the air, shaking the very ground beneath them. Louis watched Lance, his gaze lingering, as if he was comparing the man before him to the young porter who he had abandoned within the depths of the Rift all those months ago. "Back there . . . was that . . . Thomas? He looked—"

"That wasn't him," Lance's voice sliced through the air, interrupting the man with an icy anger that was almost palpable. "Thomas is dead. The three of you ensured that when you betrayed us and left us to die."

Louis faltered, his expression one of familiar remorse. With a groan, he mustered the strength to sit upright, disregarding the additional blood loss that went along with the movement. "To my great shame . . . yes, we . . . I fled. I saved my own life and left others behind. I'm sorry about what happened to you and your friend," Louis confessed, his voice heavy with regret. "It's strange. I never thought I would ever see you again, let alone here in Paris under these circumstances."

"I did," Lance's voice dripped with venom as he lowered himself into a crouched position, deliberately aligning his eyes with Louis's. The intensity of his gaze signaled just how hard he had fought to realize this moment. "I knew that our paths would cross once more. I willed it so. It's the reason I clawed my way out of that wretched Rift." With each word, Lance's grip on his revolver grew tighter, the leather handle audibly creaking under the strain.

Louis's gaze momentarily shifted to the weapon in Lance's hand before meeting his eyes once more. "And why are you here, with that person that looks like Thomas? Are you here to kill me?" A heavy silence enveloped them, Lance just staring at the wounded man in front of him as if weighing his options. "I wonder. Can you really go through with it? Executing someone is no easy task."

"I have already killed two assassins on my path to find you," Lance responded, his mind battling the surge of unfamiliar thoughts clamoring for attention, some pleading for justice, while others were steering him toward vengeance. He ignored them for now, instead focusing on what Louis had to say.

Louis offered Lance a somber smile, as if finding out something about him. "Killing in the heat of battle, with adrenaline coursing through your veins, makes things easier. It becomes a matter of survival—either you or them. But there's a stark difference between killing and executing," Louis explained, showing his bloodstained hands without any weapon on him. "Execution is crossing a line, a price paid with a sliver of your soul." Lance just stayed silent and observed him, unaffected by the weighty pause. "Lance, why did you come here? Do you even have a goal, or were you driven just—"

"To get justice for Thomas. To make the three of you confess," Lance responded.

"I see . . . Justice . . ." Louis murmured, as if tasting the word and the gravity it held for Lance. His expression softened as he placed his hands back on his stomach, trying to stem the bleeding once more. "Bringing Connor, Kira, and me to the authorities for a confession would be justice." He winced briefly before continuing. "But I doubt Connor is capable of that. Not with the pressure he's feeling. Not with that brother of his. As for Kira, your mere existence is an offense to her . . . and judging by the assassin sent after me . . . so was I." Louis's gaze turned resolute. "I'm your best chance, but my confession wouldn't earn you Connor. But beyond that, I'd rather die than publicly admit what we did to you, not after the threats Kira applied in the Rift where we all met."

"Threats?" Lance inquired.

"None that matter. I don't think the information should make any difference to the outcome here. Just know that I have someone worth protecting. It's worth dying for," he said, giving Lance the time to digest his refusal. "This means you no longer have the option between justice and revenge. You only have the option of—" Louis's words were abruptly interrupted by the crackle of his radio, bursting back to life.

"All units be advised. Rift-Breaker is approaching the target."

Louis's pained expression mutated into a weak smile as he shifted his gaze upward and closed his eyes, whispering a soft prayer because of the news. In response, Lance's grip on his revolver tightened, his resolve hardening as he spoke, "I could forcefully take you to the GRRO and the authorities, keep you there until you confess."

Louis winced, a flicker of pain crossing his face as he replied, "I doubt that. At least not at the rate I'm bleeding out." He forced his eyes open as he heard the approaching planes that moved toward the Rift, one of them carrying the weight of Paris's fate. "I'm bound to die here, whether through action or inaction," he continued, his voice betraying a blend of resignation and concealed anguish. "No reason to risk losing parts of your soul when the outcome will be the same . . . You can just . . . wait."

His gaze shifted toward the distant Rift, his hand trembling as it moved away from his body. With a shuddering breath, he opened his Inventory, retrieving several Items that materialized underneath his hand, including an expensive bow and a weathered rifle. "I hope these will buy me a little more time," he implored, his voice thick with unspoken emotion. "Just long enough to see Rift-Breaker get used, to see it liberate Paris from these monsters . . . Please."

Lance wobbled backwards, his left hand hanging at his side. His eyes fixed on the speeding airplanes closing in on the Rift while a constricting sensation gripped the area around his white-shard. Within his mind, the emotions and memories of the people he had forged clashed and swirled, confusing him further.

Iyas's voice hissed insistently, commanding Lance's arm to rise to deal with the threat. Mira's thoughts countered, protesting its movement, demanding he avoid further conflict. The traces of animals within his mind demanded decisive action, urging him to protect himself with overwhelming force or evade the potential threat. Finn and Peter's presence loomed faintly, their hesitant emotions mirroring Lance's own uncertainty.

This wasn't what I wanted for Thomas . . . I wanted justice . . . I need to . . . I have to . . . Lance's head throbbed, as if on the verge of shattering. Unfamiliar thoughts and memories, interwoven emotions, and indecisiveness assailed him even further, intensifying the pain radiating from his white-shard. Within seconds, he coughed up fresh blood, the metallic tang staining his mouth.

Immersed in the chaotic maelstrom of his own thoughts, Lance felt like he was mentally suffocating. Finding his own emotions from within the entangled web of others became harder and harder. Suddenly, a blinding white light materialized, accompanied by a thunderous shockwave that reverberated through the city with an intensity that shook the very foundations of its existence, leaving destruction in its wake.

The two injured men watched as the sudden unnatural luminescence expanded into a colossal sphere of pure white energy, whipping around itself in an unstable frenzy. Originating a mere few hundred meters above the ominous black Rift, the light grew exponentially, consuming everything in its path. All fell victim to its insatiable hunger, disintegrating beneath its unstoppable advance.

With a cataclysmic clash, the white sphere collided with the Rift, engaging in a relentless battle between opposing forces. The relentless brilliance eclipsed the colossal Rift, its expansion hiding it from sight, along with a substantial portion of the city before it stopped its expanse, content in illuminating Paris from its position. An enigmatic energy crackled through the atmosphere, causing the men's

hair to stand on end, while their white-shards throbbed and radiated heat, resonating with the white energy.

"It . . . worked," Louis whispered, his voice trembling with a mixture of awe
and disbelief. His eyes remained locked on the magnificent sight unfolding before
him, even as tears welled up, blurring his vision. "I can't believe it . . . It actually
worked!"

Don't think, just do.

The explosive surge of light momentarily silenced the chaos that had consumed
Lance's mind, demanding his full attention. In that instant, Thomas's voice fought
through the mire of emotions and memories, establishing a dominant position
and demanding the others submit to him, pulsating with an indescribable intensity that rivaled the white energy Lance was witnessing.

Thomas's presence surged, pouring into Lance's bones, muscles, and veins.
Lance's ravaged body suddenly ceased its protests and stood up straighter, surrendering to Thomas's absolute will. Slowly, Lance's left hand opened the revolver's
cylinder, revealing a single Vindicator round within one of the three chambers.
His thumb pressed against the cool, unyielding steel, reminding him of Thomas's
former shield and gift to him.

As the distinct click of a cylinder being opened reached Louis's ears, he invol-
untarily recoiled, sinking deeper into the corner as if the sound alone had drained
what little strength remained in him. With a slow turn, his gaze met Lance's while
a serene facade adorned his pale features. "I'm . . . glad I got to see this. Thank
you for this. I finally got to see Paris freed," he uttered, his voice carrying a mixture of resignation and trepidation. Behind them, the blinding light illuminated
Paris, casting a stark contrast against their silhouettes on the rooftop. "I take it
you've made your choice?"

Lance clenched his teeth, a resolute expression etched across his face.
Thomas's presence in his mind quelled the cacophony of conflicting voices,
allowing Lance to decide what he was going to do on his own. Lance went over
his path that he had traveled the last few months, ever since they had been left
to die. He recalled all the hardships he had endured in order to get justice, only
to now be robbed of that as well at the last moment, to have it corrupted by
them. With a cold anger, Lance acknowledged this last betrayal as he breathed
life into his decision. "I don't care why you abandoned us. Forgiving people is
a luxury I can no longer afford," he uttered, his voice cutting through the air
like ice.

Imbue Lightning
Imbue Lightning
Imbue Lightning

The Vindicator round nestled in the revolver suddenly became active, casting a brilliant blue glow that crackled with lightning. With each activation of Lance's Skill, the lightning surged in strength, the very air vibrating with a near-deafening spark. Lance observed Louis's lips moving, silently uttering his parting words before shifting his gaze back to the distant white energy that had purified their city. To Louis's credit, the man remained composed despite what lay ahead.

Images of a bloody knife flooded Lance's mind as he remembered it sliding across a rugged cavern floor, sealing Thomas's fate. *I should have died that day, not you*, Lance thought, flicking the cylinder back into place. Sparks of electricity roared within the weapon, yearning to be unleashed upon the world.

Lance slowly assumed a steady position, his weapon trained on Louis's pale frame, the haunting image of Thomas's bloodstained knife serving as his sole motivation. Jaw clenched, he disregarded the coppery taste of blood filling his mouth as he manifested his resolve.

"There are some oaths worth losing your soul for."

UNKNOWN

Amidst the devastation that gripped Paris, the once-impressive Eiffel Tower now stood as a haunting testament to the city's plight. Its towering form, marred and battered, bore the scars of battle and disrepair, with beams broken and twisted in a grotesque dance of decay. Nine cloaked figures adorned the fragmented structure, their silhouettes etched against the backdrop of a blinding spectacle of light.

Some stood tall, their gazes fixed upon the colossal sphere of radiant white energy that bathed the surroundings in an ethereal glow. Others crouched, their postures reflecting a mixture of anticipation and caution. A few even found solace perched upon the broken beams, observing the scene from their elevated vantage points, cradling their weapons.

Yet, amidst this gathering, one figure commanded attention. Positioned at the center, his golden irises reflected the brilliance of the white sphere. The wind teased at his hood, causing it to flutter intermittently, briefly revealing his short silver hair. Four slender fingers moved as he closed his hand into a firm fist. *Elders . . . we're so close.*

In an instant, the massive sphere of white energy collapsed in on itself. A cataclysmic implosion rippled through the air, accompanied by a thunderous shockwave that reverberated throughout the city. Some of the surrounding buildings, already weakened by the ravages of decay and war, crumbled.

In the aftermath, only the Rift remained—a dark, hissing sphere of unnatural energy. It had once been a formidable presence that had ravaged Paris. Now it quivered, a mere echo of its former size and power, barely as large as a small house. It seemed to seethe, restrained within its dwindled confines, its potency diminished but not yet extinguished.

"The portal appears to be stable, brother," the female figure beside him remarked, her similar golden gaze shifted from the now stabilized Rift to the man standing by her side. "These people . . . they remain oblivious to the magnitude of their own creation. They are blind to the very essence they have tapped into."

Her brother just stood there, a soft smile playing on his lips. "How could they?" he mused, his sharp eyes tracing the trajectory of several flying metal objects hurtling through the air, further engulfing the area near the Rift in flames and death. "These humans . . . these creatures . . . are too addicted to their own arrogance . . . their insatiable greed . . . their malice. These creatures have squandered the precious gift of life bestowed upon them, poisoning their realm, destroying their future even without portals." His attention then shifted to the massive horde of surviving monsters converging upon the Rift. He observed their desperate frenzy as they threw themselves into it, seeking sanctuary from the imminent danger of more metal fire spears thrown from the sky.

"Gvoal, Ti'vé," he suddenly called, his gaze shifting toward the left, where a massive figure lurked at the edge of a bent iron beam, accompanied by a smaller companion crouched on another above him. "Enter the Rift when the humans make their push. Confirm the visions foreseen by our seer."

"And after?" inquired the smaller figure, his tone a melodic blend of clicks and hisses. "What of the humans?"

"Kill them." Another powerful gust of wind assailed their leader, his hair swirling around his face, exposing his delicate, narrow ears. "Despite their soul crystals, they are not our brethren. They have not bled across countless realms for generations like we all have."

"Yes, my prince," replied the taller figure, his hood pushed back to reveal dark green skin and jagged teeth and tusks. As the wind swept past, a subtle glimmer emanated from the white-shard embedded within his muscular chest. Meanwhile, the smaller figure's form wavered and flickered, before finally vanishing from sight, leaving no trace.

Without hesitation, the larger figure just stepped off the metal beam, embracing gravity's pull for several seconds. The figure then collided with the ground below with enough force to shatter stone. Unbothered, he then rushed forward before disappearing amidst the ruined buildings.

Afterward, the silver-haired figure just kept watching the Rift, a subtle smile etching its way across his features. *Watch me, Elders. I shall be the spear of our people's revenge,* he silently vowed. One by one, the other figures left the ruined structure, leaving only his sister and him behind, a silent understanding passing between them. He knew she sensed the fire burning within him, the desire for retribution.

Even if I have to burn this realm to the ground in order to achieve it.

In the aftermath of Paris's victory and the stabilizing of its Rift, threads of destiny intertwined, their intricate convergence sparked by a single act of sacrifice and the echoes of crackling lightning. In response to this, unseen forces awakened, attuned to the growing anomalies that had started to occur.

[Item can be forged. Do you wish to proceed?]

CHAPTER THIRTY-THREE

Revelations

Several days later

VIVIANE

Viviane "Newton" Beaumanoir stood at the entrance of a large tent, her eyes fixed on the steady stream of vehicles passing by. Through the open flap, she stared at the vast expanse beyond, where the vehicles were headed—the Rift or Paris. Surrounding the violent black sphere of energy, she observed the sturdy walls, overlapping cables, and thick nets that were now in place.

Behind her, within the tent, dozens of voices filled the air as people discussed important matters with one another. High-profile guild leaders conferred with generals, their voices blending with the urgent whispers of politicians stationed nearby. The constant buzz of mobile phones added to the chaotic atmosphere as everyone jostled for attention and sought to make their voices heard.

"Newton?" a man by her side called, awaiting her response. She nodded, taking note of his worn chain mail, leather, and sturdy plate armor. His gaze held an intensity that mirrored the gravity of their conversation. The man, a prominent Italian guild leader, proceeded to address the matter at hand. "We've been reviewing the casualties among the Rifters during the campaign. Two—"

"Two hundred and ninety-six lost, with triple that number wounded," Viviane interjected, showing that she remembered their earlier discussion. Each loss weighed heavily on her conscience. *Even one lost Rifter is a tragedy for our world . . . but nearly three hundred casualties just to stabilize one outbreak is a devastating blow,* she pondered, her thoughts burdened by the guilt of leading many of them during this campaign. *When considering the loss of life among our fellow soldiers who fought with us, the fallen Rifters pale in comparison.*

Another officer entered the tent, delivering a document to a general. At the same time, guild leaders focused their attention on a list of volunteers for those who had come forward to tackle the Rift. Viviane slowly approached the table, her gaze scanning the names before her. Clearing the city of its monstrous inhabitants had presented its challenges, but clearing the Rift itself would prove to be a far more challenging task.

Previous attempts had been disastrous, with only one recorded instance that had resulted in survival but not success. Only two Rifters had managed to make it out by utilizing Guardian-shards. From interviews with the survivors, they had figured out that the monsters within the Rift posed less of a threat compared to the differences in the flow of time, the imposing structures, and the harsh nature of the alien world. The survivors likened it to a fortress.

Viviane thought about the task ahead, realizing that they would now have to confront this Rift with hundreds, if not thousands, of additional monsters lurking inside as she recalled how most of the remaining monsters had fled back into the Rift in the past few days.

"How many volunteers do we have?" she asked. She knew that the ones that went in would possibly never return and would be on their own the minute they stepped in. Reinforcements would be hard to orchestrate because of the significant time difference. A mere few seconds on Earth could equate to several hours inside the Rift.

"Ninety-eight Rifters have volunteered up to this point. But we anticipate that the number will increase. The Rift is still stable, so we should have a few more days," the man stated, a self-assured smile gracing his face. "And as I mentioned earlier, my guild is eager to tackle this challenge." He tapped his finger on the document, highlighting his guild's name at the top of the list.

"We'll think about it," Viviane replied, her gaze shifting toward a nearby general. She understood the delicate nature of her role as the leader of the Rifters when it came to dealing with the military and the GRRO. "Let's give it a few more days, see if we can attract additional specialists and assemble an experienced assault force. Meanwhile, we'll focus on stabilizing the area around the Rift and clear out any remaining pockets of resistance or monster nests."

With a nod in her direction, the man returned to the group, prompting Viviane to step back to her position near the tent's open flap, her gaze fixed on the Rift, seeing the violent black energy lashing out. An unsettling feeling tugged at her, a nagging sense that she was missing something. Her eyes swept the vicinity, taking in the mound of lifeless monster carcasses stacked near the Rift, the construction crews bolstering the protective barrier around it, and the multitude of soldiers fortifying their position.

Her attention shifted into focus when she noticed movement and spotted a small, elegant form landing in front of the Rift—a sleek, gray falcon. Its colorless presence stood in stark contrast against the backdrop of the violent black Rift in front of it. She wanted to dismiss it at first, but its lack of color captured her attention, causing her to arch an eyebrow in interest.

DANIEL

Stepping into the bowling alley, Daniel noticed the unmistakably Norwegian name adorning the sign above the bar. His gaze flickered to the information on his cell phone one last time before sliding the device back into his pocket. The early hour meant the venue wasn't yet bustling, although Daniel could already hear the symphony of bowling balls crashing into pins melding seamlessly with the boisterous noise of the local Norwegians chatting while drinking beer.

Making his way toward the bar, Daniel observed the bartender unpacking a few boxes of chips while his gaze remained fixed on the television, tuned to the news. Despite not understanding the Norwegian language, Daniel could see that the report was about the Rift in Paris, detailing the military and the Rifters' extraordinary milestone of destroying a Rift outbreak and turning it stable again, along with reclaiming most of the city.

The world will never be the same again, Daniel thought as he settled onto a barstool. He caught the bartender's attention with a subtle wave of his left hand and a friendly smile.

The man approached, addressing Daniel with a question in his native tongue before swiftly switching to English upon realizing Daniel's lack of understanding. "What can I get you?"

"The owner."

A smile formed on the man's face as he tapped his own chest. "You're looking at him. I'm Bjørn," he introduced himself, wiping his hands as he stepped closer to the bar. "So, anything else I can assist you with?"

"I'll have a scotch," Daniel stated frankly, slowly sliding a paper across the bar. It featured a printed image of a bald man with the name Fergus Murry written below it. "And any information you can provide about this person."

Bjørn's expression momentarily hardened. His gaze shifted to the printed photo. "And why are you looking for this particular individual?" he questioned.

Daniel maintained his calm demeanor, having expected the response. "It's part of an ongoing investigation."

"Are you with the police? If so, I might need to see some ID before I start pointing fingers at previous customers that—" Bjørn hesitated, his sentence cut short when a GRRO tag suddenly materialized in Daniel's left hand.

"I'm not with the police," Daniel clarified, fully aware of the reaction his revelation as a sanctioned Rifter under GRRO would likely elicit. "The other side of the paper contains the date of the last financial transaction associated with this individual. A transaction that took place within your establishment."

Bjørn's complexion paled slightly as he turned the page around, swiftly scanning the information presented. "I, uh . . . I wasn't working that day," he remarked. "It was my son-in-law's shift. However, we have surveillance cameras covering the bar." At that, he pointed toward the camera positioned by the entrance. "I can retrieve the footage for you," he offered with a hint of hesitation.

"Please do," Daniel replied, his gaze sharp, in order to quell any lingering resistance within the man. In response, Bjørn disappeared through a door that led to an office in the back. As minutes passed, Daniel berated himself for not getting the scotch first. His eyes scanned the surroundings, taking in a chandelier crafted from antlers, an extensive collection of liquor bottles behind the bar, and a wall adorned with Polaroid photos, capturing moments of revelry and laughter.

Suddenly, Daniel's eyes widened, and he swiftly leaped over the bar, startling a nearby man, who spilled his beer all over himself and the counter in response. Ignoring the man's complaints, Daniel made his way to the wall. Within seconds, he snatched one that had "The Sentinels" written on the white tab. His gaze focused on the picture, in which Fergus was being hugged by a younger man and woman. As he examined the photo, his eyes narrowed on several indistinct figures sitting behind them, one of whom he could barely make out but knew all too well.

"Lance."

The sound of the bar owner's return reached Daniel's ears, and he braced himself for a scolding due to his presence behind the bar. Yet, contrary to his expectations, the man didn't say a word. Instead, he kept his gaze on the television screen, as did most of the others around the bar. Curiosity piqued, Daniel shifted his gaze toward the screen, revealing more footage of Paris playing before him.

On the screen, an individual suddenly appeared in front of the Rift in an eruption of shadow and dust. Strange, dark, gray armor covered the figure's entire body. Daniel could see a billowing cloak clinging to their armor, casting an eerie visage as wisps of black smoke swirled in the air, distorting the surroundings. *A phone?* Daniel thought as he focused on the object the mysterious figure was holding in his hand. Judging by build and posture, he figured that they were male. After that the footage switched to a live feed.

Around the figure, soldiers, GRRO personnel, and Rifters reacted with panic and confusion. Some froze in their tracks, while others desperately attempted to reach the him. With a calm pace, the mysterious figure advanced toward the Rift, unaffected by the chaos unfolding around him.

A gray falcon soon landed on his shoulder, crackling with violent arcs of lightning that seemed to have no effect on him. Daniel could see the strange man pressing something on his phone before it vanished from his hands, stored in his Inventory. Within seconds, four other birds materialized, crackling with the same sparks of electricity. Then, they all moved forward, disappearing into the Rift itself, leaving no trace except for a final play of shadows and lightning dissipating in the air.

Dozens of Rifters and soldiers surged toward the Rift, coming to an abrupt halt as soon as the figure vanished from sight. A collective realization dawned upon the Rifters, who were all too aware that they had mere seconds to decide to enter before the Rift destabilized once more, preventing normal entry.

"What the hell was that?" Bjørn exclaimed, his eyes widening in unison with the others in the room. They all watched the Rift slowly destabilize again, trapping the mysterious Rifter within.

Daniel squinted, his gaze narrowing as he struggled to comprehend the unfolding event, realizing that this strange Rifter had just done something that seemed tantamount to suicide. Puzzled and grappling with what he just witnessed, he suddenly froze as his phone began to vibrate, signaling an incoming text. He retrieved the device and glanced at the screen, revealing Lance as the sender.

As comprehension dawned upon him, Daniel's eyes grew wide, his mind reeling with the realization of what had actually just happened.

Lance!

Luck Attribute

GRRO Manual, Part 9G
by Lucinda Anderson
Psychologist, London Branch

Greetings <insert_firstname>,

In the preceding sections, we thoroughly discussed the various Attributes that define a Rifter, namely Endurance, Strength, Agility, Perception, and Wisdom. Now, let's delve into the strange Attribute that is Luck.

Similar to the other Attributes, Luck undergoes evolution throughout a Rifter's journey. It can advance through the accumulation of Level points or by spending more Attribute points on it. Unlike other Attributes, Luck is harder to define, and has no direct link to a Rifter's biology, genetics, or lifestyle.

Pragmatic Benefits:

Luck manifests in various ways, often leading to significant advantages to a Rifter. Research indicates that Rifters with a high Luck Attribute tend to experience favorable outcomes in a range of situations, from finding rare and valuable loot in the Rift to encountering opportunities and avoiding hazardous circumstances. These fortuitous events can have a profound impact on a Rifter's journey, shaping their path and influencing their overall success. Beyond good fortune, Luck also directly increases Mana regeneration, which makes it a decent Attribute for hybrid Mages.

The Ripple Effect:

Beyond immediate benefits, Luck may also extend its influence to indirect outcomes. Studies conducted on Rifters have suggested that a high Luck Attribute can create a ripple effect, positively affecting the outcomes of their actions and the events surrounding them. This phenomenon can be observed in both personal endeavors and larger-scale ones such as group missions or even across an entire guild. The fortuitous outcomes brought about by a Rifter's Luck can have far-reaching consequences.

Combat and Survival:
Luck also plays a role in combat scenarios and survival situations. Although not as extensively studied as other Attributes, anecdotal evidence suggests that Rifters with a higher Luck Attribute may possess an uncanny ability to inflict more critical hits, dodge projectiles, and narrowly escape dangerous situations in ways that can be hard to explain. In some extraordinary cases that have been reported, Rifters seemingly defied the odds by surviving life-threatening encounters unscathed, as if protected by an invisible shield of good fortune. Many speculate that this isn't some act of fate, but rather tied to the strange energy emanating from within a Rifter's white-shard.

In the context of Rift-related challenges, Luck becomes a crucial asset. A Rifter with a high Luck Attribute may find themselves more adept at navigating treacherous terrains, stumbling upon hidden paths, and discovering valuable artifacts or information crucial to their progress, all manifesting in a "gut feeling." Additionally, many Rifters claim that a higher amount of Luck significantly increases the likelihood of obtaining a Skill-shard from slain Rift-guardians.

Further Research and Ethical Considerations:
Given the intrinsic nature of Luck and its elusive qualities, studying this attribute presents unique challenges. Its subjective nature and resistance to controlled experimentation make it difficult to measure and quantify accurately. Ethical concerns also arise when attempting to manipulate or influence Luck artificially, as it raises questions about the implications of tampering with an individual's path in life.

However, it could be inferred that every Rifter, whether active in the field or not, possesses an element of Luck by virtue of having survived their initial encounter with the Rift.

<Link_previous_page> <Link_index> <Link_next_page>

Kaiden Abdi's Survival Guide Part 4

Water!
by Kaiden Abdi

This chapter will delve into a singular topic: water. It not only blankets a significant portion of our own planet but also acts as an indispensable lifeline for a Rifter in the untamed wilderness of most Rifts.

As I explained in the preceding chapter, I've spent seven years as a Rifter, specializing in survivor extraction in hostile worlds devoid of most life-sustaining resources. Among the array of tools that a Rifter can carry, none is more pivotal than water for achieving success.

For a start, let's dive into some basic math. Studies reveal that in typical conditions, Rifters consume approximately 2.5 to 3 liters of water per day. The average deployment time in most Rifts lasts around eight days. So, for hydration alone, a regular deployment would require roughly 20 to 24 liters of water. Additionally, during such deployments, Rifters usually use another 8 liters for cooking, cleaning, and sterilizing wounds. Therefore, the total water requirement comes closer to 28 to 32 liters. Most Rifters should have enough inventory storage to accommodate this after a few Levels. All of this just to meet the average requirement in the field. And seeing as some Rifts take several weeks or months to clear, this number can easily skyrocket.

Reflecting on my own experiences as a Rifter tasked with rescuing survivors, we generally managed to save three to five people per Rift. It's essential to emphasize that this isn't an official tally upheld by the GRRO; instead, it's based on the average our team usually encountered. Yet, even a modest increase of three to five individuals can strain a squad's resources significantly, especially as additional survivors often impede the time it takes to clear Rifts.

Water serves a dual purpose beyond its essential role in quenching our thirst. It becomes a crucial asset for both offense and defense. Many worlds I've visited don't have abundant water, rendering the terrain and its plants and animals ill-prepared to handle it. One must never underestimate the transformative power of water on arid land, bolstering a Rifter's defensive position as once-parched ground now becomes a muddy quagmire, hindering enemy movements. Moreover, certain creatures, like Slimes, possess immunity to most cutting or concussive attacks. However, submerging them in water until they drown can prove to be an effective strategy, just as fire and Skills tend to be.

Drawing inspiration from our history books, we can adopt a technique of boiling water and storing it in fragile containers within our Inventory system. When unleashed amidst a cluster of monsters, these dozens of boiling pots of water erupt, creating a havoc that rivals the chaotic nature of a fire Skill or a high explosive grenade. The beauty of this method lies in its affordability and the fact that fresh water isn't even necessary. I highly recommend reading the after-action report of the 118-A Rift in Spain, cleared by the Black Swan Guild. It provides valuable tips on creating these boiling water explosives and insights into their effective mass utilization.

<Link_previous_page> <Link_index> <Link_next_page>

About the Author

Osirium Writes is the pen name of author Joost Lassche, whose urban fantasy LitRPG series, Death Smith, was originally released on Royal Road.

Podium
DISCOVER
STORIES UNBOUND
PodiumAudio.com